Contents

Preface

A Pleasant and Delightful History of Thomas Hickathrift

A Son of Adam

Amys and Amyle

Binnorie

Cap O' Rushes

Catskin

Coat o' Clay

Earl Mar's Daughter

Gobborn Seer

Henny-Penny

How the Cobbler Cheated the Devil

I Won't

Jack and the Beanstalk

Jack the Giant-Killer

Johnny Reed's Cat

Kate Crackernuts

Knave and Fool

Master of all Masters

Mr Fox

Mr. Miacca

Nelly The Knocker

Nix Naught Nothing

Silky

Sir Gammer Vans

Tamlane

Teeny-Tiny

The Baker's Daughter

The Blinded Giant

The Brown Man of the Moors

The Fairies' Cup

The Fiddler in the Fairy Ring

The Fish and the Ring

The Golden Arm

The Golden Snuff-Box

The Hillman and the Housewife

The History of Whittington

The King o' the Cats

The Laidly Worm

The Little Bull-Calf

The Lover's Vows

The Magician Turned Mischief-Maker

The Magpie's Nest

The Master and His Pupil

The Old Witch

The Old Woman and her Pig

The Pedlar of Swaffham

The Rose Tree

The Stars in the Sky

The Strange Visitor

Tales from the Land of Hope & Glory

Traditional tales, fables and sagas from England...

4th edition revised and updated

Compiled adapted & edited by Clive Gilson

'Tales from the World's Firesides'

The Tavistock Witch

The Three Feathers

The Three Heads of the Well

The Three Sillies

The True History of Sir Thomas Thumb

The White Lady

The Wise Men of Gotham

The Yorkshire Boggart

Titty Mouse and Tatty Mouse

Tom-Tit-Tot

Under the Sun

Guy of Warwick

Havelock and Goldborough

Hereward the Wake

King Horn

Legends of King Arthur

St Herbert, the Hermit of Derwentwater

The Compassion of Constantine

William of Cloudeslee

Historical Notes

About the Editor

Reviews

Preface

For some twenty years I have been collecting and telling stories, alongside publishing a number of my own works of short fiction in the fields of magical realism and speculative science fiction. Throughout that time, traditional folk and fairy tales have been a central source of inspiration. In working with them, I have gathered many thousands of narratives from around the world, and it has long been an ambition of mine to assemble these materials into a coherent "library" of tales, one that speaks of particular places and peoples while also revealing the continuities that run across cultures.

A major motivation behind this project is preservation. Many of the stories I draw upon survive only in older printed collections, often now long out of print, and risk slipping from common view. My sources are largely drawn from early collectors working from the late eighteenth century through the nineteenth and into the early decades of the twentieth century. Their work is invaluable, but it is also rooted in world views that differ markedly from those of many readers in the early twenty-first century. Attitudes to race, gender, class and empire, for example, are frequently expressed in ways that can be unsettling or offensive today.

In retelling these narratives I therefore attempt, as carefully as I can, to adapt them for contemporary readers while preserving the core structures, images and moods of the originals. My aim is not to erase the past, but to offer stories that can still be read with pleasure and thoughtfulness, without uncritically reproducing prejudices that distort or diminish the cultures from which they were taken. I cannot claim perfect success, but I hope the balance I seek will be evident.

It is also important to state that I do not claim to speak for any originating culture, nor to offer definitive versions of its traditions. The early collectors whose books I use as sources often imposed their own assumptions on the material they recorded. My task here is more modest: to keep the tales in active circulation in a form that is readable and enjoyable, and to acknowledge as clearly as possible where they have come from. To that end, every story in this volume carries a full attribution, naming the original collector or author, the title of the work from which this version is adapted, and, where available, details of publication and other relevant bibliographical information. Wherever I can, I also indicate cultural or regional origins, although in some cases the national framing of the original collection already makes that obvious.

This volume, *Tales from the Land of Hope and Glory*, focuses on England and forms part of a wider series covering the folk and fairy traditions of the British and Irish islands. The stories here are drawn from some of the major collectors and redactors of English popular narrative. As so often, they reveal both beauty and cruelty, humour and terror, the everyday and the uncanny. They speak to what we like to call "modern" experience just as clearly as they speak from the past.

Over time, I hope that this series will expand to encompass materials from every continent, although even then it will represent only a small sample of the world's narrative inheritance. Storytelling is one of the most enduring human practices. Since our distant ancestors sat around fires, trying to make sense of themselves and the world, we have told one another tales of magic and cleverness, of warning and desire. When I began to read more systematically across traditions, from Celtic narratives to those recorded in Indonesia, across Africa, the Middle East and the Far East, I was struck not only by their diversity but also by their deep similarities. Characters, motifs and plots recur in altered forms; beneath the local detail there is a shared grammar of story that suggests a common imaginative heritage.

The tales in this volume were once performed aloud, often by firelight, as a means of preserving communal memory and of instructing both children and adults. They are part of a shared inheritance. Witches and kings, tricksters and beasts, miracles and misfortunes, kindness and cruelty all find a place here. They can be dark and violent, or gentle and tender. In different ways they reflect us, and we, in turn, recognise ourselves in them.

It has been a pleasure to read, re-read and re-shape these stories for this collection. I offer them in the hope that you will find in them both enjoyment and a renewed sense of connection to a much older, and still very living, tradition.

Clive

Bath, 2025

A Pleasant and Delightful History of Thomas Hickathrift

A Pleasant and Delightful History of Thomas Hickathrift belongs to the late eighteenth-century English chapbook tradition, an inexpensive popular print form aimed at a broad, often juvenile, readership. The copy cited here comes from a chapbook printed in Whitehaven by Ann Dunn, whose activity as a printer and seller of chapbooks is documented for the 1790s.

This version is taken from Charles John Tibbits's anthology Folk-Lore and Legends: English, first issued by W. W. Gibbings in London around 1890 and later reissued under the title English Fairy Tales, Folklore and Legends in 1902.

Chapter I

In the reign before William the Conqueror, I have read in an ancient history that there dwelt a man in the parish of the Isle of Ely, in the county of Cambridge, whose name was Thomas Hickathrift - a poor man and a day-labourer, yet he was a very stout man, and able to perform two days' work instead of one. He having one son and no more children in the world, he called him by his own name, Thomas Hickathrift. This old man put his son to good learning, but he would take none, for he was, as we call them in this age, none of the wisest sort, but something less, and had no docility at all in him.

His father being soon called out of the world, his mother was tender of him, and maintained him by her hand labour as well as she could, he being slothful and not willing to work to get a penny for his living, but all his delight was to be in the chimney-corner, and he would eat as much at one time as would serve four or five men. He was in height, when he was but ten years of age, about eight feet; and in thickness, five feet; and his hand was like unto a shoulder of mutton; and in all his parts, from top to toe, he was like unto a monster, and yet his great strength was not known.

The first time that his strength was known was by his mother's going to a rich farmer's house (she being but a poor woman) to desire a bottle of straw for herself and her son Thomas. The farmer, being a very honest, charitable man, bid her take what she would. She going home to her son Tom, said, "I pray, go to such a place and fetch me a bottle of straw; I have asked him leave."

He swore he would not go.

"Nay, prithee, Tom, go," said his mother.

He swore again he would not go unless she would borrow him a cart-rope. She, being willing to please him, because she would have some straw, went and borrowed him a cart-rope to his desire.

He, taking it, went his way. Coming to the farmer's house, the master was in the barn, and two men a-thrashing. Said Tom, "I am come for a bottle of straw."

"Tom," said the master, "take as much as you can carry."

He laid down the cart-rope and began to make his bottle. They said, "Tom, your rope is too short," and jeered poor Tom, but he fitted the man well for it, for he made his bottle, and when he had finished it, there was supposed to be a load of straw in it of two thousand pounds weight. Said they -

"What a great fool are you. You cannot carry the tenth of it."

Tom took the bottle, and flung it over his shoulder, and made no more of it than we would do of a hundredweight, to the great admiration of master and man.

Tom Hickathrift's strength being then known in the town they would no longer let him lie baking by the fire in the chimney-corner. Everyone would be hiring him for work. They seeing him to have so much strength told him that it was a shame for him to live such a lazy course of life, and to be idle day after day, as he did.

Tom seeing them bate him in such a manner as they did, went first to one work and then to another, but at length came to a man who would hire him to go to the wood, for he had a tree to bring home, and he would content him. Tom went with him, and took with him four men besides; but when they came to the wood they set the cart to the tree, and began to draw it up with pulleys. Tom seeing them not able to stir it, said , "Stand away, you fools!" then takes it up and sets it on one end and lays it in the cart.

"Now," says he, "see what a man can do!"

"Marry, it is true," they said.

When they had done, as they came through the wood, they met the woodman. Tom asked him for a stick to make his mother a fire with.

"Ay," says the woodman. "Take one that you can carry."

Tom espied a tree bigger than that one that was in the cart, and lays it on his shoulder, and goes home with it as fast as the cart and the six horses could draw it. This was the second time that Tom's strength was known.

When Tom began to know that he had more strength than twenty men, he then began to be merry and very tractable, and would run or jump; took great delight to be amongst company, and to go to fairs and meetings, to see sports and pastimes.

Going to a feast, the young men were all met, some to cudgels, some to wrestling, some throwing the hammer, and the like. Tom stood a little to see the sport, and at last goes to them that were throwing the hammer. Standing a little to see their manlike sport, at last he takes the hammer in his hand, to feel the weight of it, and bid them stand out of the way, for he would throw it as far as he could.

"Ay," said the smith, and jeered poor Tom. "You'll throw it a great way, I'll warrant you."

Tom took the hammer in his hand and flung it. And there was a river about five or six furlongs off, and he flung it into that. When he had done, he bid the smith fetch the hammer, and laughed the smith to scorn.

When Tom had done this exploit he would go to wrestling, though he had no more skill of it than an ass but what he did by strength, yet he flung all that came to oppose him, for if he once laid hold of them they were gone. Some he would throw over his head, some he would lay down slyly and how he pleased. He would not like to strike at their heels, but flung them two or three yards from him, ready to break their necks asunder. So that none at last durst go into the ring to wrestle with him, for they took him to be some devil that was come among them. So Tom's fame spread more and more in the country.

Tom's fame being spread abroad both far and near, there was not a man durst give him an angry word, for he was something fool-hardy, and did not care what he did unto them, so that all they that knew him would not in the least displease him. At length there was a brewer at Lynn that wanted a good lusty man to carry his beer to the Marsh and to Wisbech, hearing of Tom, went to hire him, but Tom seemed coy, and would not be his man until his mother and friends persuaded him, and his master entreated him. He likewise promised him that he should have a new suit of clothes and everything answerable from top to toe, besides he should eat of the best. Tom at last yielded to be his man, and his master told him how far he must go, for you must understand there was a monstrous giant kept some part of the Marsh, and none durst go that way, for if they did he would keep them or kill them, or else he would make bond slaves of them.

But to come to Tom and his master. He did more work in one day than all his men could do in three, so that his master, seeing him very tractable, and to look well after his business, made him his head man to go into the Marsh to carry beer by himself, for he needed no man with him. Tom went every day in the week to Wisbech, which was a very good journey, and it was twenty miles the roadway.

Tom - going so long that wearisome journey, and finding that way the giant kept was nearer by half, and Tom having now got much more strength than before by being so well kept and drinking so much strong ale as he did - one day as he was going to Wisbech, and not saying anything to his master or to any of his fellow-servants, he was resolved to make the nearest way to the wood or lose his life, to win the horse or lose the saddle, to kill or be killed, if he met with the giant. And with this resolution he goes the nearest way with his cart and horses to go to Wisbech; but the giant, perceiving him, and seeing him to be bold, thought to prevent him, and came, intending to take his cart for a prize, but he cared not a bit for him.

The giant met Tom like a lion, as though he would have swallowed him up at a mouthful. "Sirrah," he said, "who gave you authority to come this way? Do you not know I make all stand in fear of my sight, and you, like an impudent rogue, must come and fling my gates open at your pleasure? How dare you presume to do this? Are you so careless of your life? I will make you an example for all rogues under the sun. Do you not care what you do? Do you see how many heads hang upon yonder tree that have offended my law? Your head shall hang higher than all the rest for an example!"

Tom made him answer, "A fig for your news, for you shall not find me like one of them."

"No?" said the giant. "Why? You are but a fool if you come to fight with such a one as I am, and bring no weapon to defend yourself with."

Said Tom, "I have a weapon here will make you understand you are a traitorous rogue."

"Ay, sirrah," said the giant; and took that word in high disdain that Tom should call him a traitorous rogue, and with that he ran into his cave to fetch out his club, intending to dash out Tom's brains at the first blow.

Tom knew not what to do for a weapon, for he knew his whip would do but little good against such a monstrous beast as he was, for he was in height about twelve feet, and six about the waist. While the giant went for his club, Tom bethought himself of two very good weapons, for he makes no more ado but takes his cart and turns it upside down, takes out the axle-tree, and a wheel for his shield and buckler, and very good weapons they were, especially in time of need. The giant, coming out again, began to stare at Tom, to see him take the wheel in one hand, and the axle-tree in the other, to defend him with.

"Oh," said the giant, "you are like to do great service with these weapons. I have here a twig that will beat you and your wheel and axle-tree to the ground."

That which the giant called a twig was as thick as some mill-posts are, but Tom was not daunted for his big and threatening speech, for he perfectly saw there was no way except one, which was to kill or be killed. So the giant made at Tom with such a vehement force that he made Tom's wheel crack again, and Tom lent the giant as good, for he took him such a weighty blow on the side of his head, that he made the giant reel again.

"What," said Tom, "are you drunk with my strong beer already?"

The giant, recovering, laid on Tom, but still as they came, Tom kept them off with his wheel, so that he had no hurt at all. In short, Tom plied his work so well, and laid such huge blows on the giant that sweat and blood together ran down his face, and being fat and foggy with fighting so long, he was almost tired out, and he asked Tom to let him drink a little water, and then he would fight him again.

"No," said Tom, "my mother did not teach me that wit. Who would be the fool then?"

Tom, seeing the giant began to grow weary, and that he failed in his blows, thought it was best to make hay while the sun did shine, for he laid on so fast as though he had been mad, till he brought the giant down to the ground.

The giant seeing himself down, and Tom laying so hard on him, made him roar in a most lamentable manner, and prayed him not to take away his life and he would do anything for him, and yield himself to him to be his servant.

But Tom, having no more mercy on him than a dog or a bear, laid still on the giant till he laid him for dead. When he had done, he cut off his head, and went into his cave, where he found great store of gold and silver, which made his heart leap.

Now, having done this action in killing the giant, he put his cart together again, loaded it, and drove it to Wisbech and delivered his beer, and, coming home to his master, he told it to him. His master was so overjoyed at the news that he would not believe him till he had seen; and, getting up the next day, he and his master went to see if he spoke the truth or not, together with most of the town of Lynn. When they came to the place and found the giant dead, he then showed the place where the head was, and what silver and gold there was in the cave. All of them leaped for joy, for this monster was a great enemy to all the country.

This news was spread all up and down the country, how Tom Hickathrift had killed the giant, and well was he that could run or go to see the giant and his cave. Then all the folks made bonfires for joy, and Tom was a better respected man than before.

Tom took possession of the giant's cave by consent of the whole country, and everyone said he deserved twice as much more. Tom pulled down the cave and built him a fine house where the cave stood, and in the ground that the giant kept by force and strength, some of which he gave to the poor for their common, the rest he made pastures of, and divided the most part into tillage to maintain him and his mother, Jane Hickathrift.

Tom's fame was spread both far and near throughout the country, and it was no longer Tom but Mr. Hickathrift, so that he was now the chiefest man among them, for the people feared Tom's anger as much as they did the giant before. Tom kept men and maid servants, and lived most bravely. He made a park to keep deer in. Near to his house he built a church and gave it the name of St. James's Church, because he killed the giant on that day, which is so called to this hour. He did many good deeds, and became a public benefactor to all persons that lived near him.

Tom having got so much money about him, and being not used to it, could hardly tell how to dispose of it, but yet he did use the means to do it, for he kept a pack of hounds and men to hunt with him, and who but Tom then? So he took such delight in sports that he would go far and near to any meetings, as cudgel-play, bear baiting, football, and the like.

Now as Tom was riding one day, he alighted off his horse to see that sport, for they were playing for a wager. Tom was a stranger, and none did know him there. But Tom spoiled their sport, for he, meeting the football, took it such a kick, that they never found their ball more. They could see it fly, but where none could tell. They all wondered at it, and began to quarrel with Tom, but some of them got nothing by it, for Tom gets a great spar which belonged to a house that was blown down, and all that stood in his way he knocked down, so that all the county was up in arms to take Tom, but all in vain, for he manfully made way wherever he came.

When he was gone from them, and returning homewards, he chanced to be somewhat late in the evening on the road. There met him four stout, lusty rogues that had been robbing passengers that way, and none could escape them, for they robbed all they met, both rich and poor. They thought when they met with Tom he would be a good prize for them, and, perceiving he was alone made cock-sure of his money, but they were mistaken, for he got a prize by them. Whereupon, meeting him, they bid him stand and deliver.

"What," said Tom, "shall I deliver?"

"Your money, sirrah," they said.

"But" said Tom, "you will give me better words for it, and you must be better armed."

"Come, come," they said, "we do not come here to parley, but we come for money, and money we will have before we stir from this place."

"Ay!" said Tom. "Is it so? Then get it and take it."

So then one of them made at him, but he presently unarmed him and took away his sword, which was made of good trusty steel, and smote so hard at the others that they began to put spurs to their horses and be-gone. But he soon stayed their journey, for one of them having a portmanteau behind him, Tom, supposing there was money in it, fought with a great deal of more courage than before, till at last he killed two of the four, and the other two he wounded very sore so that they cried out for quarter. With much ado he gave them their lives, but took all their money, which was about two hundred pounds, to bear his expenses home. Now when Tom came home he told them how he had served the football-players and the four highwaymen, which caused a laughter from his old mother. Then, refreshing himself, he went to see how all things were, and what his men had done since he went from home.

Then going into his forest, he walked up and down, and at last met with a lusty tinker that had a good staff on his shoulder, and a great dog to carry his leather bag and tools of work. Tom asked the tinker from whence he came, and where he was going, for that was no highway. The tinker, being a sturdy fellow, bid him go look, and what was that to him, for fools would be meddling.

"No," says Tom, "but I'll make you know, before you and me part, it is me."

"Ay!" said the tinker, "I have been this three long years, and have had no combat with any man, and none durst make me an answer. I think they be all cowards in this country, except it be a man who is called Thomas Hickathrift who killed a giant. Him I would fain see to have one combat with him."

"Ay!" said Tom, "but, methinks, I might be master in your mouth. I am the man, what have you to say to me?"

"Why," said the tinker, "verily, I am glad we have met so happily together, that we may have one single combat."

"Sure," said Tom, "you do but jest?"

"Marry," said the tinker, "I am in earnest."

"A match," said Tom. "Will you give me leave to get a twig?"

"Ay," says the tinker. "Hang him that will fight a man unarmed."

Tom steps to the gate, and takes one of the rails for his staff. So they fell to work. The tinker at Tom and Tom at the tinker, like unto two giants, they laid one at the other. The tinker had on a leather coat, and at every blow Tom gave the tinker his coat cracked again, yet the tinker did not give way to Tom an inch, but Tom gave the tinker a blow on the side of the head which felled the tinker to the ground. "Now, tinker, where are you?" said Tom.

But the tinker, being a man of metal, leaped up again, and gave Tom a blow which made him reel again, and followed his blows, and then took Tom on the other side, which made Tom's neck crack again. Tom flung down the weapon, and yielded the tinker to be the best man, and took him home to his house, where I shall leave Tom and the tinker to be recovered of their many wounds and bruises, which relation is more enlarged as you may read in the second part of Thomas Hickathrift.

A Son of Adam

A Son of Adam is one of the shorter moral exempla included in Joseph Jacobs's More English Fairy Tales, first published in 1894 with illustrations by John D. Batten. Like many of Jacobs's tales it was compiled from oral or printed tradition rather than authored by him in a literary sense. Structurally, this tale belongs to the international family of "trial" or "temptation" tales, in which a character's boast about superior virtue is immediately disproved by a staged experiment.

The story is usually classified under English folklore, with a light theological framework but a strongly secular, didactic tone: it illustrates human fallibility rather than offering doctrinal commentary.

A man was working one day. It was very hot, and he was digging. By-and-by he stopped to rest and wipe his face; and he was very angry to think he had to work so hard only because of Adam's sin. So he complained bitterly, and said some very hard words about Adam.

It happened that his master heard him, and he asked, "Why do you blame Adam? You'd have done just like Adam, if you'd a-been in his place."

"No, I shouldn't," said the man, "I should have known better."

"Well, I'll try you," says his master, "come to me at dinner-time."

So come dinner-time, the man came, and his master took him into a room where the table was a-set with good things of all sorts. And he said, "Now, you can eat as much as ever you like from any of the dishes on the table; but don't touch the covered dish in the middle till I come back." And with that the master went out of the room and left the man there all by himself.

So the man sat down and helped himself, and ate some o' this dish and some o' that, and enjoyed himself finely. But after a while, as his master didn't come back, he began to look at the covered dish, and to wonder whatever was in it. And he wondered more and more, and he says to himself, "It must be something very nice. Why shouldn't I just look at it? I won't touch it. There can't be any harm in just peeping." So at last he could hold back no longer, and he lifted up the cover a tiny bit; but he couldn't see anything. Then he lifted it up a bit more, and out popped a mouse. The man tried to catch it; but it ran away and jumped off the table and he ran after it. It ran first into one corner, and then, just as he thought he'd got it, into another, and under the table, and all about the room. And the man made such a clatter, jumping and banging and running round after the mouse, a-trying to catch it, that his master came in.

"Ah!" he said, "never you blame Adam again, my man!"

Amys and Amyle

The story known as Amys and Amyle is almost certainly derived from the medieval Middle-English romance Amis and Amiloun, a long tail-rhyme poem dating to about the early fourteenth century. That poem survives in a handful of manuscripts, the earliest likely from c.1330, and enjoyed a wide circulation in the Middle English tradition.

This is from The Red Romance Book, edited by Andrew Lang (with contributions by his wife, Mrs Lang) and first published in 1905 by Longmans, Green and Co.

Sometime in the middle ages there lived in the Duchy of Lombardy, which, as everybody knows, is part of Italy, two knights, who loved each other like brothers. And what is more to be wondered at, their wives were the best friends in the world. To complete the happiness of the two couples, two little boys were born to them on the same day, and they were given the names of Amys and Amyle.

Now it generally happens that when parents are very anxious for their children to be friends, because they are the same age, or neighbours, or for some equally good reason, the young people make up their minds to hate each other. However, Amys and

Amyle did not disappoint their fathers and mothers in this way. From the moment they could walk they were never seen apart; if they ever did quarrel no one ever heard of it; and by the time they were twelve years old they had grown so like each other that even their parents could hardly tell the difference between them. Indeed, the likeness between them is supposed to have given rise to the proverb, 'A miss is as good as a mile.'

It was in that year that the duke, their liege lord, bade all his vassals to a great festival to be held in his castle, and many of them took their sons with them, to show them some of the customs of chivalry. Amys and Amyle went with the rest, and endless were the mistakes made about them. The boys themselves, who were merry little fellows, delighted in increasing the confusion, and played so many pranks that the duke declared that they must remain at the court with him, as his life would be too dull without them.

Perhaps the knights thought that their homes would be dull too, but, if so, they did not dare say so; only their wives noticed, as they entered the castle gates, that their heads were bowed, as if some ill had befallen them.

At first the boys felt unhappy and lonely in this strange new world, and clung to each other more closely than ever, but, after a little, they got used to the change, and learned eagerly how to shoot at a mark and tilt at a ring, or to sing sweet love-songs to the sound of a lute.

So the years passed away till Amys and Amyle were eighteen years old, and thought themselves men, and were ready to cross lances with the bravest. The first step they took towards proving to the world that no tie of blood could bind them closer than the love they bore one to another, was to swear the oaths which made them brothers in arms, and obliged them to fight in each other's quarrels, avenge each other's wrongs - even to sacrifice what the other held most dear in the service of his friend. Marriage itself was not more sacred.

All this time the duke had been too busy with his own affairs to have the youths much in his company, though he took care that they had the best chances of learning everything that they ought to know. When, however, he heard that Amys and Amyle had sworn the solemn oaths that made them brothers in arms, he ordered a tournament to be held in their honour, and, when it was over, knighted them on the field. He further declared that henceforth Sir Amys should be his chief butler and Sir Amyle his head steward over his household, thus the steward whom Amyle displaced became their deadly enemy.

Although the young men knew a great deal about hunting, and wrestling, and other such sports, they had no idea what the duties of a butler and a steward might be. But what they did know was that they would have to be very careful, for the eyes of the old steward were watching eagerly to report any mistakes to the duke their master. Luckily for them, they were favourites with everyone, and if now and then they forgot their work, or slipped away for a day's hunting, well! the task was done by somebody, and not even the old steward could find out by whom.

Everything seemed going smoothly, and the new-made knights were in danger of being spoilt by the favour of the ladies of the court, when a sudden stop was put to all their pleasures. One day a man-at-arms riding a jaded horse appeared at the palace gateway, and demanded to be led into the presence of the good knight Sir Amyle.

'Oh, my lord,' he said, and knew not that it was Amys before whom he was kneeling, 'it is grievous news that I bear unto you. Your father and mother, that noble knight and his lady, died of a pestilence but seven days ago, and none save you can take their place. Therefore am I sent unto you.'

'My father and mother?' cried Amys, staggering back.

'Yes, my lord, yours,' answered the man. 'At least...' he stammered, as Sir Amyle came and stood by his friend, 'I know not if indeed it may be yours. It is long years since I have seen you, and this knight and you have but one face. But it is Sir Amyle with whom I would speak.'

Then Amys laid his hand on his brother's shoulder.

'Be comforted,' he said softly. 'Am I not with you? and, though I cannot go with you now, I will follow you shortly unless you quickly return to me.'

Early next morning Amyle started with a heavy heart for the home which he had left six years before; but before his departure he had caused to be made two cups of gold, delicately wrought with figures of birds and beasts, such as he and Amys had often chased in the forests and lakes of Lombardy. The cups were no more to be told from each other than were Amys and Amyle themselves, and Amyle placed them in the pockets of his saddle till the moment came for him to part from Sir Amys, who had ridden with him as far as he might. Then, drawing out one of the cups, Amyle placed it in his friend's hands.

'Farewell, my brother,' he said. 'Be true to me as I will be true to you, according to the oath which we swear, that as long as we both shall live nothing and nobody shall stand between me and you.'

And Sir Amys repeated the words of his oath, then slowly turned his horse's head towards the castle.

Seven days' hard riding brought Sir Amyle back to his native place, and for many months he had much to do in setting aside the pretenders who had sprung up to claim his father's lands. When at last peace was restored and the false traitors had been thrown into prison, a petition on the part of his vassals to take a wife and settle down amongst them, turned his thoughts in other directions.

It was the custom of the country that the ruler of those lands should choose his wife from the most beautiful maidens in the Duchy of Lombardy, no matter what their degree might be. So a herald was sent forth to proclaim that any damsel who wished to fill this high place was to present herself in the courtyard of the palace on the morning following the next new moon, where the chamberlain would receive her. Oh, what a fluttering of hearts there was in the towns and villages, as the herald, with his silver trumpet and his satin coat of red and yellow, covered with figures of strange beasts, passed up and down the streets! How the girls all ran to their mirrors, and turned themselves this way and that to see if there could possibly be a chance for them! Perhaps it was the fault of the headdress they wore that their faces seemed so long and their noses so big, or surely something was wrong with the glass that their cheeks looked so yellow! But even when it was proved beyond a doubt that neither headdress nor mirror was to blame in the matter, there were enough lovely maidens and to spare in the courtyard of the castle on the day following the new moon.

'He is certain to choose you,' said one, who in her secret heart thought it was impossible that she should be passed over.

'Oh no; fair men's eyes always rest upon dark women,' answered the girl, whose locks were brighter than the sun, though while she spoke she was really thinking that no one could bear comparison with her. And then all grew silent, for there was heard a blast of trumpets announcing that Sir Amyle was at hand.

The young knight had donned for this occasion a close-fitting coat of silver cloth, while a short blue velvet mantle hung from his shoulders. He walked slowly down the ranks of the maidens, watching each carefully, and noting the way in which she received his gaze. Some looked down and blushed; some looked up and smiled, but one there was who did neither, only stood calm and pale as the young man drew near.

She was a tall girl with dark hair and soft grey eyes, and the chamberlain had doubted long, before he told her father that she might take her stand with the rest. None would have chosen her as Queen of a Tourney, or bidden her preside over a Court of Love, yet there was that in her face which had caused Amyle to pause before her and to hold out his hand.

So they were married, and by the side of his wife Sir Amyle for a while forgot his brother.

Meanwhile Sir Amys dwelt sorrowfully at the court, defending himself as best he might against the wiles of the black-hearted steward, who now received him with smiles and fair words. Nay, he even desired that they should become brothers at arms, but to this Sir Amys replied that, having made oath to one brother at arms, the rules of chivalry did not allow him to take another.

At these words the steward threw off the mask with which he had sought to beguile Sir Amys.

'You will have cause to rue this day,' roared he, nearly choking in his wrath, 'you dog, you white-livered cur!' but Amys only smiled, and bade him do his worst.

By this time the duke's only daughter, Belisante, had reached the age of fifteen, and on her birthday her father proclaimed a great tournament, which was to last for fourteen days. Knights from far and near flocked to break a lance in honour of the fair damsel, but, though many doughty deeds were done, the prize fell to Sir Amys. When he came up to receive the golden circlet from the hands of the duchess - for the duke held his daughter to be of too tender years to be queen of the tourney - Belisante looked earnestly at the knight whose praises had rung in her ears ever since her childhood. It was almost the first time her eyes had beheld him, for she had lived in one of her father's distant castles, and had seldom visited the court.

Now we all know full well that whenever we form to ourselves the picture of a man or woman of whom great things are said, woeful is in general the disappointment. But even in that assembly Sir Amys was taller and stronger and fairer to look upon than the rest.

'He shall be my knight,' said Belisante to herself, never dreaming that any man alive could pass her by. But Sir Amys' thoughts dwelt not upon women, and he hardly so much as marked her where she sat.

This slight was more than the spoiled damsel could bear. She fell sick with love and anger, and for many days lay in bed, pondering how she should win the love of Sir Amys.

A full week went by, and still she had never had speech of him - nor had even so much as caught sight of him as he followed her father to the chase. But one morning her lady brought her word - for indeed she had guessed something of her mistress's heart - that Sir Amys had so wearied himself in pursuit of a boar the previous evening that he had let his lord ride forth alone. So Belisante bade her maiden bring her kirtle of green silk, and clasp it with her golden belt set with precious stones, and place a veil of shining white upon her hair; then seeking her mother they went down into the garden together.

It was not long before her quick-glancing eyes beheld Sir Amys lying under a tree by the side of a stream, but in her guile she took no heed of him, but turned away and entered a little wood.

'I can sleep now,' she said, stretching herself on a bank of soft moss. 'Listen to the birds, how sweetly they sing! Methinks I hear the voice of the nightingale, for the trees make such darkness that he knows not night from day.'

'Let us leave her,' answered her mother, and signing to her ladies they all returned to the castle.

For a moment Belisante lay still, feigning to sleep; then she raised herself on her arm and looked about her. Nothing was to be seen save the green darkness about her, nothing was to be heard save the songs of the birds. Softly she rose to her feet, and stole out of the wood to the orchard where Sir Amys was resting, thinking, though she guessed it not, of his brother in arms Amyle.

He sprang to his feet in surprise as Belisante the Fair drew near him; but she begged him to sit beside her, and told him how that she had been sick of love, and besought him of his grace not to withhold this good gift from her. Sir Amys hearkened to her words, not knowing if he had heard correctly, but, calling his wits to his aid, he answered that she was the daughter of a great prince while he was only the son of a poor knight, and that marriage between them might never be. This speech so wrought upon Belisante that she broke out in such tears and entreaties that Sir Amys, to gain time to ponder what best to do, replied that if in eight days her mind was still set on him, he would ask her hand in marriage.

By ill-luck for both the knight and the maiden, the steward, who had been seeking a chance of doing Sir Amys an ill turn, had seen Belisante leave the wood and go in search of Sir Amys. Creeping stealthily up to them, he hid himself behind a clump of bushes and heard all that was said. Cunningly he made his plan, and on the eighth day he waylaid the duke and told him that Sir Amys was about to repay all the kindness shown him by a secret marriage with the duke's daughter.

Sir Amys was keeping guard that day in the hall of the palace, when, sword in hand, his liege lord stood before him charging him with beguiling his daughter. In another moment Amys would have fallen dead, but behind him was a little room, and into this he stepped, shutting the door, so that the sword stuck in the hard wood as it came against it. This mischance somewhat cooled the duke's anger, and bidding Sir Amys come out and speak with him, he again accused him of having sought to steal away his daughter, whom he wished to betroth to the emperor's son.

Sir Amys was in sore straits. If he could have borne the penalty alone, he would have suffered gladly whatever sentence the duke might have passed on him; but this could not be. So, to save Belisante from her father's wrath, he swore a great oath that there was no truth in that tale, and, flinging down his glove, offered to fight any man whom the duke should appoint, and prove his innocence on his body. Then the king bade his steward pick up Sir Amys' glove, and fixed a morning, fourteen days hence, when the two should meet in single combat.

Still it was not enough that Sir Amys and the steward should agree to fight; it was needful also that sureties should be found, and such was the steward's power at court that all men feared to come forward on behalf of Sir Amys. The young man would have fared badly, and indeed would at once have been thrown into prison, had not both Belisante and her mother offered themselves as sureties for his presence when the day arrived.

But not all the wiles of the fair Belisante could chase the gloom from the face of Sir Amys. He never forgot that he had sworn a false oath, and it was to no purpose that Belisante reminded him of all the ill deeds done by the steward to him and others. 'This time,' he said sadly, 'I have the wrong and he the right, therefore I am afraid to fight,' and no other answer could she wring from him.

Way out of the tangle there seemed none. Fight Sir Amys could not, with the weight of a false oath on his soul, yet to run away were to confess all, and leave Belisante to bear her father's anger alone. Turn his thoughts which side he would, escape seemed barred, till the image of Sir Amyle flashed across him. 'Fool, why had he not remembered him earlier? Luckily there was yet time, and he could ride with full speed to his brother's castle, and bid him return to take the battle on himself.' With a gladder face than he had known for long, he sought out the duchess and her daughter, and told them his plan.

Before the sun rose Sir Amys was in the saddle, and so busy was he with all that had befallen him that he pushed on and never drew rein till his horse dropped dead under him from sheer weariness. As there was no town or house where he might find another, he was forced to proceed on foot. But by-and-by he too fell from lack of sleep, and when Sir Amyle was returning home through the forest after a day's hunting, he discovered his brother stretched across the path in the shade of a tree.

Joy at meeting gave new life to Sir Amys, and, sitting up, he told his friend all his woes, and how he dare not fight with a false oath on his conscience.

'Oh! that is easily to be managed,' cried Sir Amyle, with a great laugh. 'Go home to my castle,' he said, 'and tell my wife that you have sent the horse to Sir Amys, at court, as you heard he had sore need of one. None will know you from me, no more than they did of old, and, as to my wife, it was but now I told her that business called me to the most distant parts of my lands, so this very night you can bid her farewell.'

Sir Amys did as his brother bade him, and Sir Amyle hastened with all speed to the duke's palace.

He was only just in time. The hour for the fight had come, and the steward had entered the lists, and, looking round in triumph, proclaimed to all whom it might concern that his adversary knew himself to be a traitor to his lord, and had fled. Therefore, according to all the rules of chivalry, a fire should be made, and his sureties burned before all the people.

At these dreadful words, the hearts of the king and his wife and daughter trembled within them. For the steward had spoken truly, and the order for the execution must be given. It was in vain that the men worked right slowly; linger as they might, the pile was ready at last, and with one despairing glance round, the duchess and her daughter were bravely walking up to it, when Sir Amyle hastily pushed his way to the duke and demanded that the captives should be instantly set free. Then, followed by the duchess and Belisante, he entered the palace to gird himself with the armour of Sir Amys.

When his helmet and sword were buckled on him, he prayed them to leave him, as he would fain be alone for a short space before he mounted his horse. So the two ladies embraced him and left him, wishing him God-speed. As the door closed upon them, Sir Amyle held up his sword and muttered a prayer before it.

'Come weal or woe, I will help my brother,' he said softly; then mounting his horse he rode into the lists, and, kneeling, took the oath that he was guiltless of wrong and would prove his innocence on the body of his foe.

The fight lasted but a short time; the steward's sword was keen, and he knew how to use it, and it was not long before he had given Sir Amyle a sharp thrust through the shoulder, and the young knight reeled in his saddle. The steward uttered a cry of fierce joy, and raised his arm to deal a second blow, when Sir Amyle suddenly spurred his horse to one side and pierced his enemy to the heart. Then, all bleeding as he was, the false Amys cut off the head of the traitor, and gave it to the duke, proving to him and to all the court that the right had conquered. But hardly had he done so when, faint from loss of blood, he fell senseless on the ground, and was carried into the palace, where the duke's best leeches were called in to attend him. In a few days the fever left him, and he was able to receive a visit from the duke himself.

'O Amys, my friend, how I have misjudged you!' cried the duke, falling on his knees weeping, 'but I will let my people know that you were always true, and you shall marry my daughter as soon as you can stand upon your feet, and I will hold a feast, and proclaim you heir to my duchy.'

And the wounded man gave him thanks and grace, but sent off a messenger in all haste to Sir Amys, bidding him be by a spring in the forest, nine days hence, which message Sir Amys obeyed, wondering what had passed. Then the two knights changed their clothes once more, and Sir Amyle returned to his wife and Sir Amys to his bride, and they lived happily to the end of their lives.

27

Binnorie

Binnorie is tale IX in English Fairy Tales, collected and retold by Joseph Jacobs and first published in London by David Nutt in 1890. Jacobs credits the piece as a prose adaptation of the traditional ballad "The Twa Sisters o' Binnorie", and notes in his "Notes and References" that he follows the longer version printed in Roberts's Legendary Ballads. Modern catalogues classify the story under ATU 780, "The Singing Bone", which groups together European narratives in which a murdered person's remains reveal the crime through music or speech. Within English Fairy Tales, "Binnorie" sits alongside other items that blur the line between fairy tale, legend and ballad, reflecting Jacobs's broad conception of "fairy tales" as encompassing a range of popular narrative forms.

Once upon a time there were two king's daughters lived in a bower near the bonny mill-dams of Binnorie. And Sir William came wooing the eldest and won her love and plighted troth with glove and with ring. But after a time he looked upon the youngest, with her cherry cheeks and golden hair, and his love grew towards her till he cared no longer for the eldest one. So she hated her sister for taking away Sir William's love, and day by day her hate grew upon her, and she plotted and she planned how to get rid of her.

So one fine morning, fair and clear, she said to her sister, "Let us go and see our father's boats come in at the bonny mill-stream of Binnorie." So they went there hand in hand. And when they got to the river's bank the youngest got upon a stone to watch for the coming of the boats. And her sister, coming behind her, caught her round the waist and dashed her into the rushing mill-stream of Binnorie.

"O sister, sister, reach me your hand!" she cried, as she floated away, "and you shall have half of all I've got or shall get."

"No, sister, I'll reach you no hand of mine, for I am the heir to all your land. Shame on me if I touch the hand that has come 'twixt me and my own heart's love."

"O sister, Oh sister, then reach me your glove!" she cried, as she floated further away, "and you shall have your William again."

"Sink on," cried the cruel princess, "no hand or glove of mine you'll touch. Sweet William will be all mine when you are sunk beneath the bonny mill-stream of Binnorie." And she turned and went home to the king's castle.

And the princess floated down the mill-stream, sometimes swimming and sometimes sinking, till she came near the mill. Now the miller's daughter was cooking that day, and needed water for her cooking. And as she went to draw it from the stream, she saw something floating towards the mill-dam, and she called out, "Father! father! draw your dam. There's something white - a merry maid or a milk-white swan - coming down the stream." So the miller hastened to the dam and stopped the heavy cruel mill-wheels. And then they took out the princess and laid her on the bank.

Fair and beautiful she looked as she lay there. In her golden hair were pearls and precious stones; you could not see her waist for her golden girdle; and the golden fringe of her white dress came down over her lily feet. But she was drowned, drowned!

And as she lay there in her beauty a famous harper passed by the mill-dam of Binnorie, and saw her sweet pale face. And though he travelled on far away he never forgot that face, and after many days he came back to the bonny mill-stream of Binnorie. But then all he could find of her where they had put her to rest were her bones and her golden hair. So he made a harp out of her breast-bone and her hair, and travelled on up the hill from the mill-dam of Binnorie, till he came to the castle of the king her father.

That night they were all gathered in the castle hall to hear the great harper - king and queen, their daughter and son, Sir William and all their Court. And first the harper sang to his old harp, making them joy and be glad or sorrow and weep just as he liked. But while he sang he put the harp he had made that day on a stone in the hall. And presently it began to sing by itself, low and clear, and the harper stopped and all were hushed.

And this was what the harp sung:

"O yonder sits my father, the king,

Binnorie, Oh Binnorie;

And yonder sits my mother, the queen;

By the bonny mill-dams o' Binnorie,

"And yonder stands my brother Hugh,

Binnorie, Oh Binnorie;

And by him, my William, false and true;

By the bonny mill-dams o' Binnorie."

Then they all wondered, and the harper told them how he had seen the princess lying drowned on the bank near the bonny mill-dams o' Binnorie, and how he had afterwards made this harp out of her hair and breast-bone. Just then the harp began singing again, and this was what it sang out loud and clear:

"And there sits my sister who drowned me

By the bonny mill-dams o' Binnorie."

And the harp snapped and broke, and never sang more.

Cap O' Rushes

Cap O' Rushes is a traditional English fairy tale recorded by the folklorist Joseph Jacobs and first published in his collection English Fairy Tales (David Nutt, London, 1890), where it appears accompanied by John D. Batten's illustrations.

Jacobs notes that his text is based on a version contributed by "Mrs Walter-Thomas" to "Suffolk Notes and Queries" in the Ipswich Journal, and then reprinted in Longman's Magazine and in the journal Folk-Lore in 1890, where Andrew Lang remarks that the tale was noticed in the Suffolk material by Edward Clodd.

From a classificatory perspective, the story has attracted attention from scholars of international tale types. It is usually indexed as ATU 510B ("Unnatural Love" / persecuted heroine), a group that includes the so-called "King Lear" motif.

Well, there was once a very rich gentleman, and he'd three daughters, and he thought he'd see how fond they were of him. So he says to the first, "How much do you love me, my dear?"

"Why," says she, "as I love my life."

"That's good," says he.

So he says to the second, "How much do you love me, my dear?"

"Why," says she, "better nor all the world."

"That's good," says he.

So he says to the third, "How much do you love me, my dear?"

"Why, I love you as fresh meat loves salt," says she.

Well, he was that angry. "You don't love me at all," says he, "and in my house you stay no more." So he drove her out there and then, and shut the door in her face.

Well, she went away on and on till she came to a fen, and there she gathered a lot of rushes and made them into a kind of a sort of a cloak with a hood, to cover her from head to foot, and to hide her fine clothes. And then she went on and on till she came to a great house.

"Do you want a maid?" says she.

"No, we don't," they said.

"I haven't nowhere to go," says she, "and I ask no wages, and do any sort of work," says she.

"Well," says they, "if you like to wash the pots and scrape the saucepans you may stay," they said.

So she stayed there and washed the pots and scraped the saucepans and did all the dirty work. And because she gave no name they called her "Cap o' Rushes."

Well, one day there was to be a great dance a little way off, and the servants were allowed to go and look on at the grand people. Cap o' Rushes said she was too tired to go, so she stayed at home.

But when they were gone she offed with her cap o' rushes, and cleaned herself, and went to the dance. And no one there was so finely dressed as her.

Well, who should be there but her master's son, and what should he do but fall in love with her the minute he set eyes on her. He wouldn't dance with anyone else.

But before the dance was done Cap o' Rushes slipped off, and away she went home. And when the other maids came back she was pretending to be asleep with her cap o' rushes on.

Well, next morning they said to her, "You did miss a sight, Cap o' Rushes!"

"What was that?" says she.

"Why, the beautifullest lady you ever see, dressed right gay and ga'. The young master, he never took his eyes off her."

"Well, I should have liked to have seen her," says Cap o' Rushes.

"Well, there's to be another dance this evening, and perhaps she'll be there."

But, come the evening, Cap o' Rushes said she was too tired to go with them. Howsoever, when they were gone, she offed with her cap o' rushes and cleaned herself, and away she went to the dance.

The master's son had been reckoning on seeing her, and he danced with no one else, and never took his eyes off her. But, before the dance was over, she slipped off, and home she went, and when the maids came back she, pretended to be asleep with her cap o' rushes on.

Next day they said to her again, "Well, Cap o' Rushes, you should have been there to see the lady. There she was again, gay and ga', and the young master he never took his eyes off her."

"Well, there," says she, "I should have liked to have seen her."

"Well," says they, "there's a dance again this evening, and you must go with us, for she's sure to be there."

Well, come this evening, Cap o' Rushes said she was too tired to go, and do what they would she stayed at home. But when they were gone she offed with her cap o' rushes and cleaned herself, and away she went to the dance.

The master's son was rarely glad when he saw her. He danced with none but her and never took his eyes off her. When she wouldn't tell him her name, nor where she came from, he gave her a ring and told her if he didn't see her again he should die.

Well, before the dance was over, off she slipped, and home she went, and when the maids came home she was pretending to be asleep with her cap o' rushes on.

Well, next day they says to her, "There, Cap o' Rushes, you didn't come last night, and now you won't see the lady, for there's no more dances."

"Well I should have rarely liked to have seen her," says she.

The master's son he tried every way to find out where the lady was gone, but go where he might, and ask whom he might, he never heard anything about her. And he got worse and worse for the love of her till he had to keep his bed.

"Make some gruel for the young master," they said to the cook. "He's dying for the love of the lady." The cook she set about making it when Cap o' Rushes came in.

"What are you a-doing of?", says she.

"I'm going to make some gruel for the young master," says the cook, "for he's dying for love of the lady."

"Let me make it," says Cap o' Rushes.

Well, the cook wouldn't at first, but at last she said yes, and Cap o' Rushes made the gruel. And when she had made it she slipped the ring into it on the sly before the cook took it upstairs.

The young man he drank it and then he saw the ring at the bottom.

"Send for the cook," says he.

So up she comes.

"Who made this gruel here?" says he.

"I did," says the cook, for she was frightened.

And he looked at her,

"No, you didn't," says he. "Say who did it, and you shan't be harmed."

"Well, then, 'twas Cap o' Rushes," says she.

"Send Cap o' Rushes here," says he.

So Cap o' Rushes came.

"Did you make my gruel?" says he.

"Yes, I did," says she.

"Where did you get this ring?" says he.

"From him that gave it me," says she.

"Who are you, then?" says the young man.

"I'll show you," says she. And she offed with her cap o' rushes, and there she was in her beautiful clothes.

Well, the master's son he got well very soon, and they were to be married in a little time. It was to be a very grand wedding, and everyone was asked far and near. And Cap o' Rushes' father was asked. But she never told anybody who she was.

But before the wedding she went to the cook, and says she:

"I want you to dress every dish without a mite o' salt."

"That'll be rare nasty," says the cook.

"That doesn't signify," says she.

"Very well," says the cook.

Well, the wedding-day came, and they were married. And after they were married all the company sat down to the dinner. When they began to eat the meat, that was so tasteless they couldn't eat it. But Cap o' Rushes' father he tried first one dish and then another, and then he burst out crying.

"What is the matter?" said the master's son to him.

"Oh!" says he, "I had a daughter. And I asked her how much she loved me. And she said, 'As much as fresh meat loves salt.' And I turned her from my door, for I thought she didn't love me. And now I see she loved me best of all. And she may be dead for anything I know."

"No, father, here she is!" says Cap o' Rushes. And she goes up to him and puts her arms round him.

And so they were happy ever after.

Catskin

English Fairy Tales is a collection of more than forty traditional tales retold by Flora Annie Steel and first published by Macmillan in London in 1918, with illustrations by Arthur Rackham.

Catskin is Steel's adaptation of an English narrative that had already circulated in chapbook form and in Joseph Jacobs's More English Fairy Tales (1894). Catskin is one of the recognised "classic" English variants of the Cinderella-type story in twentieth-century popular anthologies.

Once upon a time there lived a gentleman who owned fine lands and houses, and he very much wanted to have a son to be heir to them. So when his wife brought him a daughter, though she was bonny as bonny could be, he cared nought for her, and said, "Let me never see her face."

So she grew up to be a beautiful maiden, though her father never set eyes on her till she was fifteen and was ready to be married.

Then her father said roughly, "She shall marry the first that comes for her." Now when this became known, who should come along and be first but a nasty, horrid old man! So she didn't know what to do, and went to the hen-wife and asked her advice. And the hen-wife said, "Say you will not take him unless they give you a coat of silver cloth." Well, they gave her a coat of silver cloth, but she wouldn't take him for all that, but went again to the hen-wife, who said, "Say you will not take him unless they give you a coat of beaten gold." Well, they gave her a coat of beaten gold, but still she would not take the old man, but went again to the hen-wife, who said, "Say you will not take him unless they give you a coat made of the feathers of all the birds of the air." So they sent out a man with a great heap of peas; and the man cried to all the birds of the air, "Each bird take a pea and put down a feather." So each bird took a pea and put down one of its feathers: and they took all the feathers and made a coat of them and gave it to her; but still she would not take the nasty, horrid old man, but asked the hen-wife once again what she was to do, and the hen-wife said, "Say they must first make you a coat of cat skin." Then they made her a coat of cat skin; and she put it on, and tied up her other coats into a bundle, and when it was night-time ran away with it into the woods.

Now she went along, and went along, and went along, till at the end of the wood she saw a fine castle. Then she hid her fine dresses by a crystal waterfall and went up to the castle gates and asked for work. The lady of the castle saw her, and told her, "I'm sorry I have no better place, but if you like you may be our scullion." So down she went into the kitchen, and they called her Catskin, because of her dress. But the cook was very cruel to her, and led her a sad life.

Well, soon after that the young lord of the castle came home, and there was to be a grand ball in honour of the occasion. And when they were speaking about it among the servants, "Dear me, Mrs. Cook," said Catskin, "how much I should like to go!"

"What! You dirty, impudent slut," said the cook, "you go among all the fine lords and ladies with your filthy cat skin? A fine figure you'd cut!" She took a basin of water and dashed it into Catskin's face. But Catskin only shook her ears and said nothing.

Now when the day of the ball arrived, Catskin slipped out of the house and went to the edge of the forest where she had hidden her dresses. Then she bathed herself in a crystal waterfall, and put on her coat of silver cloth, and hastened away to the ball. As soon as she entered all were overcome by her beauty and grace, while the young lord at once lost his heart to her. He asked her to be his partner for the first dance; and he would dance with none other the livelong night.

When it came to parting time, the young lord said, "Pray tell me, fair maid, where you live?"

But Catskin curtsied and said,

"Kind sir, if the truth I must tell,

At the sign of the 'Basin of Water' I dwell."

Then she flew from the castle and donned her cat skin robe again, and slipped into the scullery, unbeknown to the cook.

The young lord went the very next day and searched for the sign of the "Basin of Water"; but he could not find it. So he went to his mother, the lady of the castle, and declared he would wed none other but the lady of the silver dress, and would never rest till he had found her. So another ball was soon arranged in hopes that the beautiful maid would appear again.

So Catskin said to the cook, "Oh, how I should like to go!"

Whereupon the cook screamed out in a rage, "What, you, you dirty, impudent slut! You would cut a fine figure among all the fine lords and ladies." And with that she up with a ladle and broke it across Catskin's back. But Catskin only shook her ears, and ran off to the forest, where, first of all, she bathed, and then she put on her coat of beaten gold, and off she went to the ball-room.

As soon as she entered all eyes were upon her; and the young lord at once recognised her as the lady of the "Basin of Water," claimed her hand for the first dance, and did not leave her till the last. When that came, he again asked her where she lived. But all that she would say was:

"Kind sir, if the truth I must tell,

At the sign of the 'Broken Ladle' I dwell";

With that she curtsied and flew from the ball, off with her golden robe, on with her cat skin, and into the scullery without the cook's knowing.

Next day, when the young lord could not find where the sign of the "Basin of Water" was, he begged his mother to have another grand ball, so that he might meet the beautiful maid once more.

Then Catskin said to the cook, "Oh, how I wish I could go to the ball!" Whereupon the cook called out, "A fine figure you'd cut!" and broke the skimmer across her head. But Catskin only shook her ears, and went off to the forest, where she first bathed in the crystal spring, and then donned her coat of feathers, and so off to the ball-room.

When she entered everyone was surprised at so beautiful a face and form dressed in so rich and rare a dress; but the young lord at once recognised his beautiful sweetheart, and would dance with none but her the whole evening. When the ball came to an end he pressed her to tell him where she lived, but all she would answer was:

"Kind sir, if the truth I must tell,

At the sign of the 'Broken Skimmer' I dwell";

With that she curtsied, and was off to the forest. But this time the young lord followed her, and watched her change her fine dress of feathers for her cat skin dress, and then he knew her for his own scullery-maid.

Next day he went to his mother, and told her that he wished to marry the scullery-maid, Catskin.

"Never," said the lady of the castle, "never so long as I live."

Well, the young lord was so grieved that he took to his bed and was very ill indeed. The doctor tried to cure him, but he would not take any medicine unless from the hands of Catskin. At last the doctor went to the mother, and said that her son would die if she did not consent to his marriage with Catskin; so she had to give way. Then she summoned Catskin to her, and Catskin put on her coat of beaten gold before she went to see the lady; and she, of course, was overcome at once, and was only too glad to wed her son to so beautiful a maid.

So they were married, and after a time a little son was born to them, and grew up a fine little lad. Now one day, when he was about four years old, a beggar woman came to the door, and Lady Catskin gave some money to the little lord and told him to go and give it to the beggar woman. So he went and gave it, putting it into the hand of the woman's baby child; and the child leant forward and kissed the little lord.

Now the wicked old cook (who had never been sent away, because Catskin was too kind-hearted) was looking on, and she said, "See how beggars' brats take to one another!"

This insult hurt Catskin dreadfully: and she went to her husband, the young lord, and told him all about her father, and begged he would go and find out what had become of her parents. So they set out in the lord's grand coach, and travelled through the forest till they came to the house of Catskin's father. Then they put up at an inn near, and Catskin stopped there, while her husband went to see if her father would own she was his daughter.

Now her father had never had any other child, and his wife had died; so he was all alone in the world, and sat moping and miserable. When the young lord came in he hardly looked up, he was so miserable. Then Catskin's husband drew a chair close up to him, and asked him, "Pray, sir, had you not once a young daughter whom you would never see or own?"

And the miserable man said with tears, "It is true; I am a hardened sinner. But I would give all my worldly goods if I could but see her once before I die."

Then the young lord told him what had happened to Catskin, and took him to the inn, and afterwards brought his father-in-law to his own castle, where they lived happy ever afterwards.

Coat o' Clay

More English Fairy Tales is Joseph Jacobs's second major collection of English folk narratives, first published in 1894 as a companion volume to English Fairy Tales and illustrated by John D. Batten. It gathers a further range of stories from English oral and chapbook traditions, many of them regional or previously neglected, and presents them in a deliberately "old-fashioned" storytelling style, with dialect phrases and colloquial turns of speech.

Coat o' Clay is a comic fool tale. It follows a simple-minded hero who is told by a wise woman that he will gain true wisdom when he gets himself a "coat of clay.". The tale is short, strongly dialectal, and very typical of Jacobs's taste for stories in which verbal misunderstanding, literal-mindedness and earthy humour carry a quietly moral point about human folly.

Once on a time, in the parts of Lindsey, there lived a wise woman. Some said she was a witch, but they said it in a whisper, lest she should overhear and do them a mischief, and truly it was not a thing one could be sure of, for she was never known to hurt anyone, which, if she were a witch, she would have been sure to do. But she could tell you what your sickness was, and how to cure it with herbs, and she could mix rare possets that would drive the pain out of you in a twinkling; and she could advise you what to do if your cows were ill, or if you'd got into trouble, and tell the maids whether their sweethearts were likely to be faithful.

But she was ill-pleased if folks questioned her too much or too long, and she sore misliked fools. A many came to her asking foolish things, as was their nature, and to them she never gave counsel - at least of a kind that could aid them much.

Well, one day, as she sat at her door paring potatoes, over the stile and up the path came a tall lad with a long nose and goggle eyes and his hands in his pockets.

"That's a fool, if ever was one, and a fool's luck in his face," said the wise woman to herself with a nod of her head, and threw a potato skin over her left shoulder to keep off ill-chance.

"Good-day, missis," said the fool. "I be come to see you."

"So you are," said the wise woman, "I see that. How's all in your folk this year?"

"Oh, fairly," answered he. "But they say I be a fool."

"Ay, so you are," nodded she, and threw away a bad potato. "I see that too. But would o' me? I keep no brains for sale."

"Well, see now. Mother says I'll ne'er be wiser all my born days; but folks tell us you can do everything. Can't you teach me a bit, so they'll think me a clever fellow at home?"

"Hout-tout!" said the wise woman, "thou are a bigger fool than I thought. Nay, I can't teach you nought, lad; but I tell you something. You will be a fool all your days till you gets a coat o' clay; and then you will know more than me."

"Hi, missis; what sort of a coat's that?" he said.

"That's none o' my business," answered she, "You have to find out that."

And she took up her potatoes and went into her house.

The fool took off his cap and scratched his head.

"It's a queer kind of coat to look for, surely," he said, "I never heard of a coat o' clay. But then I be a fool, that's true."

So he walked on till he came to the drain nearby, with just a pickle of water and a foot of mud in it.

"Here's muck," said the fool, much pleased, and he got in and rolled in it spluttering. "Hi, you" said he - for he had his mouth full - "I've got a coat o' clay now to be sure. I'll go home and tell my mother I'm a wise man and not a fool any longer." And he went on home.

Presently he came to a cottage with a lass at the door.

"Morning, fool," she said, "hast you been ducked in the horse-pond?"

"Fool yourself," he said, "the wise woman says I'll know more 'n she when I get a coat o' clay, and here it is. Shall I marry you, lass?"

"Ay," she said, for she thought she'd like a fool for a husband, "when shall it be?"

"I'll come and fetch you when I've told my mother," said the fool, and he gave her his lucky penny and went on.

When he got home his mother was on the doorstep.

"Mother, I 've got a coat o' clay," he said.

"Coat o' muck," she said, "and what of that?"

"Wise woman said I'd know more than she when I got a coat o' clay," he said, "so I down in the drain and got one, and I'm not a fool any longer."

"Very good," said his mother, "now you can get a wife."

"Ay," he said, "I'm going to marry so-an'-so."

"What!" said his mother, "that lass? No, and that you will not. She's nought but a brat, with ne'er a cow or a cabbage o' her own."

"But I gave her my luck penny," said the fool.

"Then you are a bigger fool than ever, for all your coat o' clay!" said his mother, and banged the door in his face.

"Dang it!" said the fool, and scratched his head, "that's not the right sort o' clay sure-ly."

So back he went to the highroad and sat down on the bank of the river close by, looking at the water, which was cool and clear.

By-and-by he fell asleep, and before he knew what he was about - plump - he rolled off into the river with a splash, and scrambled out, dripping like a drowned rat.

"Dear, dear," he said, "I'd better go and get dry in the sun." So up he went to the highroad, and lay down in the dust, rolling about so that the sun should get at him all over.

Presently, when he sat up and looked down at himself, he found that the dust had caked into a sort of skin over his wet clothes till you could not see an inch of them, they were so well covered. "Hi, you" he said, "here's a coat o' clay ready-made, and a fine one. See now, I'm a clever fellow this time sure-ly, for I've found what I wanted without looking for it! Wow, but it's a fine feeling to be so smart!"

And he sat and scratched his head, and thought about his own cleverness.

But all of a sudden, round the corner came the squire on horseback, full gallop, as if the boggles were after him; but the fool had to jump, even though the squire pulled his horse back on his haunches.

"What the dickens," said the squire, "do you mean by lying in the middle of the road like that?"

"Well, master," said the fool, "I fell into the water and got wet, so I lay down in the road to get dry; and I lay down a fool an' got up a wise man."

"How's that?" said the squire.

So the fool told him about the wise woman and the coat o' clay.

"Ah, ah!" laughed the squire, "whoever heard of a wise man lying in the middle of the highroad to be ridden over? Lad, take my word for it, you are a bigger fool than ever," and he rode on laughing.

"Dang it!" said the fool, as he scratched his head. "I've not got the right sort of coat yet, then." And he choked and spluttered in the dust that the squire's horse had raised.

So, on he went in a melancholy mood till he came to an inn, and the landlord at his door smoking.

"Well, fool," he said, "thou are fine and dirty."

"Ay," said the fool, "I be dirty outside an' dusty in, but it's not the right thing yet."

And he told the landlord all about the wise woman and the coat o' clay.

"Hout-tout!" said the landlord, with a wink. "I know what's wrong. You have a skin o' dirt outside and all dry dust inside. You must moisten it, lad, with a good drink, and then you will have a real all-over coat o' clay."

"Hi," said the fool, "that's a good word."

So down he sat and began to drink. But it was wonderful how much liquor it took to moisten so much dust; and each time he got to the bottom of the pot he found he was still dry. At last he began to feel very merry and pleased with himself.

"Hi, you" he said. "I've got a real coat o' clay now outside and in - what a difference it do make, to be sure. I feel another man now - so smart."

And he told the landlord he was certainly a wise man now, though he couldn't speak over-distinctly after drinking so much. So up he got, and thought he would go home and tell his mother she hadn't a fool for a son anymore.

But just as he was trying to get through the inn-door which would scarcely keep still long enough for him to find it, up came the landlord and caught him by the sleeve.

"See here, master," he said, "thou hasn't paid for your score - where's your money?"

"Haven't any!" said the fool, and pulled out his pockets to show they were empty.

"What!" said the landlord, and swore, "thou have drunk all my liquor and haven't got nought to pay for it with!"

"Hi!" said the fool. "You told me to drink so as to get a coat o' clay;

but as I'm a wise man now I don't mind helping you along in the world a bit, for though I'm a smart fellow I'm not too proud to my friends."

"Wise man! smart fellow!" said the landlord, "and help me along, will you? Dang it! you are the biggest fool I ever saw, and it's I'll help you first. Get out o' this place!"

And he kicked him out of the door into the road and swore at him.

"Hum," said the fool, as he lay in the dust, "I'm not so wise as I thought. I guess I'll go back to the wise woman and tell her there's a screw loose somewhere."

So up he got and went along to her house, and found her sitting at the door.

"So you have come back," she said, with a nod. "What do you want with me now?"

So he sat down and told her how he'd tried to get a coat o' clay, and he wasn't any wiser for all of it.

"No," said the wise woman, "thou are a bigger fool than ever, my lad."

"So they all say," sighed the fool, "but where can I get the right sort of coat o' clay, then, missis?"

"When you are done with this world, and your folk put you in the ground," said the wise woman. "That's the only coat o' clay as 'll make such as you wise, lad. Born a fool, die a fool, and be a fool your life long, and that's the truth!"

And she went into the house and shut the door.

"Dang it," said the fool. "I must tell my mother she was right after all, and that she'll never have a wise man for a son!"

And he went off home.

Earl Mar's Daughter

English Fairy Tales is a classic collection of traditional narratives gathered and retold by the folklorist Joseph Jacobs, first published in London by David Nutt in 1890 with illustrations by John Dickson Batten. Aimed at children but grounded in serious comparative work, the book assembles more than forty English folk and fairy tales that Jacobs sourced from oral tradition, chapbooks and earlier antiquarian collections, and presents them in a deliberately plain, "tellable" prose style.

Earl Mar's Daughter is one of the shorter pieces and represents Jacobs's prose adaptation of a traditional ballad narrative, catalogued by Francis James Child as ballad 270, "The Earl of Mar's Daughter". The story centres on a young noblewoman who falls in love with a dove that visits her in the garden.

One fine summer's day Earl Mar's daughter went into the castle garden, dancing and tripping along. And as she played and sported she would stop from time to time to listen to the music of the birds. After a while as she sat under the shade of a green oak tree she looked up and spied a sprightly dove sitting high up on one of its branches. She looked up and said, "Coo-my-dove, my dear, come down to me and I will give you a golden cage. I'll take you home and pet you well, as well as any bird of them all." Scarcely had she said these words when the dove flew down from the branch and settled on her shoulder, nestling up against her neck while she smoothed its feathers. Then she took it home to her own room.

The day was done and the night came on and Earl Mar's daughter was thinking of going to sleep when, turning round, she found at her side a handsome young man. She was startled, for the door had been locked for hours. But she was a brave girl and said, "What are you doing here, young man, to come and startle me so? The door was barred these hours ago; however did you come here?"

"Hush! hush!" the young man whispered. "I was that cooing dove that you coaxed from off the tree."

"But who are you then?" she said quite low, "and how came you to be changed into that dear little bird?"

"My name is Florentine, and my mother is a queen, and something more than a queen, for she knows magic and spells, and because I would not do as she wished she turned me into a dove by day, but at night her spells lose their power and I become a man again. Today I crossed the sea and saw you for the first time and I was glad to be a bird that I could come near you. Unless you love me, I shall never be happy more."

"But if I love you," says she, "will you not fly away and leave me one of these fine days?"

"Never, never," said the prince, "be my wife and I'll be yours for ever. By day a bird, by night a prince, I will always be by your side as a husband, dear."

So they were married in secret and lived happily in the castle and no one knew that every night Coo-my-dove became Prince

Florentine. And every year a little son came to them as bonny as bonny could be. But as each son was born Prince Florentine carried the little thing away on his back over the sea to where the queen his mother lived and left the little one with her.

Seven years passed thus and then a great trouble came to them. For the Earl Mar wished to marry his daughter to a noble of high degree who came wooing her. Her father pressed her sore but she said, "Father dear, I do not wish to marry; I can be quite happy with Coo-my-dove here."

Then her father got into a mighty rage and swore a great big oath, and said, "Tomorrow, so sure as I live and eat, I'll twist that birdie's neck," and out he stamped from her room.

"Oh, oh!" said Coo-my-dove, "it's time that I was away," and so he jumped upon the window-sill and in a moment was flying away. And he flew and he flew till he was over the deep, deep sea, and yet on he flew till he came to his mother's castle. Now the queen his mother was taking her walk abroad when she saw the pretty dove flying overhead and alighting on the castle walls.

"Here, dancers come and dance your jigs," she called, "and pipers, pipe you well, for here's my own Florentine, come back to me to stay for he's brought no bonny boy with him this time."

"No, mother," said Florentine, "no dancers for me and no minstrels, for my dear wife, the mother of my seven, boys, is to be wed tomorrow, and sad is the day for me."

"What can I do, my son?" said the queen, "tell me, and it shall be done if my magic has power to do it."

"Well then, mother dear, turn the twenty-four dancers and pipers into twenty-four grey herons, and let my seven sons become seven white swans, and let me be a goshawk and their leader."

"Alas! alas! my son," she said, "that may not be; my magic reaches not so far. But perhaps my teacher, the spaewife of Ostree, may know better." And away she hurries to the cave of Ostree, and after a while comes out as white as white can be and muttering over some burning herbs she brought out of the cave. Suddenly Coo-my-dove changed into a goshawk and around him flew twenty-four grey herons and above them flew seven cygnets.

Without a word or a good-bye off they flew over the deep blue sea which was tossing and moaning. They flew and they flew till they swooped down on Earl Mar's castle just as the wedding party were setting out for the church. First came the men-at-arms and then the bridegroom's friends, and then Earl Mar's men, and then the bridegroom, and lastly, pale and beautiful, Earl Mar's daughter herself. They moved down slowly to stately music till they came past the trees on which the birds were settling. A word from Prince Florentine, the goshawk, and they all rose into the air, herons beneath, cygnets above, and goshawk circling above all. The wedding guests wondered at the sight when, swoop! the herons were down among them scattering the men-at-arms. The swanlets took charge of the bride while the goshawk dashed down and tied the bridegroom to a tree. Then the herons gathered themselves together into one feather bed and the cygnets placed their mother upon them, and suddenly they all rose in the air bearing the bride away with them in safety towards Prince Florentine's home. Surely a wedding party was never so disturbed in this world. What could the wedding guests do? They saw their pretty bride carried away and away till she and the herons and the swans and the goshawk disappeared, and that very day Prince Florentine brought Earl Mar's daughter to the castle of the queen his mother, who took the spell off him and they lived happy ever afterwards.

Gobborn Seer

More English Fairy Tales is Joseph Jacobs's second major collection of English traditional narratives, first published in 1894 as a sequel to English Fairy Tales (1890). It gathers forty-plus tales that Jacobs either took from oral tradition, older chapbooks or earlier antiquarian collections, and recast for a late Victorian child and family readership, with illustrations by John D. Batten.

Gobborn Seer is a short narrative about a master builder and wise man, Gobborn Seer, his son Jack, and Jack's notably clever wife. The story turns on a series of riddling tasks and threats.

Once there was a man called Gobborn Seer, and he had a son called Jack. One day he sent him out to sell a sheep skin, and Gobborn said, "You must bring me back the skin and the value of it as well."

So Jack started, but he could not find any who would leave him the skin and give him its price too. So he came home discouraged.

But Gobborn Seer said, "Never mind, you must take another turn at it tomorrow."

So he tried again, and nobody wished to buy the skin on those terms.

When he came home his father said, "You must go and try your luck tomorrow," and the third day it seemed as if it would be the same thing over again. And he had half a mind not to go back at all, his father would be so vexed. As he came to a bridge, like the Creek Road one yonder, he leaned on the parapet thinking of his trouble, and that perhaps it would be foolish to run away from home, but he could not tell which to do; when he saw a girl washing her clothes on the bank below. She looked up and said, "If it may be no offence asking, what is it you feel so badly about?"

"My father has given me this skin, and I am to fetch it back and the price of it beside."

"Is that all? Give it here, and it's easily done."

So the girl washed the skin in the stream, took the wool from it, and paid him the value of it, and gave him the skin to carry back.

His father was well pleased, and said to Jack, "That was a witty woman; she would make you a good wife. Do you think you could tell her again?"

Jack thought he could, so his father told him to go by-and-by to the bridge, and see if she was there, and if so bid her come home to take tea with them.

And sure enough Jack spied her and told her how his old father had a wish to meet her, and would she be pleased to drink tea with them.

The girl thanked him kindly, and said she could come the next day; she was too busy at the moment.

"All the better," said Jack, "I'll have time to make ready."

So when she came Gobborn Seer could see she was a witty woman, and he asked her if she would marry his Jack. She said "Yes," and they were married.

Not long after, Jack's father told him he must come with him and build the finest castle that ever was seen, for a king who wished to outdo all others by his wonderful castle.

And as they went to lay the foundation-stone, Gobborn Seer said to Jack, "Can't you shorten the way for me?"

But Jack looked ahead and there was a long road before them, and he said, "I don't see, father, how I could break a bit off."

"You're no good to me, then, and had best be off home."

So poor Jack turned back, and when he came in his wife said, "Why, how's this you've come alone?" and he told her what his father had said and his answer.

"You stupid," said his witty wife, "if you had told a tale you would have shortened the road! Now listen till I tell you a story, and then catch up with Gobborn Seer and begin it at once. He will like hearing it, and by the time you are done you will have reached the foundation-stone."

So Jack sweated and overtook his father. Gobborn Seer never said a word, but Jack began his story, and the road was shortened as his wife had said.

When they came to the end of their journey, they started building of this castle which was to outshine all others. Now the wife had advised them to be intimate with the servants, and so they did as she said, and it was "Good-morning" and "Good-day to you" as they passed in and out.

Now, at the end of a twelvemonth, Gobborn, the wise man, had built such a castle thousands were gathered to admire it.

And the king said, "The castle is done. I shall return tomorrow and pay you all."

"I have just a ceiling to finish in an upper lobby," said Gobborn, "and then it wants nothing."

But after the king was gone off, the housekeeper sent for Gobborn and Jack, and told them that she had watched for a chance to warn them, for the king was so afraid they should carry their art away and build some other king as fine a castle, he meant to take their lives on the morrow. Gobborn told Jack to keep a good heart, and they would come off all right.

When the king had come back Gobborn told him he had been unable to complete the job for lack of a tool left at home, and he should like to send Jack after it.

"No, no," said the king, "cannot one of the men do the errand?"

"No, they could not make themselves understood," said the Seer, "but Jack could do the errand."

"You and your son stop here. How will it do if I send my son?"

So Gobborn sent by him a message to Jack's wife. "Give him Crooked and Straight!"

Now there was a little hole in the wall rather high up, and Jack's wife tried to reach up into a chest there after "crooked and straight," but at last she asked the king's son to help her, because his arms were longest.

But when he was leaning over the chest she caught him by the two heels, and threw him into the chest, and fastened it down. So there he was, both "crooked and straight!"

Then he begged for pen and ink, which she brought him, but he was not allowed out, and holes were bored that he might breathe.

When his letter came, telling the king, his father, he was to be let free when Gobborn and Jack were safe home, the king saw he must settle for the building, and let them come away.

As they left Gobborn told him: Now that Jack was done with this work, he should soon build a castle for his witty wife far superior to the king's, which he did, and they lived there happily ever after.

Henny-Penny

English Fairy Tales is Flora Annie Steel's 1918 collection of forty or so traditional English folk narratives, and illustrated by Arthur Rackham. It sits within the late nineteenth- and early twentieth-century movement to gather "national" fairy tales into single, family-friendly volumes.

"Henny-Penny" in Steel's volume is her retelling of a widely known international folk tale about a hen who believes the sky is falling after an acorn hits her, and who gathers a procession of animal companions to go and tell the king.

One day Henny-penny was picking up corn in the rickyard when - whack! - an acorn hit her upon the head. "Goodness gracious me!" said Henny-penny, "the sky's a-going to fall; I must go and tell the King."

So she went along, and she went along, and she went along, till she met Cocky-locky. "Where are you going, Henny-penny?" says Cocky-locky. "Oh! I'm going to tell the King the sky's a-falling," says Henny-penny. "May I come with you?" says Cocky-locky. "Certainly," says Henny-penny. So Henny-penny and Cocky-locky went to tell the King the sky was falling.

They went along, and they went along, and they went along, till they met Ducky-daddles. "Where are you going to, Henny-penny and Cocky-locky?" says Ducky-daddles. "Oh! we're going to tell the King the sky's a-falling," said Henny-penny and Cocky-locky. "May I come with you?" says Ducky-daddles. "Certainly," said Henny-penny and Cocky-locky. So Henny-penny, Cocky-locky, and Ducky-daddles went to tell the King the sky was a-falling.

So they went along, and they went along, and they went along, till they met Goosey-poosey. "Where are you going to, Henny-penny, Cocky-locky, and Ducky-daddles?" said Goosey-poosey. "Oh! we're going to tell the King the sky's a-falling," said Henny-penny and Cocky-locky and Ducky-daddles. "May I come with you?" said Goosey-poosey. "Certainly," said Henny-penny, Cocky-locky, and Ducky-daddles. So Henny-penny, Cocky-locky, Ducky-daddles, and Goosey-poosey went to tell the King the sky was a-falling.

So they went along, and they went along, and they went along, till they met Turkey-lurkey. "Where are you going, Henny-penny, Cocky-locky, Ducky-daddles, and Goosey-poosey?" says Turkey-lurkey. "Oh! we're going to tell the King the sky's a-falling," said Henny-penny, Cocky-locky, Ducky-daddles, and Goosey-poosey. "May I come with you, Henny-penny, Cocky-locky, Ducky-daddles, and Goosey-poosey?" said Turkey-lurkey. "Oh, certainly, Turkey-lurkey," said Henny-penny, Cocky-locky, Ducky-daddles, and Goosey-poosey. So Henny-penny, Cocky-locky, Ducky-daddles, Goosey-poosey, and Turkey-lurkey all went to tell the King the sky was a-falling.

So they went along, and they went along, and they went along, till they met Foxy-woxy, and Foxy-woxy said to Henny-penny, Cocky-locky, Ducky-daddles, Goosey-poosey, and Turkey-lurkey, "Where are you going, Henny-penny, Cocky-locky, Ducky-daddles, Goosey-poosey, and Turkey-lurkey?" And Henny-penny, Cocky-locky, Ducky-daddles, Goosey-poosey, and Turkey-lurkey said to Foxy-woxy, "We're going to tell the King the sky's a-falling." "Oh! but this is not the way to the King, Henny-penny, Cocky-locky, Ducky-daddles, Goosey-poosey, and Turkey-lurkey," says Foxy-woxy, "I know the proper way; shall I show it you?" "Oh, certainly, Foxy-woxy," said Henny-penny, Cocky-locky, Ducky-daddles, Goosey-poosey, and Turkey-lurkey. So Henny-penny, Cocky-locky, Ducky-daddles, Goosey-poosey, Turkey-lurkey, and Foxy-woxy all went to tell the King the sky was a-falling. So they went along, and they went along, and they went along, till they came to a narrow and dark hole. Now this was the door of Foxy-woxy's burrow. But Foxy-woxy said to Henny-penny, Cocky-locky, Ducky-daddies, Goosey-poosey, and Turkey-lurkey, "This is the short cut to the King's palace: you'll soon get there if you follow me. I will go first and you come after, Henny-penny, Cocky-locky, Ducky-daddles, Goosey-poosey, and Turkey-lurkey." "Why, of course, certainly, without doubt, why not?" said Henny-penny, Cocky-locky, Ducky-daddles, Goosey-poosey, and Turkey-lurkey.

I will go first and you come after

So Foxy-woxy went into his burrow, and he didn't go very far but turned round to wait for Henny-penny, Cocky-locky, Ducky-daddles, Goosey-poosey, and Turkey-lurkey. Now Turkey-lurkey was the first to go through the dark hole into the burrow. He hadn't got far when, "Hrumph!"

Foxy-woxy snapped off Turkey-lurkey's head and threw his body over his left shoulder. Then Goosey-poosey went in, and "Hrumph!" Off went her head and Goosey-poosey was thrown beside Turkey-lurkey.

Then Ducky-daddles waddled down, and "Hrumph!" Foxy-woxy had snapped off Ducky-daddles' head and Ducky-daddles was thrown alongside Turkey-lurkey and Goosey-poosey.

Then Cocky-locky strutted down into the burrow, and he hadn't gone far when, "Hrumph!" But Cocky-locky will always crow whether you want him to do so or not, and so he had just time for one "Cock-a-doo-dle d..." before he went to join Turkey-lurkey, Goosey-poosey, and Ducky-daddles over Foxy-woxy's shoulders.

Now when Henny-penny, who had just got into the dark burrow, heard Cocky-locky crow, she said to herself, "My goodness! it must be dawn. Time for me to lay my egg."

So she turned round and bustled off to her nest; so she escaped, but she never told the King the sky was falling!

How the Cobbler Cheated the Devil

How the Cobbler Cheated the Devil is a neat little trickster tale where a supposedly half-witted cobbler ends up being the smartest person in town.

The story comes from Folk-Lore and Legends: English, a late-Victorian anthology edited by Charles John Tibbits and first published in London by W. W. Gibbings in 1890. The book is a small, popular collection, mixing a short "Dissertation on Fairies" with a run of English tales and legends. How the Cobbler Cheated the Devil is one of the shorter, jokey pieces, the kind of thing that would have worked well both as light reading and as a spoken story.

It chanced that once upon a time long years ago, in the days when strange things used to happen in the world, and the devil himself used sometimes to walk about in it in a bare-faced fashion, to the distraction of all good and bad folk alike, he came to a very small town where he resolved to stay a while to play some of his tricks. How it was, whether the people were better or were worse than he expected to find them, whether they would not give way to him, or whether they went beyond him and outwitted him, I don't know, and so cannot say; but sure it is that in a short while he became terribly angry with the folk, and at length was so disgusted that he threatened he would make them repent their treatment of him, for he would punish them in a manner which should show them his power. With that he flew off in a fury, and the folk, knowing with whom they had to deal, were very sad thinking what terrible thing would overtake them, and at their wits' end to imagine how they might manage to escape the claws of the Evil One.

Accordingly it was decided to call a meeting of the townsfolk, to which all, old and young, should come to deliver their opinion as to the best course to be pursued, only those too old to walk, the sick, and the foolish, being not called to the council.

Very many different courses were proposed, and while these were being debated a man rushed into the hall where the council was held, and informed them that their enemy was coming, for he had himself seen him making his way to the town, bearing on his shoulder a stone almost big enough to bury the place under it. He reported that the devil was yet a long way off, for his load hampered him sadly and he could not travel fast.

What to do the councillors did not know, when suddenly there came amongst them a poor cobbler, whom they had forgot to call to the meeting, for he was, indeed, looked upon as only half-witted.

"I will go and meet him," he said, "and stop him coming here."

"You stop him!" cried they all, "it's mad you must be to think of it."

"I'll go all the same," said the cobbler, and without saying a word more he goes out and begins to make ready for his journey.

First of all he collected together as many old boots and shoes as he could find, and when he had got them all in a bundle, he finds out the man who had seen the devil coming on, and inquired of him the way he should go to meet him. The man told him the road, and the cobbler set out. He walked, and walked, and walked, till at last he came to the devil, who was sitting by the roadside resting himself and trying to get cool, for the day was warm, and he was nearly worn out with carrying the big rock which lay beside him.

"Do you know such-and-such a place?" asks he of the man, naming the town he would be at.

"I do, indeed," says the man, "for I ought to, seeing I have lived in its neighbourhood these many years, and have only left there to travel here."

"And how many days have you been getting here?" asked the devil anxiously, for he had hoped he was near the end of his journey.

"Oh, days and days," replies the man. "See here," and he opens his bundle of old boots that he had ready, "see here," says he, "these are the boots I've worn out on the hard road in coming from the place here."

"Have you, indeed!' says the devil, looking at them amazed, little thinking that the man was lying as he showed him pair after pair, all in holes and shreds. "Well, indeed, it must be a long way off," and he looks around him, and then at the rock, and thinks what a terrible long way he has had to bring it, and begins to doubt whether, after all, since he's still got so far to go, it's worth all the trouble.

"If it had been near," says he, "it would have been a different thing, and I would have shown them what it is to treat me as they did, but as it's so far off it's another matter, and I don't think it's worth the trouble."

So he just takes up the rock and flings it aside in a field, and goes off back again. So the cobbler came home, and told all the townsfolk what he had done, and how he had cheated the devil, and I can assure you that they all admired his cleverness, and the joke of tricking the devil as he had, nor did they allow him to lose in consequence of missing his day's work.

I Won't

Old-Fashioned Fairy Tales is Juliana Horatia Ewing doing her very Victorian thing: brand-new fairy tales written to feel like old ones. The stories first appeared in Aunt Judy's Magazine in the 1870s, then were gathered into book form in 1882. They are full of ghosts, sprites, water spirits and odd little moral tests, but the tone is very homely.

I Won't centres on a child whose default answer to everything is, essentially, "no," and Ewing spins that stubborn streak into a kind of moral fairy story, where self-will and sulks are tested against the needs and feelings of other people.

"Don't care", so they say, fell into a goose-pond; and "I won't" is apt to come to no better an end. At least, my grandmother tells me that was how the Miller had to quit his native town, and leave the tip of his nose behind him.

It all came of his being allowed to say "I won't" when he was quite a little boy. His mother thought he looked pretty when he was pouting, and that wilfulness gave him an air which distinguished him from other people's children. And when she found out that his lower lip was becoming so big that it spoilt his beauty, and that his wilfulness gained his way twice and stood in his way eight times out of ten, it was too late to alter him.

Then she said, "Dearest Abinadab, do be more obliging!"

And he replied (as she had taught him), "I won't."

He always took what he could get, and would neither give nor give up to other people. This, he thought, was the way to get more out of life than one's neighbours.

Amongst other things, he made a point of taking the middle of the footpath.

"Will you allow me to pass you, sir? I am in a hurry," said a voice behind him one day.

"I won't," said Abinadab; on which a poor washerwoman, with her basket, scrambled down into the road, and Abinadab chuckled.

Next day he was walking as before.

"Will you allow me to pass you, sir? I am in a hurry," said a voice behind him.

"I won't," said Abinadab. On which he was knocked into the ditch; and the Baron walked on, and left him to get out of the mud on whichever side he liked.

He quarrelled with his friends till he had none left, and he quarrelled with the tradesmen of the town till there was only one who would serve him, and this man offended him at last.

"I'll show you who's master!" said the Miller. "I won't pay a penny of your bill - not a penny."

"Sir," said the tradesman, "my giving you offence now, is no just reason why you should refuse to pay for what you have had and been satisfied with. I must beg you to pay me at once."

"I won't," said the Miller, "and what I say I mean. I won't; I tell you, I won't."

So the tradesman summoned him before the Justice, and the Justice condemned him to pay the bill and the costs of the suit.

"I won't," said the Miller.

So they put him in prison, and in prison he would have remained if his mother had not paid the money to obtain his release. By and by she died, and left him her blessing and some very good advice, which (as is sometimes the case with bequests) would have been more useful if it had come earlier.

The Miller's mother had taken a great deal of trouble off his hands which now fell into them. She took in all the small bags of grist which the country-folk brought to be ground, and kept account of them, and spoke civilly to the customers, big and little. But these small matters irritated the Miller.

"I may be the slave of all the old women in the country-side," he said, "but I won't - they shall see that I won't."

So he put up a notice to say that he would only receive grist at a certain hour on certain days. Now, but a third of the old women could read the notice, and they did not attend to it. People came as before; but the Miller locked the door of the mill and sat in the counting-house and chuckled.

"My good friend," said his neighbours, "you can't do business in this way. If a man lives by trade, he must serve his customers. And a Miller must take in grist when it comes to the mill."

"Others may if they please," said the Miller, "but I won't. When I make a rule, I stick to it."

"Take advice, man, or you'll be ruined," said his friends.

"I won't," said the Miller.

In a few weeks all the country-folk turned their donkeys' heads towards the windmill on the heath. It was a little farther to go, but the Windmiller took custom when it came to him, gave honest measure, and added civil words gratis.

The other Miller was ruined.

"All you can do now is to leave the mill while you can pay the rent, and try another trade," said his friends.

"I won't," said the Miller. "Shall I be turned out of the house where I was born, because the country-folk are fools?"

However, he could not pay the rent, and the landlord found another tenant.

"You must quit," said he to the Miller.

"That I won't," said the Miller, "not for fifty new tenants."

So the landlord sent for the constables, and he was carried out, which is not a dignified way of changing one's residence. But then it is not easy to be obstinate and dignified at the same time.

His wrath against the landlord knew no bounds.

"Was there ever such a brute?" he cried. "Would any man of spirit hold his home at the whim of a landlord? I'll never rent another house as long as I live."

"But you must live somewhere," said his friends.

"I won't," said the Miller.

He was no longer a young man, and the new tenant pitied him.

"The poor old fellow is out of his senses," he said. And he let him sleep in one of his barns. One of the mill cats found out that there was a new warm bed in this barn, and she came and lived there too, and kept away the mice.

One night, however, Mrs. Pussy disturbed the Miller's rest. She was in and out of the window constantly, and meowed horribly into the bargain.

"It seems a man can't even sleep in peace," said the Miller. "If this happens again, you'll go into the mill-race to sing to the fishes."

The next night the cat was still on the alert, and the following morning the Miller tied a stone round her neck, and threw her into the water.

"Oh, spare the poor thing, there's a good soul," said a bystander.

"I won't," said the Miller. "I told her what would happen."

When his back was turned, however, the bystander got Pussy out, and took her home with him.

Now the cat was away, the mice could play; and they played hide-and seek over the Miller's nightcap.

It came to such a pass that there was no rest to be had.

"I won't go to bed, I declare I won't," said the Miller. So he sat up all night in an arm-chair, and threw everything he could lay his hands on at the corners where he heard the mice scuffling, till the place was topsy-turvy.

Towards morning he lit a candle and dressed himself. He was in a terrible humour; and when he began to shave, his hand shook and he cut himself. The draughts made the flame of the candle unsteady too, and the shadow of the Miller's nose (which was a large one) fell in uncertain shapes upon his cheeks, and interfered with the progress of the razor. At first he thought he would wait till daylight. Then his temper got the better of him.

"I won't," he said, "I won't; why should I?"

So he began again. He held on by his nose to steady his cheeks, and he gave it such a spiteful pinch that the tears came into his eyes.

"Matters have come to a pretty pass, when a man's own nose is to stand in his light," he said.

By and by a gust of wind came through the window. Up flared the candle, and the shadow of the Miller's nose danced half over his face, and the razor gashed his chin.

Transported with fury, he struck at it before he could think what he was doing. The razor was very sharp, and the tip of the Miller's nose came off as clean as his whiskers.

When daylight came, and he saw himself in the glass, he resolved to leave the place.

"I won't stay here to be a laughing-stock," he said.

As he trudged out on to the highway, with his bundle on his back, the Baron met him and pitied him. He dismounted from his horse, and leading it up to the Miller, he said, "Friend, you are elderly to be going far afoot. I will lend you my mare to take you to your destination. When you are there, knot the reins and throw them on her shoulder, saying, 'Home!' She will then return to me. But mark one thing, she is not used to whip or spur. Humour her, and she will carry you well and safely."

The Miller mounted willingly enough, and set forward. At first the mare was a little restive. The Miller had no spurs on, but, in spite of the Baron's warning, he kicked her with his heels. On this, she danced till the Miller's hat and bundle flew right and left, and he was very near to following them.

"Ah, you vixen!" he cried. "You think I'll humour you as the Baron does. But I won't - no, you shall see that I won't!" And gripping his walking-stick firmly in his hand, he belaboured the Baron's mare as if she had been a donkey.

On which she sent the Miller clean over her head, and cantered back to the castle; and wherever it was that he went to, he had to walk.

He never returned to his native village, and everybody was glad to be rid of him. One must bear and forbear with his neighbours if he hopes to be regretted when he departs.

But my grandmother says that long after the mill had fallen into ruin, the story was told as a warning to wilful children of the Miller who cut off his nose to spite his own face.

Jack and the Beanstalk

English Fairy Tales, first published by Macmillan in 1918, is Flora Annie Steel's collection of over forty well-known English folk and fairy tales, retold in a clear, literary style and illustrated by Arthur Rackham.

Jack and the Beanstalk appears as one of the central narratives, presenting the now familiar story of a poor boy who trades a cow for magic beans. Steel's adaptation follows the established English tradition of the tale, already shaped by earlier print versions in the eighteenth and nineteenth centuries, while giving it a smooth, readable prose and placing it alongside other canonical stories such as "The Three Little Pigs" and "Little Red Riding Hood".

A long, long time ago, when most of the world was young and folk did what they liked because all things were good, there lived a boy called Jack.

His father was bed-ridden, and his mother, a good soul, was busy early morns and late eyes planning and placing how to support her sick husband and her young son by selling the milk and butter which Milky-White, the beautiful cow, gave them without stint. For it was summer-time. But winter came on; the herbs of the fields took refuge from the frosts in the warm earth, and though his mother sent Jack to gather what fodder he could get in the hedgerows, he came back as often as not with a very empty sack; for Jack's eyes were so often full of wonder at all the things he saw that sometimes he forgot to work!

So it came to pass that one morning Milky-White gave no milk at all - not one drain! Then the good hard-working mother threw her apron over her head and sobbed, "What shall we do? What shall we do?"

Now Jack loved his mother; besides, he felt just a bit sneaky at being such a big boy and doing so little to help, so he said, "Cheer up! Cheer up! I'll go and get work somewhere." And he felt as he spoke as if he would work his fingers to the bone; but the good woman shook her head mournfully.

"You've tried that before, Jack," she said, "and nobody would keep you. You are quite a good lad but your wits go a-wool-gathering. No, we must sell Milky-White and live on the money. It is no use crying over milk that is not here to spill!"

You see, she was a wise as well as a hard-working woman, and Jack's spirits rose.

"Just so," he cried. "We will sell Milky-White and be richer than ever. It's an ill wind that blows no one good. So, as it is market-day, I'll just take her there and we shall see what we shall see."

"But - " began his mother.

"But doesn't butter parsnips," laughed Jack. "Trust me to make a good bargain."

So, as it was washing-day, and her sick husband was more ailing than usual, his mother let Jack set off to sell the cow.

"Not less than ten pounds," she bawled after him as he turned the corner.

Ten pounds, indeed! Jack had made up his mind to twenty! Twenty solid golden sovereigns!

He was just settling what he should buy his mother as a fairing out of the money, when he saw a queer little old man on the road who called out, "Good-morning, Jack!"

"Good-morning," replied Jack, with a polite bow, wondering how the queer little old man happened to know his name; though, to be sure, Jacks were as plentiful as blackberries.

"And where may you be going?" asked the queer little old man. Jack wondered again - he was always wondering, you know - what the queer little old man had to do with it; but being always polite, he replied:

"I am going to market to sell Milky-White - and I mean to make a good bargain."

"So you will! So you will!" chuckled the queer little old' man. "You look the sort of chap for it. I bet you know how many beans make five?"

"Two in each hand and one in my mouth," answered Jack readily. He really was sharp as a needle.

"Just so, just so!" chuckled the queer little old man; and as he spoke he drew out of his pocket five beans. "Well, here they are, so give us Milky-White."

Jack was so flabbergasted that he stood with his mouth open as if he expected the fifth bean to fly into it.

"What!" he said at last. "My Milky-White for five common beans! Not if I know it!"

"But they aren't common beans," put in the queer little old man, and there was a queer little smile on his queer little face. "If you plant these beans over-night, by morning they will have grown up right into the very sky."

Jack was too flabbergasted this time even to open his mouth; his eyes opened instead. As he spoke he drew out of his pocket five beans.

"Did you say right into the very sky?" he asked at last; for, see you, Jack had wondered more about the sky than about anything else.

"RIGHT UP INTO THE VERY SKY" repeated the queer old man, with a nod between each word. "It's a good bargain, Jack; and as fair play's a jewel, if they don't - why! meet me here tomorrow morning and you shall have Milky-White back again. Will that please you?"

"Right as a trivet," cried Jack, without stopping to think, and the next moment he found himself standing on an empty road.

"Two in each hand and one in my mouth," repeated Jack. "That is what I said, and what I'll do. Everything in order, and if what the queer little old man said isn't true, I shall get Milky-White back tomorrow morning."

So whistling and munching the bean he trudged home cheerfully, wondering what the sky would be like if he ever got there.

"What a long time you've been!" exclaimed his mother, who was watching anxiously for him at the gate. "It is past sun-setting; but I see you have sold Milky-White. Tell me quick how much you got for her."

"You'll never guess," began Jack.

"Laws-a-mercy! You don't say so," interrupted the good woman.

"And I worrying all day lest they should take you in. What was it? Ten pounds - fifteen - sure it can't be twenty!"

Jack held out the beans triumphantly.

"There," he said. "That's what I got for her, and a jolly good bargain too!"

It was his mother's turn to be flabbergasted; but all she said was:

"What! Them beans!"

"Yes," replied Jack, beginning to doubt his own wisdom, "but they're magic beans. If you plant them over-night, by morning they - grow - right up - into - the - sky - Oh! Please don't hit so hard!"

For Jack's mother for once had lost her temper, and was belabouring the boy for all she was worth. And when she had finished scolding and beating, she flung the miserable beans out of window and sent him, supperless, to bed.

If this was the magical effect of the beans, thought Jack ruefully, he didn't want any more magic, if you please.

However, being healthy and, as a rule, happy, he soon fell asleep and slept like a top.

When he woke he thought at first it was moonlight, for everything in the room showed greenish. Then he stared at the little window. It was covered as if with a curtain by leaves. He was out of bed in a trice, and the next moment, without waiting to dress, was climbing up the biggest beanstalk you ever saw. For what the queer little old man had said was true! One of the beans which his mother had chucked into the garden had found soil, taken root, and grown in the night....

Where?... Up to the very sky? Jack meant to see at any rate.

So he climbed, and he climbed, and he climbed. It was easy work, for the big beanstalk with the leaves growing out of each side was like a ladder; for all that he soon was out of breath. Then he got his second wind, and was just beginning to wonder if he had a third when he saw in front of him a wide, shining white road stretching away, and away, and away.

So he took to walking, and he walked, and walked, and walked, till he came to a tall, shining white house with a wide white doorstep.

And on the doorstep stood a great big woman with a black porridge-pot in her hand. Now Jack, having had no supper, was hungry as a hunter, and when he saw the porridge-pot he said quite politely, "Good-morning, 'm. I wonder if you could give me some breakfast?"

"Breakfast!" echoed the woman, who, in truth, was an ogre's wife. "If it is breakfast you're wanting, it's breakfast you'll likely be; for I expect my man home every instant, and there is nothing he likes better for breakfast than a boy - a fat boy grilled on toast."

Now Jack was not a bit of a coward, and when he wanted a thing he generally got it, so he said cheerful-like:

"I'd be fatter if I'd had my breakfast!" Whereat the ogre's wife laughed and bade Jack come in; for she was not, really, half as bad as she looked. But he had hardly finished the great bowl of porridge and milk she gave him when the whole house began to tremble and quake. It was the ogre coming home!

Thump! THUMP!! THUMP!!!

"Into the oven with you, sharp!" cried the ogre's wife; and the iron oven door was just closed when the ogre strode in. Jack could see him through the little peep-hole slide at the top where the steam came out.

He was a big one for sure. He had three sheep strung to his belt, and these he threw down on the table. "Here, wife," he cried, "roast me these snippets for breakfast; they are all I've been able to get this morning, worse luck! I hope the oven's hot?" And he went to touch the handle, while Jack burst out all of a sweat, wondering what would happen next.

"Roast!" echoed the ogre's wife. "Pooh! the little things would dry to cinders. Better boil them."

So she set to work to boil them; but the ogre began sniffing about the room. "They don't smell - mutton meat," he growled. Then he frowned horribly and began the real ogre's rhyme:

"Fee-fi-fo-fum,

I smell the blood of an Englishman.

Be he alive, or be he dead,

I'll grind his bones to make my bread."

"Don't be silly!" said his wife. "It's the bones of the little boy you had for supper that I'm boiling down for soup! Come, eat your breakfast, there's a good ogre!"

So the ogre ate his three sheep, and when he had done he went to a big oaken chest and took out three big bags of golden pieces. These he put on the table, and began to count their contents while his wife cleared away the breakfast things. And by and by his head began to nod, and at last he began to snore, and snored so loud that the whole house shook.

Then Jack nipped out of the oven and, seizing one of the bags of gold, crept away, and ran along the straight, wide, shining white road as fast as his legs would carry him till he came to the beanstalk. He couldn't climb down it with the bag of gold, it was so heavy, so he just flung his burden down first, and, helter-skelter, climbed after it.

And when he came to the bottom, there was his mother picking up gold pieces out of the garden as fast as she could; for, of course, the bag had burst.

"Laws-a-mercy me!" she says. "Wherever have you been? See! It's been raining gold!"

"No, it hasn't," began Jack. "I climbed up - "

Then he turned to look for the beanstalk; but, lo and behold! it wasn't there at all! So he knew, then, it was all real magic.

After that they lived happily on the gold pieces for a long time, and the bed-ridden father got all sorts of nice things to eat; but, at last, a day came when Jack's mother showed a doleful face as she put a big yellow sovereign into Jack's hand and bade him be careful marketing, because there was not one more in the coffer. After that they must starve.

That night Jack went supperless to bed of his own accord. If he couldn't make money, he thought, at any rate he could eat less money. It was a shame for a big boy to stuff himself and bring no grist to the mill.

He slept like a top, as boys do when they don't overeat themselves, and when he woke....

Hey, presto! the whole room showed greenish, and there was a curtain of leaves over the window! Another bean had grown in the night, and Jack was up it like a lamp-lighter before you could say knife.

This time he didn't take nearly so long climbing until he reached the straight, wide, white road, and in a trice he found himself before the tall white house, where on the wide white steps the ogre's wife was standing with the black porridge-pot in her hand.

And this time Jack was as bold as brass. "Good-morning, 'm," he said. "I've come to ask you for breakfast, for I had no supper, and I'm as hungry as a hunter."

"Go away, bad boy!" replied the ogre's wife. "Last time I gave a boy breakfast my man missed a whole bag of gold. I believe you are the same boy."

"Maybe I am, maybe I'm not," said Jack, with a laugh. "I'll tell you true when I've had my breakfast; but not till then."

So the ogre's wife, who was dreadfully curious, gave him a big bowl full of porridge; but before he had half-finished it he heard the ogre coming:

Thump! THUMP! THUMP!

"In with you to the oven," shrieked the ogre's wife. "You shall tell me when he has gone to sleep."

This time Jack saw through the steam peep-hole that the ogre had three fat calves strung to his belt.

"Better luck today, wife!" he cried, and his voice shook the house. "Quick! Roast these trifles for my breakfast! I hope the oven's hot?"

And he went to feel the handle of the door, but his wife cried out sharply, "Roast! Why, you'd have to wait hours before they were done! I'll broil them - see how bright the fire is!"

"Umph!" growled the ogre. And then he began sniffing and calling out:

"Fee-fi-fo-fum,

I smell the blood of an Englishman.

Be he alive, or be he dead,

I'll grind his bones to make my bread."

"Twaddle!" said the ogre's wife. "It's only the bones of the boy you had last week that I've put into the pig-bucket!"

"Umph!" said the ogre harshly; but he ate the broiled calves, and then he said to his wife, "Bring me my hen that lays the magic eggs. I want to see gold."

So the ogre's wife brought him a great big black hen with a shiny red comb. She plumped it down on the table and took away the breakfast things.

Then the ogre said to the hen, "Lay!" and it promptly laid - what do you think? - a beautiful, shiny, yellow, golden egg!

"None so dusty, henny-penny," laughed the ogre. "I shan't have to beg as long as I've got you." Then he said, "Lay!" once more; and, lo and behold! there was another beautiful, shiny, yellow, golden egg!

Jack could hardly believe his eyes, and made up his mind that he would have that hen, come what might. So, when the ogre began to doze, he just out like a flash from the oven, seized the hen, and ran for his life! But, you see, he reckoned without his prize; for hens, you know, always cackle when they leave their nests after laying an egg, and this one set up such a scrawing that it woke the ogre.

"Where's my hen?" he shouted, and his wife came rushing in, and they both rushed to the door; but Jack had got the better of them by a good start, and all they could see was a little figure right away down the wide white road, holding a big, scrawing, cackling, fluttering black hen by the legs!

How Jack got down the beanstalk he never knew. It was all wings, and leaves, and feathers, and cacklings; but get down he did, and there was his mother wondering if the sky was going to fall!

But the very moment Jack touched ground he called out, "Lay!" and the black hen ceased cackling and laid a great, big, shiny, yellow, golden egg.

So everyone was satisfied; and from that moment everybody had everything that money could buy. For, whenever they wanted anything, they just said, "Lay!" and the black hen provided them with gold.

But Jack began to wonder if he couldn't find something else besides money in the sky. So one fine moonlight midsummer night he refused his supper, and before he went to bed stole out to the garden with a big watering-can and watered the ground under his window; for, thought he, "there must be two more beans somewhere, and perhaps it is too dry for them to grow." Then he slept like a top.

And, lo and behold! when he woke, there was the green light shimmering through his room, and there he was in an instant on the beanstalk, climbing, climbing, climbing for all he was worth.

But this time he knew better than to ask for his breakfast; for the ogre's wife would be sure to recognise him. So he just hid in some bushes beside the great white house, till he saw her in the scullery, and then he slipped out and hid himself in the copper; for he knew she would be sure to look in the oven first thing.

And by and by he heard:

Thump! THUMP! THUMP!

And peeping through a crack in the copper-lid, he could see the ogre stalk in with three huge oxen strung at his belt. But this time, no sooner had the ogre got into the house than he began shouting:

"Fee-fi-fo-fum,

I smell the blood of an Englishman.

Be he alive, or be he dead,

I'll grind his bones to make my bread."

For, see you, the copper-lid didn't fit tight like the oven door, and ogres have noses like a dogs for scent.

"Well, I declare, so do I!" exclaimed the ogre's wife. "It will be that horrid boy who stole the bag of gold and the hen. If so, he's hid in the oven!"

But when she opened the door, lo and behold! Jack wasn't there! Only some joints of meat roasting and sizzling away. Then she laughed and said, "You and I be fools for sure. Why, it's the boy you caught last night as I was getting ready for your breakfast. Yes, we be fools to take dead meat for live flesh! So eat your breakfast, there's a good ogre!"

But the ogre, though he enjoyed roast boy very much, wasn't satisfied, and every now and then he would burst out with "Fee-fi-fo-fum," and get up and search the cupboards, keeping Jack in a fever of fear lest he should think of the copper.

But he didn't. And when he had finished his breakfast he called out to his wife, "Bring me my magic harp! I want to be amused."

So she brought out a little harp and put it on the table. And the ogre leant back in his chair and said lazily, "Sing!"

And, lo and behold! the harp began to sing. If you want to know what it sang about? Why! It sang about everything! And it sang so beautifully that Jack forgot to be frightened, and the ogre forgot to think of "Fee-fi-fo-fum," and fell asleep and did not snore...

Then Jack stole out of the copper like a mouse and crept hands and knees to the table, raised himself up ever so softly and laid hold of the magic harp; for he was determined to have it.

But no sooner had he touched it, than it cried out quite loud, "Master! Master!" So the ogre woke, saw Jack making off, and rushed after him.

My goodness, it was a race! Jack was nimble, but the ogre's stride was twice as long. So, though Jack turned, and twisted, and doubled like a hare, yet at last, when he got to the beanstalk, the ogre was not a dozen yards behind him. There wasn't time to think, so Jack just flung himself on to the stalk and began to go down as fast as he could, while the harp kept calling, "Master! Master!" at the very top of its voice. He had only got down about a quarter of the way when there was the most awful lurch you can think of, and Jack nearly fell off the beanstalk. It was the ogre beginning to climb down, and his weight made the stalk sway like a tree in a storm. Then Jack knew it was life or death, and he climbed down faster and faster, and as he climbed he shouted, "Mother! Mother! Bring an axe! Bring an axe!"

Now his mother, as luck would have it, was in the backyard chopping wood, and she ran out thinking that this time the sky must have fallen. Just at that moment Jack touched ground, and he flung down the harp - which immediately began to sing of all sorts of beautiful things - and he seized the axe and gave a great chop at the beanstalk, which shook and swayed and bent like barley before a breeze.

"Have a care!" shouted the ogre, clinging on as hard as he could. But Jack did have a care, and he dealt that beanstalk such a shrewd blow that the whole of it, ogre and all, came toppling down, and, of course, the ogre broke his crown, so that he died on the spot.

After that everyone was quite happy. For they had gold to spare and if the bedridden father was dull, Jack just brought out the harp

and said, "Sing!"And lo and behold, it sang about everything under the sun. So Jack ceased his wonderings and became quite a useful person.

And the last bean still hasn't grown yet. It is still in the garden? I wonder if it will ever grow? And what little child will climb its beanstalk into the sky? And what will that child find?

Jack the Giant-Killer

English Fairy Tales is a 1918 collection of forty-one traditional tales retold by Flora Annie Steel and published by Macmillan, with illustrations by Arthur Rackham. It gathers together many of the now "standard" English narratives, and draws heavily on the earlier compilations of Joseph Jacobs from the 1890s

Jack the Giant-Killer appears as one of the heroic wonder tales, retelling the exploits of the Cornish farm boy Jack who destroys a succession of man-eating giants in the time of King Arthur.

Chapter I

When good king Arthur reigned with Guinevere his Queen, there lived, near the Land's End in Cornwall, a farmer who had one only son called Jack. Now Jack was brisk and ready; of such a lively wit that none nor nothing could worst him.

In those days, the Mount of St. Michael in Cornwall was the fastness of a hugeous giant whose name was Cormoran.

He was full eighteen feet in height, some three yards about his middle, of a grim fierce face, and he was the terror of all the country-side. He lived in a cave amidst the rocky Mount, and when he desired victuals he would wade across the tides to the mainland

and furnish himself forth with all that came in his way. The poor folk and the rich folk alike ran out of their houses and hid themselves when they heard the swish-swash of his big feet in the water; for if he saw them, he would think nothing of broiling half-a-dozen or so of them for breakfast. As it was, he seized their cattle by the score, carrying off half-a-dozen fat oxen on his back at a time, and hanging sheep and pigs to his waist belt like bunches of dip-candles. Now this had gone on for long years, and the poor folk of Cornwall were in despair, for none could put an end to the giant Cormoran.

It so happened that one market day Jack, then quite a young lad, found the town upside down over some new exploit of the giants. Women were weeping, men were cursing, and the magistrates were sitting in Council over what was to be done. But none could suggest a plan. Then Jack, blithe and gay, went up to the magistrates, and with a fine courtesy - for he was ever polite - asked them what reward would be given to him who killed the giant Cormoran.

"The treasures of the Giant's Cave," they said.

"Every whit of it?" said Jack, who was never to be done.

"To the last farthing," they said.

"Then will I undertake the task," said Jack, and forthwith set about the business.

It was winter-time, and having got himself a horn, a pickaxe, and a shovel, he went over to the Mount in the dark evening, set to work, and before dawn he had dug a pit, no less than twenty-two feet deep and nigh as big across. This he covered with long thin sticks and straw, sprinkling a little loose mould over all to make it look like solid ground. So, just as dawn was breaking, he planted himself fair and square on the side of the pit that was farthest from the giant's cave, raised the horn to his lips, and with full blast sounded, "Tantivy! Tantivy! Tantivy!" just as he would have done had he been hunting a fox.

Of course this woke the giant, who rushed in a rage out of his cave, and seeing little Jack, fair and square blowing away at his horn, as calm and cool as may be, he became still more angry, and made for the disturber of his rest, bawling out, "I'll teach you to wake a giant, you little whipper-snapper. You shall pay dearly for your taunts, I'll take you and broil you whole for break…"

He had only got as far as this when crash - he fell into the pit! So there was a break indeed; such a one that it caused the very foundations of the Mount to shake.

But Jack shook with laughter. "Ho, ho!" he cried, "how about breakfast now, Sir Giant? Will you have me broiled or baked? And will no diet serve you but poor little Jack? Faith! I've got you in Lob's pound now! You're in the stocks for bad behaviour, and I'll plague you as I like. Would I had rotten eggs; but this will do as well." And with that he up with his pickaxe and dealt the giant Cormoran such a most weighty knock on the very crown of his head, that he killed him on the spot.

Whereupon Jack calmly filled up the pit with earth again and went to search the cave, where he found much treasure.

Now when the magistrates heard of Jack's great exploit, they proclaimed that henceforth he should be known as "Jack The giant Killer!", and they presented him with a sword and belt, on which these words were embroidered in gold:

"Here's the valiant Cornishman

Who slew the giant Cormoran."

Chapter II

Of course the news of Jack's victory soon spread over all England, so that another giant named Blunderbore who lived to the north, hearing of it, vowed if ever he came across Jack he would be revenged upon him. Now this giant Blunderbore was lord of an enchanted castle that stood in the middle of a lonesome forest.

It so happened that Jack, about four months after he had killed Cormoran, had occasion to journey into Wales, and on the road he passed this forest. Weary with walking, and finding a pleasant fountain by the wayside, he lay down to rest and was soon fast asleep.

Now the giant Blunderbore, coming to the well for water, found Jack sleeping, and knew by the lines embroidered on his belt that here was the far-famed giant-killer. Rejoiced at his luck, the giant, without more ado, lifted Jack to his shoulder and began to carry him through the wood to the enchanted castle.

But the rustling of the boughs awakened Jack, who, finding himself already in the clutches of the giant, was terrified; nor was his alarm decreased by seeing the courtyard of the castle all strewn with men's bones.

"Yours will be with them ere long," said Blunderbore as he locked poor Jack into an immense chamber above the castle gateway. It had a high-pitched, beamed roof, and one window that looked down the road. Here poor Jack was to stay while Blunderbore went to fetch his brother-giant, who lived in the same wood, that he might share in the feast.

Now, after a time, Jack, watching through the window, saw the two giants tramping hastily down the road, eager for their dinner.

"Now," said Jack to himself, "my death or my deliverance is at hand." For he had thought out a plan. In one corner of the room he had seen two strong cords. These he took, and making a cunning noose at the end of each, he hung them out of the window, and, as the giants were unlocking the iron door of the gate, managed to slip them over their heads without their noticing it. Then, quick as thought, he tied the other ends to a beam, so that as the giants moved on the nooses tightened and throttled them until they grew black in the face. Seeing this, Jack slid down the ropes, and drawing his sword, slew them both.

So, taking the keys of the castle, he unlocked all the doors and set free three beauteous ladies who, tied by the hair of their heads, he found almost starved to death. "Sweet ladies," said Jack, kneeling on one knee - for he was ever polite - "here are the keys of this enchanted castle. I have destroyed the giant Blunderbore and his brutish brother, and thus have restored to you your liberty. These keys should bring you all else you require."

So saying he proceeded on his journey to Wales.

Chapter III

He travelled as fast as he could; perhaps too fast, for, losing his way, he found himself benighted and far from any habitation. He wandered on always in hopes, until on entering a narrow valley he came on a very large, dreary-looking house standing alone. Being anxious for shelter he went up to the door and knocked. You may imagine his surprise and alarm when the summons was answered by a giant with two heads. But though this monster's look was exceedingly fierce, his manners were quite polite; the truth being that he was a Welsh giant, and as such double-faced and smooth, given to gaining his malicious ends by a show of false friendship.

So he welcomed Jack heartily in a strong Welsh accent, and prepared a bedroom for him, where he was left with kind wishes for a good rest. Jack, however, was too tired to sleep well, and as he lay awake, he overheard his host muttering to himself in the next room. Having very keen ears he was able to make out these words, or something like them:

"Though here you lodge with me this night

You shall not see the morning light.

My club shall dash your brains outright."

"Say'st you so!" said Jack to himself, starting up at once, "So that is your Welsh trick, is it? But I will be even with you." Then, leaving his bed, he laid a big billet of wood among the blankets, and taking one of these to keep himself warm, made himself snug in a corner of the room, pretending to snore, so as to make Mr. Giant think he was asleep.

And sure enough, after a little time, in came the monster on tiptoe as if treading on eggs, and carrying a big club. Then: WHACK! WHACK! WHACK!

Jack could hear the bed being belaboured until the Giant, thinking every bone of his guest's skin must be broken, stole out of the room again; whereupon Jack went calmly to bed once more and slept soundly! Next morning the giant couldn't believe his eyes when he saw Jack coming down the stairs fresh and hearty.

Taking the keys of the castle, Jack unlocked all the doors.

"Odds splutter and nails!" he cried, astonished. "Did she sleep well? Was there not nothing felt in the night?"

"Oh," replied Jack, laughing in his sleeve, "I think a rat did come and give me two or three flaps of his tail."

On this the giant was dumbfounded, and led Jack to breakfast, bringing him a bowl which held at least four gallons of hasty-pudding, and bidding him, as a man of such mettle, eat the lot. Now Jack when travelling wore under his cloak a leather bag to carry his things with; so, quick as thought, he hitched this round in front with the opening just under his chin; thus, as he ate, he could slip the best part of the pudding into it without the giant's being any the wiser. So they sat down to breakfast, the giant gobbling down his own measure of hasty-pudding, while Jack made away with his.

"Odds splutter and nails!" cried the giant, not to be outdone. "She can do that herself!"

"See," says crafty Jack when he had finished. "I'll show you a trick worth two of yours," and with that he up with a carving-knife and, ripping up the leather bag, out fell all the hasty-pudding on the floor!

"Odds splutter and nails!" cried the giant, not to be outdone. "She can do that herself!" Whereupon he seized the carving-knife, and ripping open his own belly fell down dead.

Thus was Jack quit of the Welsh giant.

Chapter IV

Now it so happened that in those days, when gallant knights were always seeking adventures, King Arthur's only son, a very valiant Prince, begged of his father a large sum of money to enable him to journey to Wales, and there strive to set free a certain beautiful lady who was possessed by seven evil spirits. In vain the King denied him; so at last he gave way and the Prince set out with two horses, one of which he rode, the other laden with gold pieces. Now after some days' journey the Prince came to a market-town in Wales where there was a great commotion. On asking the reason for it he was told that, according to law, the corpse of a very generous man had been arrested on its way to the grave, because, in life, it had owed large sums to the money-lenders.

"That is a cruel law," said the young Prince. "Go, bury the dead in peace, and let the creditors come to my lodgings; I will pay the debts of the dead."

So the creditors came, but they were so numerous that by evening the Prince had but tuppence left for himself, and could not go further on his journey.

Now it so happened that Jack the Giant-Killer on his way to Wales passed through the town, and, hearing of the Prince's plight, was so taken with his kindness and generosity that he determined to be the Prince's servant. So this was agreed upon, and next morning, after Jack had paid the reckoning with his last farthing, the two set out together. But as they were leaving the town, an old woman ran after the Prince and called out, "Justice! Justice! The dead man owed me tuppence these seven years. Pay me as well as the others."

And the Prince, kind and generous, put his hand to his pocket and gave the old woman the tuppence that was left to him. So now they had not a penny between them, and when the sun grew low the Prince said, "Jack! Since we have no money, how are we to get a night's lodging?"

Then Jack replied, "We shall do well enough, Master; for within two or three miles of this place there lives a huge and monstrous giant with three heads, who can fight four hundred men in armour and make them fly from him like chaff before the wind.

"And what good will that be to us?" said the Prince. "He will for sure chop us up in a mouthful."

"Nay," said Jack, laughing. "Let me go and prepare the way for you. By all accounts this giant is a dolt. Mayhap I may manage better than that."

So the Prince remained where he was, and Jack pricked his steed at full speed till he came to the giant's castle, at the gate of which he knocked so loud that he made the neighbouring hills resound.

On this the giant roared from within in a voice like thunder, "Who's there?"

Then said Jack as bold as brass, "None but your poor cousin Jack."

"Cousin Jack!" said the giant, astounded. "And what news with my poor cousin Jack?" For, see you, he was quite taken aback; so Jack made haste to reassure him

"Dear coz, heavy news, God wot!"

"Heavy news," echoed the giant, half afraid. "God wot, no heavy news can come to me. Have I not three heads? Can I not fight five hundred men in armour? Can I not make them fly like chaff before the wind?"

"True," replied crafty Jack, "but I came to warn you because the great King Arthur's son with a thousand men in armour is on his way to kill you."

At this the giant began to shiver and to shake. "Ah! Cousin Jack!

Kind cousin Jack! This is heavy news indeed," he said. "Tell me, what am I to do?"

Ah! Cousin Jack! Kind cousin Jack! This is heavy news indeed

"Hide yourself in the vault," says crafty Jack, "and I will lock and bolt and bar you in; and keep the key till the Prince has gone. So you will be safe."

Then the giant made haste and ran down into the vault, and Jack locked, and bolted, and barred him in. Then being thus secure, he went and fetched his master, and the two made themselves heartily merry over what the giant was to have had for supper, while the miserable monster shivered and shook with fright in the underground vault.

Well, after a good night's rest Jack woke his master in the early morning, and having furnished him well with gold and silver from the giant's treasure, bade him ride three miles forward on his journey. So when Jack judged that the Prince was pretty well out of the smell of the giant, he took the key and let his prisoner out. He was half dead with cold and damp, but very grateful; and he begged Jack to let him know what he would be given as a reward for saving the giant's life and castle from destruction, and he should have it.

"You're very welcome," said Jack, who always had his eyes about him. "All I want is the old coat and cap, together with the rusty old sword and slippers which are at your bed-head."

When the giant heard this he sighed and shook his head. "You don't know what you are asking," he said. "They are the most precious things I possess, but as I have promised, you must have them. The coat will make you invisible, the cap will tell you all you want to know, the sword will cut asunder whatever you strike, and the slippers will take you wherever you want to go in the twinkling of an eye!"

So Jack, overjoyed, rode away with the coat and cap, the sword and the slippers, and soon overtook his master; and they rode on together until they reached the castle where the beautiful lady lived whom the Prince sought.

Now she was very beautiful, for all she was possessed of seven devils, and when she heard the Prince sought her as a suitor, she smiled and ordered a splendid banquet to be prepared for his reception. And she sat on his right hand, and plied him with food and drink.

And when the repast was over she took out her own handkerchief and wiped his lips gently, and said, with a smile, "I have a task for you, my lord! You must show me that kerchief tomorrow morning or lose your head."

And with that she put the handkerchief in her bosom and said, "Good-night!"

The Prince was in despair, but Jack said nothing till his master was in bed. Then he put on the old cap he had got from the giant, and lo! in a minute he knew all that he wanted to know. So, in the dead of the night, when the beautiful lady called on one of her familiar spirits to carry her to Lucifer himself, Jack was beforehand with her, and putting on his coat of darkness and his slippers of swiftness, was there as soon as she was. And when she gave the handkerchief to the Devil, bidding him keep it safe, and he put it away on a high shelf, Jack just up and nipped it away in a trice!

So the next morning, when the beauteous enchanted lady looked to see the Prince crestfallen, he just made a fine bow and presented her with the handkerchief.

At first she was terribly disappointed, but, as the day drew on, she ordered another and still more splendid repast to be got ready. And this time, when the repast was over, she kissed the Prince full on the lips and said, "I have a task for you, my lover. Show me tomorrow morning the last lips I kiss tonight or you lose your head."

Then the Prince, who by this time was head over ears in love, said tenderly, "If you will kiss none but mine, I will." Now the beauteous lady, for all she was possessed by seven devils, could not but see that the Prince was a very handsome young man; so she blushed a little, and said, "That is neither here nor there: you must show me them, or death is your portion."

So the Prince went to his bed, sorrowful as before; but Jack put on the cap of knowledge and knew in a moment all he wanted to know.

Thus when, in the dead of the night, the beauteous lady called on her familiar spirit to take her to Lucifer himself, Jack in his coat of darkness and his shoes of swiftness was there before her.

"You have betrayed me once," said the beauteous lady to Lucifer, frowning, "by letting go my handkerchief. Now will I give you something none can steal, and so best the Prince, King's son though he be."

With that she kissed the loathly demon full on the lips, and left him. Whereupon Jack with one blow of the rusty sword of strength cut off Lucifer's head, and, hiding it under his coat of darkness, brought it back to his master.

Thus next morning when the beauteous lady, with malice in her beautiful eyes, asked the Prince to show her the lips she had last kissed, he pulled out the demon's head by the horns. On that the seven devils, which possessed the poor lady, gave seven dreadful shrieks and left her. Thus the enchantment being broken, she appeared in all her perfect beauty and goodness.

So she and the Prince were married the very next morning. After which they journeyed back to the court of King Arthur, where Jack the Giant-Killer, for his many exploits, was made one of the Knights of the Round Table.

Chapter V

This, however, did not satisfy our hero, who was soon on the road again searching for giants. Now he had not gone far when he came upon one, seated on a huge block of timber near the entrance to a dark cave. He was a most terrific giant. His goggle eyes were as coals of fire, his countenance was grim and gruesome; his cheeks, like huge flitches of bacon, were covered with a stubbly beard, the bristles of which resembled rods of iron wire, while the locks of hair that fell on his brawny shoulders showed like curled snakes or hissing adders. He held a knotted iron club, and breathed so heavily you could hear him a mile away. Nothing daunted by this fearsome sight, Jack alighted from his horse and, putting on his coat of darkness, went close up to the giant and said softly, "Hullo! is that you? It will not be long before I have you fast by your beard."

So saying he made a cut with the sword of strength at the giant's head, but, somehow, missing his aim, cut off the nose instead, clean as a whistle! My goodness! How the giant roared! It was like claps of thunder, and he began to lay about him with the knotted iron club, like one possessed. But Jack in his coat of darkness easily dodged the blows, and running in behind, drove the sword up to the hilt into the giant's back, so that he fell stone dead.

Jack then cut off the head and sent it to King Arthur by a waggoner whom he hired for the purpose. After which he began to search the giant's cave to find his treasure. He passed through many windings and turnings until he came to a huge hall paved and roofed with freestone. At the upper end of this was an immense fireplace where hung an iron cauldron, the like of which, for size, Jack had never seen before. It was boiling and gave out a savoury steam; while beside it, on the right hand, stood a big, massive table set out with huge platters and mugs. Here it was that the giants used to dine. Going a little further he came upon a sort of window barred with iron, and looking within beheld a vast number of miserable captives.

"Alas! Alack!" they cried on seeing him. "Are you come, young man, to join us in this dreadful prison?"

"That depends," said Jack, "but first tell me wherefore you are thus held imprisoned?"

"Through no fault," they cried at once. "We are captives of the cruel giants and are kept here and well-nourished until such time as the monsters desire a feast. Then they choose the fattest and sup off them."

On hearing this Jack straightway unlocked the door of the prison and set the poor fellows free. Then, searching the giants' coffers, he divided the gold and silver equally amongst the captives as some redress for their sufferings, and taking them to a neighbouring castle gave them a right good feast.

Chapter VI

Now as they were all making merry over their deliverance, and praising Jack's prowess, a messenger arrived to say that one Thunderdell, a huge giant with two heads, having heard of the death of his kinsman, was on his way from the northern dales to be revenged, and was already within a mile or two of the castle, the country folk with their flocks and herds flying before him like chaff before the wind.

Now the castle with its gardens stood on a small island that was surrounded by a moat twenty feet wide and thirty feet deep, having very steep sides. And this moat was spanned by a drawbridge. This, without a moment's delay, Jack ordered should be sawn on both sides at the middle, so as to only leave one plank uncut over which he in his invisible coat of darkness passed swiftly to meet his enemy, bearing in his hand the wonderful sword of strength.

Now though the giant could not, of course, see Jack, he could smell him, for giants have keen noses. Therefore Thunderdell cried out in a voice like his name:

"Fee, fi, fo, fum!

I smell the blood of an Englishman.

Be he alive, or be he dead,

I'll grind his bones to make my bread!"

"Is that so?" said Jack, cheerful as ever. "Then are you a monstrous miller for sure!"

On this the giant, peering round everywhere for a glimpse of his foe, shouted out:

"Are you, indeed, the villain who has killed so many of my kinsmen? Then, indeed, will I tear you to pieces with my teeth, suck your blood, and grind your bones to powder."

"You'll have to catch me first," said Jack, laughing, and throwing off his coat of darkness and putting on his slippers of swiftness, he began nimbly to lead the giant a pretty dance, he leaping and doubling light as a feather, the monster following heavily like a walking tower, so that the very foundations of the earth seemed to shake at every step. At this game the onlookers nearly split their sides with laughter, until Jack, judging there had been enough of it, made for the drawbridge, ran neatly over the single plank, and reaching the other side waited in teasing fashion for his adversary.

On came the giant at full speed, foaming at the mouth with rage, and flourishing his club. But when he came to the middle of the bridge his great weight, of course, broke the plank, and there he was fallen headlong into the moat, rolling and wallowing like a whale, plunging from place to place, yet unable to get out and be revenged.

The spectators greeted his efforts with roars of laughter, and Jack himself was at first too overcome with merriment to do more than scoff. At last, however, he went for a rope, cast it over the giant's two heads, so, with the help of a team of horses, drew them shorewards, where two blows from the sword of strength settled the matter.

Chapter VII

After some time spent in mirth and pastimes, Jack began once more to grow restless, and taking leave of his companions set out for fresh adventures.

He travelled far and fast, through woods, and vales, and hills, till at last he came, late at night, on a lonesome house set at the foot of a high mountain. Knocking at the door, it was opened by an old man whose head was white as snow.

"Father," said Jack, ever courteous, "can you lodge a benighted traveller?"

"Ay, that will I, and welcome to my poor cottage," replied the old man.

Whereupon Jack came in, and after supper they sat together chatting in friendly fashion. Then it was that the old man, seeing by Jack's belt that he was the famous Giant-Killer, spoke in this wise, "My son! You are the great conqueror of evil monsters. Now close by there lives one well worthy of your prowess. On the top of yonder high hill is an enchanted castle kept by a giant named Galligantua, who, by the help of a wicked old magician, inveigles many beautiful ladies and valiant knights into the castle, where they are transformed into all sorts of birds and beasts, yea, even into fishes and insects. There they live pitiably in confinement; but most of all do I grieve for a duke's daughter whom they kidnapped in her father's garden, bringing her here in a burning chariot drawn by fiery dragons. Her form is that of a white hind; and though many valiant knights have tried their utmost to break the spell and work her deliverance, none have succeeded; for, see you, at the entrance to the castle are two dreadful griffins who destroy everyone who attempts to pass them by."

Now Jack bethought him of the coat of darkness which had served him so well before, and he put on the cap of knowledge, and in an instant he knew what had to be done. Then the very next morning, at dawn-time, Jack arose and put on his invisible coat and his slippers of swiftness. And in the twinkling of an eye there he was on the top of the mountain! And there were the two griffins guarding the castle gates - horrible creatures with forked tails and tongues. But they could not see him because of the coat of darkness, so he passed them by unharmed.

And hung to the doors of the gateway he found a golden trumpet on a silver chain, and beneath it was engraved in red lettering:

"Whoever shall this trumpet blow

Will cause the giant's overthrow.

The black enchantment he will break,

And gladness out of sadness make."

No sooner had Jack read these words than he put the horn to his lips and blew a loud

"Tantivy! Tantivy! Tantivy!"

Now at the very first note the castle trembled to its vast foundations, and before he had finished the measure, both the giant and the magician were biting their thumbs and tearing their hair, knowing that their wickedness must now come to an end. But the giant showed fight and took up his club to defend himself; whereupon Jack, with one clean cut of the sword of strength, severed his head from his body, and would doubtless have done the same to the magician, but that the latter was a coward, and, calling up a whirlwind, was swept away by it into the air, nor has he ever been seen or heard of since. The enchantments being thus broken, all the valiant knights and beautiful ladies, who had been transformed into birds and beasts and fishes and reptiles and insects, returned to their proper shapes, including the duke's daughter, who, from being a white hind, showed as the most beauteous maiden upon whom the sun ever shone. Now, no sooner had this occurred than the whole castle vanished away in a cloud of smoke, and from that moment giants vanished also from the land.

So Jack, when he had presented the head of Galligantua to King Arthur, together with all the lords and ladies he had delivered from enchantment, found he had nothing more to do. As a reward for past services, however, King Arthur bestowed the hand of the duke's daughter upon honest Jack the Giant-Killer. So married they were, and the whole kingdom was filled with joy at their wedding. Furthermore, the King bestowed on Jack a noble castle with a magnificent estate belonging thereto, whereon he, his lady, and their children lived in great joy and content for the rest of their days.

Johnny Reed's Cat

Folk-Lore and Legends: English is a late nineteenth-century anthology compiled and edited by Charles John Tibbits, first published in London by W. W. Gibbings in 1890. It gathers a mixed selection of English folk narratives, from fairy lore and nursery tales to regional legends and anecdotes, framed by an introductory Dissertation on Fairies.

Johnny Reed's Cat is one of the shorter prose legends, set in the north of England near Newcastle-upon-Tyne. Told in a conversational, frame-narrative style, it recounts the curious and increasingly uncanny behaviour of the sexton Johnny Reed's seemingly ordinary black cat.

"Yes, cats are queer folk, sure enough, and often know more than a simple beast ought to by knowledge that's rightly come by. There's that cat there, you've been looking at, will stand at a door on its hind legs with its front paws on the handle trying like a Christian to open the door, and mewling in a manner that's almost like talking. He's a London cat, he is, being brought me by a cousin who lives there, and is called Gilpin, after, I'm told, a mayor who was christened the same. He's a knowing cat, sure enough; but it's not the London cats that are cleverer than the country ones. Who knows, he may be a relative of Johnny Reed's own tom-cat himself."

"And who was Johnny Reed? and what was there remarkable about his cat?"

"Have you never heard tell of Johnny Reed's cat? It's an old tale they have in the north country, and it's true enough, though folk may not believe it in these days when the Bible's not gospel enough for some of them. I've heard my father often tell the story, and he came from Newcastle way, which is the very part where Johnny Reed used to live, being a parish sexton in a village not far away.

"Well, Johnny Reed was the sexton, as I've already said, and he and his wife kept a cat, a well enough behaved creature, sure enough, and a beast as he had no fault to set on, saving a few of the tricks which all cats play at times, and which seem born in the blood of the creatures. It was all black except one white paw, and seemed as honest and decent a beast as could be, and Tom would as soon have suspected it of being any more than it really seemed to be as he would one of his own children themselves, like many other folk, perhaps, who, may be, have cats of the same kind, little thinking it.

"Well, the cat had been with him some years when a strange thing occurred.

"One night Johnny was going home late from the churchyard, where he had been digging a grave for a person who had died on a sudden, throwing the grave on Johnny's hands unexpectedly, so that he had to stop working at it by the light of a lantern to have it ready for the next day's burying. Well, having finished his work, and having put his tools in the shed in a corner of the yard, and having locked them up safe, he began to walk home pretty brisk, thinking would his wife be up and have a bit of fire for him, for the night was cold, a keen wind blowing over the fields.

"He hadn't gone far before he comes to a gate at the roadside, and there seemed to be a strange shadow about it, in which Johnny saw, as it might be, a lot of little gleaming fires dancing about, while some stood steady, just like flashes of light from little windows in buildings all on fire inside. Says Johnny to himself, for he was not a man to be easily frightened, being accustomed by his calling to face things which might upset other folk.

"Hullo! What's here? Here's a thing I never saw before,' and with that he walks straight up to the gate, while the shadow got deeper and the fires brighter the nearer he came to it.

"Well, when he came right up to the gate he finds that the shadow was just none at all, but nine black cats, some sitting and some dancing about, and the lights were the flashes from their eyes. When he came nearer he thought to scare them off, and he calls out, "Sh…sh…sh,' but never a cat stirs for all of it.

"I'll soon scatter you, you ugly vermin," says Johnny, looking about him for a stone, which was not to be found, the night being dark and preventing him seeing one.

Just then he hears a voice calling, "Johnny Reed!'

"Hullo!' says he, 'who's that wants me?'

"Johnny Reed,' says the voice again.

"Well,' says Johnny, 'I'm here,' and looking round and seeing no one, for no one was about 'tis true. 'Was it one of you,' says he, joking like, to the cats, 'as was calling me?'

"Yes, of course,' answers one of them, as plain as ever Christian spoke. 'It's me as has called you these three times.'

"Well, with that, you may be sure, Johnny begins to feel curious, for 'twas the first time he had ever been spoken to by a cat, and he didn't know what it might lead to exactly. So he takes off his hat to the cat, thinking that it was, perhaps, best to show it respect, and, seeing that he was unable to guess with whom he was dealing, hoping to come off all the better for a little civility.

"Well, sir,' says he, 'what can I do for you?'

"It's not much as I want with you,' says the cat, 'but it's better it'll be with you if you do what I tell you. Tell Dan Ratcliffe that Peggy Poyson's dead.'

"I will, sir,' says Johnny, wondering at the same time how he was to do it, for who Dan Ratcliffe was he knew no more than the dead. Well, with that all the cats vanished, and Johnny, running the rest of the way home, rushes into his house, smoking hot from the fright and the distance he had to go over.

"Nan,' says he to his wife, the first words he spoke, 'who's Dan Ratcliffe?'

"Dan Ratcliffe,' says she. 'I never heard of him, and don't know there's any one such living about here.'

"No more do I,' says he, 'but I must find him wherever he is.'

"Then he tells his wife all about how he had met the cats, and how they had stopped him and given him the message. Well, his cat sits there in front of the fire looking as snug and comfortable as a cat could be, and nearly half-asleep, but when Johnny comes to telling his wife the message the cats had given him, then it jumped up on its feet, and looks at Johnny, and says, "What! is Peggy Poyson dead? Then it's no time for me to be here;' and with that it springs through the door and vanishes, nor was ever seen again from that day to this."

"And did the sexton ever find Dan Ratcliffe," I asked.

"Never. He searched high and low for him about, but no one could tell him of such a person, though Johnny looked long enough, thinking it might be the worse for him if he didn't do his best to please the cats. At last, however, he gave the matter up."

"Then, what was the meaning of the cat's message?"

"It's hard to tell; but many folk thought, and I'm inclined to agree with them, that Dan Ratcliffe was Johnny's own cat, and no one else, looking at the way he acted, and no other of the name being known. Who Peggy Poyson was no one could tell, but likely enough it was some relative of the cat, or may be someone it was interested in, for it's little we know concerning the creatures and their ways, and with whom and what they're mixed up."

Kate Crackernuts

English Fairy Tales is Joseph Jacobs's influential 1890 collection of forty-three traditional narratives, drawn from printed and oral sources and issued by David Nutt with illustrations by John D. Batten. Jacobs's stated aim was to provide England with a national fairy-tale book to stand alongside the collections of the Brothers Grimm and others.

Kate Crackernuts has attracted particular critical attention because of its unusually active heroine and its blending of motifs. Originating as a Scottish tale from the Orkney Islands, Kate Crackernuts is seen as a key example of a strong female protagonist within the British fairy-tale tradition.

Once upon a time there was a king and a queen, as in many lands have been. The king had a daughter, Anne, and the queen had one named Kate, but Anne was far bonnier than the queen's daughter, though they loved one another like real sisters. The queen was jealous of the king's daughter being bonnier than her own, and cast about to spoil her beauty. So she took counsel of the henwife, who told her to send the lassie to her next morning fasting.

So next morning early, the queen said to Anne, "Go, my dear, to the henwife in the glen, and ask her for some eggs." So Anne set out, but as she passed through the kitchen she saw a crust, and she took and munched it as she went along.

When she came to the henwife's she asked for eggs, as she had been told to do; the henwife said to her, "Lift the lid off that pot there and see." The lassie did so, but nothing happened. "Go home to your minnie and tell her to keep her larder door better locked," said the henwife. So she went home to the queen and told her what the henwife had said. The queen knew from this that the lassie had had something to eat, so watched the next morning and sent her away fasting; but the princess saw some country-folk picking peas by the roadside, and being very kind she spoke to them and took a handful of the peas, which she ate by the way.

When she came to the henwife's, she said, "Lift the lid off the pot and you'll see." So Anne lifted the lid but nothing happened. Then the henwife was angry and said to Anne, "Tell your minnie the pot won't boil if the fire's away." So Anne went and told the queen.

The third day the queen goes along with the girl herself to the henwife. Now, this time, when Anne lifted the lid off the pot, off falls her own pretty head, and on jumps a sheep's head. And so the queen was now quite satisfied, and went back home.

Her own daughter, Kate, however, took a fine linen cloth and wrapped it round her sister's head and took her by the hand and they both went out to seek their fortune. They went on, and they went on, and they went on, till they came to a castle. Kate knocked at the door and asked for a night's lodging for herself and a sick sister. They went in and found it was a king's castle, who had two sons, and one of them was sickening away to death and no one could find out what ailed him. And the curious thing was that whoever watched him at night was never seen again. So the king had offered a peck of silver to anyone who would stop up with him. Now Katie was a very brave girl, so she offered to sit up with him.

Till midnight all goes well. As twelve o clock rings, however, the sick prince rises, dresses himself, and slips downstairs. Kate followed, but he didn't seem to notice her. The prince went to the stable, saddled his horse, called his hound, jumped into the saddle, and Kate leapt lightly up behind him. Away rode the prince and Kate through the greenwood, Kate, as they pass, plucking nuts from the trees and filling her apron with them. They rode on and on till they came to a green hill. The prince here drew bridle and spoke, "Open, open, green hill, and let the young prince in with his horse and his hound," and Kate added, "and his lady him behind."

Immediately the green hill opened and they passed in. The prince entered a magnificent hall, brightly lighted up, and many beautiful fairies surrounded the prince and led him off to the dance. Meanwhile, Kate, without being noticed, hid herself behind the door. There she sees the prince dancing, and dancing, and dancing, till he could dance no longer and fell upon a couch. Then the fairies would fan him till he could rise again and go on dancing.

At last the cock crew, and the prince made all haste to get on horseback; Kate jumped up behind, and home they rode. When the morning sun rose they came in and found Kate sitting down by the fire and cracking her nuts. Kate said the prince had a good night; but she would not sit up another night unless she was to get a peck of gold. The second night passed as the first had done. The prince got up at midnight and rode away to the green hill and the fairy ball, and Kate went with him, gathering nuts as they rode through the forest. This time she did not watch the prince, for she knew he would dance and dance, and dance. But she sees a fairy baby playing with a wand, and overhears one of the fairies say, "Three strokes of that wand would make Kate's sick sister as bonnie as ever she was." So Kate rolled nuts to the fairy baby, and rolled nuts till the baby toddled after the nuts and let fall the wand, and Kate took it up and put it in her apron. And at cockcrow they rode home as before, and the moment Kate got home to her room she rushed and touched Anne three times with the wand, and the nasty sheep's head fell off and she was her own pretty self again. The third night Kate consented to watch, only if she should marry the sick prince. All went on as on the first two nights. This time the fairy baby was playing with a birdie; Kate heard one of the fairies say, "Three bites of that birdie would make the sick prince as well as ever he was." Kate rolled all the nuts she had to the fairy baby till the birdie was dropped, and Kate put it in her apron.

At cockcrow they set off again, but instead of cracking her nuts as she used to do, this time Kate plucked the feathers off and cooked the birdie. Soon there arose a very savoury smell. "Oh!" said the sick prince, "I wish I had a bite of that birdie," so Kate gave him a bite of the birdie, and he rose up on his elbow. By-and-by he cried out again, "Oh, if I had another bite of that birdie!" so Kate gave him another bite, and he sat up on his bed. Then he said again, "Oh! if I only had a third bite of that birdie!" So Kate gave him a third bite, and he rose quite well, dressed himself, and sat down by the fire, and when the folk came in next morning they found Kate and the young prince cracking nuts together. Meanwhile his brother had seen Annie and had fallen in love with her, as everybody did who saw her sweet pretty face. So the sick son married the well sister, and the well son married the sick sister, and they all lived happy and died happy, and never drank out of a dry cappy.

Knave and Fool

Old-Fashioned Fairy Tales is a collection of original literary fairy stories by Juliana Horatia Ewing, first published in the later nineteenth century, with an 1890 Society for Promoting Christian Knowledge edition often cited as an early standard printing.

The book brings together a series of moral and imaginative tales written for a juvenile audience but in a style that also appealed to adult readers of Victorian "home" literature.

Knave and Fool is a short moral fable about two contrasting characters, a Knave and a Fool, who set up house together and quickly reveal the dangers of trusting cunning over sound judgement.

A fool and a knave once set up house together; which shows what a fool the Fool was.

The Knave was delighted with the agreement; and the Fool thought himself most fortunate to have met with a companion who would supply his lack of mother-wit.

As neither of them liked work, the Knave proposed that they should live upon their joint savings as long as these should last; and, to avoid disputes, that they should use the Fool's share till it came to an end, and then begin upon the Knave's stocking

So, for a short time, they lived in great comfort at the Fool's expense, and were very good company; for easy times make easy tempers.

Just when the store was exhausted, the Knave came running to the Fool with an empty bag and a wry face, crying, "Dear friend, what shall we do? This bag, which I had safely buried under a gooseberry-bush, has been taken up by some thief, and all my money stolen. My savings were twice as large as yours; but now that they are gone, and I can no longer perform my share of the bargain, I fear our partnership must be dissolved."

"Not so, dear friend," said the Fool, who was very good-natured, "we have shared good luck together, and now we will share poverty. But as nothing is left, I fear we must seek work."

"You speak very wisely," said the Knave, "And what, for instance, can you do?"

"Very little," said the Fool, "but that little I do well."

"So do I," said the Knave. "Now can you plough, or sow, or feed cattle, or plant crops?"

"Farming is not my business," said the Fool.

"Nor mine," said the Knave, "but no doubt you are a handicraftsman. Are you clever at carpentry, mason's work, tailoring, or shoemaking?"

"I do not doubt that I should have been had I learned the trades," said the Fool, "but I never was bound apprentice."

"It is the same with me," said the Knave, "but you may have finer talents. Can you paint, or play the fiddle?"

"I never tried," said the Fool, "so I don't know."

"Just my case," said the Knave. "And now, since we can't find work, I propose that we travel till work finds us."

The two comrades accordingly set forth, and they went on and on, till they came to the foot of a hill, where a merchantman was standing by his wagon, which had broken down.

"You seem two strong men," he said, as they advanced, "if you will carry this chest of valuables up to the top of the hill, and down to the bottom on the other side, where there is an inn, I will give you two gold pieces for your trouble."

The Knave and the Fool consented to this, saying, "Work has found us at last;" and they lifted the box on to their shoulders.

"Turn, and turn about," said the Knave, "but the best turn between friends is a good turn; so I will lead the way up-hill, which is the hardest kind of travelling, and you shall go first down-hill, the easy half of our journey."

The Fool thought this proposal a very generous one, and, not knowing that the lower end of their burden was the heavy one, he carried it all the way. When they got to the inn, the merchant gave each of them a gold piece, and, as the accommodation was good, they remained where they were till their money was spent. After this, they lived there awhile on credit; and when that was exhausted, they rose one morning whilst the landlord was still in bed, and pursued their journey, leaving old scores behind them.

They had been a long time without work or food, when they came upon a man who sat by the roadside breaking stones, with a quart of porridge and a spoon in a tin pot beside him.

"You look hungry, friends," he said, "and I, for my part, want to get away. If you will break up this heap, you shall have the porridge for supper. But when you have eaten it, put the pot and spoon under the hedge, that I may find them when I return."

"If we eat first, we shall have strength for our work," said the Knave, "and as there is only one spoon, we must eat by turns. But fairly divide, friendly abide. As you went first the latter part of our journey, I will begin on this occasion. When I stop, you fall to, and eat as many spoonfuls as I eat. Then I will follow you in like fashion, and so on till the pot is empty."

"Nothing could be fairer," said the Fool; and the Knave began to eat, and went on till he had eaten a third of the porridge. The Fool, who had counted every spoonful, now took his turn, and ate precisely as much as his comrade. The Knave then began again, and was exact to a mouthful; but it emptied the pot. Thus the Knave had twice as much as the Fool, who could not see where he had been cheated.

They then set to work.

"As there is only one hammer," said the Knave, "we must work, as we supped, by turns; and as I began last time, you shall begin this. After you have worked awhile, I will take the hammer from you, and do as much myself whilst you rest. Then you shall take it up again, and so on till the heap is finished."

"It is not everyone who is as just as you," said the Fool; and taking up the hammer, he set to work with a will.

The Knave took care to let him go on till he had broken a third of the stones, and then he did as good a share himself; after which the Fool began again, and finished the heap.

By this means the Fool did twice as much work as the Knave, and yet he could not complain.

As they moved on again, the Fool perceived that the Knave was taking the can and the spoon with him.

"I am sorry to see you do that, friend," he said.

"It's a very small theft," said the Knave. "The can cannot have cost more than sixpence when new."

"That was not what I meant," said the Fool, "so much as that I fear the owner will find it out."

"He will only think the things have been stolen by some vagrant," said the Knave - "which, indeed, they would be if we left them. But as you seem to have a tender conscience, I will keep them myself."

After a while they met with a farmer, who offered to give them supper and a night's lodging, if they would scare the birds from a field of corn for him till sunset.

"I will go into the outlying fields," said the Knave, "and as I see the birds coming, I will turn them back. You, dear friend, remain in the corn, and scare away the few that may escape me."

But whilst the Fool clapped and shouted till he was tired, the Knave went to the other side of the hedge, and lay down for a nap.

As they sat together at supper, the Fool said, "Dear friend, this is laborious work. I propose that we ask the farmer to let us tend sheep, instead. That is a very different affair. One lies on the hillside all day. The birds do not steal sheep; and all this shouting and clapping is saved."

The Knave very willingly agreed, and next morning the two friends drove a flock of sheep on to the downs. The sheep at once began to nibble, the dog sat with his tongue out, panting, and the Knave and

Fool lay down on their backs, and covered their faces with their hats to shield them from the sun.

Thus they lay till evening, when, the sun being down, they uncovered their faces, and found that the sheep had all strayed away, and the dog after them.

"The only plan for us is to go separate ways in search of the flock," said the Knave, "only let us agree to meet here again." They accordingly started in opposite directions; but when the Fool was fairly off, the Knave returned to his place, and lay down as before.

By and by the dog brought the sheep back; so that, when the Fool returned, the Knave got the credit of having found them; for the dog scorned to explain his part in the matter.

As they sat together at supper, the Fool said, "The work is not so easy as I thought. Could we not find a better trade yet?"

"Can you beg?" said the Knave. "A beggar's trade is both easy and profitable. Nothing is required but walking and talking. Then one walks at his own pace, for there is no hurry, and no master, and the same tale does for every door. And, that all may be fair and equal, you shall beg at the front door, whilst I ask an alms at the back."

To this the Fool gladly agreed; and as he was as lean as a hunted cat, charitable people gave him a penny or two from time to time. Meanwhile, the Knave went round to the back yard, where he picked up a fowl, or turkey, or anything that he could lay his hands upon.

When he returned to the Fool, he would say, "See what has been given to me, whilst you have only got a few pence."

At last this made the Fool discontented, and he said, "I should like now to exchange with you. I will go to the back doors, and you to the front."

The Knave consented, and at the next house the Fool went to the back door; but the mistress of the farm only rated him, and sent him away. Meanwhile, the Knave, from the front, had watched her leave the parlour, and slipping in through the window, he took a ham and a couple of new loaves from the table, and so made off.

When the friends met, the Fool was crestfallen at his ill luck, and the Knave complained that all the burden of their support fell upon him. "See," he said, "what they give me, where you get only a mouthful of abuse!" And he dined heartily on what he had stolen; but the Fool only had bits of the breadcrust, and the parings of the ham.

At the next place the Fool went to the front door as before, and the Knave secured a fat goose and some plums in the back yard, which he popped under his cloak. The Fool came away with empty hands, and the Knave scolded him, saying, "Do you suppose that I mean to share this fat goose with a lazy beggar like you? Go on, and find for yourself." With which he sat down and began to eat the plums, whilst the Fool walked on alone.

After a while, however, the Knave saw a stir in the direction of the farm they had left, and he quickly perceived that the loss of the goose was known, and that the farmer and his men were in pursuit of the thief. So, hastily picking up the goose, he overtook the Fool, and pressed it into his arms, saying, "Dear friend, pardon a passing ill humour, of which I sincerely repent. Are we not partners in good luck and ill? I was wrong, dear friend; and, in token of my penitence, the goose shall be yours alone. And here are a few plums with which you may refresh yourself by the wayside. As for me, I will hasten on to the next farm, and see if I can beg a bottle of wine to wash down the dinner, and drink to our good-fellowship." And before the Fool could thank him, the Knave was off like the wind.

By and by the farmer and his men came up, and found the Fool eating the plums, with the goose on the grass beside him.

They hurried him off to the justice, where his own story met with no credit. The woman of the next farm came up also, and recognized him for the man who had begged at her door the day she lost a ham and two new loaves. In vain he said that these things also had been given to his friend. The friend never appeared; and the poor Fool was whipped and put in the stocks.

Towards evening the Knave hurried up to the village green, where his friend sat doing penance for the theft.

"My dear friend," he said, "what do I see? Is such cruelty possible? But I hear that the justice is not above a bribe, and we must at any cost obtain your release. I am going at once to pawn my own boots and cloak, and everything about me that I can spare, and if you have anything to add, this is no time to hesitate."

The poor Fool begged his friend to draw off his boots, and to take his hat and coat as well, and to make all speed on his charitable errand.

The Knave took all that he could get, and, leaving his friend sitting in the stocks in his shirt-sleeves, he disappeared as swiftly as one could wish a man to carry a reprieve.

For those good folks to whom everything must be explained in full, it may be added that the Knave did not come back, and that he kept the clothes.

It was very hard on the Fool; but what can one expect if he keeps company with a Knave?

Master of all Masters

English Fairy Tales is a 1918 collection of forty-one traditional stories retold by Flora Annie Steel and published by Macmillan, with illustrations by Arthur Rackham. It belongs to the early twentieth-century movement to present English folk narratives in polished literary form for family and juvenile reading.

Master of all Masters is a brief comic tale about a maidservant who is required to learn her eccentric employer's private names for everyday objects, with the humour arising when she later has to use this invented vocabulary in an emergency.

A girl once went to the fair to hire herself for servant. At last a funny-looking old gentleman engaged her and took her home to his house. When she got there, he told her that he had something to teach her, for that in his house he had his own names for things.

He said to her, "What will you call me?"

"Master or mister, or whatever you please, sir," says she.

He said, "You must call me 'master of all masters.' And what would you call this?" pointing to his bed.

"Bed or couch, or whatever you please, sir."

"No, that's my 'barnacle'. And what do you call these?" he said, pointing to his pantaloons.

"Breeches or trousers, or whatever you please, sir."

"You must call them 'squibs and crackers.' And what would you call her?" pointing to the cat.

"Cat or kit, or whatever you please, sir.'

"You must call her 'white-faced simminy' And this now," showing the fire, "what would you call this?"

"Fire or flame, or whatever you please, sir."

"You must call it 'hot cockalorum'; and what's this?" he went on, pointing to the water.

"Water or wet, or whatever you please, sir."

"No, 'pondalorum' is its name. And what do you call all this?" asked he, as he pointed to the house.

"House or cottage, or whatever you please, sir."

"You must call it 'high topper mountain.”

That very night the servant woke her master up in a fright and said, "Master of all masters, get out of your barnacle and put on your squibs and crackers. For white-faced simminy has got a spark of hot cockalorum on its tail, and unless you get some pondalorum high topper mountain will be all on hot cockalorum...."

Mr Fox

English Fairy Tales is a collection of forty-one traditional English stories retold by Flora Annie Steel and first published by Macmillan in London in 1918, with illustrations by Arthur Rackham.

Mr Fox is Steel's version of a long-circulating English tale about a young gentlewoman, Lady Mary, who discovers that her apparently charming suitor is in fact a serial murderer. The story belongs to the international "robber bridegroom" group of narratives, related to the better-known "Bluebeard" cycle, in which a heroine uncovers her future husband's violence, escapes, and exposes him before a public audience.

Lady Mary was young and Lady Mary was fair, and she had more lovers than she could count on the fingers of both hands.

She lived with her two brothers, who were very proud and very fond of their beautiful sister, and very anxious that she should choose well amongst her many suitors.

Now amongst them there was a certain Mr. Fox, handsome and young and rich; and though nobody quite knew who he was, he was so gallant and so gay that everyone liked him. And he wooed

Lady Mary so well that at last she promised to marry him. But though he talked much of the beautiful home to which he would take her, and described the castle and all the wonderful things that furnished it, he never offered to show it to her, neither did he invite Lady Mary's brothers to see it.

Now this seemed to her very strange indeed; and, being a lass of spirit, she made up her mind to see the castle if she could.

So one day, just before the wedding, when she knew Mr. Fox would be away seeing the lawyers with her brothers, she just kilted up her skirts and set out unbeknownst - for, see you, the whole household was busy preparing for the marriage feastings - to see for herself what Mr. Fox's beautiful castle was like.

After many searchings, and much travelling, she found it at last; and a fine strong building it was, with high walls and a deep moat to it. A bit frowning and gloomy, but when she came up to the wide gateway she saw these words carved over the arch: BE BOLD - BE BOLD.

So she plucked up courage, and the gate being open, went through it and found herself in a wide, empty, open courtyard. At the end of this was a smaller door, and over this was carved: BE BOLD, BE BOLD; BUT NOT TOO BOLD.

So she went through it to a wide, empty hall, and up the wide, empty staircase. Now at the top of the staircase there was a wide, empty gallery at one end of which were wide windows with the sunlight streaming through them from a beautiful garden, and at the other end a narrow door, over the archway of which was carved: BE BOLD, BE BOLD; BUT NOT TOO BOLD, LEST THAT YOUR HEART'S BLOOD SHOULD RUN COLD.

Now Lady Mary was a lass of spirit, and so, of course, she turned her back on the sunshine, and opened the narrow, dark door. And there she was in a narrow, dark passage. But at the end there was a chink of light. So she went forward and put her eye to the chink - and what do you think she saw?

Why, a wide saloon lit with many candles, and all round it, some hanging by their necks, some seated on chairs, some lying on the floor, were the skeletons and bodies of numbers of beautiful young maidens in their wedding-dresses that were all stained with blood.

Now Lady Mary, for all she was a lass of spirit, and brave as brave, could not look for long on such a horrid sight, so she turned and fled. Down the dark narrow passage, through the dark narrow door (which she did not forget to close behind her), and along the wide gallery she fled like a hare, and was just going down the wide stairs into the wide hall when, what did she see, through the window, but Mr. Fox dragging a beautiful young lady across the wide courtyard! There was nothing for it, Lady Mary decided, but to hide herself as quickly and as best she might; so she fled faster down the wide stairs, and hid herself behind a big wine-butt that stood in a corner of the wide hall. She was only just in time, for there at the wide door was Mr. Fox dragging the poor young maiden along by the hair; and he dragged her across the wide hall and up the wide stairs. And when she clutched at the bannisters to stop herself, Mr. Fox cursed and swore dreadfully; and at last he drew his sword and brought it down so hard on the poor young lady's wrist that the hand, cut off, jumped up into the air so that the diamond ring on the finger flashed in the sunlight as it fell, of all places in the world, into Lady Mary's very lap as she crouched behind the wine-butt!

Then she was fair frightened, thinking Mr. Fox would be sure to find her; but after looking about a little while in vain (for, of course, he coveted the diamond ring), he continued his dreadful task of dragging the poor, beautiful young maiden upstairs to the horrid chamber, intending, doubtless, to return when he had finished his loathly work, and seek for the hand.

But by that time Lady Mary had fled; for no sooner did she hear the awful, dragging noise pass into the gallery, than she upped and ran for dear life - through the wide door with: BE BOLD, BE BOLD; BUT NOT TOO BOLD engraved over the arch, across the wide courtyard past the wide gate with: BE BOLD - BE BOLD engraved over it, never stopping, never thinking till she reached her own chamber. And all the while the hand with the diamond ring lay in her kilted lap.

Now the very next day, when Mr. Fox and Lady Mary's brothers returned from the lawyers, the marriage-contract had to be signed. And all the neighbourhood was asked to witness it and partake of a splendid breakfast. And there was Lady Mary in bridal array, and there was Mr. Fox, looking so gay and so gallant. He was seated at the table just opposite Lady Mary, and he looked at her and said, "How pale you are this morning, dear heart."

Then Lady Mary looked at him quietly and said, "Yes, dear sir! I had a bad night's rest, for I had horrible dreams."

Then Mr. Fox smiled and said, "Dreams go by contraries, dear heart; but tell me your dream, and your sweet voice will speed the time till I can call you mine."

"I dreamed," said Lady Mary, with a quiet smile, and her eyes were clear, "that I went yesterday to seek the castle that is to be my home, and I found it in the woods with high walls and a deep dark moat. And over the gateway were carved these words: BE BOLD - BE BOLD."

Then Mr. Fox spoke in a hurry. "But it is not so - nor it was not so."

"Then I crossed the wide courtyard and went through a wide door over which was carved: BE BOLD, BE BOLD; BUT NOT TOO BOLD,", went on Lady Mary, still smiling, and her voice was cold, "but, of course, it is not so, and it was not so."

And Mr. Fox said nothing; he sat like a stone.

"Then I dreamed," continued Lady Mary, still smiling, though her eyes were stern, "that I passed through a wide hall and up a wide stair and along a wide gallery until I came to a dark narrow door, and over it was carved: BE BOLD, BE BOLD; BUT NOT TOO BOLD, LEST THAT YOUR HEART'S BLOOD SHOULD RUN COLD.

"But it is not so, of course, and it was not so."

And Mr. Fox said nothing; he sat frozen.

"Then I dreamed that I opened the door and went down a dark narrow passage," said Lady Mary, still smiling, though her voice was ice. "And at the end of the passage there was a door, and the door had a chink in it. And through the chink I saw a wide saloon lit with many candles, and all round it were the bones and bodies of poor dead maidens, their clothes all stained with blood; but of course it is not so, and it was not so."

By this time all the neighbours were looking Mr. Fox-ways with all their eyes, while he sat silent.

But Lady Mary went on, and her smiling lips were set, "Then I dreamed that I ran downstairs and had just time to hide myself when you, Mr. Fox, came in dragging a young lady by the hair. And the sunlight glittered on her diamond ring as she clutched the stair-rail, and you out with your sword and cut off the poor lady's hand."

Then Mr. Fox rose in his seat stonily and glared about him as if to escape, and his eye-teeth showed like a fox beset by the dogs, and he grew pale.

And he said, trying to smile, though his whispering voice could scarcely be heard, "But it is not so, dear heart, and it was not so, and God forbid it should be so!"

Then Lady Mary rose in her seat also, and the smile left her face, and her voice rang as she cried, "But it is so, and it was so; Here's hand and ring I have to show."

And with that she pulled out the poor dead hand with the glittering ring from her bosom and pointed it straight at Mr. Fox.

At this all the company rose, and drawing their swords cut Mr. Fox to pieces, which served him very well and ight.

Mr. Miacca

English Fairy Tales is a landmark collection of traditional English narratives compiled and retold by Joseph Jacobs, first published in 1890. It gathers a wide range of material, from well-known plots to colloquial prose that Jacobs intended to sound like spoken storytelling.

Mr. Miacca" is one of the shorter tales in the volume, a cautionary story about Tommy Grimes, a disobedient child who ignores his mother's warnings and is seized by the child-eating ogre-figure Mr Miacca.

Tommy Grimes was sometimes a good boy, and sometimes a bad boy; and when he was a bad boy, he was a very bad boy. Now his mother used to say to him, "Tommy, Tommy, be a good boy, and don't go out of the street, or else Mr. Miacca will take you." But still when he was a bad boy he would go out of the street; and one day, sure enough, he had scarcely got round the corner, when Mr. Miacca did catch him and popped him into a bag upside down, and took him off to his house.

When Mr. Miacca got Tommy inside, he pulled him out of the bag and set him down, and felt his arms and legs. "You're rather tough," says he, "but you're all I've got for supper, and you'll not taste bad boiled. But body o' me, I've forgot the herbs, and it's bitter you'll taste without herbs. Sally! Here, I say, Sally!" and he called Mrs. Miacca.

So Mrs. Miacca came out of another room and said, "What do you want, my dear?"

"Oh, here's a little boy for supper," said Mr. Miacca, "and I've forgot the herbs. Mind him, will ye, while I go for them."

"All right, my love," says Mrs. Miacca, and off he goes.

Then Tommy Grimes said to Mrs. Miacca, "Does Mr. Miacca always have little boys for supper?"

"Mostly, my dear," said Mrs. Miacca, "if little boys are bad enough, and get in his way."

"And don't you have anything else but boy-meat? No pudding?" asked Tommy.

"Ah, I loves pudding," says Mrs. Miacca. "But it's not often the likes of me gets pudding."

"Why, my mother is making a pudding this very day," said Tommy Grimes, "and I am sure she'd give you some, if I ask her. Shall I run and get some?"

"Now, that's a thoughtful boy," said Mrs. Miacca, "only don't be long and be sure to be back for supper."

So off Tommy pelted, and right glad he was to get off so cheap; and for many a long day he was as good as good could be, and never went round the corner of the street. But he couldn't always be good; and one day he went round the corner, and as luck would have it, he hadn't scarcely got round it when Mr. Miacca grabbed him up, popped him in his bag, and took him home.

When he got him there, Mr. Miacca dropped him out; and when he saw him, he said, "Ah, you're the youngster what served me and my missus that shabby trick, leaving us without any supper. Well, you shan't do it again. I'll watch over you myself. Here, get under the sofa, and I'll set on it and watch the pot boil for you."

So poor Tommy Grimes had to creep under the sofa, and Mr. Miacca sat on it and waited for the pot to boil. And they waited, and they waited, but still the pot didn't boil, till at last Mr. Miacca got tired of waiting, and he said, "Here, you under there, I'm not going to wait any longer; put out your leg, and I'll stop your giving us the slip."

So Tommy put out a leg, and Mr. Miacca got a chopper, and chopped it off, and pops it in the pot.

Suddenly he calls out, "Sally, my dear, Sally!" and nobody answered. So he went into the next room to look out for Mrs. Miacca, and while he was there, Tommy crept out from under the sofa and ran out of the door. For it was a leg of the sofa that he had put out.

So Tommy Grimes ran home, and he never went round the corner again till he was old enough to go alone.

Nelly The Knocker

Nelly the Knocker is a short Northumbrian ghost legend included early in Charles John Tibbits's anthology Folk-Lore and Legends: English. The story tells of a female spectre who appears by night near a farmstead close to Haltwhistle in Northumberland.

The book itself, Folk-Lore and Legends: English, was first published in London by W. W. Gibbings in 1890 and gathers a range of English folk narratives, from fairy lore and ghost stories to hero legends such as "Jack and the Giants" and "The Worm of Lambton". Tibbits frames the volume as an attempt to preserve tales he felt were "fast dying out", and Nelly the Knocker appears near the beginning of the collection, after a short "Dissertation on Fairies.

A farm-steading situated near the borders of Northumberland, a few miles from Haltwhistle, was once occupied by a well-established local family. In front of the dwelling-house, and at about sixty yards' distance, lay a stone of vast size, as ancient, for so tradition amplifies the date, as the flood. On this stone, at the dead hour of the night, might be discerned a female figure, wrapped in a grey cloak, with one of those low-crowned black bonnets, so familiar to our grandmothers, upon her head. She was incessantly knock, knock, knocking, in a fruitless endeavour to split the impenetrable rock. Duly as night came round, she occupied her lonely station, in the same low crouching attitude, and pursued the dreary obligations of her destiny, till the grey streaks of the dawn gave admonition to depart. From this, the only perceptible action in which she engaged, she obtained the name of Nelly, the Knocker. So perfectly had the inmates of the farmhouse in the lapse of time, which will reconcile sights and events the most disagreeable and alarming, become accustomed to Nelly's undeviating nightly din, that the work went forward unimpeded and undisturbed by any apprehension accruing from her shadowy presence. Did the servant-man make his punctual resort to the neighbouring cottages, he took the liberty of scrutinising Nelly's antiquated garb that varied not with the vicissitudes of seasons, or he pried sympathetically into the progress of her monotonous occupation, and though her pale, ghastly, contracted features gave a momentary pang of terror, it was rapidly effaced in the vortex of good fellowship into which he was speedily drawn. Did the loon venture an appointment with his mistress at the rustic style of the stack-garth, Nelly's unwearied hammer, instead of proving a barrier, only served, by imparting a grateful sense of mutual danger, to render more intense the raptures of the hour of meeting. So apathetic were the feelings cherished towards her, and so little jealousy existed of her power to injure, that the relater of these circumstances states that on several occasions she has passed Nelly at her laborious toil, without evincing the slightest perturbation, beyond a hurried step, as she stole a glance at the inexplicable and mysterious form.

An event, in the course of years, disclosed the secrets that marvellous stone shrouded, and drove poor Nelly forever from the scene so inscrutably linked with her fate.

Two of the sons of the farmer were rapidly approaching maturity, when one of them, more reflecting and shrewder than his compeers, suggested the idea of relieving Nelly from her toilsome avocation, and of taking possession of the alluring legacy to which she was evidently and urgently summoning. He proposed, conjointly with his father and brother, to blast the stone, as the most expeditious mode of gaining access to her arcana, and this in the open daylight, in order that any tutelary protection she might be disposed to extend to her favourite haunt might, as she was a thing of darkness and the night, be effectually countervailed. Nor were their hopes frustrated, for, upon clearing away the earth and fragments that resulted from the explosion, there was revealed to their elated and admiring gaze, a precious booty of closely packed urns copiously enriched with gold. Anxious that no intimation of their good fortune should transpire, they had taken the precaution to despatch the female servant on a needless errand, and ere her return the whole treasure was efficiently and completely secured. So completely did they succeed in keeping their own counsel, and so successfully did their reputation keep pace with the cautious production of their undivulged treasures, that for many years afterwards they were never suspected of gaining any advantage from poor Nelly's "knocking"; their improved appearance, and the somewhat imposing figure they made in their little district, being solely attributed to their superior judgment, and to the good management of their lucky farm.

Nix Naught Nothing

English Fairy Tales, retold by Flora Annie Steel and first published by Macmillan in 1918 with illustrations by Arthur Rackham, is a canonical early-twentieth-century anthology of forty-plus "national" tales presented for children and families.

Nix Naught Nothing (Steel's spelling varies slightly from the more common "Nix Nought Nothing") is her retelling of a tale that, in Jacobs's earlier English Fairy Tales (1890s), had already been framed as an English version of a Scottish original, "Nicht Nought Nothing". The story is an example of the "Magic Flight" type. Steel's adaptation preserves the core pattern of enchantment, labour and escape that marks the tale's place in the wider European wonder-tale tradition.

Once upon a time there lived a King and a Queen who didn't differ much from all the other kings and queens who have lived since Time began. But they had no children, and this made them very sad indeed. Now it so happened that the King had to go and fight battles in a far country, and he was away for many long months. And, lo and behold! while he was away the Queen at long last bore him a little son. As you may imagine, she was fair delighted, and thought how pleased the King would be when he came home and found that his dearest wish had been fulfilled. And all the courtiers were fine and pleased too, and set about at once to arrange a grand festival for the naming of the little Prince. But the Queen said, "No! The child shall have no name till his father gives it to him. Till then we will call him 'Nix! Naught! Nothing!' because his father knows nothing about him!"

So little Prince Nix Naught Nothing grew into a strong, hearty little lad; for his father did not come back for a long time, and did not even know that he had a son.

But at long last he turned his face homewards. Now, on the way, he came to a big rushing river which neither he nor his army could cross, for it was flood-time and the water was full of dangerous whirlpools, where nixies and water-wraiths lived, always ready to drown men.

So they were stopped, until a huge giant appeared, who could take the river, whirlpool and all, in his stride; and he said kindly, "I'll carry you all over, if you like." Now, though the giant smiled and was very polite, the King knew enough of the ways of giants to think it wiser to have a hard and fast bargain. So he said, quite curt, "What's your pay?"

"Pay?" echoed the giant, with a grin, "what do you take me for? Give me Nix Naught Nothing, and I'll do the job with a glad heart."

Now the King felt just a trifle ashamed at the giant's generosity; so he said, "Certainly, certainly. I'll give you nix naught nothing and my thanks into the bargain."

So the giant carried them safely over the stream and past the whirlpools, and the King hastened homewards. If he was glad to see his dear wife, the Queen, you may imagine how he felt when she showed him his young son, tall and strong for his age.

"And what's your name, young sir?" he asked of the child fast clasped in his arms.

"Nix Naught Nothing," answered the boy, "that's what they call me till my father gives me a name."

Well! the King nearly dropped the child, he was so horrified. "What have I done?" he cried. "I promised to give nix naught nothing to the giant who carried us over the whirlpools where the nixies and water-wraiths live."

At this the Queen wept and wailed; but being a clever woman she thought out a plan whereby to save her son. So she said to her husband the King, "If the giant comes to claim his promise, we will give him the hen-wife's youngest boy. She has so many she will not mind if we give her a crown piece, and the giant will never know the difference."

Now sure enough the very next morning the giant appeared to claim Nix Naught Nothing, and they dressed up the hen-wife's boy in the Prince's clothes and wept and wailed when the giant, fine and satisfied, carried his prize off on his back. But after a while he came to a big stone and sat down to ease his shoulders. And he fell a-dozing. Now, when he woke, he started up in a fluster, and called out:

"Hodge, Hodge, on my shoulders! Say

What do you make the time o' day?"

And the hen-wife's little boy replied:

"Time that my mother the hen-wife takes

The eggs for the wise Queen's breakfast cakes!"

Then the giant saw at once the trick that had been played on him, and he threw the hen-wife's boy on the ground, so that his head hit on the stone and he was killed.

Then the giant strode back to the palace in a tower of a temper, and demanded "Nix Naught Nothing." So this time they dressed up the gardener's boy, and wept and wailed when the giant, fine and satisfied, carried his prize off on his back. Then the same thing happened. The giant grew weary of his burden, and sat down on the big stone to rest. So he fell a-dozing, woke with a start, and called out:

"Hodge, Hodge, on my shoulders! Say

What do you make the time o' day?"

And the gardener's boy replied:

"Time that my father the gardener took

Greens for the wise Queen's dinner to cook!"

So the giant saw at once that a second trick had been played on him and became quite mad with rage. He flung the boy from him so that he was killed, and then strode back to the palace, where he cried with fury, "Give me what you promised to give, Nix Naught

Nothing, or I will destroy you all, root and branch."

So then they saw they must give up the dear little Prince, and this time they really wept and wailed as the giant carried off the boy on his back. And this time, after the giant had had his rest at the big stone, and had woken up and called:

"Hodge, Hodge, on my shoulders! Say

What do you make the time o' day?"

the little Prince replied:

"Time for the King my father to call,

'Let supper be served in the banqueting hall."

Then the giant laughed with glee and rubbed his hands saying, "I've got the right one at last." So he took Nix Naught Nothing to his own house under the whirlpools; for the giant was really a great Magician who could take any form he chose. And the reason he wanted a little prince so badly was that he had lost his wife, and had only one little daughter who needed a playmate sorely. So Nix Naught Nothing and the Magician's daughter grew up together, and every year made them fonder and fonder of each other, until she promised to marry him.

Now the Magician had no notion that his daughter should marry just an ordinary human prince, the like of whom he had eaten a thousand times, so he sought some way in which he could quietly get rid of Nix Naught Nothing. So he said one day, "I have work for you, Nix Naught Nothing! There is a stable hard by which is seven miles long, and seven miles broad, and it has not been cleaned for seven years. By tomorrow evening you must have cleaned it, or I will have you for my supper."

Well, before dawn, Nix Naught Nothing set to work at his task; but, as fast as he cleared the muck, it just fell back again. So by breakfast-time he was in a terrible sweat; yet not one whit nearer the end of his job was he. Now the Magician's daughter, coming to bring him his breakfast, found him so distraught and distracted that he could scarce speak to her.

"We'll soon set that to rights," she said. So she just clapped her hands and called:

"Beasts and birds o' each degree,

Clean me this stable for love o' me."

And, lo and behold! in a minute the beasts of the fields came trooping, and the sky was just dark with the wings of birds, and they carried away the muck, and the stable was clean as a new pin before the evening.

Now when the Magician saw this, he grew hot and angry, and he guessed it was his daughter's magic that had wrought the miracle. So he said, "Shame on the wit that helped you; but I have a harder job for you tomorrow. Yonder is a lake seven miles long, seven miles broad, and seven miles deep. Drain it by nightfall, so that not one drop remains, or, of a certainty, I eat you for supper."

So once again Nix Naught Nothing rose before dawn, and began his task; but though he baled out the water without ceasing, it ever ran back, so that though he sweated and laboured, by breakfast-time he was no nearer the end of his job.

But when the Magician's daughter came with his breakfast she only laughed and said, "I'll soon mend that!" Then she clapped her hands and called:

"Oh! all you fish of river and sea,

Drink me this water for love of me!"

And, lo and behold! the lake was thick with fishes. And they drank and drank, till not one drop remained.

Now when the Magician returned in the morning and saw this he was as angry as angry. And he knew it was his daughter's magic, so he said, "Double shame on the wit that helped you! Yet it betters you not, for I will give you a yet harder task than the last. If you do that, you may have my daughter. See you, yonder is a tree, seven miles high, and no branch to it till the top, and there on the fork is a nest with some eggs in it. Bring those eggs down without breaking one or, sure as fate, I'll eat you for my supper."

Then the Magician's daughter was very sad; for with all her magic she could think of no way of helping her lover to fetch the eggs and bring them down unbroken. So she sat with Nix Naught Nothing underneath the tree, and thought, and thought, and thought; until an idea came to her, and she clapped her hands and cried:

"Fingers of mine, for love of me,

Help my true lover to climb the tree."

Then her fingers dropped off her hands one by one and ranged themselves like the steps of a ladder up the tree; but they were not quite enough of them to reach the top, so she cried again:

"Oh! toes of mine, for love o' me,

Help my true lover to climb the tree."

Then her toes began to drop off one by one and range themselves like the rungs of a ladder; but when the toes of one foot had gone to their places the ladder was tall enough. So Nix Naught Nothing climbed up it, reached the nest, and got the seven eggs. Now, as he was coming down with the last, he was so overjoyed at having finished his task, that he turned to see if the Magician's daughter was overjoyed too: and lo! the seventh egg slipped from his hand and fell, Crash!

"Quick! Quick!" cried the Magician's daughter, who, as you will observe, always had her wits about her. "There is nothing for it now but to fly at once. But first I must have my magic flask, or I shall be unable to help. It is in my room and the door is locked. Put your fingers, since I have none, in my pocket, take the key, unlock the door, get the flask, and follow me fast. I shall go slower than you, for I have no toes on one foot!"

So Nix Naught Nothing did as he was bid, and soon caught up the Magician's daughter. But alas! they could not run very fast, so ere long the Magician, who had once again taken a giant's form in order to have a long stride, could be seen behind them. Nearer and nearer he came until he was just going to seize Nix Naught Nothing, when the Magician's daughter cried, "Put your fingers, since I have none, into my hair, take my comb and throw it down." So Nix Naught Nothing did as he was bid, and, lo and behold! out of every one of the comb-prongs there sprang up a prickly briar, which grew so fast that the Magician found himself in the middle of a thorn hedge! You may guess how angry and scratched he was before he tore his way out. So Nix Naught Nothing and his sweetheart had time for a good start; but the Magician's daughter could not run fast because she had lost her toes on one foot! Therefore the Magician in giant form soon caught them up, and he was just about to grip Nix Naught Nothing when the Magician's daughter cried, "Put your fingers, since I have none, to my breast. Take out my veil-dagger and throw it down."

So he did as he was bid, and in a moment the dagger had grown to thousands and thousands of sharp razors, criss-cross on the ground, and the Magician giant was howling with pain as he trod among them. You may guess how he danced and stumbled and how long it took for him to pick his way through as if he were walking on eggs!

So Nix Naught Nothing and his sweetheart were nearly out of sight ere the giant could start again; yet it wasn't long before he was like to catch them up; for the Magician's daughter, you see, could not run fast because she had lost her toes on one foot! She did what she could, but it was no use. So just as the giant was reaching out a hand to lay hold of Nix Naught Nothing she cried breathlessly, "There's nothing left but the magic flask. Take it out and sprinkle some of what it holds on the ground."

And Nix Naught Nothing did as he was bid; but in his hurry he nearly emptied the flask altogether; and so the big, big wave of water which instantly welled up, swept him off his feet, and would have carried him away, had not the Magician's daughter's loosened veil caught him and held him fast. But the wave grew, and grew, and grew behind them, until it reached the giant's waist; then it grew and grew until it reached his shoulders; and it grew and grew until it swept over his head: a great big sea-wave full of little fishes and crabs and sea-snails and all sorts of strange creatures.

So that was the last of the Magician giant. But the poor little Magician's daughter was so weary that, after a time she couldn't move a step further, and she said to her lover, "Yonder are lights burning. Go and see if you can find a night's lodging: I will climb this tree by the pool where I shall be safe, and by the time you return I shall be rested."

Now, by chance, it happened that the lights they saw were the lights of the castle where Nix Naught Nothing's father and mother, the King and Queen, lived (though of course, he did not know this); so, as he walked towards the castle, he came upon the hen-wife's cottage and asked for a night's lodging.

"Who are you?" asked the hen-wife suspiciously.

"I am Nix Naught Nothing," replied the young man.

Now the hen-wife still grieved over her boy who had been killed, so she instantly resolved to be revenged.

"I cannot give you a night's lodging," she said, "but you shall have a drink of milk, for you look weary. Then you can go on to the castle and beg for a bed there."

So she gave him a cup of milk; but, being a witch-woman, she put a potion to it so that the very moment he saw his father and mother he should fall fast asleep, and none should be able to waken him so he would be no use to anybody, and would not recognize his father and mother.

Now the King and Queen had never ceased grieving for their lost son. They were always very kind to wandering young men, and when they heard that one was begging a night's lodging, they went down to the hall to see him. And lo, the moment Nix Naught Nothing caught sight of his father and mother, there he was on the floor fast asleep, and none could waken him! He did not recognize his father and mother nor they did not recognize him.

But Prince Nix Naught Nothing had grown into a very handsome young man, so they pitied him very much, and when none, do what they would, could waken him, the King said, "A maiden will likely take more trouble to waken him than others, seeing how handsome he is. Send forth a proclamation that if any maiden in my realm can waken this young man, she shall have him in marriage, and a handsome dowry to boot."

So the proclamation was sent forth, and all the pretty maidens of the realm came to try their luck, but they had no success.

Now the gardener whose boy had been killed by the giant had a daughter who was very ugly indeed - so ugly that she thought it no use to try her luck, and went about her work as usual. So she took her pitcher to the pool to fill it. Now the Magician's daughter was still hiding in the tree waiting for her lover to return. Thus it came to pass that the gardener's ugly daughter, bending down to fill her pitcher in the pool, saw a beautiful shadow in the water, and thought it was her own!

"If I am as pretty as that," she cried, "I'll draw water no longer!"

So she threw down her pitcher, and went straight to the castle to see if she hadn't a chance of the handsome stranger and the handsome dowry. But of course she hadn't; though at the sight of Nix Naught Nothing she fell so much in love with him, that, knowing the hen-wife to be a witch, she went straight to her, and offered all her savings for a charm by which she could awaken the sleeper.

Now when the hen-wife witch heard her tale, she thought it would be a rare revenge to marry the King and Queen's long-lost son to a gardener's ugly daughter; so she straightway took the girl's savings and gave her a charm by which she could unspell the Prince or spell him again at her pleasure.

So away went the gardener's daughter to the castle, and sure enough, no sooner had she sung her charm, than Nix Naught Nothing awoke.

"I am going to marry you, my charmer," she said coaxingly; but Nix Naught Nothing said he would prefer sleep. So she thought it wiser to put him to sleep again till the marriage feast was ready and she had got her fine clothes. So she spelled him asleep again.

Now the gardener had, of course, to draw the water himself, since his daughter would not work. And he took the pitcher to the pool; and he also saw the Magician's daughter's shadow in the water; but he did not think the face was his own, for, see you, he had a beard!

Then he looked up and saw the lady in the tree.

She, poor thing, was half dead with sorrow, and hunger, and fatigue, so, being a kind man, he took her to his house and gave her food. And he told her that that very day his daughter was to marry a handsome young stranger at the castle, and to get a handsome dowry to boot from the King and Queen, in memory of their son, Nix Naught Nothing, who had been carried off by a giant when he was a little boy.

Then the Magician's daughter felt sure that something had happened to her lover; so she went to the castle, and there she found him fast asleep in a chair.

But she could not waken him, for, see you, her magic had gone from her with the magic flask which Nix Naught Nothing had emptied.

So, though she put her fingerless hands on his and wept and sang:

"I cleaned the stable for love o' you,

I laved the lake and I clomb the tree,

Will you not waken for love o' me?"

He never stirred nor woke.

Now one of the old servants there, seeing how she wept, took pity on her and said, "She that is to marry the young man will be back before long, and unspell him for the wedding. Hide yourself and listen to her charm."

So the Magician's daughter hid herself, and, by and by, in comes the gardener's daughter in her fine wedding-dress, and begins to sing her charm. But the Magician's daughter didn't wait for her to finish it; for the moment Nix Naught Nothing opened his eyes, she rushed out of her hiding-place, and put her fingerless hands in his.

Then Nix Naught Nothing remembered everything. He remembered the castle, he remembered his father and mother, he remembered the Magician's daughter and all that she had done for him.

Then he drew out the magic flask and said, "Surely, surely there must be enough magic in it to mend your hands." And there was. There were just fourteen drops left, ten for the fingers and four for the toes; but there was not one for the little toe, so it could not be brought back. Of course, after that there was great rejoicing, and Prince Nix Naught Nothing and the Magician's daughter were married and lived happy ever after, even though she only had four toes on one foot. As for the hen-wife witch, she was burnt, and so the gardener's daughter got back her earnings; but she was not happy, because her shadow in the water was ugly again.

Silky

Folk-Lore and Legends: English is an 1890 anthology of English popular tales, edited by Charles John Tibbitts and published by W. W. Gibbings in London. It gathers together a mixture of fairy lore, local legends, nursery tales and antiquarian notes, framed by an introductory essay and a "Dissertation on Fairies".

Silky is a short legend centred on a haunting figure, a household or local spirit of the north of England, and fits into the collection's interest in ghost stories and localised supernatural beings rather than moralised fairy tales.

About the commencement of the present century the inhabitants of the quiet village of Black Heddon, near Stamfordham, and of its vicinity, who lived, as most other villagers do, with all possible harmony amongst themselves, and relishing no more external disturbance than was consistent with their gentle and sequestered mode of existence, were dreadfully annoyed by the pranks of a preternatural being called Silky. This name it had obtained from its manifesting a marked predilection to make itself visible in the semblance of a female dressed in silk. Many a time, when one of the more timorous of the community had a night journey to perform, have they unawares and invisibly been dogged and watched by this spectral tormentor, who, at the dreariest part of the road - the most suitable for thrilling surprises - would suddenly break forth in dazzling splendour. If the person happened to be on horseback, a sort of exercise for which she evinced a strong partiality, she would unexpectedly seat herself behind, "rattling in her silks." There, after enjoying a comfortable ride, with instantaneous abruptness she would, like a thing destitute of continuity, dissolve away and become incorporate with the nocturnal shades, leaving the bewildered horseman in blank amazement.

At Belsay, some two or three miles from Black Heddon, she had a favourite resort. This was a romantic crag finely studded with trees, under the gloomy umbrage of which, "like one forlorn," she loved to wander all the live-long night. Here often has the belated peasant, with awe-stricken vision, beheld her dimly through the sombre twilight as if engaged in splitting great stones, or hewing with many a repeated stroke some stately "monarch of the grove." While he thus stood and gazed, and listened to intimations, impossible to be misapprehended, of the dread reality of that mysterious being, concerning whom so various conjectures were awake, all at once, excited by that wondrous agency, he would hear the howling of a resistless tempest rushing through the woodland - the branches creaking in violent concussion, or rent into pieces by the impetuous fury of the blast - while, to the eye, not a leaf was seen to quiver, or a pensile spray to bend. The bottom of this crag is washed by a picturesque lake or fish-pond, at whose outlet is a waterfall, over which a venerable tree, sweeping its leafy arms, adds impressiveness to the scene. Amid the complicated and contorted limbs of this tree, Silky possessed a rude chair, where she was wont, in her moody moments, to sit - wind-rocked - enjoying the rustling of the storm in the dark woods, or the gush of the cascade. The tree, so consecrated in the sympathies and terrors of the people of the vicinity, has been preserved. Though now no longer tenanted by its aerial visitant, it yet spreads majestically its time-hallowed canopy over the spot, awakening in the love-versed rustic, when the winter's wind waves gusty and sonorous through its leafless boughs, the soul-harrowing recollection of the exploits of the ancient fay, but in the springtime, beautiful with the full-flushed verdure of that exuberant season, recipient of the kindling emotions of reverence and affection. It still bears the name of "Silky's seat," in memory of its once wonderful occupant.

Silky exercised a marvellous influence over the brute creation. Horses, which indisputably possess a discernment of spirits superior to that of man, and are more sharp-sighted in the dark, were in an extraordinary degree sensitive of her presence and control. Having once perceived the effects of her power she seems to have had a perverse pleasure in meddling with and arresting those poor defenceless animals, while engaged in the most exemplary performance of their labours. When this misfortune occurred there was no remedy that brute-force could devise. Expostulation, soothing, whipping, and kicking, were all exerted in vain to make the restive beast resume the proper and intended direction. The ultimate resource, unless it might be the whim of Silky to revoke the spell, was the magic dispelling witchwood, which, it is satisfactory to learn, was of unfailing efficacy. One poor wight, a farm-servant, was once the selected victim of her mischievous frolics. He had to go to a colliery at some distance for coals, and it was late in the evening before he could return. Silky, with spirit-like prescience, having intimation of the circumstance, waylaid him at a bridge - a "ghastly, ghost-alluring edifice," since called "Silky's Brig," lying a little to the south of Black Heddon, on the road between that place and Stamfordham. Just as he had arrived at "the height of that bad eminence," the keystone, horses and cart became fixed and immovable as fate. In that melancholy plight might both man and horses have continued - quaking, and sweating, and paralysed - till the morning light had thrown around them its mantle of protection - had not a neighbour's servant come to the rescue, who opportunely carried some of the potent witchwood (mountain-ash) about his person. On the arrival of this seasonable aid, the perplexed driver rallied his scattered senses, and the helpless animals, being duly seasoned after the fashion prescribed on such occasions, he had the heart-felt satisfaction of seeing them apply themselves, with the customary alacrity, to the draught. The charm was effectually overcome, and in a short time both the man and the coals reached home in safety. Ever afterwards, however, as long as he lived, he took the precaution of rendering himself spell-proof, by being furnished with a sufficient quantity of witchwood, being by no means disposed that Silky should a second time amuse herself at his expense and that of his team.

She was wayward and capricious. Sometimes she installed herself in the office of that old familiar Lar - Brownie, but, with characteristic misdirection, in a manner exactly the reverse of that useful species of hobgoblin. Here it may be remarked that, throughout her disembodied career, she can scarcely be said to have performed one benevolent action for the sake of its moral qualities. She had, from first to last, a perpetual latent hankering for mischief, and gloried in withering surprises and unforeseen movements. As is customary with that "sturdy fairy," as she is designated by the great English Lexicographer, her works were performed at night, or between the hours of sunset and day-dawn. If the good old dames had thoroughly cleaned their houses, which country people make a practice of doing, especially on Saturdays, so that they may have a comfortable and decent appearance on the Sabbath-day, after they had retired to rest, Silky would silently turn everything topsy-turvy, and the morning presented a scene of indescribable confusion. On the contrary, if the house had been left in a disorderly state, a plan which the folk generally found it best to adopt, everything would have been arranged with the greatest nicety.

At length a term had arrived in her erratic course, and both she and the peaceably disposed inhabitants whom she disquieted obtained the repose so long mutually desired. She abruptly disappeared. It had long been surmised, by those who paid attention to those dark matters, that she was the troubled phantom of some person, who had died very miserable, in consequence of having great treasure, which, before being taken by her mortal agony, had not been disclosed, and on that account Silky could not rest in her grave. About the period referred to a domestic female servant being alone in one of the rooms of a house in Black Heddon, was frightfully alarmed by the ceiling above suddenly giving way, and from it there dropped, with a prodigious clash, something quite black, shapeless, and uncouth. The servant did not stop to scrutinise an object so hideous and startling, but fled to her mistress, screaming at the pitch of her voice, "The devil's in the house! The devil's in the house! He's come through the ceiling!"

With this terrible announcement the whole family were speedily convoked, and great was the consternation at the idea of the foe of mankind being amongst them in visible form. In this appalling extremity, a considerable time elapsed before anyone could brace up courage to face the enemy, or be prevailed on to go and inspect the cause of their alarm. At last the mistress, who chanced to be the most stout-hearted, ventured into the room when, instead of the personage, on account of whom such awful apprehensions were entertained, a great dog or calf-skin lay on the floor, sufficiently black and uncomely, but filled with gold.

After this Silky was never more heard or seen. Her destiny was accomplished, her spirit laid, and she now sleeps with her ancestors.

Sir Gammer Vans

More English Fairy Tales is Joseph Jacobs's second major collection of English folk narratives, first published in 1894 as a companion to his earlier English Fairy Tales and illustrated by John D. Batten. It gathers a wide range of lesser-known stories from oral, chapbook and printed sources.

Sir Gammer Vans is one of the briefest and most playful pieces, a nonsense or "lying" tale that strings together a series of impossible, self-contradictory incidents as the first-person narrator goes to visit the giant bottle-maker Sir Gammer Vans, whose house and hunting exploits all defy logic.

Last sunday morning at six o'clock in the evening as I was sailing over the tops of the mountains in my little boat, I met two men on horseback riding on one mare: So I asked them, "Could they tell me whether the little old woman was dead yet who was hanged last Saturday week for drowning herself in a shower of feathers?" They said they could not positively inform me, but if I went to Sir Gammer Vans he could tell me all about it. "But how am I to know the house?" said I. "Ho, 't is easy enough," they said, "for 't is a brick house, built entirely of flints, standing alone by itself in the middle of sixty or seventy others just like it."

"Oh, nothing in the world is easier," said I.

"Nothing can be easier," said they: so I went on my way.

Now this Sir G. Vans was a giant, and a bottle-maker. And as all giants who are bottle-makers usually pop out of a little thumb-bottle from behind the door, so did Sir G. Vans.

"How do you do?" says he.

"Very well, I thank you," says I.

"Have some breakfast with me?"

"With all my heart," says I.

So he gave me a slice of beer, and a cup of cold veal; and there was a little dog under the table that picked up all the crumbs.

"Hang him," says I.

"No, don't hang him," says he, "for he killed a hare yesterday. And if you don't believe me, I'll show you the hare alive in a basket."

So he took me into his garden to show me the curiosities. In one corner there was a fox hatching eagle's eggs; in another there was an iron apple tree, entirely covered with pears and lead; in the third there was the hare which the dog killed yesterday alive in the basket; and in the fourth there were twenty-four hipper switches threshing tobacco, and at the sight of me they threshed so hard that they drove the plug through the wall, and through a little dog that was passing by on the other side. I, hearing the dog howl, jumped over the wall; and turned it as neatly inside out as possible, when it ran away as if it had not an hour to live. Then he took me into the park to show me his deer: and I remembered that I had a warrant in my pocket to shoot venison for his majesty's dinner. So I set fire to my bow, poised my arrow, and shot amongst them. I broke seventeen ribs on one side, and twenty-one and a half on the other; but my arrow passed clean through without ever touching it, and the worst was I lost my arrow: however, I found it again in the hollow of a tree. I felt it; it felt clammy. I smelt it; it smelt honey. "Oh, ho," said I, "here's a bee's nest," when out sprang a covey of partridges. I shot at them; some say I killed eighteen; but I am sure I killed thirty-six, besides a dead salmon which was flying over the bridge, of which I made the best apple-pie I ever tasted.

Tamlane

Tamlane in More English Fairy Tales is Joseph Jacobs's prose retelling of the old Scottish Border ballad better known as "Tam Lin" or "Tam Lin(e)". In his version, young Tamlane, the son of Earl Murray, has vanished just before his marriage to Burd Janet, daughter of the Earl of March.

As in the ballad tradition, Jacobs's version combines a love story with themes of courage, ordeal and release from the otherworld, and it helped to make this Border legend part of the standard English-language fairy-tale canon for later readers.

Young Tamlane was son of Earl Murray, and Burd Janet was daughter of Dunbar, Earl of March. And when they were young they loved one another and plighted their troth. But when the time came near for their marrying, Tamlane disappeared, and none knew what had become of him.

Many, many days after he had disappeared, Burd Janet was wandering in Carterhaugh Wood, though she had been warned not to go there. And as she wandered she plucked the flowers from the bushes. She came at last to a bush of broom and began plucking it. She had not taken more than three flowerets when by her side up started young Tamlane.

"Where come you from, Tamlane, Tamlane?" Burd Janet said, "and why have you been away so long?"

"From Elfland I come," said young Tamlane. "The Queen of Elfland has made me her knight."

"But how did you get there, Tamlane?" said Burd Janet.

"I was hunting one day, and as I rode widershins round yon hill, a deep drowsiness fell upon me, and when I awoke, behold! I was in Elfland. Fair is that land and gay, and fain would I stop but for you and one other thing. Every seven years the Elves pay their tithe to the Nether world, and for all the Queen makes much of me, I fear it is myself that will be the tithe."

"Oh can you not be saved? Tell me if anything I can do will save you, Tamlane?"

"One only thing is there for my safety. Tomorrow night is Hallowe'en, and the fairy court will then ride through England and Scotland, and if you would borrow me from Elfland you must take your stand by Miles Cross between twelve and one o' the night, and with holy water in your hand you must cast a compass all around you."

"But how shall I know you, Tamlane?" said Burd Janet, "amid so many knights I've ne'er seen before? The first court of Elves that come by let pass. The next court you shall pay reverence to, but do naught nor say anything. But the third court that comes by is the chief court of them, and at the head rides the Queen of all Elfland. And I shall ride by her side upon a milk-white steed with a star in my crown; they give me this honour as being a christened knight. Watch my hands, Janet, the right one will be gloved but the left one will be bare, and by that token you will know me."

"But how to save you, Tamlane?" said Burd Janet.

"You must spring upon me suddenly, and I will fall to the ground. Then seize me quick, and whatever change befall me, for they will exercise all their magic on me, cling hold to me till they turn me into red-hot iron. Then cast me into this pool and I will be turned back into a mother-naked man. Cast then your green mantle over me, and I shall be yours, and be of the world again."

So Burd Janet promised to do all for Tamlane, and next night at midnight she took her stand by Miles Cross and cast a compass round her with holy water.

Soon there came riding by the Elfin court, first over the mound went a troop on black steeds, and then another troop on brown. But in the third court, all on milk-white steeds, she saw the Queen of Elfland, and by her side a knight with a star in his crown, with right hand gloved and the left bare. Then she knew this was her own Tamlane, and springing forward she seized the bridle of the milk-white steed and pulled its rider down. And as soon as he had touched the ground she let go the bridle and seized him in her arms.

"He's won, he's won amongst us all," shrieked out the eldritch crew, and all came around her and tried their spells on young Tamlane.

First they turned him in Janet's arms like frozen ice, then into a huge flame of roaring fire. Then, again, the fire vanished and an adder was skipping through her arms, but still she held on; and then they turned him into a snake that reared up as if to bite her, and yet she held on. Then suddenly a dove was struggling in her arms, and almost flew away. Then they turned him into a swan, but all was in vain, till at last he was turned into a red-hot glaive, and this she cast into a well of water and then he turned back into a mother-naked man. She quickly cast her green mantle over him, and young Tamlane was Burd Janet's for ever.

Then sang the Queen of Elfland as the court turned away and began to resume its march:

"She that has borrowed young Tamlane

Has gotten a stately groom,

She's taken away my bonniest knight,

Left nothing in his room.

"But had I known, Tamlane, Tamlane,

A lady would borrow you,

I'd hae ta'en out your two grey eyne,

Put in two eyne of tree.

"Had I but known, Tamlane, Tamlane,

Before we came from home,

I'd hae ta'en out your heart o' flesh,

Put in a heart of stone.

"Had I but had the wit yestreen

That I have got today,

I'd paid the Fiend seven times his teind

Ere you'd been won away."

And then the Elfin court rode away, and Burd Janet and young Tamlane went their way homewards and were soon after married after young Tamlane had again been sainted by the holy water and made Christian once more.

Teeny-Tiny

Teeny-Tiny is a very short, comic-ghost tale from Joseph Jacobs's English Fairy Tales (1890). It follows a "teeny-tiny" woman who lives in a "teeny-tiny" house, in a "teeny-tiny" village, and whose whole world is described in that same repetitive formula.

The piece works less through plot than through rhythm and sound. The incessant repetition of "teeny-tiny" builds a sing-song pattern that makes the story ideal for telling aloud, especially to children, who can anticipate and join in the refrain. At the same time, the graveyard setting, the bone, and the ghostly voice give it a faintly eerie edge, although the sharp, almost throwaway ending pushes it back into humour rather than outright horror.

Once upon a time there was a teeny-tiny woman lived in a teeny-tiny house in a teeny-tiny village. Now, one day this teeny-tiny woman put on her teeny-tiny bonnet, and went out of her teeny-tiny house to take a teeny-tiny walk. And when this teeny-tiny woman had gone a teeny-tiny way she came to a teeny-tiny gate; so the teeny-tiny woman opened the teeny-tiny gate, and went into a teeny-tiny churchyard. And when this teeny-tiny woman had got into the teeny-tiny churchyard, she saw a teeny-tiny bone on a teeny-tiny grave, and the teeny-tiny woman said to her teeny-tiny self, "This teeny-tiny bone will make me some teeny-tiny soup for my teeny-tiny supper." So the teeny-tiny woman put the teeny-tiny bone into her teeny-tiny pocket, and went home to her teeny-tiny house.

Now when the teeny-tiny woman got home to her teeny-tiny house she was a teeny-tiny bit tired; so she went up her teeny-tiny stairs to her teeny-tiny bed, and put the teeny-tiny bone into a teeny-tiny cupboard. And when this teeny-tiny woman had been to sleep a teeny-tiny time, she was awakened by a teeny-tiny voice from the teeny-tiny cupboard, which said, "Give me my bone!"

And this teeny-tiny woman was a teeny-tiny frightened, so she hid her teeny-tiny head under the teeny-tiny clothes and went to sleep again. And when she had been to sleep again a teeny-tiny time, the teeny-tiny voice again cried out from the teeny-tiny cupboard a teeny-tiny louder, "Give me my bone!"

This made the teeny-tiny woman a teeny-tiny more frightened, so she hid her teeny-tiny head a teeny-tiny further under the teeny-tiny clothes. And when the teeny-tiny woman had been to sleep again a teeny-tiny time, the teeny-tiny voice from the teeny-tiny cupboard said again a teeny-tiny louder, "Give me my bone!"

And this teeny-tiny woman was a teeny-tiny bit more frightened, but she put her teeny-tiny head out of the teeny-tiny clothes, and said in her loudest teeny-tiny voice, "TAKE IT!"

The Baker's Daughter

The Baker's Daughter is a short moral tale from Charles John Tibbits's Folk-Lore and Legends: English, retold here in adapted form. It usually centres on a baker and his daughter in Herefordshire, whose greed and meanness are exposed when a poor stranger (often a disguised holy figure or powerful being) asks for bread.

In broader folklore, this story belongs to a well-known English legend cycle that Shakespeare alludes to in Hamlet when Ophelia remarks that "the owl was a baker's daughter." In that tradition, the visitor is often identified explicitly as Christ, reinforcing the tale's Christian moral about charity, proper hospitality, and the danger of petty greed.

A very long time ago, I cannot tell you when, it is so long since, there lived in a town in Herefordshire a baker who used to sell bread to all the folk around. He was a mean, greedy man, who sought in every way to put money by, and who did not scruple to cheat such people as he was able when they came to his shop.

He had a daughter who helped him in his business, being unmarried and living with him, and seeing how her father treated the people, and how he succeeded in getting money by his bad practices, she, too, in time came to do the like.

One day when her father was away, and the girl remained alone in the shop, an old woman came in and said, "My pretty girl," she said, "give me a bit of dough I beg of you, for I am old and hungry."

The girl at first told her to be off, but as the old woman would not go, and begged harder than before for a piece of bread, at last the baker's daughter took up a piece of dough, and giving it to her, said, "There now, be off, and do not trouble me anymore."

"My dear," says the woman, "you have given me a piece of dough, let me bake it in your oven, for I have no place of my own to bake it in."

"Very well," replied the girl, and, taking the dough, she placed it in the oven, while the old woman sat down to wait till it was baked.

When the girl thought the bread should be ready she looked in the oven expecting to find there a small cake, and was very much amazed to find instead a very large loaf of bread. She pretended to look about the oven as if in search of something.

"I cannot find the cake," she said. "It must have tumbled into the fire and got burnt."

"Very well," said the old woman, "give me another piece of dough instead and I will wait while it bakes."

So the girl took another piece of dough, smaller than the first piece, and having put it in the oven, shut to the door. At the end of a few minutes or so she looked in again, and found there another loaf, larger than the last.

"Dear me," she said, pretending to look about her, "I have surely lost the dough again. There's no cake here."

"Tis a pity," said the old woman, "but never mind. I will wait while you bake me another piece."

So the baker's daughter took a piece of dough as small as one of her fingers and put it in the oven, while the old woman sat near. When she thought it ought to be baked, she looked into the oven and there saw a loaf, larger than either of the others.

"That is mine," said the old woman.

"No," replied the girl. "How could such a large loaf have grown out of a little piece of dough?"

"It is mine, it is sure," said the woman.

"It is not," said the girl, "and you shall not have it."

Well, when the old woman saw that the girl would not give her the loaf, and saw how she had tried to cheat her, for she was a fairy, and knew all the tricks that the baker's daughter had put upon her, she draws out from under her cloak a stick, and just touches the girl with it. Then a wonderful thing occurred, for the girl became all of a sudden changed into an owl, and flying about the room, at last, made for the door, and, finding it open, she flew out and was never seen again.

The Blinded Giant

The Blinded Giant is one of the quick, punchy tales Joseph Jacobs included in More English Fairy Tales. It is tied to Dalton Mill near Thirsk in Yorkshire, where people used to point out a "giant's grave" and a long iron blade said to be the giant's knife.

Jacobs did not invent the story from scratch; he polished it from older northern English folklore, but he clearly enjoyed the way it echoes the famous episode of Odysseus and Polyphemus. This version is an English spin on a very old idea; a village-sized retelling of a much larger myth.

At Dalton, near Thirsk, in Yorkshire, there is a mill. It has quite recently been rebuilt; but when I was at Dalton, six years ago, the old building stood. In front of the house was a long mound which went by the name of "the giant's grave," and in the mill you can see a long blade of iron something like a scythe-blade, but not curved, which was called "the giant's knife," because of a very curious story which is told of this knife. Would you like to hear it? Well, it isn't very long.

There once lived a giant at this mill who had only one eye in the middle of his forehead, and he ground men's bones to make his bread. One day he captured on Pilmoor a lad named Jack, and instead of grinding him in the mill he kept him grinding as his servant, and never let him get away. Jack served the giant seven years, and never was allowed a holiday the whole time. At last he could bear it no longer. Topcliffe fair was coming on, and Jack begged that he might be allowed to go there.

"No, no," said the giant, "stop at home and mind your grinding."

"I've been grinding and grinding these seven years," said Jack, "and not a holiday have I had. I'll have one now, whatever you say."

"We'll see about that," said the giant.

Well, the day was hot, and after dinner the giant lay down in the mill with his head on a sack and dozed. He had been eating in the mill, and had laid down a great loaf of bone bread by his side, and the knife I told you about was in his hand, but his fingers relaxed their hold of it in sleep. Jack seized the knife, and holding it with both his hands drove the blade into the single eye of the giant, who woke with a howl of agony, and starting up, barred the door. Jack was again in difficulties, for he couldn't get out, but he soon found a way out of them. The giant had a favourite dog, which had also been sleeping when his master was blinded. So Jack killed the dog, skinned it, and threw the hide over his back.

"Bow, wow," says Jack.

"At him, Truncheon," said the giant, "at the little wretch that I've fed these seven years, and now has blinded me."

"Bow, wow," says Jack, and ran between the giant's legs on all-fours, barking till he got to the door. He unlatched it and was off, and never more was seen at Dalton Mill.

The Brown Man of the Moors

The Brown Man of the Moors appears in Charles John Tibbits's anthology Folk-Lore and Legends: English, first published in London by W. W. Gibbings in 1890. Tibbits prints it as a brief prose legend set "in the year before the Great Rebellion", when two young sportsmen from Newcastle encounter a "brown dwarf" on the moors above Elsdon.

Behind Tibbits's text lies an earlier literary record of the same narrative, usually cited under the form "Brown Man of the Muirs". William Henderson included it in Folklore of the Northern Counties of England and the Borders (1879), acknowledging a letter from the historian Robert Surtees to Sir Walter Scott as his source.

In the year before the great rebellion two young men from Newcastle were sporting on the high moors above Elsdon, and, after pursuing their game several hours, sat down to dine in a green glen, near one of the mountain streams. After their repast, the younger lad ran to the brook for water, and, after stooping to drink, was surprised, on lifting his head again, by the appearance of a brown dwarf, who stood on a crag covered with brackens across the burn.

This extraordinary personage did not appear to be above half the stature of a common man, but was uncommonly stout and broad-built, having the appearance of vast strength. His dress was entirely brown, the colour of the brackens, and his head covered with frizzled red hair. His countenance was expressive of the most savage ferocity, and his eyes glared like those of a bull.

It seems he addressed the young man, first threatening him with his vengeance for having trespassed on his demesnes, and asking him if he knew in whose presence he stood.

The youth replied that he supposed him to be the lord of the moors; that he had offended through ignorance; and offered to bring him the game he had killed. The dwarf was a little mollified by this submission, but remarked that nothing could be more offensive to him than such an offer, as he considered the wild animals as his subjects, and never failed to avenge their destruction. He condescended further to inform the young man that he was, like himself, mortal, though of years far exceeding the lot of common humanity, and that he hoped for salvation. He never, he added, fed on anything that had life, but lived in the summer on whortle berries, and in winter on nuts and apples, of which he had great store in the woods. Finally, he invited his new acquaintance to accompany him home and partake his hospitality, an offer which the youth was on the point of accepting, and was just going to spring across the brook (which if he had done, the dwarf would certainly have torn him to pieces) when his foot was arrested by the voice of his companion, who thought he had tarried long. On his looking round again "the wee brown man was fled."

The story adds that the young man was imprudent enough to slight the admonition, and to sport over the moors on his way homewards, but soon after his return he fell into a lingering disorder, and died within a year.

The Fairies' Cup

The Fairies' Cup in Folk-Lore and Legends: English is a short prose legend, first published in London by W. W. Gibbings in 1890 and reissued in later impressions. The tale sits among a cluster of "fairy" narratives in the.

Behind Tibbits, however, lies a much older source. The story is his lightly edited reprinting of a passage from the Historia rerum Anglicarum of the twelfth-century chronicler William of Newburgh (or Newbridge), Book I, chapter 28, in which William records the marvel of a peasant near the waters of Gipse in Deira (Yorkshire) who steals a supernatural drinking vessel from a barrow-dwelling company and ultimately presents it to King Henry I, from whom it passes into Scottish royal and then back into English royal hands.

"In the province of the Deiri (Yorkshire), not far from my birthplace," says William of Newbury, "a wonderful thing occurred, which I have known from my boyhood. There is a town a few miles distant from the Eastern Sea, near which are those celebrated waters commonly called Gipse....

A peasant of this town went once to see a friend who lived in the next town, and it was late at night when he was coming back, not very sober, when, lo! from the adjoining barrow, which I have often seen, and which is not much over a quarter of a mile from the town, he heard the voices of people singing, and, as it were, joyfully feasting. He wondered who they could be that were breaking in that place, by their merriment, the silence of the dead night, and he wished to examine into the matter more closely.

Seeing a door open in the side of the barrow he went up to it and looked in, and there he beheld a large and luminous house, full of people, women as well as men, who were reclining as at a solemn banquet. One of the attendants, seeing him standing at the door, offered him a cup. He took it, but would not drink, and pouring out the contents, kept the vessel. A great tumult arose at the banquet on account of his taking away the cup, and all the guests pursued him, but he escaped by the fleetness of the beast he rode, and got into the town with his booty.

"Finally this vessel of unknown material, of unusual colour, and of extraordinary form, was presented to Henry the Elder, King of the English, as a valuable gift; was then given to the Queen's brother, David, King of the Scots, and was kept for several years in the treasury of Scotland. A few years ago, as I have heard from good authority, it was given by William, King of the Scots, to Henry the Second, who wished to see it."

The Fiddler in the Fairy Ring

The Fiddler in the Fairy Ring is a literary fairy tale by Juliana Horatia Ewing (1841–1885), one of the most significant writers for children in late Victorian Britain. The story first appeared in January 1873 in connection with Old-fashioned Fairy Tales, a series associated with the Society for Promoting Christian Knowledge (S.P.C.K.), and is also listed in contemporary contents for Aunt Judy's Magazine, which frequently served as an initial vehicle for Ewing's work. As part of Old-Fashioned Fairy Tales, The Fiddler in the Fairy Ring has enjoyed a long reprint history.

Generations ago, there once lived A farmer's son, who had no great harm in him, and no great good either. He always meant well, but he had a poor spirit, and was too fond of idle company.

One day his father sent him to market with some sheep for sale, and when business was over for the day, the rest of the country-folk made ready to go home, and more than one of them offered the lad a lift in his cart.

"Thank you kindly, all the same," he said, "but I am going back across the downs with Limping Tim."

Then out spoke a steady old farmer and bade the lad go home with the rest, and by the main road. For Limping Tim was an idle, graceless kind of fellow, who fiddled for his livelihood, but what else he did to earn the money he squandered, no one knew. And as to the sheep path over the downs, it stands to reason that the highway is better travelling after sunset, for the other is no such very short cut; and has a big fairy ring so near it, that a butter-woman might brush it with the edge of her market cloak, as she turned the brow of the hill.

But the farmer's son would go his own way, and that was with Limping Tim, and across the downs.

So they started, and the fiddler had his fiddle in his hand, and a bundle of marketings under his arm, and he sang snatches of strange songs, the like of which the lad had never heard before. And the moon drew out their shadows over the short grass till they were as long as the great stones of Stonehenge.

At last they turned the hill, and the fairy ring looked dark under the moon, and the farmer's son blessed himself that they were passing it quietly, when Limping Tim suddenly pulled his cloak from his back, and handing it to his companion, cried, "Hold this for a moment, will you? I'm wanted. They're calling for me."

"I hear nothing," said the farmer's son. But before he had got the words out of his mouth, the fiddler had completely disappeared. He shouted aloud, but in vain, and had begun to think of proceeding on his way, when the fiddler's voice cried, "Catch!" and there came, flying at him from the direction of the fairy ring, the bundle of marketings which the fiddler had been carrying.

"It's in my way," he then heard the fiddler cry. "Ah, this is dancing! Come in, my lad, come in!"

But the farmer's son was not totally without prudence, and he took good care to keep at a safe distance from the fairy ring.

"Come back, Tim! Come back!" he shouted, and, receiving no answer, he adjured his friend to break the bonds that withheld him, and return to the right way, as wisely as one man can counsel another.

After talking for some time to no purpose, he again heard his friend's voice, crying, "Take care of it for me! The money dances out of my pocket." And therewith the fiddler's purse was hurled to his feet, where it fell with a heavy chinking of gold within.

He picked it up, and renewed his warnings and entreaties, but in vain; and, after waiting for a long time, he made the best of his way home alone, hoping that the fiddler would follow, and come to reclaim his property.

The fiddler never came. And when at last there was a fuss about his disappearance, the farmer's son, who had but a poor spirit, began to be afraid to tell the truth of the matter. "Who knows but they may accuse me of theft?" he said. So he hid the cloak, and the bundle, and the money-bag in the garden.

But when three months passed, and still the fiddler did not return, it was whispered that the farmer's son had been his last companion; and the place was searched, and they found the cloak, and the bundle, and the money-bag and the lad was taken to prison.

Now, when it was too late, he plucked up a spirit, and told the truth; but no one believed him, and it was said that he had murdered the fiddler for the sake of his money and goods. And he was taken before the judge, found guilty, and sentenced to death.

Fortunately, his old mother was a Wise Woman. And when she heard that he was condemned, she said, "Only follow my directions, and we may save you yet; for I guess how it is."

So she went to the judge, and begged for her son three favours before his death.

"I will grant them," said the judge, "if you do not ask for his life."

"The first," said the old woman, "is, that he may choose the place where the gallows shall be erected; the second, that he may fix the hour of his execution; and the third favour is, that you will not fail to be present."

"I grant all three," said the judge. But when he learned that the criminal had chosen a certain hill on the downs for the place of execution, and an hour before midnight for the time, he sent to beg the sheriff to bear him company on this important occasion.

The sheriff placed himself at the judge's disposal, but he commanded the attendance of the gaoler as some sort of protection; and the gaoler, for his part, implored his reverence the chaplain to be of the party, as the hill was not in good spiritual repute. So, when the time came, the four started together, and the hangman and the farmer's son went before them to the foot of the gallows.

Just as the rope was being prepared, the farmer's son called to the judge, and said, "If your Honour will walk twenty paces down the hill, to where you will see a bit of paper, you will learn the fate of the fiddler."

"That is, no doubt, a copy of the poor man's last confession," thought the judge.

"Murder will out, Mr. Sheriff," said he; and in the interests of truth and justice he hastened to pick up the paper.

But the farmer's son had dropped it as he came along, by his mother's direction, in such a place that the judge could not pick it up without putting his foot on the edge of the fairy ring. No sooner had he done so than he perceived an innumerable company of little people dressed in green cloaks and hoods, who were dancing round in a circle as wide as the ring itself.

They were all about two feet high, and had aged faces, brown and withered, like the knots on gnarled trees in hedge bottoms, and they squinted horribly; but, in spite of their seeming age, they flew round and round like children.

"Mr. Sheriff! Mr. Sheriff!" cried the judge, "come and see the dancing. And hear the music, too, which is so lively that it makes the soles of my feet tickle."

"There is no music, my Lord Judge," said the sheriff, running down the hill. "It is the wind whistling over the grass that your lordship hears."

But when the sheriff had put his foot by the judge's foot, he saw and heard the same, and he cried out, "Quick, Gaoler, and come down! I should like you to be witness to this matter. And you may take my arm, Gaoler, for the music makes me feel unsteady."

"There is no music, sir," said the gaoler, "but your worship doubtless hears the creaking of the gallows."

But no sooner had the gaoler's feet touched the fairy ring, than he saw and heard like the rest, and he called lustily to the chaplain to come and stop the unhallowed measure.

"It is a delusion of the Evil One," said the parson, "there is not a sound in the air but the distant croaking of some frogs." But when he too touched the ring, he perceived his mistake.

At this moment the moon shone out, and in the middle of the ring they saw Limping Tim the fiddler, playing till great drops stood out on his forehead, and dancing as madly as he played.

"Ah, you rascal!" cried the judge. "Is this where you've been all the time, and a better man than you as good as hanged for you? But you shall come home now."

Saying which, he ran in, and seized the fiddler by the arm, but Limping Tim resisted so stoutly that the sheriff had to go to the judge's assistance, and even then the fairies so pinched and hindered them that the sheriff was obliged to call upon the gaoler to put his arms about his waist, who persuaded the chaplain to add his strength to the string. But as ill luck would have it, just as they were getting off, one of the fairies picked up Limping Tim's fiddle, which had fallen in the scuffle, and began to play. And as he began to play, everyone began to dance - the fiddler, and the judge, and the sheriff, and the gaoler, and even the chaplain.

"Hangman! hangman!" screamed the judge, as he lifted first one leg and then the other to the tune, "come down, and catch hold of his reverence the chaplain. The prisoner is pardoned, and he can lay hold too."

The hangman knew the judge's voice, and ran towards it; but as they were now quite within the ring he could see nothing, either of him or his companions.

The farmer's son followed, and warning the hangman not to touch the ring, he directed him to stretch his hands forwards in hopes of catching hold of some one. In a few minutes the wind blew the chaplain's cassock against the hangman's fingers, and he caught the parson round the waist. The farmer's son then seized him in like fashion, and each holding firmly by the other, the fiddler, the judge, the sheriff, the gaoler, the parson, the hangman, and the farmer's son all got safely out of the charmed circle.

"Oh, you scoundrel!" cried the judge to the fiddler, "I have a very good mind to hang you up on the gallows without further ado."

But the fiddler only looked like one possessed, and upbraided the farmer's son for not having the patience to wait three minutes for him.

"Three minutes!" cried he, "why, you've been here three months and a day."

This the fiddler would not believe, and as he seemed in every way beside himself, they led him home, still upbraiding his companion, and crying continually for his fiddle.

His neighbours watched him closely, but one day he escaped from their care and wandered away over the hills to seek his fiddle, and came back no more.

His dead body was found upon the downs, face downwards, with the fiddle in his arms. Some said he had really found the fiddle where he had left it, and had been lost in a mist, and died of exposure. But others held that he had perished differently, and laid his death at the door of the fairy dancers.

As to the farmer's son, it is said that thenceforward he went home from market by the high-road, and spoke the truth straight out, and was more careful of his company.

The Fish and the Ring

The Fish and the Ring is an English fairy tale that entered print in Joseph Jacobs's English Fairy Tales (David Nutt, London, 1890), one of the foundational late-Victorian collections of English folk narrative. This version is taken from Flora Annie Steel's English Fairy Tales (Macmillan, London, 1918), a volume of forty-one tales in which Steel reshaped many of Jacobs's texts in a slightly fuller, more literary style, accompanied by Arthur Rackham's illustrations.

The tale itself belongs to the widespread "child of destiny" complex, in which a child of humble birth is prophesied to marry into high rank, and the very attempts to thwart that fate ensure its fulfilment.

Once upon a time there lived a Baron who was a great magician, and could tell by his arts and charms everything that was going to happen at any time.

Now this great lord had a little son born to him as heir to all his castles and lands. So, when the little lad was about four years old, wishing to know what his fortune would be, the Baron looked in his Book of Fate to see what it foretold.

And, lo and behold! it was written that this much-loved, much-prized heir to all the great lands and castles was to marry a low-born maiden. So the Baron was dismayed, and set to work by more arts and charms to discover if this maiden were already born, and if so, where she lived.

And he found out that she had just been born in a very poor house, where the poor parents were already burdened with five children.

So he called for his horse and rode away, and away, until he came to the poor man's house, and there he found the poor man sitting at his doorstep very sad and doleful.

"What is the matter, my friend?" asked he; and the poor man replied, "May it please your honour, a little lass has just been born to our house; and we have five children already, and where the bread is to come from to fill the sixth mouth, we know not."

"If that be all your trouble," said the Baron readily, "mayhap I can help you: so don't be down-hearted. I am just looking for such a little lass to companion my son, so, if you will, I will give you ten crowns for her."

Well! the man he nigh jumped for joy, since he was to get good money, and his daughter, so he thought, a good home. Therefore he brought out the child then and there, and the Baron, wrapping the babe in his cloak, rode away. But when he got to the river he flung the little thing into the swollen stream, and said to himself as he galloped back to his castle, "There goes Fate!"

But, you see, he was just sore mistaken. For the little lass didn't sink. The stream was very swift, and her long clothes kept her up till she caught in a snag just opposite a fisherman, who was mending his nets.

Now the fisherman and his wife had no children, and they were just longing for a baby; so when the good man saw the little lass he was overcome with joy, and took her home to his wife, who received her with open arms.

And there she grew up, the apple of their eyes, into the most beautiful maiden that ever was seen.

Now, when she was about fifteen years of age, it so happened that the Baron and his friends went a-hunting along the banks of the river and stopped to get a drink of water at the fisherman's hut. And who should bring the water out but, as they thought, the fisherman's daughter.

Now the young men of the party noticed her beauty, and one of them said to the Baron, "She should marry well; read us her fate, since you are so learned in the art."

Then the Baron, scarce looking at her, said carelessly, "I could guess her fate! Some wretched yokel or other. But, to please you, I will cast her horoscope by the stars; so tell me, girl, what day you were born?"

"That I cannot tell, sir," replied the girl, "for I was picked up in the river about fifteen years ago."

Then the Baron grew pale, for he guessed at once that she was the little lass he had flung into the stream, and that Fate had been stronger than he was. But he kept his own counsel and said nothing at the time. Afterwards, however, he thought out a plan, so he rode back and gave the girl a letter.

"See you!" he said. "I will make your fortune. Take this letter to my brother, who needs a good girl, and you will be settled for life."

Now the fisherman and his wife were growing old and needed

help; so the girl said she would go, and took the letter.

And the Baron rode back to his castle saying to himself once more, "There goes Fate!"

For what he had written in the letter was this:

"Dear Brother,

"Take the bearer and put her to death immediately."

But once again he was sore mistaken; since on the way to the town where his brother lived, the girl had to stop the night in a little inn. And it so happened that that very night a gang of thieves broke into the inn, and not content with carrying off all that the innkeeper possessed, they searched the pockets of the guests, and found the letter which the girl carried. And when they read it, they agreed that it was a mean trick and a shame. So their captain sat down and, taking pen and paper, wrote instead:

"Dear Brother,

"Take the bearer and marry her to my son without delay."

Then, after putting the note into an envelope and sealing it up, they gave it to the girl and bade her go on her way. So when she arrived at the brother's castle, though rather surprised, he gave orders for a wedding feast to be prepared. And the Baron's son, who was staying with his uncle, seeing the girl's great beauty, was nothing loth, so they were fast wedded.

Well! when the news was brought to the Baron, he was nigh beside himself; but he was determined not to be done by Fate. So he rode post-haste to his brother's and pretended to be quite pleased. And then one day, when no one was nigh, he asked the young bride to come for a walk with him, and when they were close to some cliffs, seized hold of her, and was for throwing her over into the sea. But she begged hard for her life.

"It is not my fault," she said. "I have done nothing. It is Fate. But if you will spare my life I promise that I will fight against Fate also. I will never see you or your son again until you desire it. That will be safer for you; since, see you, the sea may preserve me, as the river did."

Well! the Baron agreed to this. So he took off his gold ring from his finger and flung it over the cliffs into the sea and said, "Never dare to show me your face again till you can show me that ring likewise."

And with that he let her go.

Well! the girl wandered on, and she wandered on, until she came to a nobleman's castle; and there, as they needed a kitchen girl, she engaged as a scullion, since she had been used to such work in the fisherman's hut.

Now one day, as she was cleaning a big fish, she looked out of the kitchen window, and who should she see driving up to dinner but the Baron and his young son, her husband. At first she thought that, to keep her promise, she must run away; but afterwards she remembered they would not see her in the kitchen, so she went on with her cleaning of the big fish.

And, lo and behold! she saw something shine in its inside, and there, sure enough, was the Baron's ring! She was glad enough to see it, I can tell you; so she slipped it on to her thumb. But she went on with her work, and dressed the fish as nicely as ever she could, and served it up as pretty as may be, with parsley sauce and butter.

Well! when it came to table the guests liked it so well that they asked the host who cooked it. And he called to his servants, "Send up the cook who cooked that fine fish, that she may get her reward."

Well! when the girl heard she was wanted she made herself ready, and with the gold ring on her thumb, went boldly into the dining-hall. And all the guests when they saw her were struck dumb by her wonderful beauty. And the young husband started up gladly; but the Baron, recognising her, jumped up angrily and looked as if he would kill her. So, without one word, the girl held up her hand before his face, and the gold ring shone and glittered on it; and she went straight up to the Baron, and laid her hand with the ring on it before him on the table.

Then the Baron understood that Fate had been too strong for him; so he took her by the hand, and, placing her beside him, turned to the guests and said, "This is my son's wife. Let us drink a toast in her honour."

And after dinner he took her and his son home to his castle, where they all lived as happy as could be for ever afterwards.

The Golden Arm

The Golden Arm in English Fairy Tales is Joseph Jacobs's late nineteenth-century literary redaction of a much older and widely diffused folktale. Jacobs first published the story in English Fairy Tales (London, 1890), presenting it in a concise prose form as part of his broader project to define a specifically "English" fairy-tale canon

Beyond Jacobs's version, The Golden Arm has a long oral and print history in Britain, Europe and North America, with numerous variants in which a stolen item is reclaimed by a returning corpse. The story became especially famous in American tradition through Mark Twain, who used it as a model "jump tale" in his essay How to Tell a Story, and it continues to appear in folklore anthologies and performance repertoires as a classic camp-fire ghost story.

Here was once a man who travelled the land all over in search of a wife. He saw young and old, rich and poor, pretty and plain, and could not meet with one to his mind. At last he found a woman, young, fair, and rich, who possessed a right arm of solid gold. He married her at once, and thought no man so fortunate as he was. They lived happily together, but, though he wished people to think otherwise, he was fonder of the golden arm than of all his wife's gifts besides.

At last she died. The husband put on the blackest black, and pulled the longest face at the funeral; but for all that he got up in the middle of the night, dug up the body, and cut off the golden arm. He hurried home to hide his treasure, and thought no one would know.

The following night he put the golden arm under his pillow, and was just falling asleep, when the ghost of his dead wife glided into the room. Stalking up to the bedside it drew the curtain, and looked at him reproachfully. Pretending not to be afraid, he spoke to the ghost, and said, "What have you done with your cheeks so red?"

"All withered and wasted away," replied the ghost, in a hollow tone.

"What have you done with your red, rosy lips?"

"All withered and wasted away."

"What have you done with your golden hair?"

"All withered and wasted away."

"What have you done with your Golden Arm?"

"YOU HAVE IT!"

The Golden Snuff-Box

The Golden Snuff-Box is a retitled and slightly reshaped version of the tale more commonly known as Jack and his Golden Snuff-box. Flora Annie Webster Steel's collection, illustrated by Arthur Rackham, gathers forty-one English narratives and was intended as a popular yet "national" anthology of English folk material during and just after the First World War.

Behind Steel's version lies a well-documented chain of transmission. The core narrative is a Romani fairy tale, first printed in Francis Hindes Groome's In Gypsy Tents (1880), and then taken over by Joseph Jacobs as Jack and his Golden Snuff-box in his influential English Fairy Tales (1890).

Once upon a time, and a very good time too, though it was not in my time, nor your time, nor for the matter of that in any one's time, there lived a man and a woman who had one son called Jack, and he was just terribly fond of reading books. He read, and he read, and then, because his parents lived in a lonely house in a lonely forest and he never saw any other folk but his father and his mother, he became quite crazy to go out into the world and see charming princesses and the like.

So one day he told his mother he must be off, and she called him an air-brained addle-pate, but added that, as he was no use at home, he had better go seek his fortune. Then she asked him if he would rather take a small cake with her blessing to eat on his journey, or a large cake with her curse? Now Jack was a very hungry lad, so he just up and said, "A big cake, if you please"

So his mother made a great big cake, and when he started she just off to the top of the house and cast malisons on him, till he got out of sight. You see she had to do it, but after that she sat down and cried.

Well, Jack hadn't gone far till he came to a field where his father was ploughing. Now the good man was dreadfully put out when he found his son was going away, and still more so when he heard he had chosen his mother's malison. So he cast about what to do to put things straight, and at last he drew out of his pocket a little golden snuff-box, and gave it to the lad, saying, "If ever you are in danger of sudden death you may open the box; but not till then. It has been in our family for years and years; but, as we have lived, father and son, quietly in the forest, none of us have ever been in need of help - perhaps you may."

So Jack pocketed the golden snuff-box and went on his way.

Now, after a time, he grew very tired, and very hungry, for he had eaten his big cake first thing, and night closed in on him so that he could scarce see his way.

But at last he came to a large house and begged board and lodging at the back door. Now Jack was a good-looking young fellow, so the maid-servant at once called him in to the fireside and gave him plenty good meat and bread and beer. And it so happened that while he was eating his supper the master's gay young daughter came into the kitchen and saw him. So she went to her father and said that there was the prettiest young fellow she had ever seen in the back kitchen, and that if her father loved her he would give the young man some employment. Now the gentleman of the house was exceedingly fond of his gay young daughter, and did not want to vex her; so he went into the back kitchen and questioned Jack as to what he could do.

"Anything," said Jack gaily, meaning, of course, that he could do any foolish bit of work about a house.

But the gentleman saw a way of pleasing his gay young daughter and getting rid of the trouble of employing Jack; so he laughs and says, "If you can do anything, my good lad," says he, "you had better do this. By eight o'clock tomorrow morning you must have dug a lake four miles round in front of my mansion, and on it there must be floating a whole fleet of vessels. And they must range up in front of my mansion and fire a salute of guns. And the very last shot must break the leg of the four-post bed on which my daughter sleeps, for she is always late of a morning!"

Well! Jack was terribly flabbergasted, but he faltered out, "And if I don't do it?"

"Then," said the master of the house quite calmly, "your life will be the forfeit."

So he bade the servants take Jack to a turret-room and lock the door on him.

Well! Jack sat on the side of his bed and tried to think things out, but he felt as if he didn't know b from a battledore, so he decided to think no more, and after saying his prayers he lay down and went to sleep. And he did sleep! When he woke it was close on eight o'clock, and he had only time to fly to the window and look out, when the great clock on the tower began to whirr before it struck the hour. And there was the lawn in front of the house all set with beds of roses and stocks and marigolds! Well! all of a sudden he remembered the little golden snuff-box.

"I'm near enough to death," said he to himself, as he drew it out and opened it.

And no sooner had he opened it than out hopped three funny little red men in red night-caps, rubbing their eyes and yawning; for, see you, they had been locked up in the box for years, and years, and years.

"What do you want, Master?" they said between their yawns. But Jack heard that clock a-whirring and knew he hadn't a moment to lose, so he just gabbled off his orders. Then the clock began to strike, and the little men flew out of the window, and suddenly, Bang! bang! bang! bang! bang! bang!

went the guns, and the last one must have broken the leg of the four-post bed, for there at the window was the gay young daughter in her nightcap, gazing with astonishment at the lake four miles round, with the fleet of vessels floating on it!

And so did Jack! He had never seen such a sight in his life, and he was quite sorry when the three little red men disturbed him by flying in at the window and scrambling into the golden snuff-box.

"Give us a little more time when you want us next, Master," they said sulkily. Then they shut down the lid, and Jack could hear them yawning inside as they settled down to sleep.

As you may imagine, the master of the house was fair astonished, while as for the gay young daughter, she declared at once that she would never marry anyone else but the young man who could do such wonderful things; the truth being that she and Jack had fallen in love with each other at first sight.

But her father was cautious. "It is true, my dear," says he, "that the young fellow seems a bully boy; but for anything we know it may be chance, not skill, and he may have a broken feather in his wing. So we must try him again."

Then he said to Jack, "My daughter must have a fine house to live in. Therefore by tomorrow morning at eight o'clock there must be a magnificent castle standing on twelve golden pillars in the middle of the lake, and there must be a church beside it. And all things must be ready for the bride, and at eight o'clock precisely a peal of bells from the church must ring out for the wedding. If not you will have to forfeit your life."

This time Jack intended to give the three little red men more time for their task; but what with having enjoyed himself so much all day, and having eaten so much good food, he overslept himself, so that the big clock on the tower was whirring before it struck eight when he woke, leapt out of bed, and rushed to the golden snuff-box. But he had forgotten where he had put it, and so the clock had really begun to strike before he found it under his pillow, opened it, and gabbled out his orders. And then you never saw how the three little red men tumbled over each other and yawned and stretched and made haste all at one time, so that Jack thought his life would surely be forfeit. But just as the clock struck its last chime, out rang a peal of merry bells, and there was the Castle standing on twelve golden pillars and a church beside it in the middle of the lake. And the Castle was all decorated for the wedding, and there were crowds and crowds of servants and retainers, all dressed in their Sunday best.

Never had Jack seen such a sight before; neither had the gay young daughter who, of course, was looking out of the next window in her nightcap. And she looked so pretty and so gay that Jack felt quite cross when he had to step back to let the three little red men fly to their golden snuff-box. But they were far crosser than he was, and mumbled and grumbled at the hustle, so that Jack was quite glad when they shut the box down and began to snore.

Well, of course, Jack and the gay young daughter were married, and were as happy as the day is long; and Jack had fine clothes to wear, fine food to eat, fine servants to wait on him, and as many fine friends as he liked.

So he was in luck; but he had yet to learn that a mother's malison is sure to bring misfortune some time or another.

Thus it happened that one day when he was going a-hunting with all the ladies and gentlemen, Jack forgot to change the golden snuff-box (which he always carried about with him for fear of accidents) from his waistcoat pocket to that of his scarlet hunting-coat; so he left it behind him. And what should happen but that the servant let it fall on the ground when he was folding up the clothes, and the snuff-box flew open and out popped the three little red men yawning and stretching.

Well! when they found out that they hadn't really been summoned, and that there was no fear of death, they were in a towering temper and said they had a great mind to fly away with the Castle, golden pillars and all.

On hearing this the servant pricked up his ears.

"Could you do that?" he asked.

"Could we?" they said, and they laughed loud. "Why, we can do anything."

Then the servant said ever so sharp, "Then move me this Castle and all it contains right away over the sea where the master can't disturb us."

Now the little red men need not really have obeyed the order, but they were so cross with Jack that hardly had the servant said the words before the task was done; so when the hunting-party came back, lo and behold! the Castle, and the church, and the golden pillars had all disappeared!

At first all the rest set upon Jack for being a knave and a cheat; and, in particular, his wife's father threatened to have at him for deceiving the gay young daughter; but at last he agreed to let Jack have twelve months and a day to find the Castle and bring it back.

So off Jack starts on a good horse with some money in his pocket.

And he travelled far and he travelled fast, and he travelled east and west, north and south, over hills, and dales, and valleys, and mountains, and woods, and sheepwalks, but never a sign of the missing castle did he see. Now at last he came to the palace of the King of all the Mice in the Wide World. And there was a little mousie in a fine hauberk and a steel cap doing sentry at the front gate, and he was not for letting Jack in until he had told his errand. And when Jack had told it, he passed him on to the next mouse sentry at the inner gate; so by degrees he reached the King's chamber, where he sat surrounded by mice courtiers.

Now the King of the Mice received Jack very graciously, and said that he himself knew nothing of the missing Castle, but, as he was King of all the Mice in the whole world, it was possible that some of his subjects might know more than he. So he ordered his chamberlain to command a Grand Assembly for the next morning, and in the meantime he entertained Jack right royally.

But the next morning, though there were brown mice, and black mice, and grey mice, and white mice, and piebald mice, from all parts of the world, they all answered with one breath:

"If it please your Majesty, we have not seen the missing Castle."

Then the King said, "You must go and ask my elder brother the King of all the Frogs. He may be able to tell you. Leave your horse here and take one of mine. It knows the way and will carry you safe."

So Jack set off on the King's horse, and as he passed the outer gate he saw the little mouse sentry coming away, for its guard was up. Now Jack was a kind-hearted lad, and he had saved some crumbs from his dinner in order to recompense the little sentry for his kindness. So he put his hand in his pocket and pulled out the crumbs.

"Here you are, mousekin," he said. "That's for your trouble!"

Then the mouse thanked him kindly and asked if he would take him along to the King of the Frogs.

"Not I," says Jack. "I should get into trouble with your King."

But the mousekin insisted. "I may be of some use to you," it said. So it ran up the horse's hind leg and up by its tail and hid in Jack's pocket. And the horse set off at a hard gallop, for it didn't half like the mouse running over it.

So at last Jack came to the palace of the King of all the Frogs, and there at the front gate was a frog doing sentry in a fine coat of mail and a brass helmet. And the frog sentry was for not letting Jack in; but the mouse called out that they came from the King of all the Mice and must be let in without delay. So they were taken to the King's chamber, where he sat surrounded by frog courtiers in fine clothes; but alas! he had heard nothing of the Castle on golden pillars, and though he summoned all the frogs of all the world to a Grand Assembly next morning, they all answered his question with, "Kro kro, Kro kro", which everyone knows stands for "No" in frog language.

So the King said to Jack, "There remains but one thing. You must go and ask my eldest brother, the King of all the Birds. His subjects are always on the wing, so mayhap they have seen something. Leave the horse you are riding here, and take one of mine. It knows the way, and will carry you safe."

So Jack set off, and being a kind-hearted lad he gave the frog sentry, whom he met coming away from his guard, some crumbs he had saved from his dinner. And the frog asked leave to go with him, and when Jack refused to take him he just gave one hop on to the stirrup, and a second hop on to the crupper, and the next hop he was in Jack's other pocket.

Then the horse galloped away like lightning, for it didn't like the slimy frog coming down "plop" on its back.

Well, after a time, Jack came to the palace of the King of all the Birds, and there at the front gate were a sparrow and a crow marching up and down with matchlocks on their shoulders. Now at this Jack laughed fit to split, and the mouse and the frog from his pockets called out, "We come from the King! Sirrahs! Let us pass."

So that the sentries were right mazed, and let them pass in without more ado.

But when they came to the King's chamber, where he sat surrounded by all manner of birds, tomtits, wrens, cormorants, turtle-doves, and the like, the King said he was sorry, but he had no news of the missing Castle. And though he summoned all the birds of all the world to a Grand Assembly next morning, not one of them had seen or heard tell of it.

So Jack was quite disconsolate till the King said, "But where is the eagle? I don't see my eagle."

Then the Chamberlain - he was a tomtit - stepped forward with a bow and said, "May it please your Majesty he is late."

"Late?" says the King in a fume. "Summon him at once."

So two larks flew up into the sky till they couldn't be seen and sang ever so loud, till at last the eagle appeared all in a perspiration from having flown so fast.

Then the King said, "Sirrah! Have you seen a missing Castle that stands upon twelve pillars of gold?"

And the eagle blinked its eyes and said, "May it please your Majesty that is where I've been."

Then everybody rejoiced exceedingly, and when the eagle had eaten a whole calf so as to be strong enough for the journey, he spread his wide wings, on which Jack stood, with the mouse in one pocket and the frog in the other, and started to obey the King's order to take the owner back to his missing Castle as quickly as possible.

And they flew over land and they flew over sea, until at last in the far distance they saw the Castle standing on its twelve golden pillars. But all the doors and windows were fast shut and barred, for, see you, the servant-master who had run away with it had gone out for the day a-hunting, and he always bolted doors and windows while he was absent lest someone else should run away with it.

Then Jack was puzzled to think how he should get hold of the golden snuff-box, until the little mouse said, "Let me fetch it. There is always a mouse-hole in every castle, so I am sure I shall be able to get in."

So it went off, and Jack waited on the eagle's wings in a fume; till at last mousekin appeared.

"Have you got it?" shouted Jack, and the little mousie cried, "Yes!"

So everyone rejoiced exceedingly, and they set off back to the palace of the King of all the Birds, where Jack had left his horse; for now that he had the golden snuff-box safe he knew he could get the Castle back whenever he chose to send the three little red men to fetch it. But on the way over the sea, while Jack, who was dead tired with standing so long, lay down between the eagle's wings and fell asleep, the mouse and the eagle fell to quarrelling as to which of them had helped Jack the most, and they quarrelled so much that at last they laid the case before the frog. Then the frog, who made a very wise judge, said he must see the whole affair from the very beginning; so the mouse brought out the golden snuff-box from Jack's pocket, and began to relate where it had been found and all about it. Now, at that very moment Jack awoke, kicked out his leg, and plump went the golden snuff-box down to the very bottom of the sea!

"I thought my turn would come," said the frog, and went plump in after it.

Well, they waited, and waited, and waited for three whole days and three whole nights; but froggie never came up again, and they had just given him up in despair when his nose showed above the water.

"Have you got it?" they shouted.

"No!" says he, with a great gasp.

"Then what do you want?" they cried in a rage.

"My breath," says froggie, and with that he sinks down again.

Well, they waited two days and two nights more, and at last up comes the little frog with the golden snuff-box in its mouth.

Then they all rejoiced exceedingly, and the eagle flew ever so fast to the palace of the King of the Birds.

But alas and alack-a-day! Jack's troubles were not ended; his mother's malison was still bringing him ill-luck, for the King of the Birds flew into a fearsome rage because Jack had not brought the Castle of the golden pillars back with him. And he said that unless he saw it by eight o'clock next morning Jack's head should come off as a cheat and a liar.

Then Jack being close to death opened the golden snuff-box, and out tumbled the three little red men in their three little red caps. They had recovered their tempers and were quite glad to be back with a master who knew that they would only, as a rule, work under fear of death; for, see you, the servant-master had been for ever disturbing their sleep with opening the box to no purpose.

So before the clock struck eight next morning, there was the Castle on its twelve golden pillars, and the King of the Birds was fine and pleased, and let Jack take his horse and ride to the palace of the King of the Frogs. But there exactly the same thing happened, and poor Jack had to open the snuff-box again and order the Castle to come to the palace of the King of the Frogs. At this the little red men were a wee bit cross; but they said they supposed it could not be helped; so, though they yawned, they brought the Castle all right, and Jack was allowed to take his horse and go to the palace of the King of all the Mice in the World. But here the same thing happened, and the little red men tumbled out of the golden snuff-box in a real rage, and said fellows might as well have no sleep at all! However, they did as they were bidden; they brought the Castle of the golden pillars from the palace of the King of the Frogs to the palace of the King of the Birds, and Jack was allowed to take his own horse and ride home.

But the year and a day which he had been allowed was almost gone, and even his gay young wife, after almost weeping her eyes out after her handsome young husband, had given up Jack for lost; so everyone was astounded to see him, and not over-pleased either to see him come without his Castle. Indeed his father-in-law swore with many oaths that if it were not in its proper place by eight o'clock next morning Jack's life should be forfeit.

Now this, of course, was exactly what Jack had wanted and intended from the beginning; because when death was nigh he could open the golden snuff-box and order about the little red men. But he had opened it so often of late and they had become so cross that he was in a stew what to do; whether to give them time to show their temper, or to hustle them out of it. At last he decided to do half and half. So just as the hands of the clock were at five minutes to eight he opened the box, and stopped his ears!

Well! you never heard such a yawning, and scolding, and threatening, and blustering. What did he mean by it? Why should he take four bites at one cherry? If he was always in fear of death why didn't he die and have done with it?

In the midst of all this the tower clock began to whirr. "Gentlemen!" says Jack, who was really quaking with fear. "Do as you are told."

"For the last time," they shrieked. "We won't stay and serve a master who thinks he is going to die every day."

And with that they flew out of the window and they never came back.

The golden snuff-box remained empty for evermore.

But when Jack looked out of window there was the Castle in the middle of the lake on its twelve golden pillars, and there was his young wife ever so pretty and gay in her nightcap looking out of the window too.

So they lived happily ever after.

The Hillman and the Housewife

The Hillman and the Housewife is one of Juliana Horatia Ewing's original literary fairy tales, first published in Aunt Judy's Magazine in May 1870 and later collected in Old-Fashioned Fairy Tales, issued by the Society for Promoting Christian Knowledge (S.P.C.K.) in volume form in the 1870s.

As with many of Ewing's pieces, the tale has also been loosely retold in newspapers and children's features, which mediates its style and moral emphasis for different audiences.

It is well known that the Good People cannot abide meanness. They like to be liberally dealt with when they beg or borrow of the human race; and, on the other hand, to those who come to them in need, they are invariably generous.

Now there once lived a certain Housewife who had a sharp eye to her own interests in temporal matters, and gave alms of what she had no use for, for the good of her soul. One day a Hillman knocked at her door.

"Can you lend us a saucepan, good Mother?" he said. "There's a wedding in the hill, and all the pots are in use."

"Is he to have one?" asked the servant lass who had opened the door.

"Aye, to be sure," answered the Housewife. "One must be neighbourly."

But when the maid was taking a saucepan from the shelf, she pinched her arm, and whispered sharply - "Not that, you slut! Get the old one out of the cupboard. It leaks, and the Hillmen are so neat, and such nimble workers, that they are sure to mend it before they send it home. So one obliges the Good People, and saves sixpence in tinkering. But you'll never learn to be notable whilst your head is on your shoulders."

Thus reproached, the maid fetched the saucepan, which had been laid by till the tinker's next visit, and gave it to the dwarf, who thanked her, and went away.

In due time the saucepan was returned, and, as the Housewife had foreseen, it was neatly mended and ready for use.

At supper-time the maid filled the pan with milk, and set it on the fire for the children's supper. But in a few minutes the milk was so burnt and smoked that no one could touch it, and even the pigs refused the wash into which it was thrown.

"Ah, good-for-nothing hussy!" cried the Housewife, as she refilled the pan herself, "you would ruin the richest with your carelessness. There's a whole quart of good milk wasted at once!"

"And that's tuppence," cried a voice which seemed to come from the chimney, in a whining tone, like some nattering discontented old body going over her grievances.

The Housewife had not left the saucepan for two minutes, when the milk boiled over, and it was all burnt and smoked as before.

"The pan must be dirty," muttered the good woman, in great

vexation, "and there are two full quarts of milk as good as thrown to the dogs."

"And that's fourpence," added the voice in the chimney.

After a thorough cleaning, the saucepan was once more filled and set on the fire, but with no better success. The milk was hopelessly spoilt, and the housewife shed tears of vexation at the waste, crying, "Never before did such a thing befall me since I kept house! Three quarts of new milk burnt for one meal!"

"And that's sixpence," cried the voice from the chimney. "You didn't save the tinkering after all Mother!"

With which the Hillman himself came tumbling down the chimney, and went off laughing through the door.

But thenceforward the saucepan was as good as any other.

The History of Whittington

The History of Whittington in Andrew Lang's Coloured Fairy Books is less a simple rags-to-riches yarn and more a carefully curated piece of late-Victorian moral instruction. Lang was not collecting raw folklore so much as shaping a canon of "improving" tales for children, and Whittington fits that purpose neatly.

Within the broader context of the Coloured Fairy Books, Whittington sits alongside tales from many cultures that have been filtered through Lang's distinctly British, middle-class lens. His retellings tend to smooth away rougher edges, heighten the elements of courage, obedience and providence, and present the stories as part of a shared moral heritage suitable for nursery shelves.

Dick Whittington was a very little boy when his father and mother died; so little, indeed, that he never knew them, nor the place where he was born. He strolled about the country as ragged as a colt, till he met with a wagoner who was going to London, and who gave him leave to walk all the way by the side of his wagon without paying anything for his passage. This pleased little Whittington very much, as he wanted to see London sadly, for he had heard that the streets were paved with gold, and he was willing to get a bushel of it; but how great was his disappointment, poor boy! when he saw the streets covered with dirt instead of gold, and found himself in a strange place, without a friend, without food, and without money.

Though the wagoner was so charitable as to let him walk up by the side of the wagon for nothing, he took care not to know him when he came to town, and the poor boy was, in a little time, so cold and hungry that he wished himself in a good kitchen and by a warm fire in the country.

In his distress he asked charity of several people, and one of them bid him "Go to work for an idle rogue." "That I will," said Whittington, "with all my heart; I will work for you if you let me."

The man, who thought this savoured of wit and impertinence (though the poor lad intended only to show his readiness to work), gave him a blow with a stick which broke his head so that the blood ran down. In this situation, and fainting for want of food, he laid himself down at the door of one Mr. Fitzwarren, a merchant, where the cook saw him, and being an ill-natured hussy, ordered him to go about his business or she would scald him. At this time Mr. Fitzwarren came from the Exchange, and began also to scold at the poor boy, bidding him to go to work.

Whittington answered that he should be glad to work if anybody would employ him, and that he should be able if he could get some victuals to eat, for he had had nothing for three days, and he was a poor country boy, and knew nobody, and nobody would employ him.

He then endeavoured to get up, but he was so very weak that he fell down again, which excited so much compassion in the merchant that he ordered the servants to take him in and give him some meat and drink, and let him help the cook to do any dirty work that she had to set him about. People are too apt to reproach those who beg with being idle, but give themselves no concern to put them in the way of getting business to do, or considering whether they are able to do it, which is not charity.

But we return to Whittington, who could have lived happy in this worthy family had he not been bumped about by the cross cook, who must be always roasting and basting, or when the spit was idle employed her hands upon poor Whittington! At last Miss Alice, his master's daughter, was informed of it, and then she took compassion on the poor boy, and made the servants treat him kindly.

Besides the crossness of the cook, Whittington had another difficulty to get over before he could be happy. He had, by order of his master, a flock-bed placed for him in a garret, where there was a number of rats and mice that often ran over the poor boy's nose and disturbed him in his sleep. After some time, however, a gentleman who came to his master's house gave Whittington a penny for brushing his shoes. This he put into his pocket, being determined to lay it out to the best advantage; and the next day, seeing a woman in the street with a cat under her arm, he ran up to know the price of it. The woman (as the cat was a good mouser) asked a deal of money for it, but on Whittington's telling her he had but a penny in the world, and that he wanted a cat sadly, she let him have it.

This cat Whittington concealed in the garret, for fear she should be beat about by his mortal enemy the cook, and here she soon killed or frightened away the rats and mice, so that the poor boy could now sleep as sound as a top.

Soon after this the merchant, who had a ship ready to sail, called for his servants, as his custom was, in order that each of them might venture something to try their luck; and whatever they sent was to pay neither freight nor custom, for he thought justly that God Almighty would bless him the more for his readiness to let the poor partake of his fortune.

All the servants appeared but poor Whittington, who, having neither money nor goods, could not think of sending anything to try his luck; but his good friend Miss Alice, thinking his poverty kept him away, ordered him to be called.

She then offered to lay down something for him, but the merchant told his daughter that would not do, it must be something of his own. Upon which poor Whittington said he had nothing but a cat which he bought for a penny that was given him. "Fetch your cat, boy," said the merchant, "and send her." Whittington brought poor puss and delivered her to the captain, with tears in his eyes, for he said he should now be disturbed by the rats and mice as much as ever. All the company laughed at the adventure but Miss Alice, who pitied the poor boy, and gave him something to buy another cat.

While puss was beating the billows at sea, poor Whittington was severely beaten at home by his tyrannical mistress the cook, who used him so cruelly, and made such game of him for sending his cat to sea, that at last the poor boy determined to run away from his place, and having packed up the few things he had, he set out very early in the morning on All-Hallows day. He travelled as far as Holloway, and there sat down on a stone to consider what course he should take; but while he was thus ruminating, Bow bells, of which there were only six, began to ring; and he thought their sounds addressed him in this manner:

"Turn again, Whittington,

Thrice Lord Mayor of London."

"Lord Mayor of London!" said he to himself, "what would not one endure to be Lord Mayor of London, and ride in such a fine coach? Well, I'll go back again, and bear all the pummelling and ill-usage of Cicely rather than miss the opportunity of being Lord Mayor!" So home he went, and happily got into the house and about his business before Mrs. Cicely made her appearance.

We must now follow Miss Puss to the coast of Africa. How perilous are voyages at sea, how uncertain the winds and the waves, and how many accidents attend a naval life!

The ship that had the cat on board was long beaten at sea, and at last, by contrary winds, driven on a part of the coast of Barbary which was inhabited by Moors unknown to the English. These people received our countrymen with civility, and therefore the captain, in order to trade with them, showed them the patterns of the goods he had on board, and sent some of them to the King of the country, who was so well pleased that he sent for the captain and the factor to come to his palace, which was about a mile from the sea. Here they were placed, according to the custom of the country, on rich carpets, flowered with gold and silver; and the King and Queen being seated at the upper end of the room, dinner was brought in, which consisted of many dishes; but no sooner were the dishes put down but an amazing number of rats and mice came from all quarters and devoured all the meat in an instant.

The factor, in surprise, turned round to the nobles and asked if these vermin were not offensive. "Oh! yes," they said, "very offensive; and the King would give half his treasure to be freed of them, for they not only destroy his dinner, as you see, but they assault him in his chamber, and even in bed, so that he is obliged to be watched while he is sleeping, for fear of them."

The factor jumped for joy; he remembered poor Whittington and his cat, and told the King he had a creature on board the ship that would despatch all these vermin immediately. The King's heart heaved so high at the joy which this news gave him that his turban dropped off his head. "Bring this creature to me," he said, "vermin are dreadful in a court, and if she will perform what you say I will load your ship with gold and jewels in exchange for her." The factor, who knew his business, took this opportunity to set forth the merits of Miss Puss. He told his Majesty that it would be inconvenient to part with her, as, when she was gone, the rats and mice might destroy the goods in the ship - but to oblige his Majesty he would fetch her. "Run, run," said the Queen, "I am impatient to see the dear creature."

Away flew the factor, while another dinner was providing, and returned with the cat just as the rats and mice were devouring that also. He immediately put down Miss Puss, who killed a great number of them.

The King rejoiced greatly to see his old enemies destroyed by so small a creature, and the Queen was highly pleased, and desired the cat might be brought near that she might look at her. Upon which the factor called "Pussy, pussy, pussy!" and she came to him. He then presented her to the Queen, who started back, and was afraid to touch a creature who had made such havoc among the rats and mice; however, when the factor stroked the cat and called "Pussy, pussy!" the Queen also touched her and cried "Putty, putty!" for she had not learned English.

He then put her down on the Queen's lap, where she, purring, played with her Majesty's hand, and then sang herself to sleep.

The King, having seen the exploits of Miss Puss, and being informed that her kittens would stock the whole country, bargained with the captain and factor for the whole ship's cargo, and then gave them ten times as much for the cat as all the rest amounted to. On which, taking leave of their Majesties and other great personages at court, they sailed with a fair wind for England, where we must now attend them.

The morn had scarcely dawned when Mr. Fitzwarren arose to count over the cash and settle the business for that day. He had just entered the counting-house, and seated himself at the desk, when somebody came, tap, tap, at the door. "Who's there?" said Mr. Fitzwarren. "A friend," answered the other. "What friend can come at this unseasonable time?" "A real friend is never unseasonable," answered the other. "I come to bring you good news of your ship Unicorn." The merchant bustled up in such a hurry that he forgot his gout; instantly opened the door, and who should be seen waiting but the captain and factor, with a cabinet of jewels, and a bill of lading, for which the merchant lifted up his eyes and thanked heaven for sending him such a prosperous voyage. Then they told him the adventures of the cat, and showed him the cabinet of jewels which they had brought for Mr. Whittington. Upon which he cried out with great earnestness, but not in the most poetical manner:

"Go, send him in, and tell him of his fame,

And call him Mr. Whittington by name."

It is not our business to animadvert upon these lines; we are not critics, but historians. It is sufficient for us that they are the words of Mr. Fitzwarren; and though it is beside our purpose, and perhaps not in our power to prove him a good poet, we shall soon convince the reader that he was a good man, which was a much better character; for when some who were present told him that this treasure was too much for such a poor boy as Whittington, he said, "God forbid that I should deprive him of a penny; it is his own, and he shall have it to a farthing." He then ordered Mr. Whittington in, who was at this time cleaning the kitchen and would have excused himself from going into the counting-house, saying the room was swept and his shoes were dirty and full of hob-nails. The merchant, however, made him come in, and ordered a chair to be set for him. Upon which, thinking they intended to make sport of him, as had been too often the case in the kitchen, he besought his master not to mock a poor simple fellow, who intended them no harm, but let him go about his business. The merchant, taking him by the hand, said, "Indeed, Mr. Whittington, I am in earnest with you, and sent for you to congratulate you on your great success. Your cat has procured you more money than I am worth in the world, and may you long enjoy it and be happy!"

At length, being shown the treasure, and convinced by them that all of it belonged to him, he fell upon his knees and thanked the Almighty for his providential care of such a poor and miserable creature. He then laid all the treasure at his master's feet, who refused to take any part of it, but told him he heartily rejoiced at his prosperity, and hoped the wealth he had acquired would be a comfort to him, and would make him happy. He then applied to his mistress, and to his good friend Miss Alice, who refused to take any part of the money, but told him she heartily rejoiced at his good success, and wished him all imaginable felicity. He then gratified the captain, factor, and the ship's crew for the care they had taken of his cargo. He likewise distributed presents to all the servants in the house, not forgetting even his old enemy the cook, though she little deserved it.

After this Mr. Fitzwarren advised Mr. Whittington to send for the necessary people and dress himself like a gentleman, and made him the offer of his house to live in till he could provide himself with a better.

Now it came to pass when Mr. Whittington's face was washed, his hair curled, and he dressed in a rich suit of clothes, that he turned out a genteel young fellow; and, as wealth contributes much to give a man confidence, he in a little time dropped that sheepish behaviour which was principally occasioned by a depression of spirits, and soon grew a sprightly and good companion, insomuch that Miss Alice, who had formerly pitied him, now fell in love with him.

When her father perceived they had this good liking for each other he proposed a match between them, to which both parties cheerfully consented, and the Lord Mayor, Court of Aldermen, Sheriffs, the Company of Stationers, the Royal Academy of Arts, and a number of eminent merchants attended the ceremony, and were elegantly treated at an entertainment made for that purpose.

History further relates that they lived very happy, had several children, and died at a good old age. Mr. Whittington served as Sheriff of London and was three times Lord Mayor. In the last year of his mayoralty he entertained King Henry V and his Queen, after his conquest of France, upon which occasion the King, in consideration of Whittington's merit, said, "Never had prince such a subject"; to which Whittington replied, "Never had subject such a king." His Majesty, out of respect to his good character, conferred the honour of knighthood on him soon after.

Sir Richard many years before his death constantly fed a great number of poor citizens, built a church and a college to it, with a yearly allowance for poor scholars, and near it erected a hospital. He also built Newgate for criminals, and gave liberally to St. Bartholomew's Hospital and other public charities.

The King o' the Cats

The King o' the Cats, in Joseph Jacobs's More English Fairy Tales, is a tiny story with a long shadow. It works as a classic "fireside shiver" rather than as a full quest or wonder tale; almost nothing happens in narrative terms, yet everything shifts in the last line. The piece trades on the idea that the ordinary domestic cat is not ordinary at all, but a participant in a hidden kingdom that runs alongside human life.

Within Jacobs's project, the tale shows his interest in preserving short, anecdotal pieces of folklore as carefully as the grander stories. He gives it with very little decoration, in a brisk conversational style, which keeps the focus on tone: half comic, half unsettling. There is no explicit moral, no explanation of cat-kings or their courts. Instead the story carries a quieter cultural work, reflecting long-standing English and wider European beliefs about cats as liminal creatures, associated with witchcraft, churchyards and the dead, yet also curled up by the fire.

One winter's evening the sexton's wife was sitting by the fireside with her big black cat, Old Tom, on the other side, both half asleep and waiting for the master to come home. They waited and they waited, but still he didn't come, till at last he came rushing in, calling out, "Who's Tommy Tildrum?" in such a wild way that both his wife and his cat stared at him to know what the matter was.

"Why, what's the matter?" said his wife, "and why do you want to know who Tommy Tildrum is?"

"Oh, I've had such an adventure. I was digging away at old Mr. Fordyce's grave when I suppose I must have dropped asleep, and only woke up by hearing a cat's Miaou."

"Miaou!" said Old Tom in answer.

"Yes, just like that! So I looked over the edge of the grave, and what do you think I saw?"

"Now, how can I tell?" said the sexton's wife.

"Why, nine black cats all like our friend Tom here, all with a white spot on their chests. And what do you think they were carrying? Why, a small coffin covered with a black velvet pall, and on the pall was a small coronet all of gold, and at every third step they took they cried all together, Miaou…"

"Miaou!" said Old Tom again.

"Yes, just like that!" said the Sexton, "and as they came nearer and nearer to me I could see them more distinctly, because their eyes shone out with a sort of green light. Well, they all came towards me, eight of them carrying the coffin, and the biggest cat of all walking in front for all the world like - but look at our Tom, how he's looking at me. You'd think he knew all I was saying."

"Go on, go on," said his wife, "never mind Old Tom."

"Well, as I was a-saying, they came towards me slowly and solemnly, and at every third step crying all together, Miaou…"

"Miaou!" said Old Tom again.

"Yes, just like that, till they came and stood right opposite Mr. Fordyce's grave, where I was, when they all stood still and looked straight at me. I did feel queer, that I did! But look at Old Tom; he's looking at me just like they did."

"Go on, go on," said his wife, "never mind Old Tom."

"Where was I? Oh, they all stood still looking at me, when the one that wasn't carrying the coffin came forward and, staring straight at me, said to me - yes, I tell 'ee, said to me, with a squeaky voice, 'Tell Tom Tildrum that Tim Toldrum's dead,' and that's why I asked you if you knew who Tom Tildrum was, for how can I tell Tom Tildrum Tim Toldrum's dead if I don't know who Tom Tildrum is?"

"Look at Old Tom, look at Old Tom!" screamed his wife.

And well he might look, for Tom was swelling and Tom was staring, and at last Tom shrieked out, "What - old Tim dead! then I'm the King o' the Cats!" and rushed up the chimney and was never more seen.

The Laidly Worm

The Laidly Worm, in Flora Annie Steel's English Fairy Tales, is a tale about the terrors and possibilities of transformation, especially where young women and maternal figures are concerned. The princess turned into a dragon is both victim and threat; she embodies the way female power is often made monstrous when it escapes the narrow roles laid down for it. At the same time, her draconic form lets the story explore anger, hunger and destructive potential in a way that would be impossible if she remained a conventional heroine.

Within Steel's collection, the story also shows her interest in giving English material the same kind of literary polish that the Grimms gave German tales. She keeps the ballad flavour of the old Northumbrian legend, yet smooths the language and narrative so that it sits comfortably on the nursery shelf of her own time.

In Bamborough castle there once lived a King who had two children, a son named Childe Wynde, and a daughter who was called May Margret. Their mother, a fair woman, was dead, and the King mourned her long and faithfully. But, after his son Childe Wynde went to seek his fortune, the King, hunting in the forest, came across a lady of such great beauty that he fell in love with her at once and determined to marry her.

Now Princess May Margret was not over-pleased to think that her mother's place should be taken by a strange woman, nor was she pleased to think that she would have to give up keeping house for her father the King. For she had always taken a pride in her work. But she said nothing, though she stood long on the castle walls looking out across the sea wishing for her dear brother's return; for, see you, they had mothered each other.

Still no news came of Childe Wynde; so on the day when the old King was to bring the new Queen home, May Margret counted over the keys of the castle chambers, knotted them on a string, and after casting them over her left shoulder for luck - more for her father's sake than for the new Queen's regard - she stood at the castle gate ready to hand over the keys to her stepmother.

Now as the bridal procession approached with all the lords of the north country, and some of the Scots lords in attendance, she looked so fair and so sweet, that the lords whispered to one another of her beauty. And when, after saying in a voice like a mavis:

"Oh welcome, welcome, father,

Unto your halls and towers!

And welcome too, my stepmother,

For all that's here is yours!"

she turned upon the step and tripped into the yard, the Scots lords said aloud:

"Forsooth! May Margret's grace

Surpasses all that we have met, she has so fair a face!"

Now the new Queen overheard this, and she stamped her foot and her face flushed with anger as she turned her about and called:

"You might have excepted me,

But I will bring May Margret to a Laidly Worm's degree;

I'll bring her low as a Laidly Worm

That warps about a stone,

And not till the Childe of Wynde come back

Will the witching be undone."

Well! hearing this May Margret laughed, not knowing that her new stepmother, for all her beauty, was a witch; and the laugh made the wicked woman still more angry. So that same night she left her royal bed, and, returning to the lonely cave where she had ever done her magic, she cast Princess May Margret under a spell with charms three times three, and passes nine times nine. And this was her spell:

"I weird you to a Laidly Worm,

And such sail you ever be

Until Childe Wynde the King's dear son

Comes home across the sea.

Until the world comes to an end

Unspelled ye'll never be,

Unless Childe Wynde of his own free will

Sail give you kisses three!"

So it came to pass that Princess May Margret went to her bed a beauteous maiden, full of grace, and rose next morning a Laidly Worm; for when her tire-women came to dress her they found coiled up in her bed an awesome dragon, which uncoiled itself and came towards them. And when they ran away terrified, the Laidly Worm crawled and crept, and crept and crawled down to the sea till it reached the rock of the Spindlestone which is called the Heugh. And there it curled itself round the stone, and lay basking in the sun.

Then for seven miles east and seven miles west and seven miles north and south the whole country-side knew the hunger of the Laidly Worm of Spindlestone Heugh, for it drove the awesome beast to leave its resting-place at night and devour everything it came across.

At last a wise warlock told the people that if they wished to be quit of these horrors, they must take every drop of the milk of seven white milch kine every morn and every eve to the trough of stone at the foot of the Heugh, for the Laidly Worm to drink. And this they did, and after that the Laidly Worm troubled the country-side no longer; but lay warped about the Heugh, looking out to sea with its terrible snout in the air.

But the word of its doings had gone east and had gone west; it had even gone over the sea and had come to Childe Wynde's ears; and the news of it angered him; for he thought perchance it had something to do with his beloved sister May Margret's disappearance. So he called his men-at-arms together and said, "We must sail to Bamborough and land by Spindlestone, so as to quell and kill this Laidly Worm."

Then they built a ship without delay, laying the keel with wood from the rowan tree. And they made masts of rowan wood also, and oars likewise; and, so furnished, set forth.

Now the wicked Queen knew by her arts they were coming, so she sent out her imps to still the winds so that the fluttering sails of silk hung idle on the masts. But Childe Wynde was not to be bested; so he called out the oarsmen. Thus it came to pass that one morn the wicked Queen, looking from the Keep, saw the gallant ship in Bamborough Bay, and she sent out all her witch-wives and her impetus to raise a storm and sink the ship; but they came back unable to hurt it, for, see you, it was built of rowan wood, over which witches have no power.

Then, as a last device, the Witch Queen laid spells upon the Laidly Worm saying:

"Oh! Laidly Worm! Go make their topmast heel,

Go! Worm the sand, and creep beneath the keel."

Now the Laidly Worm had no choice but to obey. So:

"The Worm leapt up, the Worm leapt down

And plaited round each plank,

And aye as the ship came close to shore

She heeled as if she sank."

Three times three did Childe Wynde attempt to land, and three times three the Laidly Worm kept the good ship from the shore. At last Childe Wynde gave the word to put the ship about, and the Witch Queen, who was watching from the Keep, thought he had given up: but he was not to be bested: for he only rounded the next point to Budley sands. And there, jumping into the shoal water, he got safely to land, and drawing his sword of proof, rushed up to fight the awesome Worm. But as he raised his sword to strike he heard a voice, soft as the western wind:

"Oh quit your sword, unbend your bow,

And give me kisses three,

For though I seem a Laidly Worm

No harm I'll do to thee!"

And the voice seemed to him like the voice of his dear sister May Margret. So he stayed his hand. Then once again the Laidly Worm said:

"Oh quit your sword, unbend your bow,

My laidly form forget.

Forgive the wrong and kiss me thrice

For love of May Margret."

Then Childe Wynde, remembering how he had loved his sister, put his arms round the Laidly Worm and kissed it once. And he kissed the loathly thing twice. And he kissed it yet a third time as he stood with the wet sand at his feet.

Then with a hiss and a roar the Laidly Worm sank to the sand, and in his arms was May Margret!

He wrapped her in his mantle, for she trembled in the cold sea air, and carried her to Bamborough Castle, where the wicked Queen, knowing her hour was come, stood, all deserted by her imps and witch-wives, on the stairs, twisting her hands.

Then Childe Wynde looking at her cried:

"Woe! Woe to you, you wicked Witch!

An ill fate shalt your be!

The doom you dreed on May Margret

The same doom shalt you dree.

Henceforth thou'lt be a Laidly Toad

That in the clay doth wend,

And unspelled you will never be

Till this world has an end."

And as he spoke the wicked Queen began to shrivel, and she

shrivelled and shrivelled to a horrid, wrinkled toad that hopped down the castle steps and disappeared in a crevice.

But to this day a loathsome toad is sometimes seen haunting Bamborough Keep; and that Laidly Toad is the wicked Witch Queen!

But Childe Wynde and Princess May Margret loved each other as much as ever, and lived happily ever after.

The Little Bull-Calf

The Little Bull-Calf, as Joseph Jacobs presents it in More English Fairy Tales, plays with the old folktale pleasure of grotesque exaggeration, but it is really concerned with luck, appetite and the instability of "deserving."

Set within Jacobs's wider project of defining what counts as "English" in the fairy-tale tradition, the story also has a strongly local, almost rustic texture. His retelling keeps the language brisk and colloquial, with a faintly comic edge that undercuts sentimentality; for all the wonders involved, there is a sharp awareness of how hard life is for ordinary people, and how quickly they will try to turn the marvellous into meat or money.

Centuries of years ago, when almost all this part of the country was wilderness, there was a little boy, who lived in a poor bit of property and his father gave him a little bull-calf, and with it he gave him everything he wanted for it.

But soon after his father died, and his mother got married again to a man that turned out to be a very vicious step-father, who couldn't abide the little boy. So at last the step-father said, "If you bring that bull-calf into this house, I'll kill it." What a villain he was, wasn't he?

Now this little boy used to go out and feed his bull-calf every day with barley bread, and when he did so this time, an old man came up to him - we can guess who that was, eh? - and said to him, "You and your bull-calf had better go away and seek your fortune."

So he went on and he went on and he went on, as far as I could tell you till tomorrow night, and he went up to a farmhouse and begged a crust of bread, and when he got back he broke it in two and gave half of it to the bull-calf. And he went to another house and begged a bit of cheese crud, and when he went back he wanted to give half of it to the bull-calf. "No," says the bull-calf, "I'm going across the field, into the wild-wood wilderness country, where there'll be tigers, leopards, wolves, monkeys, and a fiery dragon, and I'll kill them all except the fiery dragon, and he'll kill me."

The little boy did cry, and said, "Oh, no, my little bull-calf; I hope he won't kill you."

"Yes, he will," said the little bull-calf, "so you climb up that tree, so that no one can come nigh you but the monkeys, and if they come the cheese crud will save you. And when I'm killed, the dragon will go away for a bit, then you must come down the tree and skin me, and take out my bladder and blow it out, and it will kill everything you hit with it. So when the fiery dragon comes back, you hit it with my bladder and cut its tongue out."

(We know there were fiery dragons in those days, like George and his dragon in the legend; but there! it's not the same world nowadays. The world is turned topsy-turvy since then, like as if you'd turn it over with a spade!)

Of course, he did all the little bull-calf told him. He climbed up the tree, and the monkeys climbed up the tree after him. But he held the cheese crud in his hand, and said, "I'll squeeze your heart like the flint-stone." So the monkey cocked his eye as much as to say, "If you can squeeze a flint-stone to make the juice come out of it, you can squeeze me." But he didn't say anything, for a monkey's cunning, but down he went. And all the while the little bull-calf was fighting all the wild beasts on the ground, and the little lad was clapping his hands up the tree, and calling out, "Go in, my little bull-calf! Well fought, little bull-calf!" And he mastered everything except the fiery dragon, but the fiery dragon killed the little bull-calf.

But the lad waited and waited till he saw the dragon go away, then he came down and skinned the little bull-calf, and took out its bladder and went after the dragon. And as he went on, what should he see but a king's daughter, staked down by the hair of her head, for she had been put there for the dragon to destroy her.

So he went up and untied her hair, but she said, "My time has come for the dragon to destroy me; go away, you can do no good." But he said, "No! I can master it, and I won't go"; and for all her begging and praying he would stop.

And soon he heard it coming, roaring and raging from afar off, and at last it came near, spitting fire, and with a tongue like a great spear, and you could hear it roaring for miles, and it was making for the place where the king's daughter was staked down. But when it came up to them, the lad just hit it on the head with the bladder and the dragon fell down dead, but before it died, it bit off the little boy's forefinger.

Then the lad cut out the dragon's tongue and said to the king's daughter, "I've done all I can, I must leave you." And sorry she was he had to go, and before he went she tied a diamond ring in his hair, and said good-bye to him.

By-and-by, who should come along but the old king, lamenting and weeping, expecting to see nothing of his daughter but the prints of the place where she had been. But he was surprised to find her there alive and safe, and he said, "How came you to be saved?" So she told him how she had been saved, and he took her home to his castle again.

Well, he put it into all the papers to find out who saved his daughter, and who had the dragon's tongue and the princess's diamond ring, and was without his forefinger. Whoever could show these signs should marry his daughter and have his kingdom after his death. Well, any number of gentlemen came from all parts of England, with forefingers cut off, and with diamond rings and all kinds of tongues, wild beasts' tongues and foreign tongues. But they couldn't show any dragons' tongues, so they were turned away.

At last the little boy turned up, looking very ragged and desolated like, and the king's daughter cast her eye on him, till her father grew very angry and ordered them to turn the little beggar boy away. "Father," says she, "I know something of that boy."

Well, still the fine gentlemen came, bringing up their dragons' tongues that weren't dragons' tongues, and at last the little boy came up, dressed a little better. So the old king says, "I see you've got an eye on that boy. If it has to be him it must be him." But all the others were fit to kill him, and cried out, "Pooh, pooh, turn that boy out, it can't be him." But the king said, "Now, my boy, let's see what you have to show." Well, he showed the diamond ring with her name on it, and the fiery dragon's tongue. How the others were thunderstruck when he showed his proofs! But the king told him, "You shall have my daughter and my estate."

So he married the princess, and afterwards got the king's estate. Then his step-father came and wanted to own him, but the young king didn't know such a man.

239

The Lover's Vows

The Lover's Vows is really a mood piece built around Furness Abbey as much as it is a love story. Armistead uses the lovers' oath as a way to charge the ruined monastery with emotional meaning: the abbey is not simply a relic of medieval piety, it becomes a kind of open-air chapel for lay devotion, where private affection borrows the language and setting of sacred ritual.

At the same time, the story is quietly about absence and repetition. The second "picture" the narrator proposes is of Matilda returning alone to the same spot, long after her lover's death, her vigil before the ruined altar echoing the earlier vow. The abbey thus becomes a fixed point through which time and memory move: first a stage for hope, then a shrine for grief.

I can just remember the circumstance; it happened when I was a boy and went to Urswick school. Matilda was one of the loveliest females I ever knew. Her father had a small estate near Stainton; and she being his only child, he fondly imagined that her beauty and her fortune would procure her a respectable match. But alas! how often do your parents err in their calculations on the happiness which, they fondly imagine, will arise from the conduct of their children?

Matilda had accompanied James, a neighbouring farmer's son, to school, when infancy gave room to no other thoughts but those of play. James had ever distinguished the lovely Matilda for his playmate; for her he had collected the deepest tinged May gowlings that grew in the meadows below the village; he spared no pains to procure the finest specimens of hawthorn blossoms, to place in her bonnet; and would artlessly compliment her on her appearance under the flowery wreath. He was always ready to assist her in conning her lessons at school, and oftener wrought her questions than she did herself.

At an early age James was removed from school, and bound to an Ulverstone trader. Matilda and James met or heard of each other no more, till he had completed his eighteenth year, and the hard and active service in which he was employed had given his fine manly form an appearance at once imposing and captivating. Matilda, too, was improved in every eye, but particularly in James'. Never had James seen so lovely a maid as his former playmate. That friendship which had been so closely cemented in infancy, required very little assistance from the blind god to ripen it into love. Their youthful hearts were disengaged; they had neither of them ever felt an interest for any person, equal to what they had felt for each other; and they soon resolved to render their attachment as binding and as permanent, as it was pure and undivided.

The period had arrived when James must again trust himself to the faithless deep, when he must leave his Matilda to have her fidelity tried by other suitors; and she must trust her James to the temptation of foreign beauties. Both, therefore, were willing to bind themselves by some solemn pledge to live but for each other.

For this purpose, they repaired, on the evening before James' departure, to the ruins of Furness Abbey. It was a fine autumnal evening; the sun had set in the greatest beauty; and the moon was hastening up the eastern sky, through a track slightly interspersed with thin fleecy clouds, which added to its beauty, rather than impaired it. They knelt in the roofless quire, near where the altar formerly stood; and, fondly locked in each other's arms, they repeated, in the presence of heaven, their vows of deathless love. James was dressed in his best seaman's dress - a blue jacket, with a multitude of silver-plated buttons, and white trousers; while Matilda leaned on his neck in a dress of the purest white muslin, carelessly wrapped in a shawl of light blue.

I have been thus particular, said the narrator in describing their dresses, because this is the picture I would paint, I would sketch an east view of the abbey, looking in at the large east window, where two lovers were kneeling, folded in each other's arms - the moonbeams just striking upon the most prominent parts of their figures - the deep shadows occasioned by the broken columns and scattered fragments, should recede into the distance - the dark grey ruins, and the deep green and brown of the oaks, slightly but brilliantly gilded by the moon, should peep out of the lengthened gloom with sparkling effect. But on the figures I would bestow the greatest attention. What manly vigour I would give to his attitude! What sweetness, what loveliness to hers!

But what became of the betrothed lovers? Their fate was a melancholy one. James returned to his ship, and never returned from his voyage. He was killed by the first broadside of a French privateer, which the captain foolishly ventured to engage with. For Matilda, she regularly went to the Abbey to visit the spot where she last saw him; and there she would stand for hours, with her hands clasped on her breast, gazing on that heaven which alone had been witness to their mutual vows. Indeed, I think this would make a picture almost equal to the other. How fine a contrast would the light and fairy form of Matilda make with the broken fragments of the ruined Abbey; it would give a life and effect to the picture which you have no conception of. I am confident if you once drew a picture of this kind, you would never again sketch a scene without a story to it.

The Magician Turned Mischief-Maker

The Magician Turned Mischief-Maker in Juliana Horatia Ewing's Old-Fashioned Fairy Tales plays with the figure of the magician in a very Victorian way; it takes raw, awe-inspiring power and steadily domesticates it into a moral problem. The story is less interested in spectacular feats of magic than in what happens when cleverness, unrestrained by conscience, slides into cruelty, vanity and self-indulgence.

Within Ewing's wider project, the tale is part of a quiet campaign to align imaginative delight with ethical growth. Old-Fashioned Fairy Tales looks back to earlier moral stories, but Ewing softens the harsh didacticism by making the magician's humiliation and correction feel almost like a natural law of her invented world; actions curve back on their maker. In that sense, the story is less a warning against magic itself than a parable about how any special gift, if used merely to tease and unsettle others, will eventually turn back into a lesson for its owner.

There was once a wicked magician who prospered, and did much evil for many years. But there came a day when Vengeance, disguised as a blind beggar, overtook him, and outwitted him, and stole his magic wand. With this he had been accustomed to turn those who offended him into any shape he pleased; and now that he had lost it he could only transform himself.

As Vengeance was returning to his place, he passed through a village, the inhabitants of which had formerly lived in great terror of the magician, and told them of the downfall of his power. But they only said, "Blind beggars have long tongues. One must not believe all one hears," and shrugged their shoulders, and left him.

Then Vengeance waved the wand and said, "As you have doubted me, distress each other;" and so departed.

By and by he came to another village, and told the news. But here the villagers were full of delight, and made a feast, and put the blind beggar in the place of honour; who, when he departed, said, "As you have done by me, deal with each other always!" and went on to the next village.

In this place he was received with even warmer welcome; and when the feast was over, the people brought him to the bridge which led out of the village, and gave him a guide-dog to help him on his way.

Then the blind beggar waved the wand once more and said,

"Those who are so good to strangers must needs be good to each other. But that nothing may be wanting to the peace of this place, I grant to the beasts and birds in it that they may understand the language of men."

Then he broke the wand in pieces, and threw it into the stream. And when the people turned their heads back again from watching the bits as they floated away, the blind beggar was gone.

Meanwhile the magician was wild with rage at the loss of his wand, for all his pleasure was to do harm and hurt. But when he came to himself he said, "One can do a good deal of harm with his tongue. I will turn mischief-maker; and when the place is too hot to hold me, I can escape in what form I please."

Then he came to the first village, where Vengeance had gone before, and here he lived for a year and a day in various disguises; and he made more misery with his tongue than he had ever accomplished in any other year with his magic wand. For everyone distrusted his neighbour, and was ready to believe ill of him. So parents disowned their children, and husband and wives parted, and lovers broke faith; and servants and masters disagreed; and old friends became bitter enemies, till at last the place was intolerable even to the magician, and he changed himself into a cockchafer, and flew to the next village, where, Vengeance had gone before.

Here also he dwelt for a year and a day, and then he left it because he could do no harm. For those who loved each other trusted each other, and the magician made mischief in vain. In one of his disguises he was detected, and only escaped with his life from the enraged villagers by changing himself into a cockchafer and flying on to the next place, where Vengeance had gone before.

In this village he made less mischief than in the first, and more than in the second. And he exercised all his art, and changed his disguises constantly; but the dogs knew him under all.

One dog - the oldest dog in the place - was keeping watch over the miller's house, when he saw the magician approaching, in the disguise of an old woman.

"Do you see that old witch?" said he to the sparrows, who were picking up stray bits of grain in the yard. "With her evil tongue she is parting my master's daughter and the finest young fellow in the country-side. She puts lies and truth together, with more skill than you patch moss and feathers to build nests. And when she is asked where she heard this or that, she says, 'A little bird told me so.'

"We never told her," said the sparrows indignantly, "and if we had your strength, Master Keeper, she should not malign us long!"

"I believe you are right!" said Master Keeper. "Of what avail is it that we have learned the language of men, if we do not help them to the utmost of our powers? She shall torment my young mistress no more."

Saying which he flew upon the disguised magician as he entered the gate, and would have torn him limb from limb, but that the mischief-maker changed himself as before into a cockchafer, and flew hastily from the village.

And thus he might doubtless have escaped to do yet further harm, had not three cock-sparrows overtaken him just before he crossed the bridge.

From three sides they hemmed him in, crying, "Which of us told you?" "Which of us told you?" "Which of us told you?", and pecked him to pieces before he could transform himself again.

After which peace and prosperity befell all the neighbourhood.

The Magpie's Nest

The Magpie's Nest is a brief, comic little aetiological tale that sets out to explain why birds' nests look so various, and why so many of them seem oddly put together. Instead of grand adventure, it offers a wry observation about impatience and half-learning: the birds grow bored before the magpie has finished her lesson, each flying off with only a fragment of knowledge.

In Joseph Jacobs's English Fairy Tales, the story also serves a wider purpose. Jacobs wanted to show that England possessed its own stock of distinctive folk narratives, as worthy of preservation as the better known tales of the Continent, and The Magpie's Nest is one of those homely, local pieces that support his case.

Once upon a time when pigs spoke rhyme

And monkeys chewed tobacco,

And hens took snuff to make them tough,

And ducks went quack, quack, quack, O!

All the birds of the air came to the magpie and asked her to teach them how to build nests. For the magpie is the cleverest bird of all at building nests. So she put all the birds round her and began to show them how to do it. First of all she took some mud and made a sort of round cake with it.

"Oh, that's how it's done," said the thrush; and away it flew, and so that's how thrushes build their nests.

Then the magpie took some twigs and arranged them round in the mud.

"Now I know all about it," says the blackbird, and off he flew; and that's how the blackbirds make their nests to this very day.

Then the magpie put another layer of mud over the twigs.

"Oh that's quite obvious," said the wise owl, and away it flew; and owls have never made better nests since.

After this the magpie took some twigs and twined them round the outside.

"The very thing!" said the sparrow, and off he went; so sparrows make rather slovenly nests to this day.

Well, then Madge Magpie took some feathers and stuff and lined the nest very comfortably with it.

"That suits me," cried the starling, and off it flew; and very comfortable nests have starlings.

So it went on, every bird taking away some knowledge of how to build nests, but none of them waiting to the end. Meanwhile Madge Magpie went on working and working without, looking up till the only bird that remained was the turtle-dove, and that hadn't paid any attention all along, but only kept on saying its silly cry "Take two, Taffy, take two-o-o-o."

At last the magpie heard this just as she was putting a twig across.

So she said, "One's enough."

But the turtle-dove kept on saying, "Take two, Taffy, take two-oo."

Then the magpie got angry and said, "One's enough I tell you."

Still the turtle-dove cried, "Take two, Taffy, take two-o-o-o."

At last, and at last, the magpie looked up and saw nobody near her but the silly turtle-dove, and then she got rare angry and flew away and refused to tell the birds how to build nests again. And that is why different birds build their nests differently.

The Master and His Pupil

In Joseph Jacobs's English Fairy Tales, "The Master and His Pupil" reads like a compact moral fable about unauthorised knowledge and the dangers of dabbling in powers you do not understand. The tale turns the traditional relationship between master and apprentice into a warning about curiosity unmoored from discipline: the pupil is not condemned for wanting to know, but for trying to shortcut the long, supervised process that makes knowledge safe.

Set within Jacobs's wider project, the story also reflects a late nineteenth-century fascination with "old English" superstition, neatly packaged for modern readers. Jacobs presents this kind of narrative as part of a national heritage, yet his retellings shave away some of the rougher, more local detail in favour of clear structure and pointed lesson.

There was once a very learned man in the north-country who knew all the languages under the sun, and who was acquainted with all the mysteries of creation. He had one big book bound in black calf and clasped with iron, and with iron corners, and chained to a table which was made fast to the floor; and when he read out of this book, he unlocked it with an iron key, and none but he read from it, for it contained all the secrets of the spiritual world. It told how many angels there were in heaven, and how they marched in their ranks, and sang in their quires, and what were their several functions, and what was the name of each great angel of might. And it told of the demons, how many of them there were, and what were their several powers, and their labours, and their names, and how they might be summoned, and how tasks might be imposed on them, and how they might be chained to be as slaves to man.

Now the master had a pupil who was but a foolish lad, and he acted as servant to the great master, but never was he suffered to look into the black book, hardly to enter the private room.

One day the master was out, and then the lad, as curious as could be, hurried to the chamber where his master kept his wondrous apparatus for changing copper into gold, and lead into silver, and where was his mirror in which he could see all that was passing in the world, and where was the shell which when held to the ear whispered all the words that were being spoken by anyone the master desired to know about. The lad tried in vain with the crucibles to turn copper and lead into gold and silver - he looked long and vainly into the mirror; smoke and clouds passed over it, but he saw nothing plain, and the shell to his ear produced only indistinct murmurings, like the breaking of distant seas on an unknown shore. "I can do nothing," he said, "as I don't know the right words to utter, and they are locked up in yon book."

He looked round, and see! the book was unfastened; the master had forgotten to lock it before he went out. The boy rushed to it, and unclosed the volume. It was written with red and black ink, and much of it he could not understand; but he put his finger on a line and spelled it through.

At once the room was darkened, and the house trembled; a clap of thunder rolled through the passage and the old room, and there stood before him a horrible, horrible form, breathing fire, and with eyes like burning lamps. It was the demon Beelzebub, whom he had called up to serve him.

"Set me a task!" he said, with a voice like the roaring of an iron furnace.

The boy only trembled, and his hair stood up.

"Set me a task, or I shall strangle thee!"

But the lad could not speak. Then the evil spirit stepped towards him, and putting forth his hands touched his throat. The fingers burned his flesh. "Set me a task!"

"Water yon flower," cried the boy in despair, pointing to a geranium which stood in a pot on the floor. Instantly the spirit left the room, but in another instant he returned with a barrel on his back, and poured its contents over the flower; and again and again he went and came, and poured more and more water, till the floor of the room was ankle-deep.

"Enough, enough!" gasped the lad; but the demon heeded him not; the lad didn't know the words by which to send him away, and still he fetched water.

It rose to the boy's knees and still more water was poured. It mounted to his waist, and Beelzebub still kept on bringing barrels full. It rose to his armpits, and he scrambled to the table-top. And now the water in the room stood up to the window and washed against the glass, and swirled around his feet on the table. It still rose; it reached his breast. In vain he cried; the evil spirit would not be dismissed, and to this day he would have been pouring water, and would have drowned all Yorkshire. But the master remembered on his journey that he had not locked his book, and therefore returned, and at the moment when the water was bubbling about the pupil's chin, rushed into the room and spoke the words which cast Beelzebub back into his fiery home.

The Old Witch

The Old Witch, in Joseph Jacobs's More English Fairy Tales, is a small but pointed exploration of work, reciprocity and domestic power. At its heart is the figure of the child who labours for an older woman, caught in a household economy where care and exploitation sit very close together.

Within Jacobs's project, the tale shows his preference for compact narratives that carry clear ethical weight without heavy preaching. He trims the story to its essentials so that the pattern is easy for a child reader to grasp: kindness to the lowly and overlooked, including the tools of work themselves, will be remembered; selfishness and slovenliness will not.

Once upon a time there were two girls who lived with their mother and father. Their father had no work, and the girls wanted to go away and seek their fortunes. Now one girl wanted to go to service, and her mother said she might if she could find a place. So she started for the town. Well, she went all about the town, but no one wanted a girl like her. So she went on farther into the country, and she came to the place where there was an oven where there was lots of bread baking.

And the bread said, "Little girl, little girl, take us out, take us out.

We have been baking seven years, and no one has come to take us out." So the girl took out the bread, laid it on the ground, and went on her way.

Then she met a cow, and the cow said, "Little girl, little girl, milk me, milk me! Seven years have I been waiting, and no one has come to milk me." The girl milked the cow into the pails that stood by. As she was thirsty she drank some, and left the rest in the pails by the cow.

Then she went on a little bit farther, and came to an apple tree, so loaded with fruit that its branches were breaking down, and the tree said, "Little girl, little girl, help me shake my fruit. My branches are breaking, it is so heavy."

And the girl said, "Of course I will, you poor tree." So she shook the fruit all off, propped up the branches, and left the fruit on the ground under the tree.

She went on again till she came to a house. Now in this house there lived a witch, and this witch took girls into her house as servants. And when she heard that this girl had left her home to seek service, she said that she would try her, and give her good wages.

The witch told the girl what work she was to do. "You must keep the house clean and tidy, sweep the floor and the fireplace; but there is one thing you must never do. You must never look up the chimney, or something bad will befall you."

So the girl promised to do as she was told, but one morning as she was cleaning, and the witch was out, she forgot what the witch said, and looked up the chimney. When she did this a great bag of money fell down in her lap. This happened again and again. So the girl started to go off home.

When she had gone some way she heard the witch coming after her. So she ran to the apple tree and cried:

"Apple-tree, apple-tree hide me,

So the old witch can't find me;

If she does she'll pick my bones,

And bury me under the marble stones."

So the apple-tree hid her. When the witch came up she said:

"Tree of mine, tree of mine,

Have you seen a girl

With a willy-willy wag, and a long-tailed bag,

Who stole my money, all I had?"

And the apple-tree said, "No, mother; not for seven year."

When the witch had gone down another way, the girl went on again, and just as she got to the cow heard the witch coming after her again, so she ran to the cow and cried:

"Cow, cow, hide me,

So the old witch can't find me;

If she does she'll pick my bones,

And bury me under the marble stones."

So the cow hid her.

When the old witch came up, she looked about and said to the cow:

"Cow of mine, cow of mine,

Have you seen a girl

With a willy-willy wag, and a long-tailed bag,

Who's stole my money, all I had?"

And the cow said, "No, mother, not for seven year."

When the witch had gone off another way, the little girl went on again, and when she was near the oven she heard the witch coming after her again, so she ran to the oven and cried:

"Oven, oven, hide me,

So the old witch can't find me;

If she does she'll break my bones,

And bury me under the marble stones."

And the oven said, "I've no room, ask the baker," and the baker hid her behind the oven.

When the witch came up she looked here and there and everywhere, and then said to the baker:

"Man of mine, man of mine,

Have you seen a girl,

With a willy-willy wag, and a long-tailed bag,

Who's stole my money, all I had?"

So the baker said, "Look in the oven." The old witch went to look, and the oven said, "Get in and look in the furthest corner." The witch did so, and when she was inside the oven shut her door, and the witch was kept there for a very long time.

The girl then went off again, and reached her home with her money bags, married a rich man, and lived happy ever afterwards.

The other sister then thought she would go and do the same. And she went the same way. But when she reached the oven, and the bread said, "Little girl, little girl, take us out. Seven years have we been baking, and no one has come to take us out," the girl said, "No, I don't want to burn my fingers."

So she went on till she met the cow, and the cow said, "Little girl, little girl, milk me, milk me, do. Seven years have I been waiting, and no one has come to milk me." But the girl said, "No, I can't milk you, I'm in a hurry," and went on faster.

 Then she came to the apple-tree, and the apple-tree asked her to help shake the fruit. "No, I can't; another day perhaps I may," and went on till she came to the witch's house. Well, it happened to her just the same as to the other girl - she forgot what she was told, and one day when the witch was out, looked up the chimney, and down fell a bag of money. Well, she thought she would be off at once.

When she reached the apple-tree, she heard the witch coming after her, and she cried:

"Apple-tree, apple-tree, hide me,

So the old witch can't find me;

If she does she'll break my bones,

And bury me under the marble stones."

But the tree didn't answer, and she ran on further. Presently the witch came up and said:

"Tree of mine, tree of mine,

Have you seen a girl,

With a willy-willy wag, and a long-tailed bag,

Who's stole my money, all I had?"

The tree said, "Yes, mother; she's gone down that way."

So the old witch went after her and caught her, she took all the money away from her, beat her, and sent her off home just as she was.

The Old Woman and her Pig

The Old Woman and her Pig, in Flora Annie Steel's English Fairy Tales, is a small but very clear example of the cumulative or "chain" tale, built almost entirely out of repetition, rhythm and frustration. Nothing much "happens" in grand narrative terms; instead, the story walks the listener through a sequence of refusals and conditional bargains, each hinging on the last.

In Steel's hands the tale also reveals something about social relations and dependence, though very lightly. The old woman's problem is trivial, yet to solve it she must appeal in turn to animals, objects and people, each of whom has its own narrow interest and its own conditions. The world is shown as a chain of mutual obligations; nothing moves without something else being moved first.

An old woman was sweeping her house, and she found a little crooked sixpence. "What," she said, "shall I do with this little sixpence? I will go to market, and buy a little pig."

So she bought a little pig; but as she was coming home, she came to a stile, and the piggy would not go over the stile.

She went a little further, and she met a dog. So she said to him,

"Dog! dog! bite pig; piggy won't go over the stile; and I shan't get home till midnight." But the dog wouldn't.

She went a little further, and she met a stick. So she said, "Stick! stick! beat dog; dog won't bite pig; piggy won't get over the stile; and I shan't get home till midnight." But the stick wouldn't.

She went a little further, and she met a fire. So she said, "Fire! fire! burn stick; stick won't beat dog; dog won't bite pig; pig won't get over the stile; and I shan't get home till midnight." But the fire wouldn't.

She went a little further, and she met some water. So she said, "Water! water! quench fire; fire won't burn stick; stick won't beat dog; dog won't bite pig; pig won't get over the stile; and I shan't get home till midnight." But the water wouldn't.

She went a little further, and she met an ox. So she said, "Ox! ox! drink water; water won't quench fire; fire won't burn stick; stick won't beat dog; dog won't bite pig; pig won't get over the stile; and I shan't get home till midnight." But the ox wouldn't.

She went a little further, and she met a butcher. So she said, "Butcher! butcher! kill ox; ox won't drink water; water won't quench fire; fire won't burn stick; stick won't beat dog; dog won't bite pig; pig won't get over the stile; and I shan't get home till midnight." But the butcher wouldn't.

She went a little further, and she met a rope. So she said, "Rope! rope! hang butcher; butcher won't kill ox; ox won't drink water; water won't quench fire; fire won't burn stick; stick won't beat dog; dog won't bite pig; pig won't get over the stile; and I shan't get home till midnight." But the rope wouldn't.

She went a little further, and she met a rat. So she said, "Rat! rat!

gnaw rope; rope won't hang butcher; butcher won't kill ox; ox won't drink water; water won't quench fire; fire won't burn stick; stick won't beat dog; dog won't bite pig; pig won't get over the stile; and I shan't get home till midnight." But the rat wouldn't.

She went a little further, and she met a cat. So she said, "Cat! cat! kill rat; rat won't gnaw rope; rope won't hang butcher; butcher won't kill ox; ox won't drink water; water won't quench fire; fire won't burn stick; stick won't beat dog; dog won't bite pig; pig won't get over the stile; and I shan't get home till midnight." But the cat said to her, "If you will go to yonder cow, and fetch me a saucer of milk, I will kill the rat." So away went the old woman to the cow.

But the cow said to her, "If you will go to yonder haystack, and fetch me a handful of hay, I'll give you the milk." So away went the old woman to the haystack; and she brought the hay to the cow.

As soon as the cow had eaten the hay, she gave the old woman the milk; and away she went with it in a saucer to the cat.

As soon as the cat had lapped up the milk, the cat began to kill the rat; the rat began to gnaw the rope; the rope began to hang the butcher; the butcher began to kill the ox; the ox began to drink the water; the water began to quench the fire; the fire began to burn the stick; the stick began to beat the dog; the dog began to bite the pig; the little pig squealed and jumped over the stile; and so the old woman got home before midnight.

The Pedlar of Swaffham

In The Pedlar of Swaffham as told by Joseph Jacobs, the story becomes a meditation on the irony that what we seek far away is often waiting at home. The tale reassures its listeners that obscurity and provincial life are no barrier to good fortune or to grace; indeed, they may be the very ground in which it lies buried.

Within More English Fairy Tales, Jacobs treats The Pedlar of Swaffham as part of a consciously English myth-making, rooted in specific localities and tied to physical landmarks, in this case the church at Swaffham. The tale becomes a kind of charter-legend explaining how a particular building or feature came to be.

In the old days when London Bridge was lined with shops from one end to the other, and salmon swam under the arches, there lived at Swaffham, in Norfolk, a poor pedlar. He'd much ado to make his living, trudging about with his pack at his back and his dog at his heels, and at the close of the day's labour was but too glad to sit down and sleep. Now it fell out that one night he dreamed a dream, and therein he saw the great bridge of London town, and it sounded in his ears that if he went there he should hear joyful news. He made little count of the dream, but on the following night it come back to him, and again on the third night.

Then he said within himself, "I must needs try the issue of it," and so he trudged up to London town. Long was the way and right glad was he when he stood on the great bridge and saw the tall houses on right hand and left, and had glimpses of the water running and the ships sailing by. All day long he paced to and fro, but he heard nothing that might yield him comfort. And again on the morrow he stood and he gazed - he paced afresh the length of London Bridge, but naught did he see and naught did he hear.

On the third day he still stood and gazed. A shopkeeper asked him, "Friend, I wonder at your fruitless standing. Have you no wares to sell?"

"No, indeed," said the pedlar.

"And you do not beg for alms."

"Not so long as I can keep myself."

"Then what, do you want here, and what may your business be?"

"Well, I dreamed that if I came here, I should hear good news."

Right heartily did the shopkeeper laugh.

"Nay, you must be a fool to take a journey on such a silly errand. I'll tell you, poor silly country fellow, that I myself dream too o' nights, and that last night I dreamt myself to be in Swaffham, a place clean unknown to me, but in Norfolk if I mistake not, and methought I was in an orchard behind a pedlar's house, and in that orchard was a great oak-tree. Then I thought that if I dug I should find beneath that tree a great treasure. But think you I'm such a fool as to take on me a long and wearisome journey and all for a silly dream. No, my good fellow, learn wit from a wiser man than yourself. Get you home, and mind your business."

When the pedlar heard this he spoke no word, but was exceeding glad in himself, and returning home speedily, dug underneath the great oak-tree, and found a prodigious great treasure. He grew exceeding rich, but he did not forget his duty in the pride of his riches. For he built up again the church at Swaffham, and when he died they put a statue of him therein all in stone with his pack at his back and his dog at his heels. And there it stands to this day to witness if I lie.

The Rose Tree

The Rose Tree in Flora Annie Steel's English Fairy Tales is one of the starkest pieces in the collection, a domestic horror tale that turns the commonplace figure of the stepmother into an instrument of absolute violence. It belongs to the European family of stories where a mother kills a child and serves the body up in a meal, a pattern also seen in the Grimms' Juniper Tree.

In turning raw brutality into a pattern of crime, haunting and punishment, the story gives readers a way to look at buried anger and grief without naming them directly; it dramatizes fears about stepfamilies, replacement children and the fragility of parental protection.

Once upon a time, long, long years ago, in the days when one had to be careful about witches, there lived a good man, whose young wife died, leaving him a baby girl.

Now this good man felt he could not look after the baby properly, so he married a young woman whose husband had died leaving her with a baby boy.

Thus the two children grew up together, and loved each other dearly, dearly.

But the boy's mother was really a wicked witch-woman, and so jealous that she wanted all the boy's love for herself, and when the girl-baby grew white as milk, with cheeks like roses and lips like cherries, and when her hair, shining like golden silk, hung down to her feet so that her father and all the neighbours began to praise her looks, the stepmother fairly hated her, and did all in her power to spoil her looks. She would set the child hard tasks, and send her out in all weathers to do difficult messages, and if they were not well performed would beat her and scold her cruelly.

Now one cold winter evening when the snow was drifting fast, and the wild rose tree in the garden under which the children used to play in summer was all brown and barren save for snowflake flowers, the stepmother said to the little girl:

"Child! go and buy me a bunch of candles at the grocers. Here is some money; go quickly, and don't loiter by the way."

So the little girl took the money and set off quickly through the snow, for already it was growing dark. Now there was such a wind blowing that it nearly blew her off her feet, and as she ran her beautiful hair got all tangled and almost tripped her up. However, she got the candles, paid for them, and started home again. But this time the wind was behind her and blew all her beautiful golden hair in front of her like a cloud, so that she could not see her steps, and, coming to a stile, had to stop and put down the bundle of candles in order to see how to get over it. And when she was climbing it a big black dog came by and ran off with the bunch of candles! Now she was so afraid of her stepmother that she durst not go home, but turned back and bought another bunch of candles at the grocers, and when she arrived at the stile once more, the same thing happened. A big black dog came down the road and ran away with the bunch of candles. So yet once again she journeyed back to the grocers through wind and snow, and, with her last penny, bought yet another bunch of candles. To no purpose, for alas, and alack-a-day! when she laid them down in order to part her beautiful golden hair and to see how to get over the stile, a big black dog ran away with them.

So nothing was left save to go back to her stepmother in fear and trembling. But, for a wonder, her stepmother did not seem very angry. She only scolded her for being so late, for, see you, her father and her little playmate had gone to their beds and were in the Land of Nod.

Then she said to the child, "I must take the tangles out of your hair before you go to sleep. Come, put your head on my lap."

So the little girl put her head on her stepmother's lap, and, lo and behold! her beautiful yellow-silk hair rolled right over the woman's knees and lay upon the ground.

Then the beauty of it made the stepmother more jealous than before, so she said, "I cannot part your hair properly on my knee, fetch me a billet of wood."

So the little girl fetched one. Then said the stepmother, "Your hair is so thick I cannot part it with a comb; fetch me an axe!"

So the child fetched an axe.

"Now," said that wicked, wicked woman, "lay your head down on the billet while I part your hair."

And the child did as she was bid without fear; and lo! the beautiful little golden head was off in a second, by one blow of the axe.

Now the wicked stepmother had thought it all out before, so she took the poor little dead girl out to the garden, dug a hollow in the snow under the rose tree, and said to herself, "When spring comes and the snow melts if people find her bones, they will say she lost her way and fell asleep in the snow."

But first, because she was a wicked witch-woman, knowing spells and charms, she took out the heart of the little girl and made it into two savoury pasties, one for her husband's breakfast and one for the little boys, for thus would the love they bore to the little girl become hers. Nevertheless, she was mistaken, for when morning came and the little child could not be found, the father sent away his breakfast barely tasted, and the little boy wept so that he could eat nothing.

So they grieved and grieved. And when the snow melted and they found the bones of the poor child, they said, "She must have lost her way that dark night going to the grocers to buy candles." So they buried the bones under the children's rose tree, and every day the little boy sat there and wept and wept for his lost playmate.

Now when summer came the wild rose tree flowered. It was covered with white roses, and amongst the flowers there sat a beautiful white bird. And it sang and sang and sang like an angel out of heaven; but what it sang the little boy could never make out, for he could hardly see for weeping, hardly hear for sobbing.

So at last the beautiful white bird unfolded its broad white wings and flew to a cobbler's shop, where a myrtle bush hung over the man and his last, on which he was making a dainty little pair of rose-red shoes. Then it perched on a bough and sang ever so sweetly:

"Stepmother slew me,

Father nigh ate me,

He whom I dearly love

Sits below, I sing above,

Stick! Stock! Stone dead!"

"Sing that beautiful song again," said the cobbler. "It is better than a nightingale's."

"That will I gladly," sang the bird, "if you will give me the little rose-red shoes you are making."

And the cobbler gave them willingly, so the white bird sang its song once more. Then with the rose-red shoes in one foot it flew to an ash tree that grew close beside a goldsmith's bench, and sang:

"Stepmother slew me,

Father nigh ate me,

He whom I dearly love

Sits below, I sing above,

Stick! Stock! Stone dead!"

"Oh, what a beautiful song!" cried the goldsmith.

"Sing again, dear bird, it is sweeter than a nightingale's."

"That will I gladly," sang the bird, "if you will give me the gold chain you're making."

And the goldsmith gave the bauble willingly, and the bird sang its song once more. Then with the rose-red shoes in one foot and the golden chain in the other, the bird flew to an oak tree which overhung the mill stream, beside which three millers were busy picking out a millstone, and, perching on a bough, sang its song ever so sweetly:

"My stepmother slew me,

My father nigh ate me,

He whom I dearly love

Sits below, I sing above,

Stick!"

Just then one of the millers put down his tool and listened.

"Stock!" sang the bird.

And the second miller put aside his tool and listened.

"Stone," sang the bird.

Then the third miller put aside his tool and listened.

"Dead!" sang the bird so sweetly that with one accord the millers looked up and cried with one voice, "Oh, what a beautiful song! Sing it again, dear bird, it is sweeter than a nightingale's."

"That will I gladly," answered the bird, "if you will hang the millstone you are picking round my neck."

So the millers hung it as they were asked; and when the song was finished, the bird spread its wide white wings and, with the millstone round its neck and the little rose-red shoes in one foot, the golden chain in the other, it flew back to the rose tree. But the little playmate was not there; he was inside the house eating his dinner.

Then the bird flew to the house, and rattled the millstone about the eaves until the stepmother cried, "Hearken! How it thunders!"

So the little boy ran out to see, and down dropped the dainty rose-red shoes at his feet.

"See what fine things the thunder has brought!" he cried with glee as he ran back.

Then the white bird rattled the millstone about the eaves once more, and once again the stepmother said, "Hearken! How it thunders!"

So this time the father went out to see, and down dropped the golden chain about his neck.

"It is true," he said when he came back. "The thunder does bring fine things!"

Then once more the white bird rattled the millstone about the eaves, and this time the stepmother said hurriedly, "Hark! there it is again! Perhaps it has got something for me!"

Then she ran out; but the moment she stepped outside the door, down fell the millstone right on her head and killed her.

So that was an end of her. And after that the little boy was ever so much happier, and all the summertime he sat with his little rose-coloured shoes under the wild rose tree and listened to the white bird's song. But when winter came and the wild rose tree was all barren and bare save for snowflake flowers, the white bird came no longer and the little boy grew tired of waiting for it. So one day he gave up altogether, and they buried him under the rose tree beside his little playmate.

Now when the spring came and the rose tree blossomed, the flowers were no longer white. They were edged with rose colour like the little boy's shoes, and in the centre of each blossom there was a beautiful tuft of golden silk like the little girl's hair.

And if you look in a wild rose you will find these things there still.

The Stars in the Sky

In The Stars in the Sky, Joseph Jacobs offers what is essentially a devotional wonder-tale framed as an English fireside story. At heart it is about radical generosity in conditions of absolute poverty. The stars themselves become active agents of grace, suggesting a world in which the cosmos notices small acts of kindness and answers them with beauty and protection.

Within More English Fairy Tales, the story reveals Jacobs's interest in aligning "English" tradition with a moral and, at points, gently Christian sensibility, without turning the tale into a sermon. He preserves the simplicity and spareness of a folk narrative, yet selects and shapes the material so that sacrifice, charity and trust are presented as central communal virtues.

Once on a time and twice on a time, and all times together as ever I heard tell of, there was a tiny lassie who would weep all day to have the stars in the sky to play with; she wouldn't have this, and she wouldn't have that, but it was always the stars she would have. So one fine day off she went to find them. And she walked and she walked and she walked, till by-and-by she came to a mill-dam.

"Good evening to you," says she, "I'm seeking the stars in the sky to play with. Have you seen any?"

"Oh, yes, my bonnie lassie," said the mill-dam. "They shine in my own face o' nights till I can't sleep for them. Jump in and perhaps you'll find one."

So she jumped in, and swam about and swam about and swam about, but ne'er a one could she see. So she went on till she came to a brooklet.

"Good evening to you, Brooklet, Brooklet," says she, "I'm seeking the stars in the sky to play with. Have you seen any?"

"Yes, indeed, my bonny lassie," said the Brooklet. "They glint on my banks at night. Paddle about, and maybe you'll find one."

So she paddled and she paddled and she paddled, but ne'er a one did she find. So on she went till she came to the Good Folk.

"Good evening to you, Good Folk," says she, "I'm looking for the stars in the sky to play with. Have you seen ever a one?"

"Why, yes, my bonny lassie," said the Good Folk. "They shine on the grass here o' night. Dance with us, and maybe you'll find one."

And she danced and she danced and she danced, but ne'er a one did she see. So down she sate; I suppose she wept.

"Oh dearie me, oh dearie me," says she, "I've swam and I've paddled and I've danced, and if ye'll not help me I shall never find the stars in the sky to play with."

But the Good Folk whispered together, and one of them came up to her and took her by the hand and said, "If you won't go home to your mother, go forward, go forward; mind you take the right road. Ask Four Feet to carry you to No Feet at all, and tell No Feet at all to carry you to the stairs without steps, and if you can climb that…"

"Oh, shall I be among the stars in the sky then?" cried the lassie.

"If you'll not be, then you'll be elsewhere," said the Good Folk, and set to dancing again.

So, on she went again with a light heart, and by-and-by she came to a saddled horse, tied to a tree.

"Good evening to you, Beast," she said, "I'm seeking the stars in the sky to play with. Will you give me a lift, for all my bones are an-aching."

"Nay," said the horse, "I know nought of the stars in the sky, and I'm here to do the bidding of the Good Folk, and not my own will."

"Well," she said, "it's from the Good Folk I come, and they bade me tell Four Feet to carry me to No Feet at all."

"That's another story," he said, "jump up and ride with me."

So, they rode and they rode and they rode, till they got out of the forest and found themselves at the edge of the sea. And on the water in front of them was a wide glistening path running straight out towards a beautiful thing that rose out of the water and went up into the sky, and was all the colours in the world, blue and red and green, and wonderful to look at.

"Now get you down," said the horse, "I've brought you to the end of the land, and that's as much as Four Feet can do. I must away home to my own folk."

"But," said the lassie, "where's No Feet at all, and where's the stair without steps?"

"I know not," said the horse, "it's none of my business neither. So good evening to you, my bonny lassie;" and off he went.

So the lassie stood still and looked at the water, till a strange kind of fish came swimming up to her feet.

"Good evening to you, big Fish," says she, "I'm looking for the stars in the sky, and for the stairs that climb up to them. Will you show me the way?"

"Nay," said the Fish, "I can't unless you bring me word from the Good Folk."

"Yes, indeed," she said. "They said Four Feet would bring me to No Feet at all, and No Feet at all would carry me to the stairs without steps."

"Get on my back and hold fast."

"Ah, well," said the Fish, "that's all right then. Get on my back and hold fast."

And off he went - Kerplash! - into the water, along the silver path, towards the bright arch. And the nearer they came the brighter the sheen of it, till she had to shade her eyes from the light of it.

And as they came to the foot of it, she saw it was a broad bright road, sloping up and away into the sky, and at the far, far end of it she could see wee shining things dancing about.

"Now," said the Fish, "here you are, and yon is the stair; climb up, if you can, but hold on fast. I'll warrant you find the stair easier at home than by such a way, 't was ne'er meant for lassies' feet to travel;" and off he splashed through the water.

So, she climbed and she climbed and she climbed, but ne'er a step higher did she get: the light was before her and around her, and the water behind her, and the more she struggled the more she was forced down into the dark and the cold, and the more she climbed the deeper she fell.

But she climbed and she climbed, till she got dizzy in the light and shivered with the cold, and dazed with the fear; but still she climbed, till at last, quite dazed and silly-like, she let clean go, and sank down, down, down.

And bang she came on to the hard boards, and found herself sitting, weeping and wailing, by the bedside at home all alone.

The Strange Visitor

The Strange Visitor, as Joseph Jacobs presents it in English Fairy Tales, sits very close to the border between folktale and fireside ghost story. Its power lies less in plot than in rhythm and accumulation: the slow assembling of the uncanny figure, bit by bit, as it draws nearer to the solitary woman at her work.

Within Jacobs's collection, the story also shows his interest in preserving the eerie and the grotesque as part of English tradition, not just the merry or sentimental. He gives the narrative with a light editorial touch, keeping the language plain enough for children while allowing the horror to remain just sharp enough to tingle.

A woman was sitting at her reel one night; And still she sat, and still she reeled, and still she wished for company.

In came a pair of broad, broad soles, and sat down at the fireside;

And still she sat, and still she reeled, and still she wished for company.

In came a pair of small, small legs, and sat down on the broad, broad soles;

And still she sat, and still she reeled, and still she wished for company.

In came a pair of thick, thick knees, and sat down on the small, small legs;

And still she sat, and still she reeled, and still she wished for company.

In came a pair of thin, thin thighs, and sat down on the thick, thick knees;

And still she sat, and still she reeled, and still she wished for company.

In came a pair of huge, huge hips, and sat down on the thin, thin thighs;

And still she sat, and still she reeled, and still she wished for company.

In came a wee, wee waist, and sat down on the huge, huge hips;

And still she sat, and still she reeled, and still she wished for company.

In came a pair of broad, broad shoulders, and sat down on the wee, wee waist;

And still she sat, and still she reeled, and still she wished for company.

In came a pair of small, small arms, and sat down on the broad, broad shoulders;

And still she sat, and still she reeled, and still she wished for company.

In came a pair of huge, huge hands, and sat down on the small,

small arms;

And still she sat, and still she reeled, and still she wished for company.

In came a small, small neck, and sat down on the broad, broad shoulders;

And still she sat, and still she reeled, and still she wished for company.

In came a huge, huge head, and sat down on the small, small neck.

"How did you get such broad, broad feet?" said the woman.

"Much tramping, much tramping" (gruffly).

"How did you get such small, small legs?"

"Aih-h-h!-late - and wee-e-e - moul" (whiningly).

"How did you get such thick, thick knees?"

"Much praying, much praying" (piously).

"How did you get such thin, thin thighs?"

"Aih-h-h! - late - and wee-e-e - moul" (whiningly).

"How did you get such big, big hips?"

"Much sitting, much sitting" (gruffly).

"How did you get such a wee, wee waist?"

"Aih-h-h! - late - and wee-e-e-moul" (whiningly).

"How did you get such broad, broad shoulders?"

"With carrying broom, with carrying broom" (gruffly).

"How did you get such small, small arms?"

"Aih-h-h! - late - and wee-e-e - moul" (whiningly.)

"How did you get such huge, huge hands?"

 "Threshing with an iron flail, threshing with an iron flail" (gruffly).

"How did you get such a small, small neck?"

"Aih-h-h! - late - wee-e-e - moul" (pitifully).

"How did you get such a huge, huge head?"

"Much knowledge, much knowledge" (keenly).

"What do you come for?"

"FOR YOU!" (At the top of the voice)

The Tavistock Witch

The Tavistock Witch sits at the crossroads between witchcraft legend and rural anecdote. In Tibbits's hands it becomes a neat little study in how superstition, poverty and local cunning intersect.

The piece works almost like a case-study from Dartmoor lore, and Tibbits presents it as a local curiosity rather than a full-blown moral exemplum. There is a faint air of amusement in the way the story is told, characteristic of late Victorian treatment of witch traditions: the terror is softened, the witch is more trickster than existential threat, and the narrative moves briskly towards exposure and containment.

An old witch in days of yore lived in the neighbourhood of Tavistock, and whenever she wanted money she would assume the shape of a hare, and would send out her grandson to tell a certain huntsman, who lived hard by, that he had seen a hare sitting at such a particular spot, for which he always received the reward of sixpence. After this deception had been practised many times, the dogs turned out the hare pursued, often seen but never caught, a sportsman of the party began to suspect "that the devil was in the dance," and there would be no end to it. The matter was discussed, a justice consulted, and a clergyman to boot, and it was thought that however clever the devil might be, law and church combined would be more than a match for him. It was therefore agreed that, as the boy was singularly regular in the hour at which he came to announce the sight of the hare, all should be in readiness for a start the instant such information was given, and a neighbour of the witch, nothing friendly to her, promised to let the parties know directly that the old woman and her grandson left the cottage and went off together, the one to be hunted, and the other to set on the hunt.

The news came, the hounds were unkennelled, and huntsmen and sportsmen set off with surprising speed. The witch, now a hare, and her little colleague in iniquity, did not expect so very speedy a turn out, so that the game was pursued at a desperate rate, and the boy, forgetting himself in a moment of alarm, was heard to exclaim, "Run, granny, run; run for your life!"

At last the pursuers lost the hare, and she once more got safe into the cottage by a little hole in the bottom of the door, but not large enough to admit a hound in chase. The huntsman and the squires, with their train, lent a hand to break open the door, but could not do it till the parson and the justice came up, but as law and church were certainly designed to break through iniquity, even so did they now succeed in bursting the magic bonds that opposed them. Upstairs they all went. There they found the old hag, bleeding and covered with wounds, and still out of breath. She denied she was a hare, and railed at the whole party.

"Call up the hounds," said the huntsman, "and let us see what they take her to be. Maybe we may yet have another hunt."

On hearing this, the old woman cried quarter. The boy dropped on his knees and begged hard for mercy. Mercy was granted on condition of its being received with a good whipping, and the huntsman, having long practised amongst the hounds, now tried his hand on their game. Thus the old woman escaped a worse fate for the time being, but on being afterwards put on trial for bewitching a young woman, and making her spit pins, the above was given as evidence against her, and the old woman finished her days, like a martyr, at the stake.

The Three Feathers

The Three Feathers, as retold by Flora Annie Steel in English Fairy Tales, is one of those "simpleton triumphs" narratives that quietly questions who gets to count as wise or worthy. On the surface it is about three brothers set a test, but beneath that it works to unpick assumptions about rank, cleverness and entitlement.

The Three Feathers also serves as a kind of gentle corrective to rigid class and gender expectations. Her prose is crisp, often lightly humorous, and she tends to give the "simple" hero a dignity that earlier chapbook versions do not always grant. The story thus becomes both a defence of the underestimated and a small manifesto for looking twice at people and things that seem unpromising.

Once upon a time there lived a girl who was wooed and married by a man she never saw; for he came a-courting her after nightfall, and when they were married he never came home till it was dark, and always left before dawn.

Still he was good and kind to her, giving her everything her heart could desire, so she was well content for a while. But, after a bit, some of her friends, doubtless full of envy for her good luck, began to whisper that the unseen husband must have something dreadful the matter with him which made him averse to being seen.

Now from the very beginning the girl had wondered why her lover did not come a-courting her as other girls' lovers came, openly and by day, and though, at first, she paid no heed to her neighbours' nods and winks, she began at last to think there might be something in what they said. So she determined to see for herself, and one night when she heard her husband come into her room, she lit her candle suddenly and saw him.

And, lo and behold! he was handsome as handsome; beautiful enough to make every woman in the world fall in love with him on the spot. But even as she got her glimpse of him, he changed into a big brown bird which looked at her with eyes full of anger and blame.

"Because you have done this faithless thing," it said, "you will see me no more, unless for seven long years and a day you serve for me faithfully."

And she cried with tears and sobs, "I will serve seven times seven years and a day if you will only come back. Tell me what I am to do."

Then the bird-husband said, "I will place you in service, and there you must remain and do good work for seven years and a day, and you must listen to no man who may seek to beguile you to leave that service. If you do I will never return."

To this the girl agreed, and the bird, spreading its broad brown wings, carried her to a big mansion.

"Here they need a laundry-maid," said the bird-husband. "Go in, ask to see the mistress, and say you will do the work; but remember you must do it for seven years and a day."

"But I cannot do it for seven days," answered the girl. "I cannot wash or iron."

"That matters nothing," replied the bird. "All you have to do is to pluck three feathers from under my wing close to my heart, and these feathers will do your bidding whatever it may be. You will only have to put them on your hand, and say, 'By virtue of these three feathers from over my true love's heart may this be done,' and it will be done."

So the girl plucked three feathers from under the bird's wing, and after that the bird flew away.

Then the girl did as she was bidden, and the lady of the house engaged her for the place. And never was such a quick laundress; for, see you, she had only to go into the wash-house, bolt the door and close the shutters, so that no one should see what she was at; then she would out with the three feathers and say, "By virtue of these three feathers from over my true love's heart may the copper be lit, the clothes sorted, washed, boiled, dried, folded, mangled, ironed," and lo! there they came tumbling on to the table, clean and white, quite ready to be put away. So her mistress set great store by her and said there never was such a good laundry-maid. Thus four years passed and there was no talk of her leaving. But the other servants grew jealous of her, all the more so, because, being a very pretty girl, all the men-servants fell in love with her and wanted to marry her.

But she would have none of them, because she was always waiting and longing for the day when her bird-husband would come back to her in man's form.

Now one of the men who wanted her was the stout butler, and one day as he was coming back from the cider-house he chanced to stop by the laundry, and he heard a voice say, "By virtue of these three feathers from over my true love's heart may the copper be lit, the clothes sorted, boiled, dried, folded, mangled, and ironed."

He thought this very queer, so he peeped through the keyhole. And there was the girl sitting at her ease in a chair, while all the clothes came flying to the table ready and fit to put away.

Well, that night he went to the girl and said that if she turned up her nose at him and his proposal any longer, he would up and tell the mistress that her fine laundress was nothing but a witch; and then, even if she were not burnt alive, she would lose her place.

Now the girl was in great distress what to do, since if she were not faithful to her bird-husband, or if she failed to serve her seven years and a day in one service, he would alike fail to return; so she made an excuse by saying she could think of no one who did not give her enough money to satisfy her.

At this the stout butler laughed. "Money?" he said. "I have seventy pounds laid by with master. Won't that satisfy you?"

"Happen it would," she replied.

So the very next night the butler came to her with the seventy pounds in golden sovereigns, and she held out her apron and took them, saying she was content; for she had thought of a plan. Now as they were going upstairs together she stopped and said, "Mr. Butler, excuse me for a minute. I have left the shutters of the wash-house open, and I must shut them, or they will be banging all night and disturb master and missus!"

Now though the butler was stout and beginning to grow old, he was anxious to seem young and gallant; so he said at once:

"Excuse me, my beauty, you shall not go. I will go and shut them. I shan't be a moment!"

So off he set, and no sooner had he gone than she out with her three feathers, and putting them on her hand, said in a hurry:

"By virtue of the three feathers from over my true love's heart may the shutters never cease banging till morning, and may Mr. Butler's hands be busy trying to shut them."

And so it happened.

Mr. Butler shut the shutters, but—bru-u-u! there they were hanging open again. Then he shut them once more, and this time they hit him on the face as they flew open. Yet he couldn't stop; he had to go on. So there he was the whole livelong night. Such a cursing, and banging, and swearing, and shutting, never was, until dawn came, and, too tired to be really angry, he crept back to his bed, resolving that come what might he would not tell what had happened to him and thus get the laugh on him. So he kept his own counsel, and the girl kept the seventy pounds, and laughed in her sleeve at her would-be lover.

Now after a time the coachman, a spruce middle-aged man, who had long wanted to marry the clever, pretty laundry-maid, going to the pump to get water for his horses overheard her giving orders to the three feathers, and peeping through the keyhole as the butler had done, saw her sitting at her ease in a chair while the clothes, all washed and ironed and mangled, came flying to the table.

So, just as the butler had done, he went to the girl and said, "I have you now, my pretty. Don't dare to turn up your nose at me, for if you do I'll tell mistress you are a witch."

Then the girl said quite calmly, "I look on none who has no

money."

"If that is all," replied the coachman, "I have forty pounds laid by with master. That I'll bring and ask for payment tomorrow night."

So when the night came the girl held out her apron for the money, and as she was going up the stairs she stopped suddenly and said, "Goody me! I've left my clothes on the line. Stop a bit till I fetch them in."

Now the coachman was really a very polite fellow, so he said at once, "Let me go. It is a cold, windy night and you'll be catching your death."

So off he went, and the girl out with her feathers and said, "By virtue of the three feathers from over my true love's heart may the clothes slash and blow about till dawn, and may Mr. Coachman not be able to gather them up or take his hand from the job."

And when she had said this she went quietly to bed, for she knew what would happen. And sure enough it did. Never was such a night as Mr. Coachman spent with the wet clothes flittering and fluttering about his ears, and the sheets wrapping him into a bundle, and tripping him up, while the towels slashed at his legs. But though he smarted all over he had to go on till dawn came, and then a very weary, woebegone coachman couldn't even creep away to his bed, for he had to feed and water his horses! And he, also, kept his own counsel for fear of the laugh going against him; so the clever laundry-maid put the forty pounds with the seventy in her box, and went on with her work gaily. But after a time the footman, who was quite an honest lad and truly in love, going by the laundry peeped through the keyhole to get a glimpse of his dearest dear, and what should he see but her sitting at her ease in a chair, and the clothes coming already folded and ironed on to the table.

Now when he saw this he was greatly troubled. So he went to his master and drew out all his savings; and then he went to the girl and told her that he would have to tell the mistress what he had seen, unless she consented to marry him.

"You see," he said, "I have been with master this while back, and have saved up this bit, and you have been here this long while back and must have saved as well. So let us put the two together and make a home, or else stay on at service as pleases you."

Well, she tried to put him off; but he insisted so much that at last she said, "James! there's a dear, run down to the cellar and fetch me a drop of brandy. You've made me feel so queer!" And when he had gone she out with her three feathers, and said, "By virtue of the three feathers from over my true love's heart may James not be able to pour the brandy straight, except down his throat."

Well! so it happened. Try as he would, James could not get the brandy into the glass. It splashed a few drops into it, then it trickled over his hand, and fell on the floor. And so it went on and on till he grew so tired that he thought he needed a dram himself. So he tossed off the few drops and began again; but he fared no better. So he took another little drain, and went on, and on, and on, till he got quite fuddled. And who should come down into the cellar but his master to know what the smell of brandy meant!

Now James the footman was truthful as well as honest, so he told the master how he had come down to get the sick laundry-maid a drop of brandy, but that his hand had shaken so that he could not pour it out, and it had fallen on the ground, and that the smell of it had got to his head.

"A likely tale," said the master, and beat James soundly.

Then the master went to the mistress, his wife, and said, "Send away that laundry-maid of yours. Something has come over my men. They have all drawn out their savings as if they were going to be married, yet they don't leave, and I believe that girl is at the bottom of it."

But his wife would not hear of the laundry-maid being blamed; she was the best servant in the house, and worth all the rest of them put together; it was his men who were at fault. So they quarrelled over it; but in the end the master gave in, and after this there was peace, since the mistress bade the girl keep herself to herself, and none of the men would say ought of what had happened for fear of the laughter of the other servants.

So it went on until one day when the master was going a-driving, the coach was at the door, and the footman was standing to hold the coach open, and the butler on the steps all ready, when who should pass through the yard, so saucy and bright with a great basket of clean clothes, but the laundry-maid. And the sight of her was too much for James, the footman, who began to blub.

"She is a wicked girl," he said. "She got all my savings, and got me a good thrashing besides."

Then the coachman grew bold. "Did she?" he said. "That was nothing to what she served me." So he up and told all about the wet clothes and the awful job he had had the livelong night. Now the butler on the steps swelled with rage until he nearly burst, and at last he out with his night of banging shutters.

"And one," he said, "hit me on the nose."

This settled the three men, and they agreed to tell their master the moment he came out, and get the girl sent about her business. Now the laundry-maid had sharp ears and had paused behind a door to listen; so when she heard this she knew she must do something to stop it. So she out with her three feathers and said, "By virtue of the three feathers from over my true love's heart may there be striving as to who suffered most between the men so that they get into the pond for a ducking."

Well! no sooner had she said the words than the three men began disputing as to which of them had been served the worst; then James up and hit the stout butler, giving him a black eye, and the fat butler fell upon James and pommelled him hard, while the coachman scrambled from his box and belaboured them both, and the laundry-maid stood by laughing.

So out comes the master, but none of them would listen, and each wanted to be heard, and fought, and shoved, and pommelled away until they shoved each other into the pond, and all got a fine ducking.

Then the master asked the girl what it was all about, and she said,

"They all wanted to tell a story against me because I won't marry them, and one said his was the best, and the next said his was the best, so they fell a-quarrelling as to which was the likeliest story to get me into trouble. But they are well punished, so there is no need to do more."

Then the master went to his wife and said, "You are right. That laundry-maid of yours is a very wise girl."

So the butler and the coachman and James had nothing to do but look sheepish and hold their tongues, and the laundry-maid went on with her duties without further trouble.

Then when the seven years and a day were over, who should drive up to the door in a fine gilded coach but the bird-husband restored to his shape as a handsome young man. And he carried the laundry-maid off to be his wife again, and her master and mistress were so pleased at her good fortune that they ordered all the other servants to stand on the steps and give her good luck. So as she passed the butler she put a bag with seventy pounds in it into his hand and said sweetly, "That is to recompense you for shutting the shutters."

And when she passed the coachman she put a bag with forty pounds into his hand and said, "That is your reward for bringing in the clothes." But when she passed the footman she gave him a bag with a hundred pounds in it, and laughed, saying, "That is for the drop of brandy you never brought me!"

So she drove off with her handsome husband, and lived happy ever after.

The Three Heads of the Well

The Three Heads of the Well, in Flora Annie Steel's English Fairy Tales, sits firmly in the great international family of "kind and unkind girls" stories, where two young women are tested and rewarded or punished according to their behaviour.

Placed in Steel's early twentieth-century collection, with Arthur Rackham's illustrations helping to fix its imagery for a modern audience, the tale becomes part of a consciously national anthology of "English" stories, even though its plot-type is shared with many European and non-European traditions.

Once upon a time there reigned a King in Colchester, valiant, strong, wise, famous as a good ruler.

But in the midst of his glory his dear Queen died, leaving him with a daughter just touching woman's estate; and this maiden was renowned, far and wide, for beauty, kindness, grace. Now strange things happen, and the King of Colchester, hearing of a lady who had immense riches, had a mind to marry her, though she was old, ugly, hook-nosed, and ill-tempered; and though she was, furthermore, possessed of a daughter as ugly as herself. None could give the reason why, but only a few weeks after the death of his dear Queen, the King brought this loathly bride to Court, and married her with great pomp and festivities. Now the very first thing she did was to poison the King's mind against his own beautiful, kind, gracious daughter, of whom, naturally, the ugly Queen and her ugly daughter were dreadfully jealous.

Now when the young Princess found that even her father had turned against her, she grew weary of Court life, and longed to get away from it; so, one day, happening to meet the King alone in the garden, she went down on her knees, and begged and prayed him to give her some help, and let her go out into the world to seek her fortune. To this the King agreed, and told his consort to fit the girl out for her enterprise in proper fashion. But the jealous woman only gave her a canvas bag of brown bread and hard cheese, with a bottle of small-beer.

Though this was but a pitiful dowry for a King's daughter, the Princess was too proud to complain; so she took it, returned her thanks, and set off on her journey through woods and forests, by rivers and lakes, over mountain and valley.

At last she came to a cave at the mouth of which, on a stone, sate an old, old man with a white beard.

"Good morrow, fair damsel," he said, "where away so fast?"

"Reverend father," replies she, "I go to seek my fortune."

"And what have you for dowry, fair damsel," he said, "in your bag and bottle?"

"Bread and cheese and small-beer, father," says she, smiling. "Will it please you to partake of either?"

"With all my heart," says he, and when she pulled out her provisions he ate them nearly all. But once again she made no complaint, but bade him eat what he needed, and welcome.

Now when he had finished he gave her many thanks, and said, "For your beauty, and your kindness, and your grace, take this wand. There is a thick thorny hedge before you which seems impassable. But strike it thrice with this wand, saying each time, 'Please, hedge, let me through,' and it will open a pathway for you. Then, when you come to a well, sit down on the brink of it; do not be surprised at anything you may see, but whatever you are asked to do, that do!"

So saying the old man went into the cave, and she went on her way. After a while she came to a high, thick thorny hedge; but when she struck it three times with the wand, saying, "Please, hedge, let me through," it opened a wide pathway for her. So she came to the well, on the brink of which she sat down, and no sooner had she done so, than a golden head without any body came up through the water, singing as it came:

"Wash me, and comb me, lay me on a bank to dry

Softly and prettily to watch the passers-by."

"Certainly," she said, pulling out her silver comb. Then, placing the head on her lap, she began to comb the golden hair. When she had combed it, she lifted the golden head softly, and laid it on a primrose bank to dry. No sooner had she done this than another golden head appeared, singing as it came:

"Wash me, and comb me, lay me on a bank to dry

Softly and prettily to watch the passers-by."

"Certainly," says she, and after combing the golden hair, placed the golden head softly on the primrose bank, beside the first one.

Then came a third head out of the well, and it said the same thing:

"Wash me, and comb me, lay me on a bank to dry

Softly and prettily to watch the passers-by."

"With all my heart," says she graciously, and after taking the head on her lap, and combing its golden hair with her silver comb, there were the three golden heads in a row on the primrose bank. And she sat down to rest herself and looked at them, they were so quaint and pretty; and as she rested she cheerfully ate and drank the meagre portion of the brown bread, hard cheese, and small-beer which the old man had left to her; for, though she was a king's daughter, she was too proud to complain.

Then the first head spoke. "Brothers, what shall we weird for this damsel who has been so gracious unto us? I weird her to be so beautiful that she shall charm everyone she meets."

"And I," said the second head, "weird her a voice that shall exceed the nightingale in sweetness."

"And I," said the third head, "weird her to be so fortunate that she shall marry the greatest King that reigns."

"Thank you with all my heart," says she, "but don't you think I had better put you back in the well before I go on? Remember you are golden, and the passers-by might steal you."

To this they agreed; so she put them back. And when they had thanked her for her kind thought and said good-bye, she went on her journey.

Now she had not travelled far before she came to a forest where the King of the country was hunting with his nobles, and as the gay cavalcade passed down the glade she stood back to avoid them; but the King caught sight of her, and drew up his horse, fairly amazed at her beauty.

"Fair maid," he said, "who are you, and where goest you through the forest thus alone?"

"I am the King of Colchester's daughter, and I go to seek my fortune," says she, and her voice was sweeter than the nightingale's.

Then the King jumped from his horse, being so struck by her that he felt it would be impossible to live without her, and falling on his knee begged and prayed her to marry him without delay.

And he begged and prayed so well that at last she consented. So, with all courtesy, he mounted her on his horse behind him, and commanding the hunt to follow, he returned to his palace, where the wedding festivities took place with all possible pomp and merriment. Then, ordering out the royal chariot, the happy pair started to pay the King of Colchester a bridal visit: and you may imagine the surprise and delight with which, after so short an absence, the people of Colchester saw their beloved, beautiful, kind, and gracious princess return in a chariot all gemmed with gold, as the bride of the most powerful King in the world. The bells rang out, flags flew, drums beat, the people huzzaed, and all was gladness, save for the ugly Queen and her ugly daughter, who were ready to burst with envy and malice; for, see you, the despised maiden was now above them both, and went before them at every

Court ceremonial.

So, after the visit was ended, and the young King and his bride had gone back to their own country, there to live happily ever after, the ugly ill-natured princess said to her mother, the ugly Queen, "I also will go into the world and seek my fortune. If that drab of a girl with her mincing ways got so much, what may I not get?"

So her mother agreed, and furnished her forth with silken dresses and furs, and gave her as provisions sugar, almonds, and sweetmeats of every variety, besides a large flagon of Malaga sack. Altogether a right royal dowry.

Armed with these she set forth, following the same road as her step-sister. Thus she soon came upon the old man with a white beard, who was seated on a stone by the mouth of a cave.

"Good morrow," says he. "Where away so fast?"

"What's that to you, old man?" she replied rudely.

"And what have you for dowry in bag and bottle?" he asked quietly.

"Good things with which you shall not be troubled," she answered pertly.

"Will you do not spare an old man something?" he said.

Then she laughed. "Not a bite, not a sup, lest they should choke you: though that would be small matter to me," she replied, with a toss of her head.

"Then ill luck go with you," remarked the old man as he rose and went into the cave.

So she went on her way, and after a time came to the thick thorny hedge, and seeing what she thought was a gap in it, she tried to pass through; but no sooner had she got well into the middle of the hedge than the thorns closed in around her so that she was all scratched and torn before she won her way. Thus, streaming with blood, she went on to the well, and seeing water, sate on the brink intending to cleanse herself. But just as she dipped her hands, up came a golden head singing as it came:

"Wash me, and comb me, lay me on the bank to dry

Softly and prettily to watch the passers-by."

"A likely story," says she. "I'm going to wash myself." And with that she gave the head such a bang with her bottle that it bobbed below the water. But it came up again, and so did a second head, singing as it came:

"Wash me, and comb me, lay me on the bank to dry

Softly and prettily to watch the passers-by."

"Not I," scoffs she. "I'm going to wash my hands and face and have my dinner." So she fetches the second head a cruel bang with the bottle, and both heads ducked down in the water.

But when they came up again all draggled and dripping, the third head came also, singing as it came:

"Wash me, and comb me, lay me on the bank to dry

Softly and prettily to watch the passers-by."

By this time the ugly princess had cleansed herself, and, seated on the primrose bank, had her mouth full of sugar and almonds.

"Not I," says she as well as she could. "I'm not a washerwoman nor a barber. So take that for your washing and combing."

And with that, having finished the Malaga sack, she flung the empty bottle at the three heads.

But this time they didn't duck. They looked at each other and said, "How shall we weird this rude girl for her bad manners?" Then the first head said, "I weird that to her ugliness shall be added blotches on her face."

And the second head said, "I weird that she shall ever be hoarse as a crow and speak as if she had her mouth full."

Then the third head said, "And I weird that she shall be glad to marry a cobbler."

Then the three heads sank into the well and were no more seen, and the ugly princess went on her way. But, lo and behold! when she came to a town, the children ran from her ugly blotched face screaming with fright, and when she tried to tell them she was the King of Colchester's daughter, her voice squeaked like a corn-crake, was hoarse as a crow, and folk could not understand a word she said, because she spoke as if her mouth was full!

Now in the town there happened to be a cobbler who not long before had mended the shoes of a poor old hermit; and the latter, having no money, had paid for the job by the gift of a wonderful ointment which would cure blotches on the face, and a bottle of medicine that would banish any hoarseness.

So, seeing the miserable, ugly princess in great distress, he went up to her and gave her a few drops out of his bottle; and then understanding from her rich attire and clearer speech that she was indeed a King's daughter, he craftily said that if she would take him for a husband he would undertake to cure her.

"Anything! Anything!" sobbed the miserable princess.

So they were married, and the cobbler straightway set off with his bride to visit the King of Colchester. But the bells did not ring, the drums did not beat, and the people, instead of huzzaing, burst into loud guffaws at the cobbler in leather, and his wife in silks and satins.

As for the ugly Queen, she was so enraged and disappointed that she went mad, and hanged herself in wrath. Whereupon the King, really pleased at getting rid of her so soon, gave the cobbler a hundred pounds and bade him go about his business with his ugly bride.

Which he did quite contentedly, for a hundred pounds means much to a poor cobbler. So they went to a remote part of the kingdom and lived unhappily for many years, he cobbling shoes, and she spinning the thread for him.

The Three Sillies

The Three Sillies, in Flora Annie Steel's English Fairy Tales, is a deliberately lightweight piece, but it has quite a sharp edge. It belongs to the class of "fool" tales that test the boundary between ordinary human muddle and absurdity, inviting the listener to measure their own common sense against the behaviour on the page.

The tale also reflects her sense of what counted as suitably "English" humour for a child reader: broad, physical, and rooted in domestic life rather than in enchantment or high romance. She keeps the tone brisk and conversational, so that the narrative feels like something heard in a kitchen or by the fireside.

Once upon a time, when folk were not so wise as they are nowadays, there lived a farmer and his wife who had one daughter. And she, being a pretty lass, was courted by the young squire when he came home from his travels.

Now every evening he would stroll over from the Hall to see her and stop to supper in the farm-house, and every evening the daughter would go down into the cellar to draw the cider for supper.

So one evening when she had gone down to draw the cider and had turned the tap as usual, she happened to look up at the ceiling, and there she saw a big wooden mallet stuck in one of the beams.

It must have been there for ages and ages, for it was all covered with cobwebs; but somehow or another she had never noticed it before, and at once she began thinking how dangerous it was to have the mallet just there.

"For," thought she, "supposing him and me was married, and supposing we was to have a son, and supposing he were to grow up to be a man, and supposing he were to come down to draw cider like as I'm doing, and supposing the mallet were to fall on his head and kill him, how dreadful it would be!"

And with that she put down the candle she was carrying and, seating herself on a cask, began to cry. And she cried and cried and cried.

Now, upstairs, they began to wonder why she was so long drawing the cider; so after a time her mother went down to the cellar to see what had come to her, and found her, seated on the cask, crying ever so hard, and the cider running all over the floor.

"Lawks a mercy me!" cried her mother, "whatever is the matter?"

"O mother!" says she between her sobs, "it's that horrid mallet. Supposing him and me was married, and supposing we was to have a son, and supposing he was to grow up to be a man, and supposing he was to come down to draw cider like as I'm doing, and supposing the mallet were to fall on his head and kill him, how dreadful it would be!"

"Dear heart!" said the mother, seating herself beside her daughter and beginning to cry, "How dreadful it would be!"

So they both sat a-crying.

Now after a time, when they did not come back, the farmer began to wonder what had happened, and going down to the cellar found them seated side by side on the cask, crying hard, and the cider running all over the floor.

"Zounds!" says he, "whatever is the matter?"

"Just look at that horrid mallet up there, father," moaned the mother. "Supposing our daughter was to marry her sweetheart, and supposing they was to have a son, and supposing he was to grow to man's estate, and supposing he was to come down to draw cider like as we're doing, and supposing that there mallet was to fall on his head and kill him, how dreadful it would be!"

"Dreadful indeed!" said the father and, seating himself beside his wife and daughter, started a-crying too.

Now upstairs the young squire wanted his supper; so at last he lost patience and went down into the cellar to see for himself what they were all after. And there he found them seated side by side on the cask a-crying, with their feet all a-wash in cider, for the floor was fair flooded. So the first thing he did was to run straight and turn off the tap. Then he said, "What are you three after, sitting there crying like babies, and letting good cider run over the floor?"

Then they all three began with one voice, "Look at that horrid mallet! Supposing you and me/she was married, and supposing we/you had a son, and supposing he was to grow to man's estate, and supposing he was to come down here to draw cider like as we be, and supposing that there mallet was to fall down on his head and kill him, how dreadful it would be!"

Then the young squire burst out a-laughing, and laughed till he was tired. But at last he reached up to the old mallet and pulled it out, and put it safe on the floor. And he shook his head and said, "I've travelled far and I've travelled fast, but never have I met with three such sillies as you three. Now I can't marry one of the three biggest sillies in the world. So I shall start again on my travels, and if I can find three bigger sillies than you three, then I'll come back and be married and not otherwise."

So he wished them good-bye and started again on his travels, leaving them all crying; this time because the marriage was off!

Well, the young man travelled far and he travelled fast, but never did he find a bigger silly, until one day he came upon an old woman's cottage that had some grass growing on the thatched roof.

And the old woman was trying her best to cudgel her cow into going up a ladder to eat the grass. But the poor thing was afraid and durst not go. Then the old woman tried coaxing, but it wouldn't go. You never saw such a sight! The cow getting more and more flustered and obstinate, the old woman getting hotter and hotter.

At last the young squire said, "It would be easier if you went up the ladder, cut the grass, and threw it down for the cow to eat."

"A likely story that," says the old woman. "A cow can cut grass for herself. And the foolish thing will be quite safe up there, for I'll tie a rope round her neck, pass the rope down the chimney, and fasten t'other end to my wrist, so as when I'm doing my bit o' washing, she can't fall off the roof without my knowing it. So mind your own business, young sir."

Well, after a while the old woman coaxed and codgered and bullied and badgered the cow up the ladder, and when she got it on to the roof she tied a rope round its neck, passed the rope down the chimney, and fastened t'other end to her wrist. Then she went about her bit of washing, and young squire he went on his way.

But he hadn't gone but a bit when he heard the awfullest hullabaloo. He galloped back, and found that the cow had fallen off the roof and got strangled by the rope round its neck, while the weight of the cow had pulled the old woman by her wrist up the chimney, where she had got stuck half-way and been smothered by the soot!

"That is one bigger silly," said the young squire as he journeyed on. "So now for two more!"

He did not find any, however, till late one night he arrived at a little inn. And the inn was so full that he had to share a room with another traveller. Now his room-fellow proved quite a pleasant fellow, and they forgathered, and each slept well in his bed.

But next morning, when they were dressing, what does the stranger do but carefully hang his breeches on the knobs of the tallboy!

"What are you doing?" asks young squire.

"I'm putting on my breeches," says the stranger; and with that he goes to the other end of the room, takes a little run, and tried to jump into the breeches.

But he didn't succeed, so he took another run and another try, and another and another and another, until he got quite hot and flustered, as the old woman had got over her cow that wouldn't go up the ladder. And all the time young squire was laughing fit to split, for never in his life did he see anything so comical.

Then the stranger stopped a while and mopped his face with his handkerchief, for he was all in a sweat. "It's very well laughing," says he, "but breeches are the most awkward things to get into that ever were. It takes me the best part of an hour every morning before I get them on. How do you manage yours?"

Then young squire showed him, as well as he could for laughing, how to put on his breeches, and the stranger was ever so grateful and said he never should have thought of that way.

"So that," said young squire to himself, "is a second bigger silly." But he travelled far and he travelled fast without finding the third, until one bright night when the moon was shining right overhead he came upon a village. And outside the village was a pond, and round about the pond was a great crowd of villagers. And some had got rakes, and some had got pitchforks, and some had got brooms. And they were as busy as busy, shouting out, and raking, and forking, and sweeping away at the pond.

"What is the matter?" cried young squire, jumping off his horse to help. "Has anyone fallen in?"

"Aye! Matter enough," says they. "Can't 'ee see moon's fallen into the pond, an' we can't get her out nohow."

And with that they set to again raking, and forking, and sweeping away. Then the young squire burst out laughing, told them they were fools for their pains, and bade them look up over their heads where the moon was riding broad and full. But they wouldn't, and they wouldn't believe that what they saw in the water was only a reflection. And when he insisted they began to abuse him roundly and threaten to duck him in the pond. So he got on his horse again as quickly as he could, leaving them raking, and forking, and sweeping away; and for all we know they may be at it yet!

But the young squire said to himself, "There are many more sillies in this world than I thought for; so I'll just go back and marry the farmer's daughter. She is no sillier than the rest."

So they were married, and if they didn't live happy ever after, that has nothing to do with the story of the three sillies.

312

The True History of Sir Thomas Thumb

The True History of Sir Thomas Thumb, in Flora Annie Steel's English Fairy Tales, plays with the very idea of "truth" in fairy lore. Steel takes the old chapbook and nursery figure of Tom Thumb, the miniature boy who lives among giants and kings, and reframes him with a wry, almost knowing narration.

The story reflects a late-Victorian attempt to gather and domesticate English folk materials for child readers, without entirely losing their older strangeness. Her Tom Thumb is still buffeted by danger and absurdity, but the tone tilts towards humour rather than horror, and there is a gentle, companionable voice guiding the reader through his adventures.

At the court of great king Arthur, who lived, as all know, when knights were bold, and ladies were fair indeed, one of the most renowned of men was the wizard Merlin. Never before or since was there such another. All that was to be known of wizardry he knew, and his advice was ever good and kindly.

Now once when he was travelling in the guise of a beggar, he chanced upon an honest ploughman and his wife who, giving him a hearty welcome, supplied him, cheerfully, with a big wooden bowl of fresh milk and some coarse brown bread on a wooden platter.

Still, though both they and the little cottage where they dwelt were neat and tidy, Merlin noticed that neither the husband nor the wife seemed happy; and when he asked the cause they said it was because they had no children.

"Had I but a son, no matter if he were no bigger than my good man's thumb," said the poor woman, "we should be quite content."

Now this idea of a boy no bigger than a man's thumb so tickled Wizard Merlin's fancy that he promised straight away that such a son should come in due time to bring the good couple content. This done, he went off at once to pay a visit to the Queen of the Fairies, since he felt that the little people would best be able to carry out his promise. And, sure enough, the droll fancy of a mannikin no bigger than his father's thumb tickled the Fairy Queen also, and she set about the task at once.

So behold the ploughman and his wife as happy as King and Queen over the tiniest of tiny babies; and all the happier because the Fairy Queen, anxious to see the little fellow, flew in at the window, bringing with her clothes fit for the wee mannikin to wear. She sang as she flew:

An oak-leaf hat he had for his crown;

His jacket was woven of thistle-down.

His shirt was a web by spiders spun;

His breeches of softest feathers were done.

His stockings of red-apple rind were tyne

With an eyelash plucked from his mother's eyne.

His shoes were made of a mouse's skin,

Tanned with the soft furry hair within.

Dressed in this guise he looked the prettiest little fellow ever seen, and the Fairy Queen kissed him over and over again, and gave him the name of Tom Thumb.

Now as he grew older—though, mind you, he never grew bigger—he was so full of antics and tricks that he was for ever getting into trouble. Once his mother was making a batter pudding, and Tom, wanting to see how it was made, climbed up to the edge of the bowl. His mother was so busy beating the batter that she didn't notice him; and when his foot slipped, and he plumped head and ears into the bowl, she just went on beating until the batter was light enough. Then she put it into the pudding-cloth and set it on the fire to boil.

Now the batter had so filled poor Tom's mouth that he couldn't cry; but no sooner did he feel the hot water than he began to struggle and kick so much that the pudding bobbed up and down, and jumped about in such strange fashion that the ploughman's wife thought it was bewitched, and in a great fright flung it to the door.

Here a poor tinker passing by picked it up and put it in his wallet. But by this time Tom had got his mouth clear of the batter, and he began hallooing, and making such a to-do, that the tinker, even more frightened than Tom's mother had been, threw the pudding in the road, and ran away as fast as he could run. Luckily for Tom, this second fall broke the pudding string and he was able to creep out, all covered with half-cooked batter, and make his way home, where his mother, distressed to see her little dear in such a woeful state, put him into a teacup of water to clean him, and then tucked him up in bed.

Another time Tom's mother went to milk her red cow in the meadow and took Tom with her, for she was ever afraid lest he should fall into mischief when left alone. Now the wind was high, and fearful lest he should be blown away, she tied him to a thistle-head with one of her own long hairs, and then began to milk. But the red cow, nosing about for something to do while she was being milked, as all cows will, spied Tom's oak-leaf hat, and thinking it looked good, curled its tongue round the thistle-stalk and… there was Tom dodging the cow's teeth, and roaring as loud as he could, "Mother! Mother! Help! Help!"

"Lawks-a-mercy-me," cried his mother, "where's the child got to now? Where are you, you bad boy?"

"Here!" roared Tom, "in the red cow's mouth!"

With that his mother began to weep and wail, not knowing what else to do; and Tom, hearing her, roared louder than ever. Whereat the red cow, alarmed—and no wonder! —at the dreadful noise in her throat, opened her mouth, and Tom dropped out, luckily into his mother's apron; otherwise he would have been badly hurt falling so far.

Adventures like these were not Tom's fault. He could not help being so small, but he got into dreadful trouble once for which he was entirely to blame. This is what happened. He loved playing cherry-stones with the big boys, and when he had lost all his own he would creep unbeknownst into the other players' pockets or bags, and make off with cherry-stones enough and galore to carry on the game!

Now one day it so happened that one of the boys saw Master Tom on the point of coming out of a bag with a whole fistful of cherry-stones. So he just drew the string of the bag tight.

"Ha! ha! Mr. Thomas Thumb," says he jeeringly, "so you were going to pinch my cherry-stones, were you? Well! you shall have more of them than you like." And with that he gave the cherry-stone bag such a hearty shake that all Tom's body and legs were sadly bruised black and blue; nor was he let out till he had promised never to steal cherry-stones again.

So the years passed, and when Tom was a lad, still no bigger than a thumb, his father thought he might begin to make himself useful. So he made him a whip out of a barley straw, and set him to drive the cattle home. But Tom, in trying to climb a furrow's ridge—which to him, of course, was a steep hill—slipped down and lay half stunned, so that a raven, happening to fly over, thought he was a frog, and picked him up intending to eat him. Not relishing the morsel, however, the bird dropped him above the battlements of a big castle that stood close to the sea. Now the castle belonged to one Grumbo, an ill-tempered giant who happened to be taking the air on the roof of his tower. And when Tom dropped on his bald pate the giant put up his great hand to catch what he thought was an impudent fly, and finding something that smelt man's meat, he just swallowed the little fellow as he would have swallowed a pill!

He began, however, to repent very soon, for Tom kicked and struggled in the giant's inside as he had done in the red cow's throat until the giant felt quite squeamish, and finally got rid of Tom by being sick over the battlements into the sea.

And here, doubtless, would have been Tom Thumb's end by drowning, had not a big fish, thinking that he was a shrimp, rushed at him and gulped him down!

Now by good chance some fishermen were standing by with their nets, and when they drew them in, the fish that had swallowed Tom was one of the haul. Being a very fine fish it was sent to the Court kitchen, where, when the fish was opened, out popped Tom on the dresser, as spry as spry, to the astonishment of the cook and the scullions! Never had such a mite of a man been seen, while his quips and pranks kept the whole buttery in roars of laughter. What is more, he soon became the favourite of the whole Court, and when the King went out a-riding Tom sat in the Royal waistcoat pocket ready to amuse Royalty and the Knights of the Round Table.

After a while, however, Tom wearied to see his parents again; so the King gave him leave to go home and take with him as much money as he could carry. Tom therefore chose a threepenny bit, and putting it into a purse made of a water bubble, lifted it with difficulty on to his back, and trudged away to his father's house, which was some half a mile distant.

It took him two days and two nights to cover the ground, and he was fair outwearied by his heavy burden ere he reached home. However, his mother put him to rest in a walnut shell by the fire and gave him a whole hazel nut to eat; which, sad to say, disagreed with him dreadfully. However, he recovered in some measure, but had grown so thin and light that to save him the trouble of walking back to the Court, his mother tied him to a dandelion-clock, and as there was a high wind, away he went as if on wings. Unfortunately, however, just as he was flying low in order to alight, the Court cook, an ill-natured fellow, was coming across the palace yard with a bowl of hot furmenty for the King's supper. Now Tom was unskilled in the handling of dandelion horses, so what should happen but that he rode straight into the furmenty, spilt the half of it, and splashed the other half, scalding hot, into the cook's face.

He was in a fine rage, and going straight to King Arthur said that

Tom, at his old antics, had done it on purpose.

Now the King's favourite dish was hot furmenty; so he also fell into a fine rage and ordered Tom to be tried for high treason. He was therefore imprisoned in a mouse-trap, where he remained for several days tormented by a cat, who, thinking him some new kind of mouse, spent its time in sparring at him through the bars. At the end of a week, however, King Arthur, having recovered the loss of the furmenty, sent for Tom and once more received him into favour. After this Tom's life was happy and successful. He became so renowned for his dexterity and wonderful activity, that he was knighted, by the King under the name of Sir Thomas Thumb, and as his clothes, what with the batter and the furmenty, to say nothing of the insides of giants and fishes, had become somewhat shabby, His Majesty ordered him a new suit of clothes fit for a mounted knight to wear. He also gave him a beautiful prancing grey mouse as a charger.

It was certainly very diverting to see Tom dressed up to the nines, and as proud as Punch.

Of butterflies' wings his shirt was made,

His boots of chicken hide,

And by a nimble fairy blade,

All learned in the tailoring trade,

His coat was well supplied.

A needle dangled at his side,

And thus attired in stately pride

A dapper mouse he used to ride.

In truth the King and all the Knights of the Round Table were ready to expire with laughter at Tom on his fine curveting steed.

But one day, as the hunt was passing a farm-house, a big cat, lurking about, made one spring and carried both Tom and the mouse up a tree. Nothing daunted, Tom boldly drew his needle sword and attacked the enemy with such fierceness that she let her prey fall. Luckily one of the nobles caught the little fellow in his cap, otherwise he must have been killed by the fall. As it was he became very ill, and the doctor almost despaired of his life. However, his friend and guardian, the Queen of the Fairies, arrived in a chariot drawn by flying mice, and then and there carried Tom back with her to Fairyland, where, amongst folk of his own size, he, after a time, recovered. But time runs swiftly in Fairyland, and when Tom Thumb returned to Court he was surprised to find that his father and mother and nearly all his old friends were dead, and that King Thunstone reigned in King Arthur's place. So everyone was astonished at his size, and carried him as a curiosity to the Audience Hall.

"Who are you, mannikin?" asked King Thunstone. "Whence do come? And where do live?"

To which Tom replied with a bow:

"My name is well known.

From the Fairies I come.

When King Arthur shone,

This Court was my home.

By him I was knighted,

In me he delighted.

I am your servant,

Sir Thomas Thumb. "

This address so pleased His Majesty that he ordered a little golden chair to be made, so that Tom might sit beside him at table. Also a little palace of gold, but a span high, with doors a bare inch wide, in which the little fellow might take his ease.

Now King Thunstone's Queen was a very jealous woman, and could not bear to see such honours showered on the little fellow; so she up and told the King all sorts of bad tales about his favourite; amongst others, that he had been saucy and rude to her.

Whereupon the King sent for Tom; but forewarned is forearmed, and knowing by bitter experience the danger of royal displeasure, Tom hid himself in an empty snail-shell, where he lay till he was nigh starved. Then seeing a fine large butterfly on a dandelion close by, he climbed up and managed to get astride it. No sooner had he gained his seat than the butterfly was off, hovering from tree to tree, from flower to flower.

At last the royal gardener saw it and gave chase, then the nobles joined in the hunt, even the King himself, and finally the Queen, who forgot her anger in the merriment. Here and there they ran, trying in vain to catch the pair, and almost expiring with laughter, until poor Tom, dizzy with so much fluttering, and doubling, and flittering, fell from his seat into a watering-pot, where he was nearly drowned. So they all agreed he must be forgiven because he had afforded them so much amusement.

Thus Tom was once more in favour; but he did not live long to enjoy his good luck, for a spider one day attacked him, and though he fought well, the creature's poisonous breath proved too much for him; he fell dead on the ground where he stood, and the spider soon sucked every drop of his blood.

Thus ended Sir Thomas Thumb; but the King and the Court were so sorry at the loss of their little favourite that they went into mourning for him. And they put a fine white marble monument over his grave whereon was carved the following epitaph:

Here lies Tom Thumb, King Arthur's Knight,

Who died by a spider's fell despite.

He was well known in Arthur's Court,

Where he afforded gallant sport.

He rode at tilt and tournament,

And on a mouse a-hunting went.

Alive he filled the Court with mirth,

His death to sadness must give birth.

So wipe your eyes and shake your head,

And say, "Alas, Tom Thumb is dead!"

The White Lady

The White Lady sits at the crossroads of ghost story, moral tale and rural theology. In Tibbits's hands it becomes a compact Devon legend about the dangers and uses of the devil, where an ordinary old woman, caught out on the moor at the wrong hour, is allowed to outwit a very literal embodiment of evil.

At the same time the story is a neat little lesson in popular theology, the sort of thing Tibbits liked to preserve. The devil, though terrifyingly staged with sulphur, flaming hounds and a headless horse, is shown as fallible and even slightly foolish; he can be lied to and tricked, so long as one keeps one's nerve.

There was once on a time an old woman who lived near Heathfield, in Devonshire. She made a slight mistake, I do not know how, and got up at midnight, thinking it to be morning. This good woman mounted her horse, and set off, panniers, cloak, and all, on her way to market. Anon she heard a cry of hounds, and soon perceived a hare making rapidly towards her. The hare, however, took a turn and a leap and got on the top of the hedge, as if it would say to the old woman "Come, catch me." She liked such hunting as this very well, put forth her hand, secured the game, popped it into one of the panniers, covered it over, and rode forward.

She had not gone far, when great was her alarm at perceiving on the dismal and solitary waste of Heathfield, advancing at full pace, a headless horse, bearing a black and grim rider, with horns sprouting from under a little jockey-cap, and having a cloven foot thrust into one stirrup. He was surrounded by a pack of hounds which had tails that whisked about and shone like fire, while the air itself had a strong sulphurous scent. These were signs not to be mistaken, and the poor old woman knew in a moment that huntsman and hounds were taking a ride from the regions below.

It soon, however, appeared that however clever the rider might be, he was no conjuror, for he very civilly asked the old woman if she could set him right, and point out which way the hare was flown. The old woman probably thought it was no harm to pay the father of lies in his own coin, so she boldly gave him a negative, and he rode on, not suspecting the cheat. When he was out of sight the old woman perceived the hare in the pannier began to move, and at length, to her great amazement, it changed into a beautiful young lady, all in white, who thus addressed her preserver, "Good dame, I admire your courage, and I thank you for the kindness with which you have saved me from a state of suffering that must not be told to human ears. Do not start when I tell you that I am not an inhabitant of the earth. For a great crime committed during the time I dwelt upon it, I was doomed, as a punishment in the other world, to be constantly pursued either above or below ground by evil spirits, until I could get behind their tails whilst they passed on in search of me. This difficult object, by your means, I have now happily effected, and, as a reward for your kindness, I promise that all your hens shall lay two eggs instead of one, and that your cows shall yield the most plentiful store of milk all the year round, that you shall talk twice as much as you ever did before, and your husband stand no chance in any matter between you to be settled by the tongue. But beware of the devil, and don't grumble about tithes, for my enemy and yours may do you an ill-turn when he finds out you were clever enough to cheat even him, since, like all great impostors, he does not like to be cheated himself. He can assume all shapes, except those of the lamb and dove."

The lady in white then vanished. The old woman found the best possible luck that morning in her traffic. And to this day the story goes in the town, that from the Saviour of the world having hallowed the form of the lamb, and the Holy Ghost that of the dove, they can never be assumed by the mortal enemy of the human race under any circumstances.

The Wise Men of Gotham

The Wise Men of Gotham, as Flora Annie Steel presents it in English Fairy Tales, sits firmly in the long European tradition of "fool" or "numskull" stories, where a whole community becomes the butt of the joke. The tale plays with the idea that folly can be a mask. Gotham's supposed stupidity becomes a way of talking about how ordinary people deal with power, law and officialdom, either by being laughed at, or by quietly outwitting those who would rule or judge them.

Within the context of Steel's collection, the story helps to balance more earnest or magical material with a sharply comic, almost satirical note.

Of Buying Sheep

There were two men of Gotham, and one of them was going to market to Nottingham to buy sheep, and the other came from the market, and they both met together upon Nottingham bridge.

"Where are you going?" said the one who came from Nottingham.

"Marry," said he that was going to Nottingham, "I am going to buy sheep."

"Buy sheep?" said the other, "and which way will you bring them home?"

"Marry," said the other, "I will bring them over this bridge."

"By Robin Hood," said he that came from Nottingham, "but you shalt not."

"By Maid Marion," said he that was going there, "but I will."

"You will not," said the one.

"I will."

Then they beat their staves against the ground, one against the other, as if there had been a hundred sheep between them.

"Hold in," said one, "beware lest my sheep leap over the bridge."

"I care not," said the other, "they shall not come this way."

"But they shall," said the other.

Then the other said, "If that you make much to do, I will put my fingers in your mouth."

"Will you?" said the other.

Now, as they were at their contention, another man of Gotham came from the market with a sack of meal upon a horse, and seeing and hearing his neighbours at strife about sheep, though there were none between them, said, "Ah, fools! will you ever learn wisdom? Help me, and lay my sack upon my shoulders."

They did so, and he went to the side of the bridge, unloosened the mouth of the sack, and shook all his meal out into the river.

"Now, neighbours," he said, "how much meal is there in my sack?"

"Marry," they said, "there is none at all."

"Now, by my faith," he said, "even as much wit as is in your two heads to stir up strife about a thing you have not."

Which was the wisest of these three persons, judge yourself.

Of Hedging a Cuckoo

Once upon a time the men of Gotham would have kept the Cuckoo so that she might sing all the year, and in the midst of their town they made a hedge round in compass and they got a Cuckoo, and put her into it, and said, "Sing there all through the year, or you shalt have neither meat nor water." The Cuckoo, as soon as she perceived herself within the hedge, flew away. "A vengeance on her!" they said. "We did not make our hedge high enough."

Of Sending Cheeses

There was a man of Gotham who went to the market at Nottingham to sell cheese, and as he was going down the hill to Nottingham bridge, one of his cheeses fell out of his wallet and rolled down the hill. "Ah, gaffer," said the fellow, "can you run to market alone? I will send one after another after you." Then he laid down his wallet and took out the cheeses and rolled them down the hill. Some went into one bush, and some went into another.

"I charge you all to meet me near the market-place," cried he; and when the fellow came to the market to meet his cheeses, he stayed there till the market was nearly done. Then he went about to inquire of his friends and neighbours, and other men, if they did see his cheeses come to the market.

"Who should bring them?" said one of the market men.

"Marry, themselves," said the fellow, "they know the way well enough."

He said, "A vengeance on them all. I did fear, to see them run so fast, that they would run beyond the market. I am now fully persuaded that they must be now almost at York." Whereupon he forthwith hired a horse to ride to York, to seek his cheeses where they were not; but to this day no man can tell him of his cheeses.

Of Drowning Eels

When Good Friday came, the men of Gotham cast their heads together what to do with their white herrings, their red herrings, their sprats, and other salt fish. One consulted with the other, and agreed that such fish should be cast into their pond (which was in the middle of the town), that they might breed against the next year, and every man that had salt fish left cast them into the pool.

"I have many white herrings," said one.

"I have many sprats," said another.

"I have many red herrings," said the other.

"I have much salt fish. Let all go into the pond or pool, and we shall fare like lords next year."

At the beginning of next year following the men drew near the pond to have their fish, and there was nothing but a great eel. "Ah," said they all, "a mischief on this eel, for he has eaten up all our fish."

"What shall we do to him?" said one to the other.

"Kill him," said one.

"Chop him into pieces," said another.

"Not so," said another, "let us drown him."

"Be it so," said all. And they went to another pond, and cast the eel into the pond. "Lie there and shift for yourself, for no help you shalt have from us"; and they left the eel to drown.

Of Sending Rent

Once on a time the men of Gotham had forgotten to pay their landlord. One said to the other, "Tomorrow is our pay-day, and what shall we find to send our money to our landlord?"

The one said, "This day I have caught a hare, and he shall carry it, for he is light of foot."

"Be it so," said all, "he shall have a letter and a purse to put our money in, and we shall direct him the right way." So when the letters were written and the money put in a purse, they tied it round the hare's neck, saying, "First you go to Lancaster, then you must go to Loughborough, and Newarke is our landlord, and commend us to him, and there is his dues."

The hare, as soon as he was out of their hands, ran on along the country way. Some cried, "You must go to Lancaster first."

"Let the hare alone," said another, "he can tell a nearer way than the best of us all. Let him go."

Another said, "It is a subtle hare; let her alone; she will not keep the highway for fear of dogs."

Of Counting

On a certain time there were twelve men of Gotham who went fishing, and some went into the water and some on dry ground; and, as they were coming back, one of them said, "We have ventured much this day wading; I pray God that none of us that did come from home be drowned."

"Marry," said one, "let us see about that. Twelve of us came out." And every man did count eleven, and the twelfth man did never count himself.

"Alas!" said one to another, "one of us is drowned." They went back to the brook where they had been fishing, and looked up and down for him that was drowned, and made great lamentation. A courtier came riding by, and he did ask what they were seeking, and why they were so sorrowful. "Oh," they said, "this day we came to fish in this brook, and there were twelve of us, and one is drowned."

"Why," said the courtier, "count me how many of you there be"; and one counted eleven and did not count himself. "Well," said the courtier, "what will you give me if I find the twelfth man?"

"Sir," they said, "all the money we have."

"Give me the money," said the courtier; and he began with the first, and gave him a whack over the shoulders that he groaned, and said, "There is one," and he served all of them that they groaned; but when he came to the last he gave him a good blow, saying, "Here is the twelfth man."

"God bless you on your heart," said all the company, "you have found our neighbour."

The Yorkshire Boggart

The Yorkshire Boggart, in Charles John Tibbits's Folk-Lore and Legends: English, works as a study of how rural communities personify everyday fear and misfortune. The boggart itself is a shapeless household presence, neither fully ghost nor goblin, that gathers up all the small failures and accidents of domestic life and gives them a face.

The story also illustrates a late Victorian fascination with regional superstition and dialect. The Yorkshire setting is important; the boggart belongs to a particular landscape and speech, and Tibbits treats it as a specimen of local belief that is just on the edge of vanishing.

A boggart intruded himself, upon what pretext or by what authority is unknown, into the house of a quiet, inoffensive, and laborious farmer; and, when once it had taken possession, it disputed the right of domicile with the legal mortal tenant, in a very unneighbourly and arbitrary manner. In particular, it seemed to have a great aversion to children.

As there is no point on which a parent feels more acutely than that of the maltreatment of his offspring, the feelings of the father, and more particularly of his good dame, were daily, ay, and nightly, harrowed up by the malice of this malignant and invisible boggart (a boggart is seldom visible to the human eye, though it is frequently seen by cattle, particularly by horses, and then they are said to "take the boggle," a Yorkshireism for a shying horse).

The children's bread and butter would be snatched away, or their porringers of bread and milk would be dashed down by an invisible hand; or if they were left alone for a few minutes, they were sure to be found screaming with terror on the return of the parents, like the farmer's children in the tale of the Field of Terror, whom the "drudging goblin" used to torment and frighten when he was left alone with them.

The stairs led up from the kitchen; a partition of boards covered the ends of the steps, and formed a closet beneath the staircase; a large round knot was accidentally displaced from one of the boards of this partition. One day the farmer's youngest boy was playing with the shoe-horn, and, as children will do, he stuck the horn into this knot-hole.

Whether the aperture had been found by the boggart as a peep-hole to watch the motions of the family, or whether he wished to amuse himself, is uncertain, but sure it is the horn was thrown back with surprising precision at the head of the child. It was found that as often as the horn was replaced in the hole, so surely it was ejected with a straight aim at the offender's head. Time at length made familiar this wonderful occurrence, and that which at the first was regarded with terror, became at length a kind of amusement with the more thoughtless and daring of the family. Often was the horn slipped slyly into the hole, and the boggart never failed to dart it out at the head of one or the other, but most commonly he or she who placed it there was the mark at which the invisible foe launched the offending horn. They used to call this, in their provincial dialect, "laking with the boggart," i.e., playing with the boggart.

As if enraged at these liberties taken with his boggartship, the goblin commenced a series of night disturbances. Heavy steps, as of a person in wooden clogs, were often heard clattering down the stairs in the dead hour of darkness, and the pewter and earthen dishes appeared to be dashed on the kitchen floor, though, in the morning, all were found uninjured on their respective shelves.

The children were chiefly marked out as objects of dislike by their unearthly tormenter. The curtains of their beds would be violently pulled backward and forward. Anon, a heavy weight, as of a human being, would press them nearly to suffocation. They would then scream out for their "daddy" and "mammy," who occupied the adjoining room, and thus the whole family was disturbed night after night. Things could not long go on after this fashion. The farmer and his good dame resolved to leave a place where they had not the least shadow of rest or comfort.

The farmer, whose name was George Gilbertson, was following, with his wife and family, the last load of furniture, when they met a neighbouring farmer, whose name was John Marshall, between whom and the unhappy tenant the following colloquy took place:

"Well, George, and so you're leaving t'old house at last?"

"Heigh, Johnny, ma lad, I'm forced to it, for that boggart torments us so we can neither rest neet nor day for't. It seems like to have such a malice against poor bairns. It almost kills my poor dame here at thoughts on't, and so, you see, we're forced to flit like."

He had got thus far in his complaint when, behold! a shrill voice, from a deep upright churn, called out, "Ay, ay, George, we 're flitting, you see."

"Confound you," says the poor farmer, "if I'd known thou'd been there I wouldn't ha stirred a peg. Nay, nay, it's to no use, Mally," turning to his wife, "we may as well turn back again to t'old house, as be tormented in another that's not so convenient."

They are said to have turned back, but the boggart and they afterwards came to a better understanding, though it long continued its trick of shooting the horn from the knot-hole.

Titty Mouse and Tatty Mouse

Titty Mouse and Tatty Mouse, in Flora Annie Steel's English Fairy Tales, is one of those deceptively slight cumulative tales that circles around domestic space, accident and absurd grief. Two tiny household creatures perform ordinary tasks in a little shared world that feels like a caricature of a human cottage; then a trivial mishap shatters that order and sets off a chain of exaggerated reactions.

Steel's version, like much of her work, trims and tidies older folk material into a form suited to late-Victorian nurseries, but she leaves intact the odd mixture of cuteness and catastrophe that defines the tale. The names "Titty" and "Tatty", the talking objects, the almost ritualistic escalation, all belong to the oral tradition of nonsense and chant, yet the ending is startlingly complete in its destruction.

Titty Mouse and Tatty Mouse both lived in a house.

Titty Mouse went a-gleaning, and Tatty Mouse went a-gleaning.

So they both went a-gleaning.

Titty Mouse gleaned an ear of corn, and Tatty Mouse gleaned an ear of corn.

So they both gleaned an ear of corn.

Titty Mouse made a pudding, and Tatty Mouse made a pudding.

So they both made a pudding.

And Tatty Mouse put her pudding into the pot to boil.

But when Titty went to put hers in, the pot tumbled over, and scalded her to death, and Tatty sat down and wept.

Then the three-legged stool said, "Tatty, why do you weep?"

"Titty's dead," said Tatty, "and so I weep."

"Then," said the stool, "I'll hop," so the stool hopped.

Then a broom in the corner of the room said, "Stool, why do you hop?"

"Oh!" said the stool, "Titty's dead, and Tatty weeps, and so I hop."

"Then," said the broom, "I'll sweep," so the broom began to sweep.

Then said the door, "Broom, why do you sweep?"

"Oh!" said the broom, "Titty's dead, and Tatty weeps, and the stool hops, and so I sweep."

"Then," said the door, "I'll jar," so the door jarred.

Then the window said, "Door, why do you jar?"

"Oh!" said the door, "Titty's dead, and Tatty weeps, and the stool hops, and the broom sweeps, and so I jar."

"Then," said the window, "I'll creak," so the window creaked.

Now there was an old form outside the house, and when the window creaked, the form said, "Window, why do you creak?"

"Oh!" said the window, "Titty's dead, and Tatty weeps, and the stool hops, and the broom sweeps, the door jars, and so I creak!"

"Then," said the old form, "I'll gallop round the house." So the old form galloped round the house.

Now there was a fine large walnut tree growing by the cottage, and the tree said to the form, "Form, why do you gallop round the house?"

"Oh!" says the form, "Titty's dead, and Tatty weeps, and the stool hops, and the broom sweeps, the door jars, and the window creaks, and so I gallop round the house."

"Then," said the walnut tree, "I'll shed my leaves." So the walnut tree shed all its beautiful green leaves.

Now there was a little bird perched on one of the boughs of the tree, and when all the leaves fell, it said, "Walnut tree, why do you shed your leaves?"

"Oh!" said the tree, "Titty's dead, and Tatty weeps, the stool hops, and the broom sweeps, the door jars, and the window creaks, the old form gallops round the house, and so I shed my leaves."

"Then," said the little bird, "I'll moult all my feathers," so he moulted all his gay feathers.

Now there was a little girl walking below, carrying a jug of milk for her brothers' and sisters' supper, and when she saw the poor little bird moult all its feathers, she said, "Little bird, why do you moult all your feathers?"

"Oh!" said the little bird, "Titty's dead, and Tatty weeps, the stool hops, and the broom sweeps, the door jars, and the window creaks, the old form gallops round the house, the walnut tree sheds its leaves, and so I moult all my feathers."

"Then," said the little girl, "I'll spill the milk." So she dropped the pitcher and spilt the milk.

Now there was an old man just by on the top of a ladder thatching a rick, and when he saw the little girl spill the milk, he said, "Little girl, what do you mean by spilling the milk? your little brothers and sisters must go without their suppers."

Then said the little girl, "Titty's dead, and Tatty weeps, the stool hops, and the broom sweeps, the door jars, and the window creaks, the old form gallops round the house, the walnut tree sheds all its leaves, the little bird moults all its feathers, and so I spill the milk."

"Oh!" said the old man, "then I'll tumble off the ladder and break my neck."

So he tumbled off the ladder and broke his neck; and when the old man broke his neck, the great walnut tree fell down with a crash and upset the old form and house, and the house falling knocked the window out, and the window knocked the door down, and the door upset the broom, and the broom upset the stool, and poor little Tatty Mouse was buried beneath the ruins.

Tom-Tit-Tot

Tom-Tit-Tot, in Flora Annie Steel's English Fairy Tales, is a domestic nightmare turned into a sharp little comedy about power, wit and women's speech. Steel keeps the old East Anglian flavour of the tale, with its dialect title and rhythmic, almost sung refrains, but she also leans into the tension between a woman's private strategies and the public roles forced on her.

The tale sits at the crossroads of folklore and the late-Victorian nursery, and she uses it to showcase both the odd music of regional storytelling and the practical cunning of its heroines. This is not a world of shining princesses; it is a world of spinning-rooms, gossip, small boasts that get out of hand, and women working out how to survive men's expectations.

Once upon a time there was a woman and she baked five pies. But when they came out of the oven they were over-baked, and the crust was far too hard to eat. So she said to her daughter, "Daughter," says she, "put them pies on to the shelf and leave 'em there awhile. Surely they'll come again in time."

By that, you know, she meant that they would become softer; but her daughter said to herself, "If Mother says the pies will come again, why shouldn't I eat these now?" So, having good, young teeth, she set to work and ate the lot, first and last.

Now when supper-time came the woman said to her daughter, "Go and get one of the pies. They are sure to have come again by now."

Then the girl went and looked, but of course there was nothing but the empty dishes.

So back she came and said, "No, Mother, they ain't come again."

"Not one o' them?" asked the mother, taken aback like.

"Not one o' them," says the daughter, quite confident.

"Well," says the mother, "come again, or not come again, I will have one of them pies for my supper."

"But you can't," says the daughter. "How can you if they ain't come? And they ain't, as sure's sure."

"But I can," says the mother, getting angry. "Go you at once, child, and bring me the best on them. My teeth must just tackle it."

"Best or worst is all one," answered the daughter, quite sulky, "for I've ate the lot, so you can't have one till it comes again."

Well, the mother she bounced up to see; but half an eye told her there was nothing save the empty dishes.

So, having no supper, she sate her down on the doorstep, and, bringing out her distaff, began to spin. And as she span she sang:

"My daughter has ate five pies today,

My daughter has ate five pies today,

My daughter has ate five pies today,"

…for, see you, she was quite flabbergasted and fair astonished.

Now the King of that country happened to be coming down the street, and he heard the song going on and on, but could not quite make out the words. So he stopped his horse, and asked, "What is that you are singing, my good woman?"

Now the mother, though horrified at her daughter's appetite, did not want other folk, leastwise the King, to know about it, so she sang instead:

"My daughter has spun five skeins today,

My daughter has spun five skeins today,

My daughter has spun five skeins today."

"Five skeins!" cried the King. "By my garter and my crown, I never heard tell of anyone who could do that! Look you here, I have been searching for a maiden to wife, and your daughter who can spin five skeins a day is the very one for me. Only, mind you, though for eleven months of the year she shall be Queen indeed, and have all she likes to eat, all the gowns she likes to get, all the company she likes to keep, and everything her heart desires, in the twelfth month she must set to work and spin five skeins a day, and if she does not she must die. Come! is it a bargain?"

So the mother agreed. She thought what a grand marriage it was for her daughter. And as for the five skeins? Time enough to bother about them when the year came round. There was many a slip between cup and lip, and, likely as not, the King would have forgotten all about it by then.

Anyhow, her daughter would be Queen for eleven months. So they were married, and for eleven months the bride was happy as happy could be. She had everything she liked to eat, and all the gowns she liked to get, all the company she cared to keep, and everything her heart desired. And her husband the King was kind as kind could be. But in the tenth month she began to think of those five skeins and wonder if the King remembered. And in the eleventh month she began to dream about them as well. But ne'er a word did the King, her husband, say about them; so she hoped he had forgotten.

But on the very last day of the eleventh month, the King, her husband, led her into a room she had never set eyes on before. It had one window, and there was nothing in it but a stool and a spinning-wheel.

"Now, my dear," he said quite kind like, "you will be shut in here tomorrow morning with some victuals and some flax, and if by evening you have not spun five skeins, your head will come off."

Well she was fair frightened, for she had always been such a gatless thoughtless girl that she had never learnt to spin at all. So what she was to do on the morrow she could not tell; for, see you, she had no one to help her; for, of course, now she was Queen, her mother didn't live nigh her. So she just locked the door of her room, sat down on a stool, and cried and cried and cried until her pretty eyes were all red.

Now as she sat sobbing and crying she heard a queer little noise at the bottom of the door. At first she thought it was a mouse. Then she thought it must be something knocking.

So she upped and opened the door and what did she see? Why! a small, little, black Thing with a long tail that whisked round and round ever so fast.

"What are you crying for?" said that Thing, making a bow, and twirling its tail so fast that she could scarcely see it.

"What's that to you?" she said, shrinking a bit, for that Thing was very queer like.

"Don't look at my tail if you're frightened," says That, smirking. "Look at my toes. Ain't they beautiful?"

And sure enough That had on buckled shoes with high heels and big bows, ever so smart.

A small, little, black Thing with a long tail

So she kind of forgot about the tail, and wasn't so frightened, and when That asked her again why she was crying, she upped and said, "It won't do no good if I do."

"You don't know that" says That, twirling its tail faster and faster, and sticking out its toes. "Come, tell me, there's a good girl."

"Well," says she, "it can't do any harm if it doesn't do good." So she dried her pretty eyes and told That all about the pies, and the skeins, and everything from first to last.

And then that little, black Thing nearly burst with laughing. "If that is all, it's easy mended!" it says. "I'll come to your window every morning, take the flax, and bring it back spun into five skeins at night. Come! shall it be a bargain?"

Now she, for all she was so gatless and thoughtless, said, cautious like, "But what is your pay?"

Then That twirled its tail so fast you couldn't see it, and stuck out its beautiful toes, and smirked and looked out of the corners of its eyes. "I will give you three guesses every night to guess my name, and if you haven't guessed it before the month is up, why"—and

That twirled its tail faster and stuck out its toes further, and smirked and sniggered more than ever—"you shall be mine, my beauty."

Three guesses every night for a whole month! She felt sure she would be able for so much; and there was no other way out of the business, so she just said, "Yes! I agree!"

And lord! how That twirled its tail, and bowed, and smirked, and stuck out its beautiful toes.

Well, the very next day her husband led her to the strange room again, and there was the day's food, and a spinning-wheel and a great bundle of flax.

"There you are, my dear," says he as polite as polite. "And remember! if there are not five whole skeins tonight, I fear your head will come off!"

At that she began to tremble, and after he had gone away and locked the door, she was just thinking of a good cry, when she heard a queer knocking at the window. She upped at once and opened it, and sure enough there was the small, little, black Thing sitting on the window-ledge, dangling its beautiful toes and twirling its tail so that you could scarcely see it.

"Good-morning, my beauty," says That. "Come! hand over the flax, sharp, there's a good girl."

So she gave That the flax and shut the window and, you may be sure, ate her victuals, for, as you know, she had a good appetite, and the King, her husband, had promised to give her everything she liked to eat. So she ate to her heart's content, and when evening came and she heard that queer knocking at the window again, she upped and opened it, and there was the small, little, black Thing with five spun skeins on his arm!

And it twirled its tail faster than ever, and stuck out its beautiful toes, and bowed and smirked and gave her the five skeins.

Then That said, "And now, my beauty, what is That's name?"

And she answered quite easy like, "That is Bill."

"No, it ain't," says That, and twirled its tail.

"Then That is Ned," says she.

"No, it ain't," says That, and twirled its tail faster.

"Well," says she a bit more thoughtful, "That is Mark."

"No, it ain't," says That, and laughs and laughs and laughs, and twirls its tail so as you couldn't see it, as away it flew.

Well, when the King, her husband, came in, he was fine and pleased to see the five skeins all ready for him, for he was fond of his pretty wife.

"I shall not have to order your head off, my dear," says he. "And I hope all the other days will pass as happily." Then he said good-night and locked the door and left her.

But next morning they brought her fresh flax and even more delicious foods. And the small, little, black Thing came knocking at the window and stuck out its beautiful toes and twirled its tail faster and faster, and took away the bundle of flax and brought it back all spun into five skeins by evening.

Then That made her guess three times what That's name was; but she could not guess right, and That laughed and laughed and laughed as it flew away.

Now every morning and evening the same thing happened, and

every evening she had her three guesses; but she never guessed right. And every day the small, little, black Thing laughed louder and louder and smirked more and more, and looked at her quite maliceful out of the corners of its eyes until she began to get frightened, and instead of eating all the fine foods left for her, spent the day in trying to think of names to say. But she never hit upon the right one.

So it came to the last day of the month but one, and when the small, little, black Thing arrived in the evening with the five skeins of flax already spun, it could hardly say for smirking, "Ain't you got That's name yet?"

So says she - for she had been reading her Bible, "Is That Nicodemus?"

"No, it ain't," says That, and twirled its tail faster than you could see.

"Is That Samuel?" says she all of a flutter.

"No, it ain't, my beauty," chuckles That, looking maliceful.

"Well, is That Methuselah?" says she, inclined to cry.

Then That just fixes her with eyes like a coal a-fire, and says, "No, it ain't that neither, so there is only tomorrow night and then you'll be mine, my beauty."

And away the small, little, black Thing flew, its tail twirling and whisking so fast that you couldn't see it.

Well, she felt so bad she couldn't even cry; but she heard the King, her husband, coming to the door, so she made bold to be cheerful, and tried to smile when he said, "Well done, wife! Five skeins again! I shall not have to order your head off after all, my dear, of that I'm quite sure, so let us enjoy ourselves." Then he bade the servants bring supper, and a stool for him to sit beside his Queen, and down they sat, lover-like, side by side.

But the poor Queen could eat nothing; she could not forget the small, little, black Thing. And the King hadn't eaten but a mouthful or two when he began to laugh, and he laughed so long and so loud that at last the poor Queen, all lackadaisical as she was, said, "Why do you laugh so?"

"At something I saw today, my love," says the King. "I was out a-hunting, and by chance I came to a place I'd never been in before. It was in a wood, and there was an old chalk-pit there, and out of the chalk-pit there came a queer kind of a sort of a humming, bumming noise. So I got off my hobby to see what made it, and went quite quiet to the edge of the pit and looked down. And what do you think I saw? The funniest, queerest, smallest, little, black Thing you ever set eyes upon. And it had a little spinning-wheel and it was spinning away for dear life, but the wheel didn't go so fast as its tail, and that span round and round—ho-ho-ha-ha!—you never saw the like. And its little feet had buckled shoes and bows on them, and they went up and down in a desperate hurry. And all the time that small, little, black Thing kept bumming and booming away at these words:

"Name me, name me not,

Who'll guess it's Tom-Tit-Tot."

Well, when she heard these words the Queen nearly jumped out of her skin for joy; but she managed to say nothing, but ate her supper quite comfortably.

And she said no word when next morning the small, little, black Thing came for the flax, though it looked so gleeful and maliceful that she could hardly help laughing, knowing she had got the better of it. And when night came and she heard that knocking against the window-panes, she put on a wry face, and opened the window slowly as if she was afraid. But that Thing was as bold as brass and came right inside, grinning from ear to ear. And oh, my goodness! how That's tail was twirling and whisking!

"Well, my beauty," says That, giving her the five skeins already spun, "what's my name?"

Then she put down her lip, and says, tearful like, "Is…is…That called Solomon?"

"No, it ain't," laughs That, smirking out of the corner of That's eye. And the small, little, black Thing came further into the room.

So she tried again, and this time she seemed hardly able to speak for fright.

"Well…is That…Zebedee?" she says.

"No, it ain't," cried the impet, full of glee. And it came quite close and stretched out its little black hands to her, and O-oh, its tail...!!!

"Take time, my beauty," says That, sort of jeering like, and its small, little, black eyes seemed to eat her up. "Take time! Remember! next guess and you're mine!" Well, she backed just a wee bit from it, for it was just horrible to look at; but then she laughed out and pointed her finger at it and said, says she:

"Name me, name me not,

Your name is

Tom

TIT

TOT."

And you never heard such a shriek as that small, little, black Thing gave out. Its tail dropped down straight, its feet all crumpled up, and away That flew into the dark, and she never saw it no more.

And she lived happy ever after with her husband, the King.

Under the Sun

Under the Sun is one of Ewing's sharpest little moral fables, dressed up as a fairy bargain. She takes a very traditional figure, the miserly farmer, and uses him to probe ideas about greed, envy and the illusion of control. The phrase "anything under the sun" becomes a legalistic trap rather than a promise of abundance, and the dwarf's trick exposes how the farmer's obsession with gain blinds him to language, to neighbourliness and to simple sufficiency.

The story also shows Ewing's characteristic blend of humour and sermon. She borrows the shapes of older wonder tales, but the concerns are very much those of a nineteenth-century moralist writing for children and families: usury, "interest," the ethics of lending, and the corrosive effect of comparing one's lot with a more fortunate neighbour.

There once lived a farmer who was so avaricious and miserly, and so hard and close in all his dealings that, as folks say, he would skin a flint. A Jew and a Yorkshireman had each tried to bargain with him, and both had had the worst of it. It is needless to say that he never either gave or lent.

Now, by thus scraping, and saving, and grinding for many years, he had become almost wealthy; though, indeed, he was no better fed and dressed than if he had not a penny to bless himself with. But what vexed him sorely was that his next neighbour's farm prospered in all matters better than his own; and this, although the owner was as open-handed as our farmer was stingy.

When in spring he ploughed his own worn-out land, and reached the top of the furrow where his field joined one of the richly-fed fields of his neighbour, he would cast an envious glance over the hedge, and say, "So far and no farther?" for he would have liked to have had the whole under his plough. And so in the autumn, when he gathered his own scanty crop and had to stop his sickle short of the close ranks of his neighbour's corn, he would cry, "All this, and none of that?" and go home sorely discontented.

Now on the lands of the liberal farmer (whose name was Merryweather) there lived a dwarf or hill man, who made a wager that he would both beg and borrow of the covetous farmer, and out-bargain him to boot. So he went one day to his house, and asked him if he would kindly give him half a stone of flour to make hasty pudding with; adding, that if he would lend him a bag to carry it into the hill, this should be returned clean and in good condition.

The farmer saw with half an eye that this was the dwarf from his neighbour's estate, and as he had always laid the luck of the liberal farmer to his being favoured by the good people, he resolved to treat the little man with all civility.

"Look you, wife," he said, "this is no time to be saving half a stone of flour when we may make our fortunes at one stroke. I have heard my grandfather tell of a man who lent a sack of oats to one of the fairies, and got it back filled with gold pieces. And as good measure as he gave of oats so he got of gold;" saying which, the farmer took a canvas bag to the flour-bin, and began to fill it. Meanwhile the dwarf sat in the larder window and cried—"We've a big party for supper tonight; give us good measure, neighbour, and you shall have anything under the sun that you like to ask for."

When the farmer heard this he was nearly out of his wits with delight, and his hands shook so that the flour spilled all about the larder floor.

"Thank you, dear sir," he said, "it's a bargain, and I agree to it. My wife hears us, and is witness. Wife! wife!" he cried, running into the kitchen, "I am to have anything under the sun that I choose to ask for. I think of asking for neighbour Merryweather's estate, but this is a chance never likely to happen again, and I should like to make a wise choice, and that is not easy at a moment's notice."

"You will have a week to think it over in," said the dwarf, who had come in behind him, "I must be off now, so give me my flour, and come to the hill behind your house seven days hence at midnight, and you shall have your share of the bargain."

So the farmer tied up the flour-sack, and helped the dwarf with it on to his back, and as he did so he began thinking how easily the bargain had been made, and casting about in his mind whether, he could not get more where he had so easily got much.

"And half a stone of flour is half a stone of flour," he muttered to himself, "and whatever it may do with thriftless people, it goes a long way in our house. And there's the bag—and a terrible lot spilled on the larder floor—and the string to tie it with, which doubtless he'll never think of returning—and my time, which must be counted, and nothing whatever for it all for a week to come." And the outlay so weighed upon his mind that he cleared his throat and began:

"Not for seven days, did you say, sir? You know, dear sir, or perhaps, indeed, you do not know, that when amongst each other we men have to wait for the settlement of an account, we expect something over and above the exact amount. Interest we call it, my dear sir."

"And you want me to give you something extra for waiting a week?" asked the dwarf. "Pray, what do you expect?"

"Oh, dear sir, I leave it to you," said the farmer. "Perhaps you may add some trifle - in the flour-bag, or not, as you think fit - but I leave it entirely to you."

"I will give you something over and above what you shall choose," said the dwarf, "but, as you say, I shall decide what it is to be." With which he shouldered the flour-sack, and went his way.

For the next seven days, the farmer had no peace for thinking, and planning, and scheming how to get the most out of his one wish. His wife made many suggestions to which he did not agree, but he was careful not to quarrel with her, "for," he said, "we will not be like the foolish couple who wasted three wishes on black-puddings. Neither will I desire useless grandeur and unreasonable elevation, like the fisherman's wife. I will have a solid and substantial benefit."

And so, after a week of sleepless nights and anxious days, he came back to his first thought, and resolved to ask for his neighbour's estate.

At last the night came. It was full moon, and the farmer looked anxiously about, fearing the dwarf might not be true to his appointment. But at midnight he appeared, with the flour-bag neatly folded in his hand.

"You hold to the agreement," said the farmer, "of course. My wife was witness. I am to have anything under the sun that I ask for; and I am to have it now."

"Ask away," said the dwarf.

"I want neighbour Merryweather's estate," said the farmer.

"What, all this land below here, that joins on to your own?"

"Every acre," said the farmer.

"Farmer Merryweather's fields are under the moon at present," said the dwarf, coolly, "and thus not within the terms of the agreement. You must choose again."

But as the farmer could choose nothing that was not then under the moon, he soon saw that he had been outwitted, and his rage knew no bounds at the trick the dwarf had played him.

"Give me my bag, at any rate," he screamed, "and the string, and your own extra gift that you promised. Half a loaf is better than no bread," he muttered, "and I may yet come in for a few gold pieces."

"There's your bag," cried the dwarf, clapping it over the miser's head like an extinguisher, "it's clean enough for a nightcap. And there's your string," he added, tying it tightly round the farmer's throat till he was almost throttled. "And, for my part, I'll give you what you deserve;" saying which he gave the farmer such a hearty kick that he kicked him straight down from the top of the hill to his own back door.

"If that does not satisfy you, I'll give you as much again," shouted the dwarf; and as the farmer made no reply, he went chuckling back to his hill.

Historical Tales

Guy of Warwick

Guy of Warwick is a long medieval chivalric romance centred on the rise, penitence and withdrawal from the world of its eponymous hero, a legendary English knight associated with the "Matter of England". The story survives in Anglo-Norman and several Middle English verse versions, and circulated very widely from the thirteenth century onward in manuscript, print and popular chapbook form.

The original is taken from George Ellis's influential three-volume Specimens of Early English Metrical Romances (1805), in which Guy of Warwick appears in translated extracts and prose summary as part of a canon-forming survey of Middle English romance. This version is then adapted again from Andrew Lang's Red Romance Book (Longmans, Green & Co., 1905), a children's anthology of heroic tales and chivalric episodes.

Everyone knows about the famous knight Sir Guy, the slayer of the great Dun Cow which had laid waste the whole county of Warwick. But besides slaying the cow, he did many other noble deeds of which you may like to hear, so we had better begin at the beginning and learn who Sir Guy really was.

The father of Guy, Segard the Wise, was one of the most

trustworthy councillors of the powerful earl of Warwick and Oxford, who was feared as well as loved by all, as a man who would suffer no wrong through the lands which he governed.

Now the earl had long noted the beauty and strength of Segard's young son, and had enrolled him amongst his pages and taught him all manner of knightly exercises. He even was versed in the art of chess-playing, and thus whiled away many a wet and gloomy day for his master, and for his daughter the fair Felice, learned in astronomy, geometry, and music, and in all else that professors from the schools of Toulouse and Spain could teach a maiden.

It happened one Pentecost that the earl of Warwick ordered a great feast, followed by a tourney, to be held in the open space near the castle, and tents to be set up for dancing and players on the lute and harp. At these tourneys it was the custom of every knight to choose out his lady and to wear her token or colours on his helmet, as Sir Lancelot did the red sleeve of Elaine, and oftentimes, when Pentecost and the sports were over, marriages would be blessed by the priest.

At this feast of Pentecost in particular, Guy stood behind the chair of his master the earl, as was his duty, when he was bidden by the chamberlain of the castle to hasten to the chamber of the Lady Felice, and to attend upon her and her maidens, as it was not thought seemly for them to be present at the great feast.

Although, as we have said, the page had more than once been called upon to amuse the young damsel with a bout of chess, she had ever been strictly guarded by her nurse and never suffered to exchange a word with the youth whose place was so much below hers. On this evening, however, with none to hinder her, she chattered and laughed and teased her ladies, till Guy's heart was stolen from him and he quite forgot the duties he was sent to fulfil, and when he left her presence he sought his room, staggering like one blind.

Young though he was, Guy knew - none better - how wide was the gulf that lay between him and the daughter of his liege lord. If the earl, in spite of all his favour, was but to know of the passion that had so suddenly been born in him, instant death would be the portion of the over-bold youth. But, well though he knew this, Guy cared little, and vowed to himself that, come what might, as soon as the feast was over he would open his heart to Felice, and abide by her answer.

It was not easy to get a chance of speaking to her, so surrounded was she by all the princes and noble knights who had taken part in the tourney; but, as everything comes to him who waits, he one day found her sitting alone in the garden, and at once poured forth all his love and hopes.

'Are you mad to think that I should marry you?' was all she said, and Guy turned away so full of unhappiness that he grew sick with misery. The news of his illness much distressed his master, who bade all his most learned leeches go and heal his best-beloved page, but, as he answered nothing to all they asked him, they returned and told the earl that the young man had not many days to live.

But, as some of our neighbours say, 'What shall be, shall be'; and that very night Felice dreamed that an angel appeared to her and chided her for her pride, and bade her return a soft answer if Guy again told her of his love. She arose from her bed full of doubts and fears, and hurried to a rose bower in her own garden, where, dismissing her ladies, she tried to set her mind in order and find out what she really felt.

Felice was not very successful, because when she began to look into her heart there was one little door which always kept bursting open, though as often as it did so her pride shut it and bolted it again. She became so tired of telling herself that it was impossible that the daughter of a powerful noble could ever wed the simple son of a knight, that she was about to call to her maidens to cheer her with their songs and stories, when a hand pushed aside the roses and Guy himself stood before her.

'Will my love ever be in vain?' he asked, gasping painfully as he spoke and steadying himself by the walls of the arbour. 'It is for the last time that I ask it; but if you deny me, my life is done, and I die, I die!' And indeed it seemed as if he were already dead, for he sank in a swoon at Felice's feet.

Her screams brought one of her maidens running to her. 'Grammercy, my lady, and is your heart of stone,' cried the damsel, 'that it can see the fairest knight in the world lying here, and not break into pieces at his misery? Would that it were I whom he loved! I would never say him nay.'

'Would it were you, and then I should no more be plagued of him,' answered Felice; but her voice was softer than her words, and she even helped her maiden to bring the young man out of his swoon. 'He is restored now,' she said to her damsel, who curtseyed and withdrew from the bower.

Then, turning to Guy, she added, half smiling, 'It seems that in my father's court no man knows the proverb, "Faint heart never won fair lady." Yet it is old, and a good one. My hand will only be the prize of a knight who has proved himself better than other men. If you can be that knight - well, you will have your chance with the rest.'

The soul of the youth leaped into his eyes as he listened; for he knew that this was much for the proud Felice to say. But he only bowed low, and with new life in his blood he left the castle. In a few days he was as strong as ever he had been, and straightway sought the earl, whom he implored to bestow on him the honour of knighthood.

'Right gladly will I do so, my page,' answered Rohand, and gave orders that he would hold a solemn ceremony, when Guy and twenty other youths should be dubbed knights.

Like many young men, Sir Guy thought that his first step on the road was also to be his last, and instantly sought the presence of Felice, whom he expected to find in the same softened mood as he had left her. But the lady only laughed his eagerness to scorn.

'Think you that the name of knight is so rare that its ownership places you high above all men?' asked she. 'In what, I pray you tell me, does it put you above the rest who were dubbed by my father with you today? No troth of mine shall you have until your name is known from Warwick to Cathay.'

And Sir Guy confessed his folly and presumption, and went heavily unto the house of Segard.

'O my father,' he began before he had let the tapestry fall behind him, 'I would fain cross the seas and seek adventures.'

'Truly this is somewhat sudden, my fair young knight,' answered Sir Segard, with a mocking gleam in his eyes, for Guy's father had not been as blind as fathers are wont to be.

'Other knights do so,' replied Guy, drawing figures on the floor with the point of his sword. 'And I would not that I were behind them.'

'You shall go, my son,' said Segard, 'and I will give you as companions the well-tried knights Sir Thorold and Sir Leroy, and Héraud, whom I have proved in many wars. Besides these, you shall have men-at-arms with you, and such money as you may need.'

Before many days had passed, Sir Guy and his friends had sailed across the high seas, and had made their way to the noble city of Rouen. Amidst all that was strange and new to him, there was yet much that was familiar to his eyes, for there were certain signs which betokened a tournament, and on questioning the host of the inn he learned all that he desired. Next morning a tourney was to be held by order of the emperor and the prize should be a white horse, a milk-white falcon, and two white greyhounds, and, if he wished it, the hand of the princess Whiterose, the emperor's daughter.

Though he had not been made a knight a month ago, Sir Guy knew full well the customs of chivalry, and presented a palfrey, scarcely less beautiful than the one promised as a prize, to the teller of these happy tidings. Then he put on his armour and rode forth to the place of the tourney.

In the field over against Rouen was gathered the flower of Western chivalry. The emperor had sent his son, and in his train came many valiant knights, among them Otho duke of Pavia, hereafter to be Sir Guy's most bitter enemy. The fights were long and sore, but one by one the keenest swordsmen rolled in the dust, and the prize was at length adjudged to the youngest knight there present.

Full courteously he told all who might wish to hear that he might not wed Whiterose, the princess, for his faith was already plighted to another across the sea. And to Felice and to her father he sent the falcon and horse and greyhounds as tokens of his valour. After that he and his friends journeyed to many lands, fighting tournaments when there were any tournaments to fight, till the whole of Christendom rang with the name of Sir Guy.

'Surely I have proved my worth,' he said, when a whole year had gone by. 'Let us go home'; and home they went.

Joyful was the welcome bestowed on him by everyone he met - joyful, that is, from all but Felice.

'Yes, you have done well,' she said, when he knelt before her, offering some of the prizes he had won. 'It is truly spoken among men that there are not twelve knights living as valorous as you. But that is not good enough for me. It matters not that you are "one of the best"; my husband must be "the best of all."

In vain Sir Guy pleaded that with her for his wife his strength would be doubled, and his renown also.

'If you cannot conquer all men for my sake now, you will never do it after,' she answered; and Sir Guy, seeing his words were useless, went out to do her bidding.

The wrath of his father and mother was great when their son came to tell them he was going to seek a fresh quest, but, though his heart was sore rent with their tears, he only embraced them tenderly, and departed quickly, lest he should make some promise he might not keep.

For long he found no knight whose skill and strength were equal to his own, and he was beginning to hope that the day was drawing nigh that should see him stand without a peer, when, in a tourney near the city of Benevento, his foe thrust his lance deep into his shoulder, and for many days Sir Guy lay almost senseless on his bed.

Now Otho duke of Pavia had neither forgotten nor forgiven his overthrow by the young knight at Rouen, more than a year ago, and he resolved to have his revenge while his enemy was still weak from loss of blood. So he hid some men behind some bushes, which Sir Guy would needs pass while riding along the road to the north, 'and then,' thought he, 'I will cast him into prison, there to await my pleasure.'

But though his plans were well laid, the fight went against him, and in the end Sir Guy, nearly fainting with weariness and loss of blood, was again the victor, and Otho's best knight, Sir Guichard of Lombardy, owed his life to the swiftness of his horse. His victory, however, was to Sir Guy as sad as many defeats, for his constant companions lay dead before him.

'Ah, Felice, this is your doing,' he said.

Long were it to tell of the deeds done by the noble knight Sir Guy; of the tourneys that he won, of the cities that he conquered - even at the game of chess he managed to be victorious! Of course many men were sorely jealous of him and his renown, and wove plots for his ruin, but somehow or other he contrived to escape them all.

By this time Sir Guy had grown to love wandering and fighting so well that he had well-nigh forgotten who had sent him from his native land, and why he was not dwelling in his father's castle. Indeed, so wholly had the image of Felice faded from his memory, that when Ernis emperor of Constantinople, under whose banner he was serving, offered him the hand of his only daughter and half of his dominions, Sir Guy at once accepted his gifts.

The sight of the wedding-ring brought him back to his allegiance. He no longer loved Felice it is true, and he did love a younger and gentler maiden. But he must abide by the oath he had sworn, though it were to his own undoing.

His grief at the loss of the princess Lorette sent Sir Guy to his bed for many days, but as soon as the fever left him he felt that he could stay at court no longer, and began to make plans to seek other adventures in company with his friend Héraud and a lion which he had saved from the claws of a dragon.

Since that day this lion had never quitted his side, except at his master's bidding, and he always slept on the floor by his master's bed. The emperor and all his courtiers were fond of the great beast, who moved among them as freely as a kitten, but Sir Morgadour, the chief steward of the emperor of the West, who was visiting the court, had ever been Sir Guy's mortal enemy, and one evening, thinking himself unseen, gave the lion a mortal wound as he was sleeping quietly in the garden. He had just strength enough to drag himself to Sir Guy's feet, where he died, and a damsel who had marked the cruel deed proclaimed loudly that it was done by Sir Morgadour. In an instant Sir Guy's dagger was buried in his breast; but when he grew calmer he remembered that his presence at court might bring injury upon Ernis, as the emperor of the West would certainly seize the occasion to avenge the death of his steward. So the next day he left the city, and slowly turned his face towards England.

It was some months before he arrived there, so many adventures did he meet with on the way. But directly he landed he hastened to York to throw himself at the feet of Athelstan the king.

'Ah, welcome indeed, fair son,' cried he, 'the fame of your

prowess has reached us these many years past, and we have just received the news that a fearful and horrible dragon, with wings on his feet and claws on his ears, is laying waste our county of Northumberland. He is as black as any coal, and as rough as any foal, and every man who has gone out to meet him has been done to death ere he has struck a blow. Go, therefore, with all speed and deliver us from this monster, for of dragons you have slain many, and perchance this one is no more evil than the rest.'

The adventure was one after Sir Guy's own heart, and that very day he rode northwards; but even his well-proved courage failed somewhat at the sight of the dragon, ten times uglier and more loathsome than any he had ever beheld. The creature roared hideously as he drew near, and stood up at his full length, till he seemed almost to stretch as far as Warwick. 'Verily,' thought Sir Guy to himself, 'the fight of old with the great Dun Cow was as the slaying of a puppy in comparison with this!'

The dragon was covered thickly with scales all over his body, his stomach as well as his back. They were polished and shiny and hard as iron, and so closely planted that no sword could get in between them.

'No use to strike there,' muttered Sir Guy, 'a thrust down his throat is my only chance.'

But if Sir Guy knew this, the dragon knew it much better, and, though the knight managed to jump aside and avoid the swoops of his long neck and the sudden darting of his sharp claws, he had not even tried to strike a blow himself for fear lest his sword should break in two against that shining horny surface. This was not the kind of warfare to which the dragon was accustomed, and he began to grow angry, as anyone might have seen by the lashings of his tail and the jets of smoke and flame that poured out of his nostrils. Sir Guy felt that his chance would soon come, and waited patiently, keeping his eye for ever fixed on the dragon's mouth.

At length the monster gave a sudden spring forward, and if Sir Guy had not been watching he could scarcely have leaped out of the way. The failure to reach his prey enraged the dragon more than ever, and, opening his mouth, he gave a roar which the king heard on his throne at York. He opened his mouth; but he never shut it again, for Guy's sword was buried in it. The death struggles were short; and then Sir Guy cut off the head and bore it to the king.

After this, his first thought was for his parents, who, he found, had died many years ago, and having said a prayer over their graves, and put his affairs in order, he hurried off to Warwick to see Felice, and tell her that he had fulfilled the commands she had given him long years ago, when he was but a boy. He also told her of the ladies of high degree whose hands he had won in fair fight and rejected. 'All of them I forsook for you, Felice,' he said.

He had kept his word; but he had left his heart in Constantinople. Perhaps Felice did not know this, or perhaps she did not set much store by hearts, and cared more for the renown that Sir Guy had won throughout Christendom. Anyhow, she received him gladly and graciously, and so did her father, and the marriage was celebrated with great pomp, and for a space Sir Guy remained at home, and after a time a son was born to him.

But at the day of his son's birth Sir Guy was far away. In the quiet and idleness of the castle he began to think, and his conscience pricked him sore, that all the years of his life he had done ill to many a man:

And slain many a man with his hand,

Burnt and destroyed many a land.

And all was for woman's love,

And not for God's sake above.

'The end should be different from the beginning,' he said, and forthwith he put on the dress of a pilgrim, and took ship for the Holy Land, carrying with him a gold ring, given him by Felice.

Once more he came back, an old man now, summoned by Athelstan, to deliver the city of Winchester out of the hands of the Danes, who were besieging it. Once more he returned to Warwick, and, unseen, watched Felice training her son in all the duties of knighthood, and once more he spoke with her, when, dying in his hermitage, he sent her the ring by his page, and prayed her to come and give him burial.

Havelock and Goldborough

Havelock and Goldborough is Andrew Lang's prose retelling of the Middle English romance The Lay of Havelok the Dane, a c.1300 poem of about 3,000 lines, preserved in the Bodleian Library, and edited for the Early English Text Society by Walter W. Skeat in 1868.

Lang's version appears in The Red Romance Book (Longmans, Green & Co., 1905), one of his "story books" of chivalric and heroic material for children, illustrated by Henry J. Ford and drawing on medieval romances and sagas. The underlying story is a "Matter of England" romance about dispossessed heirs and the restoration of just rule.

Once upon a time there lived in England a king called Athelwold, who ruled the land so well that everyone was rich and happy: or, if they were not, it was their own fault. His people all loved him dearly, and would do anything for him, and when he went to war there was no sovereign that could count on a larger following of stout brave men. He was quite a youth when he came to the throne, and at first all sorts of traitors and robbers from other countries took refuge in his kingdom, but Athelwold sought them out so carefully and punished them so severely that they soon betook themselves and their crimes elsewhere.

Now one thing grieved the king sorely. He had no son to sit on his throne after he was dead, to protect the poor and put down the lawless. And how was his little daughter, who was not yet fourteen, to keep order, or to uphold the laws?

'If she were a woman grown, it might be different,' he thought to himself, 'for Goldborough sees clearly and acts promptly. But as yet she has little knowledge, and her ways are those of a child. And full well I know that my death is nigh at hand, and there is none to watch over her.'

Long the king pondered in his mind what he could best do for his daughter's safety and the welfare of his people, and in the end he sent messengers with letters to all his earls and barons from Roxborough to Dover, bidding them come to his castle of Winchester as swiftly as they might, for he could no more mount his horse, neither could he swallow meat or pasties.

Sadly his vassals received the summons, for each loved him as his own father, and not one lurked behind. The king gave them a glad welcome, but they could not forbear shedding tears when they saw his weakness and heard his feeble voice. Athelwold let them have their way a little while, and then he said, 'I am dying, as you see, and I have sent for you here, to ask you all to tell me which of you will best guard my daughter when I am dead, till she has come to years when she can guard herself.'

And they answered as one man, 'Earl Godrich of Cornwall.'

Then the king bade the priest bring the holy vessels, and earl Godrich swore on them that he would be faithful and true in peace and in war to Goldborough; and, further, that he would seek out a man who was better and fairer and stronger than all others to be her husband, so that the land might have peace, as in the days of Athelwold.

After the earl had sworn to fulfil what the king required of him, Athelwold made his will, and gave England into the keeping of Godrich. This done, he lay back in his bed, and that same morning he died in the arms of his daughter.

But bad indeed was the choice which king Athelwold's vassals had made when they proclaimed earl Godrich as the fittest guardian for the young princess. In the beginning, indeed, while Goldborough was still a child, everything went smoothly. The earl appointed justices and sheriffs to carry out the laws, and, though he took more heed to gather riches for himself than to protect his people, yet on the whole he governed well.

Thus six years passed away, and Goldborough was twenty years old. She had lived far away from the castle of Winchester, and had never seen her guardian since the day that her father had been buried, and, for his part, he had hardly remembered her, he was so busy making laws and amassing treasures. Still, other people recollected Goldborough, if he did not, and one Eastertide, when the princess's twentieth birthday was at hand, an old pilgrim chanced to stop at Winchester on his way to Canterbury. He had but lately passed through the town where Goldborough was living, and had many tales to tell of her fair and gracious ways.

Godrich let him talk, but his face was gloomy and he answered nought. But, though his tongue was silent, his heart was base and his thoughts were evil.

'Have I toiled all these years for nothing?' he said to himself, 'and shall England be ruled by a fool, a maiden? I have a son, a full fair knave; he shall have England and be king.'

So Goldborough was brought from her woods and gardens, and shut up in the castle of Dover, where none might visit her. And no company had she but her foster-sister, and an old woman who had been her nurse.

*

At the time when Athelwold ruled England there reigned in Denmark a king called Birkabeyn, who had three children, two girls named Swanborough and Helfled and a boy called Havelok. Birkabeyn was strong and healthy, and thought to live many years, when a wound in battle proved his death-blow. Like Goldborough, the children were all young, and he was forced to choose someone to protect them till they were of full age. The man on whom Birkabeyn's choice fell was his own close friend, who had served him all his life, and who, he thought, loved his children well. And so perhaps the earl would have done had not such power been given into his hands, but this he was not proof against. No sooner had the king died than he caused the three children to be cast into prison, where he murdered the two girls himself.

At the dreadful fate of his sisters, Havelok, who was the youngest, fell on his knees and implored the wicked earl to spare him.

'If it is Denmark you want, it shall be yours,' cried the boy, 'and never will I seek to take it from you. Nay, give me a ship, and today I will leave the country for ever.'

Even the earl's heart was for a moment softened by the child's tears and prayers, and at first he thought that he would let him go, as it would be many years before he would be old enough to be an enemy. But then he remembered that, if Havelok died unwedded, he and his sons would be heirs to the crown, for he was the king's cousin. However, he pretended to grant the child's prayer, and bade him follow him down to the shore, where dwelt an old fisherman. Havelok wandered down to the water, and wondered which of the ships drawn up on the beach he should set sail in, and where he would go. He was still terrified at the death of sisters, and shook with fear as long as their murderer was in sight.

Meanwhile the earl was speaking to the fisherman, who stood at the door of his cottage, which was built just out of reach of the waves.

'Grim,' he said, 'today you are my thrall, but tomorrow you shall be a free man if you will do my bidding. Take the boy that stands there, and throw him into the sea, that he drown. Fear nothing: the penalty will be mine, not yours.'

 'Your bidding shall be done,' answered the fisherman, 'though the deed is but little to my liking.'

 'So be it,' said the earl, and went home to hold counsel with his family how best to take possession of the crown.

Grim took down a cord from a hook in the roof, and went out to the child, who screamed with terror as he drew near, but there was no one to help him, and Grim thrust a cloth in his mouth to stifle his cries, while he bound his hands behind his back with a cord. When this was done, he put the boy in a black bag, and carried him to his wife, who flung him on the floor, where he lay for many hours, thinking every moment that he would be thrown down a well or stabbed by a dagger.

At midnight, when all was still, and the men in the ships were sleeping soundly, Grim arose, and told his wife to kindle a fire and to light a candle.

'Why, there is a light in the room already,' she said, 'and it seems to come from the farthest corner, and to shine as brightly as if it were the sun itself'; and with that she sprang out of bed and ran over the floor, calling to Grim to follow her.

And in truth it was as she had said, for round the bag which held the boy a brilliant light was shining.

'If we touch him we shall rue it all our lives,' she whispered to her husband; then, stooping, she cut the knots which held the bag, and drew out Havelok, who was well-nigh dead with fright and suffocation. Next she stripped him of his clothes, and on his shoulder she found the mark of a tiny cross, from which the light came.

'He is born to be king,' said Grim softly, 'and surely it is he and no other who is the son of Birkabeyn, and who someday shall come to his own. It is easy to see that he will grow into a man, tall and strong, who shall come back from over the sea where I shall send him, and avenge himself on the traitor.' Then Grim fell on his knees before Havelok and prayed his forgiveness.

'You shall stay here awhile,' he said, 'till I can fit out a ship, and in it we will all set sail, you, and I, and my wife and my three sons, but it must be done in secret, lest the earl should come to know of it.'

So they gave Havelok bread to eat and milk to drink, and laid him in a bed in a dark corner, where no man could see him, and the next day Grim set out for the traitor's castle to ask for the reward that had been promised him.

'Your bidding is done, and I have come to claim my freedom,' said Grim when he stood in the presence of the traitor. But the earl made answer:

'Who is there to know what lies betwixt us? Go home, and be my thrall, as you have ever been.'

Full of rage though he was, Grim dared say no more, lest his head should pay forfeit; but the earl's words had filled him with fear, and he hastened to get ready a ship and to fill it during the night with food enough to last them for three weeks. By that time, he thought, they would reach the shores of England.

When all was finished, Grim and his wife, his three sons and two daughters and little Havelok, stole away very early one morning before the sun was up, and set sail southwards. A north wind soon sprang up and drove him, in ten days, to the mouth of a great river called the Humber. Here he steered his ship on to the beach, and then they all got out and set up a tent, till they could look about for a little and see what best to do.

It was a wild place where they landed, and for many miles there was not even a hut to be seen, but Grim liked it well, and he built houses for himself and his family, and by-and-by more people came there also, and a town was built and was called Grimsby, after Grim. But that happened afterwards.

Fish were plentiful at the mouth of the river - lampreys and sturgeon and turbot and great cod - and Grim and his sons were good fishers, both with net and line, and Havelok soon learned to fish too, and was as happy as any boy could be. Sometimes he stayed at home with the women while the others carried fish round the country in baskets.

Twelve years passed in this manner, during which Grim had prospered greatly, but he began to get old, and the long journeys with heavy panniers on his back tried him sorely. This Havelok perceived, and one day he spoke:

'I am a man grown, and shall I sit at home idle mending nets while my father travels over the whole country-side carrying weights too heavy for him to bear? Not so! Tomorrow I go forth, and my father shall take his seat by the fire, and shall mend the nets.'

Whatever Havelok said he did, and early the next morning he took the panniers on his shoulders, and started for the houses where Grim was wont to sell his fish. But soon, none could tell why, a bad time came, and there was no corn in the land, and no fish in the sea. And Grim felt pity in his heart for Havelok, who was young and strong, and needed more meat than other men. So one day Grim spoke, 'Havelok, dear son, you have come upon evil days, and must stay with us no longer. Go to the city of Lincoln. It is a rich town, and there you may find work for all you need. But woe is me! no clothes can I give you, save this old sail, which the women shall fashion into doublet and hose for you.'

The sail was soon cut and fashioned by Grim's wife and daughters, but there was nothing to make into shoes, and Havelok walked into Lincoln barefoot, and he fasted from meat for two or three days; at length the earl's cook took him into his service as porter, and his chief duty was to carry the earl's fish into the castle. But the cook had many porters besides Havelok, and when the cry of 'barmen' was heard they all tried one to outdo the other in obtaining the pot in which lay the hot fish. However, Havelok was taller and stronger than the rest, and generally was able to thrust the others on one side.

Besides bearing the cauldron of fish, Havelok had many things to do. He had to fill a huge tub in the kitchen with water, and to cut wood for the fire, and to do anything the cook told him. And, whatever happened, he was full of mirth, and would jest and play with the children who ran about the back of the castle.

At last his clothes, which had been fashioned out of the old sail, fell into holes, and the cook, out of pity and liking, bought him some new ones, and when he put them on there was no man, be he who he might, that was fairer to see. Then folk began to notice that he was taller than any man in the castle, and that he was very strong. Very soon a chance came to him to prove his strength.

Godrich the earl - or the king, as he called himself - now held his court at Lincoln, and summoned a parliament to be held there to settle the affairs of the nation. They came in great companies, and everyone had a following, and so many were they that they were forced to dwell in tents outside the city walls. It was not long before they fell to wrestling and such sports.

For a while Havelok looked on, and bided his time. He took no part in the wrestling, though there was not a champion on the ground that he could not easily have overcome.

When they were tired of throwing each other, someone proposed that they should put the stone, and a large smooth piece of rock was chosen. Man after man came forward, but hardly one could raise it from the ground, far less cast it any distance from him. At this moment the cook strolled up and saw his scullion standing there.

'It is your turn,' he said to Havelok, 'show them what you can do, for the honour of Lincoln,' and Havelok obeyed him. He lifted the mighty stone to the height of his shoulder, and sent it spinning through the air.

'Measure the cast,' said the cook proudly; and when it was measured it was found to be twelve feet beyond the cast of any other man.

Little was talked of that day but the wonderful throw of the young scullion, and soon it reached the ears of the knights at court, and in time, Godrich himself. As he listened to the tale, there flashed across his memory the words of the dying Athelwold, 'Find out the man who is better and fairer and stronger than any man in the world, and give him to be husband to my daughter.' Was there any man living stronger than this Havelok? and could he himself be ill-spoken of if he should carry out Athelwold's dying wish? So thought Godrich; but far back in his heart he knew that once Goldborough was wedded to a scullion there would be small chance of her becoming queen.

Next morning a knight mounted on a big bay horse, and attended by two men-at-arms, might have been seen riding southwards through the fair county of Lincoln, and in twenty days' time he returned, bringing with him the princess. Godrich greeted her with tokens of great joy, and told her that, as her father had bidden him, he had found at last the fairest and strongest man in the world, and he should be her husband.

Goldborough listened quietly to his words, and when he had ended she looked at him.

'Let him be as strong and fair as he may,' she said, 'but if he is not a king or a king's son he is no husband for me.'

At this Godrich waxed wrath, and his whole body trembled with anger.

'Your father bade me swear to him when he was dying that you should marry the strongest man in the world, and none other,' cried he, 'and, by the Rood, it is he you seek to disobey, and not me. The man who is to be your husband is the servant of my cook, and tomorrow we will have the wedding.'

The heart of Goldborough was filled with horror when she heard the fate that was in store for her, and she fell weeping on her knees before the earl to implore him the rather to let her enter a convent; but Godrich answered her nothing, and strode out of the hall.

The bells were ringing next day when Havelok woke, and before he was dressed a message came ordering him to go at once to the earl's presence. He wondered for what cause he was wanted, for never yet had he had speech of the earl, and still more surprised was he to find Godrich clad in his most splendid robes, as if for a festival. But if Havelok was astonished at all this, he was nearly struck dumb by the words which he heard.

'Master, will you take a wife?' and the young man gazed at him in silence; for why should the ruler of all England take heed whether his scullion was wedded or not?

'Will you take a wife?' asked Godrich again, in tones of impatience; then Havelok found his voice.

'No, by heaven I will not,' he cried, 'what should I do with a wife? I could neither feed, nor clothe, nor shoe her! For myself, I should have no clothes either, had it not been for the bounty of your cook.'

In his rage Godrich seized a thick staff and laid it across his scullion's shoulder.

'Promise me that you will wed her within an hour, or I will hang you on the nearest tree,' he cried; and Havelok, who had no liking for death, consented.

His purpose thus gained with Havelok, the earl now summoned Goldborough, whom he threatened to burn if she withstood him. All night the princess had wept and pondered how to escape so dreadful a doom, but at last she took comfort in the thought that in accepting this husband, however lowly born he might be, she would be fulfilling her father's wishes. So as soon as Godrich gave her a chance to speak she said she would resist him no longer.

Then Godrich for the first time in six years felt that he was indeed King of England.

'You are a wise maiden,' cried he, his face glowing with joy, 'and, to show you how well I love you, I will give you much gold, and you shall have an archbishop to bless your marriage.' And so it was done.

Both Havelok and his wife felt that they could stay in Lincoln no longer, and the next day they bought two horses and set forth for Grimsby. To Havelok's great grief he found that the fisherman had died just before, after a few days' illness, but his sons and daughters gave them a glad greeting, and bade them stay in their house, promising that they themselves would be their servants.

Weary with travel, Havelok soon went to bed, but Goldborough knelt praying before the window, when suddenly a bright light filled the room. She turned to see what it might be, and beheld it issuing from a cross on Havelok's shoulder. While she gazed wondering, she heard a voice saying, 'Goldborough, let sorrow depart from you, for your husband is no scullion, but the son of a king, and he shall rule over England and Denmark.' At that her heart grew light again, and she kissed Havelok and woke him, and told him what the voice had said.

'Let us sail at once,' added she, 'for who knows when Godrich the traitor may change his mind? And bid the sons of Grim sail with us.'

Goldborough's counsel seemed good to Havelok, and he rose in haste and sought Grim's sons, whom he found setting forth to fish. He begged them to wait, and to listen to his story, which Grim had always hidden from them, and when they heard it, they said that they would go with him, and help him to slay the murderer of his sisters and the robber of his crown.

'You shall be rich men the day he dies,' vowed Havelok; and the boat was made ready for sea.

A fair wind blew them to Denmark, and Havelok left his wife with his three foster-brothers, and betook himself to the house of Ubbe the earl, whom his father had loved dearly. He said no word as to his birth, but asked him leave to trade on his lands, offering a ring as earnest-money.

Ubbe looked at the ring, and then at the young man who gave it.

'You look fitter to do a knight's work than to buy and sell,' he said, and Havelok answered:

'That will come, fair sir, but I must first go softly. Meanwhile I have left my wife Goldborough under the care of her foster-brothers, and can tarry here no longer.'

'Bring her here,' said Ubbe, 'and dwell with her in this castle, and if no man has dubbed you knight I will take that upon me.'

And so it was done, and the heart of Goldborough rejoiced, for by this time she loved her husband dearly.

That same midnight Ubbe was wakened by a great light, which seemed to fill the castle. He rose from his bed, and went from room to room, and all were bright as day, though he could not tell why. Then he came to the room where Havelok and Goldborough lay asleep, and out of Havelok's mouth came a flame like that of a hundred and ninety-seven candles. And on his shoulder was the cross of kingship, and that was shining too.

When Ubbe saw that, he knew that Havelok was indeed the son of Birkabeyn, his friend, and the rightful king of Denmark; and, waking the sleeping man, he bade him sit up and receive his homage. After that he sent for his lords, and commanded that they should swear fealty to their king. And when the lords had sworn, Ubbe summoned the people, and told them, what many had known before, that the earl had betrayed his trust, and that now he should pay forfeit of his wickedness.

Blithe were Havelok and Goldborough that day as they moved amidst the groups of men who shared in the sports which the people of Denmark ever loved, and once more Havelok cast the stone further than any one there could throw it. His first act, after he had been proclaimed king, was to make Grim's three faithful sons barons with fair lands. Then he bid them go and seek the earl, and bring him back with them.

This was not done without a hard fight, for the earl and his men defended themselves stoutly; but at length he was bound and placed upon an old horse and carried before Havelok, who was waiting in the castle with his lords about him.

'What judgment will you pass on him, fair lords?' asked the king.

'That he may be hanged as beseems a murderer and a traitor, and that his head be planted over the chief gate of the town as a warning to all,' they said with one voice, and this was done also.

For a while Havelok stayed in Denmark to see to the affairs of the kingdom, and then, leaving Ubbe to rule, he set sail for England with Goldborough his wife, and a large army, in many ships with high carved prows. Once again he landed at the mouth of the Humber, and his first act was to found a church in memory of Grim. Next, he placed his army in order of battle, and awaited the attack of his enemy. Godrich the earl had heard that he had come, and had hastily collected a great host, with which he marched upon

Lincoln. The attack was begun by the English, and fierce was the fight. Many were killed, both of English and Danes. At last, just as the English were being beaten slowly back, Havelok and Godrich came face to face with each other. Bitterly the earl then rued the day when he had married Goldborough to the strongest man in the world, scullion though he were! Many times Havelok might have slain him, but such was not his purpose, and, taking a cord from his waist, he bound the traitor's arms, and bade one of his knights ride and fetch Goldborough, whom he had left under a guard at a little distance.

When she drew near, Havelok commanded that a flag of truce should be waved, so that the fighting might cease. Then, taking his wife by the hand, he led her forward, and told her story to them all, and how Godrich the earl had wronged her. And the English fell on their faces and did obeisance, and vowed to serve her faithfully all the days of their lives.

'And what is the law of England respecting a traitor?' asked Havelok, when Goldborough had been proclaimed queen with trumpets and shouting.

'That he be laid on an ass and burned at the stake,' cried they. And this was done also.

After this, Havelok gave his two foster-sisters in marriage to great lords, and made the cook to whom he had owed his good fortune earl of Cornwall in place of the wicked Godrich. He left Ubbe to rule in Denmark, while he and Goldborough remained in England, but every two years he sailed across the sea to be sure that all went well in the country of his birth.

And for sixty years Havelok and Goldborough lived happily together and had many children, and wherever Havelok went,

Goldborough went too.

Hereward the Wake

Hero-Myths & Legends of the British Race is Maud Isabel Ebbutt's early twentieth-century collection of prose retellings of major medieval and heroic narratives associated (often quite broadly) with Britain. First published by G. G. Harrap in 1910, it gathers sixteen extended stories, from Beowulf and Havelok the Dane to Robin Hood and Hereward, framed by an introduction that treats them as expressions of the "British race" and its ideals of courage, loyalty and chivalry.

Hereward the Wake presents Hereward as a semi-historical Anglo-Saxon patriot, leading resistance in the Fen Country and at Ely against William the Conqueror. The tale is best thought of as a literary, early twentieth-century synthesis of chronicle tradition and later legend, designed to make Hereward a symbolic embodiment of "Anglo-Saxon sturdy manliness" for modern readers.

Introduction

In dealing with hero-legends and myths we are sometimes confronted with the curious fact that a hero whose name and date can be ascertained with exactitude has yet in his story mythological elements which seem to belong to all the ages. This anomaly arises chiefly from the fact that the imagination of a people is a myth-making thing, and that the more truly popular the hero the more likely he is to become the centre of a whole cycle of myths, which are in different ages attached to the heroes of different periods. The folk-lore of primitive races is a great storehouse whence a people can choose tales and heroic deeds to glorify its own national hero, careless that the same tales and deeds have done duty for other peoples and other heroes. Hence it happens that Hereward the Saxon, a patriot hero as real and actual as Wellington or Nelson, whose deeds were recorded in prose and verse within forty years of his death, was even then surrounded by a cloud of romance and mystery, which hid in vagueness his family, his marriage, and even his death.

The Saxon Patriot

Hereward was, naturally, the darling hero of the Saxons, and for the patriotism of his splendid defence of Ely they forgave his final surrender to William the Norman; then they attributed to him all the virtues supposed to be inherent in the free-born, and all the glorious valour on which the English prided themselves; and, lastly, they surrounded his death with a halo of desperate fighting, and made his last conflict as wonderful as that of Roland at Roncesvalles. If Roland is the ideal of Norman feudal chivalry, Hereward is equally the ideal of Anglo-Saxon sturdy manliness and knighthood, and it seems fitting that the Saxon ideal in the individual should go down before the representatives, however unworthy, of a higher ideal.

Leofric of Mercia

When the weak but saintly King Edward the Confessor nominally ruled all England the land was divided into four great earldoms, of which Mercia and Kent were held by two powerful rivals. Leofric of Mercia and Godwin of Kent were jealous not only for themselves, but for their families, of each other's power and wealth, and the sons of Leofric and of Godwin were ever at strife, though the two earls were now old and prudent men, whose wars were fought with words and craft, not with swords. The wives of the two great earls were as different as their lords. The Lady Gytha, Godwin's wife, of the royal Danish race, was fierce and haughty, a fit helpmeet for the ambitious earl who was to undermine the strength of England by his efforts to win kingly power for his children. But the Lady Godiva, Leofric's beloved wife, was a gentle, pious, loving woman, who had already won an almost saintly reputation for sympathy and pity by her sacrifice to save her husband's oppressed citizens at Coventry, where her pleading won relief for them from the harsh earl on the pitiless condition of her never-forgotten ride. Happily her gentle self-suppression awoke a nobler spirit in her husband, and enabled him to play a worthier part in England's history. She was in entire sympathy with the religious aspirations of Edward the Confessor, and would gladly have seen one of her sons become a monk, perhaps to win spiritual power and a saintly reputation like those of the great Dunstan.

Hereward's Youth

For this holy vocation she fixed on her second son, Hereward, a wild, wayward lad, with long golden curls, eyes of different colours, one grey, one blue, great breadth and strength of limb, and a wild and ungovernable temper which made him difficult of control. This reckless lad the Lady Godiva vainly tried to educate for the monkish life, but he utterly refused to adopt her scheme, would not master any but the barest rudiments of learning, and spent his time in wrestling, boxing, fighting and all manly exercises. Despairing of making him an ecclesiastic, his mother set herself to inspire him with a noble ideal of knighthood, but his wildness and recklessness increased with his years, and often his mother had to stand between the riotous lad and his father's deserved anger.

His Strength and Leadership

When he reached the age of sixteen or seventeen he became the terror of the Fen Country, for at his father's Hall of Bourne he gathered a band of youths as wild and reckless as himself, who accepted him for their leader, and obeyed him implicitly, however outrageous were his commands. The wise Earl Leofric, who was much at court with the saintly king, understood little of the nature of his second son, and looked upon his wild deeds as evidence of a cruel and lawless mind, a menace to the peace of England, while they were in reality but the tokens of a restless energy for which the comparatively peaceable life of England at that time was all too dull and tame.

Leofric and Hereward

Frequent were the disputes between father and son, and sadly did Lady Godiva forebode an evil ending to the clash of warring natures whenever Hereward and his father met; yet she could do nothing to avert disaster, for though her entreaties would soften the lad into penitence for some mad prank or reckless outrage, one hint of cold blame from his father would suffice to make him hardened and impenitent; and so things drifted from bad to worse. In all Hereward's lawless deeds, however, there was no meanness or crafty malice. He hated monks and played many a rough trick upon them, but took his punishment, when it came, with equable cheerfulness; he robbed merchants with a high hand, but made reparation liberally, counting himself well satisfied with the fun of a fight or the skill of a clever trick; his band of youths met and fought other bands, but they bore no malice when the strife was over. In one point only was Hereward less than true to his own nobility of character - he was jealous of admitting that any man was his superior in strength or comeliness, and his vanity was well supported by his extraordinary might and beauty.

Hereward at Court

The deeds which brought Earl Leofric's wrath upon his son in a terrible fashion were not matters of wanton wickedness, but of lawless personal violence. Called to attend his father to the Confessor's court, the youth, who had little respect for one so unwarlike as "the miracle-monger," uttered his contempt for saintly king, Norman prelate, and studious monks too loudly, and thereby shocked the weakly devout Edward, who thought piety the whole duty of man. But his wildness touched the king more nearly still; for in his sturdy patriotism he hated the Norman favourites and courtiers who surrounded the Confessor, and again and again his marvellous strength was shown in the personal injuries he inflicted on the Normans in mere boyish brawls, until his father could endure the disgrace no longer.

Hereward's Exile

Begging an audience of the king, Leofric formally asked for a writ of outlawry against his own son. The Confessor, surprised, but not displeased, felt some compunction as he saw the father's affection overborne by the judge's severity. Earl Godwin, Leofric's greatest rival, was present in the council, and his pleading for the noble lad, whose faults were only those of youth, was sufficient to make Leofric more urgent in his petition. The curse of family feud, which afterwards laid England prostrate at the foot of the Conqueror, was already felt, and felt so strongly that Hereward resented Godwin's intercession more than his father's sternness.

Hereward's Farewell

"What!" he cried, "shall a son of Leofric, the noblest man in England, accept intercession from Godwin or any of his family? No. I may be unworthy of my wise father and my saintly mother, but I am not yet sunk so low as to ask a favour from a Godwin. Father, I thank you. For years I have fretted against the peace of the land, and thus have incurred your displeasure; but in exile I may range abroad and win my fortune at the sword's point." "Win your fortune, foolish boy!" said his father. "And where will you fare?" "Wherever fate and my fortune lead me," he replied recklessly. "Perhaps to join Harald Hardrada at Constantinople and become one of the Emperor's Varangian Guard; perhaps to follow old Beowa out into the West, at the end of some day of glorious battle; perhaps to fight giants and dragons and all kinds of monsters. All these things I may do, but never shall Mercia see me again till England calls me home. Farewell, father; farewell, Earl Godwin; farewell, reverend king. I go. And pray you that you may never need my arm, for it may hap that you will call me and I will not come." Then Hereward rode away, followed into exile by one man only, Martin Lightfoot, who left the father's service for that of his outlawed son. It was when attending the king's court on this occasion that Hereward first saw and felt the charm of a lovely little Saxon maiden named Alftruda, a ward of the pious king.

Hereward in Northumbria

Though the king's writ of outlawry might run in Mercia, it did not carry more than nominal weight in Northumbria, where Earl

Siward ruled almost as an independent lord. There Hereward determined to go, for there dwelt his own godfather, Gilbert of Ghent, and his castle was known as a good training school for young aspirants for knighthood. Sailing from Dover, Hereward landed at Whitby, and made his way to Gilbert's castle, where he was well received, since the cunning Fleming knew that an outlawry could be reversed at any time, and Leofric's son might yet come to rule England. Accordingly Hereward was enrolled in the number of young men, mainly Normans or Flemings, who were seeking to perfect themselves in chivalry before taking knighthood. He soon showed himself a brave warrior, an unequalled wrestler, and a wary fighter, and soon no one cared to meddle with the young Mercian, who outdid them all in manly sports. The envy of the young Normans was held in check by Gilbert, and by a wholesome dread of Hereward's strong arm; until, in Gilbert's absence, an incident occurred which placed the young exile on a pinnacle so far above them that only by his death could they hope to rid themselves of their feeling of inferiority.

The Fairy Bear

Gilbert kept in his castle court an immense white Polar bear, dreaded by all for its enormous strength, and called the Fairy Bear. It was even believed that the huge beast had some kinship to old Earl Siward, who bore a bear upon his crest, and was reputed to have had something of bear-like ferocity in his youth. This white bear was so much dreaded that he was kept chained up in a strong cage. One morning as Hereward was returning with Martin from his morning ride he heard shouts and shrieks from the castle yard, and reaching the great gate, entered lightly and closed it behind him rapidly, for there outside the shattered cage, with broken chain dangling, stood the Fairy Bear, glaring savagely round the courtyard. But one human figure was in sight, that of a girl of about twelve years of age.

Hereward Slays the Bear

There were sounds of men's voices and women's shrieks from within the castle, but the doors were fast barred, while the maid, in her terror, beat on the portal with her palms, and begged them, for the love of God, to let her in. The cowards, refused, and in the meantime the great bear, irritated by the dangling chain, made a rush towards the child. Hereward dashed forward, shouting to distract the bear, and just managed to stop his charge at the girl. The savage animal turned on the new-comer, who needed all his agility to escape the monster's terrible onset. Seizing his battle-axe, the youth swung it around his head and split the skull of the furious beast, which fell dead. It was a blow so mighty that even Hereward himself was surprised at its deadly effect, and approached cautiously to examine his victim. In the meantime the little girl, who proved to be no other than the king's ward, Alftruda, had watched with fascinated eyes first the approach of the monster, and then, as she crouched in terror, its sudden slaughter; and now she summoned up courage to run to Hereward, who had always been kind to the pretty child, and to fling herself into his arms. "Kind Hereward," she whispered, "you have saved me and killed the bear. I love you for it, and I must give you a kiss, for my dame says so do all ladies that choose good knights to be their champions. Will you be mine?" As she spoke she kissed Hereward again and again.

Alftruda

"Where have they all gone, little one?" asked the young noble; and Alftruda replied, "We were all out here in the courtyard watching the young men at their exercises, when we heard a crash and a roar, and the cage burst open, and we saw the dreadful Fairy Bear. They all ran, the ladies and knights, but I was the last, and they were so frightened that they shut themselves in and left me outside; and when I beat at the door and prayed them to let me in they would not, and I thought the bear would eat me, till you came."

"The cowards!" cried Hereward. "And they think themselves worthy of knighthood when they will save their own lives and leave a child in danger! They must be taught a lesson. Martin, come here and aid me." When Martin came, the two, with infinite trouble, raised the carcase of the monstrous beast, and placed it just where the bower door, opening, would show it at once. Then Hereward bade Alftruda call to the knights in the bower that all was safe and they could come out, for the bear would not hurt them. He and Martin, listening, heard with great glee the bitter debate within the bower as to who should risk his life to open the door, the many excuses given for refusal, the mischievous fun in Alftruda's voice as she begged someone to open to her, and, best of all, the cry of horror with which the knight who had ventured to draw the bolt shut the door again on seeing the Fairy Bear waiting to enter. Hereward even carried his trick so far as to thrust the bear heavily against the bower door, making all the people within shriek and implore the protection of the saints. Finally, when he was tired of the jest, he convinced the valiant knights that they might emerge safely from their retirement, and showed how he, a stripling of seventeen, had slain the monster at one blow. From that time Hereward was the darling of the whole castle, petted, praised, beloved by all its inmates, except his jealous rivals.

Hereward Leaves Northumbria

The foreign knights grew so jealous of the Saxon youth, and so restive under his shafts of sarcastic ridicule, that they planned several times to kill him, and once or twice nearly succeeded. This insecurity, and a feeling that perhaps Earl Siward had some kinship with the Fairy Bear, and would wish to avenge his death, made Hereward decide to quit Gilbert's castle. The spirit of adventure was strong upon him, the sea seemed to call him; now that he had been acknowledged superior to the other noble youths in Gilbert's household, the castle no longer afforded a field for his ambition. Accordingly he took a sad leave of Alftruda, an affectionate one of Sir Gilbert, who wished to knight him for his brave deed, and a mocking one of his angry and unsuccessful foes.

Hereward in Cornwall

Entering into a merchant-ship, he sailed for Cornwall, and there was taken to the court of King Alef, a petty British chief, who, on true patriarchal lines, disposed of his children as he would, and had betrothed his fair daughter to a terrible Pictish giant, breaking off, in order to do it, her troth-plight with Prince Sigtryg of Waterford, son of a Danish king in Ireland. Hereward was ever chivalrous, and little Alftruda had made him feel pitiful to all maidens. Seeing speedily how the princess loathed her new betrothed, a hideous, misshapen wretch, nearly eight feet high, he determined to slay him. With great deliberation he picked a quarrel with the giant, and killed him the next day in fair fight; but King Alef was driven by the threats of the vengeful Pictish tribe to throw Hereward and his man Martin into prison, promising trial and punishment on the morrow.

Hereward Released from Prison

To the young Saxon's surprise, the released princess appeared to be as grieved and as revengeful as any follower of the Pictish giant, and she not only advocated prison and death the next day, but herself superintended the tying of the thongs that bound the two strangers. When they were left to their lonely confinement Hereward began to blame the princess for hypocrisy, and to protest the impossibility of a man's ever knowing what a woman wants. "Who would have thought," he cried, "that that beautiful maiden loved a giant so hideous as this Pict? Had I known, I would never have fought him, but her eyes said to me, 'Kill him,' and I have done so; this is how she rewards me!" "No," replied Martin, "this is how"; and he cut Hereward's bonds, laughing silently to himself. "Master, you were so indignant with the lady that you could not make allowances for her. I knew that she must pretend to grieve, for her father's sake, and when she came to test our bonds I was sure of it, for as she fingered a knot she slipped a knife into my hands, and bade me use it. Now we are free from our bonds, and must try to escape from our prison."

The Princess Visits the Captives

In vain, however, the master and man ranged round the room in which they were confined; it was a tiny chapel, with walls and doors of great thickness, and violently as Hereward exerted himself, he could make no impression on either walls or door, and, sitting sullenly down on the altar steps, he asked Martin what good was freedom from bonds in a secure prison. "Much, every way," replied the servant, "at least we die with free hands; and I, for my part, am content to trust that the princess has some good plan, if we will only be ready." While he was speaking they heard footsteps just outside the door, and the sound of a key being inserted into the lock. Hereward beckoned silently to Martin, and the two stood ready, one at each side of the door, to make a dash for freedom, and Martin was prepared to slay any who should hinder. To their great surprise, the princess entered, accompanied by an old priest bearing a lantern, which he set down on the altar step, and then the princess turned to Hereward, crying, "Pardon me, my deliverer!" The Saxon was still aggrieved and bewildered, and replied, "Do you now say 'deliverer'? This afternoon it was 'murderer, villain, cut-throat.' How shall I know which is your real mind?" The princess almost laughed as she said, "How stupid men are! What could I do but pretend to hate you, since otherwise the Picts would have slain you then and us all afterwards, but I claimed you as my victims, and you have been given to me. How else could I have come here tonight? Now tell me, if I set you free will you swear to carry a message for me?"

Hereward and the Princess

"Where shall I go, lady, and what shall I say?" asked Hereward. "Take this ring, my ring of betrothal, and go to Prince Sigtryg, son of King Ranald of Waterford. Say to him that I am beset on every side, and beg him to come and claim me as his bride; otherwise I fear I may be forced to marry some man of my father's choosing, as I was being driven to wed the Pictish giant. From him you have rescued me, and I thank you; but if my betrothed delays his coming it may be too late, for there are other hateful suitors who would make my father bestow my hand upon one of them. Beg him to come with all speed." "Lady, I will go now," said Hereward, "if you will set me free from this vault."

Hereward Binds the Princess

"Go quickly, and safely," said the princess, "but ere you go you have one duty to fulfil: you must bind me hand and foot, and fling me, with this old priest, on the ground." "Never," said Hereward, "will I bind a woman; it were foul disgrace to me for ever." But Martin only laughed, and the maiden said again, "How stupid men are! I must pretend to have been overpowered by you, or I shall be accused of having freed you, but I will say that I came here to question you, and you and your man set on me and the priest, bound us, took the key, and so escaped. So shall you be free, and I shall have no blame, and my father no danger; and may Heaven forgive the lie."

Hereward reluctantly agreed, and, with Martin's help, bound the two hand and foot and laid them before the altar; then, kissing the maiden's hand, and swearing loyalty and truth, he turned to depart. But the princess had one question to ask. "Who are you, noble stranger, so gallant and strong? I would fain know for whom to pray." "I am Hereward Leofricsson, and my father is the Earl of Mercia." "Are you that Hereward who slew the Fairy Bear? Little wonder is it that you have slain my monster and set me free." Then master and man left the chapel, after carefully turning the key in the lock. Making their way to the shore, they succeeded in getting a ship to carry them to Ireland, and in course of time reached Waterford.

Prince Sigtryg

The Danish kingdom of Waterford was ruled by King Ranald, whose only son, Sigtryg, was about Hereward's age, and was as noble-looking a youth as the Saxon hero. The king was at a feast, and Hereward, entering the hall with the captain of the vessel, sat down at one of the lower tables; but he was not one of those who can pass unnoticed. The prince saw him, distinguished at once his noble bearing, and asked him to come to the king's own table. He gladly obeyed, and as he drank to the prince and their goblets touched together he contrived to drop the ring from the Cornish princess into Sigtryg's cup. The prince saw and recognised it as he drained his cup, and, watching his opportunity, left the hall, and was soon followed by his guest.

Hereward and Sigtryg

Outside in the darkness Sigtryg turned hurriedly to Hereward, saying, "You bring me a message from my betrothed?" "Yes, if you are that Prince Sigtryg to whom the Princess of Cornwall was affianced." "Was affianced! What do you mean? She is still my lady and my love." "Yet you leave her there unaided, while her father gives her in marriage to a hideous giant of a Pict, breaking her betrothal, and driving the hapless maiden to despair. What kind of love is yours?" Hereward said nothing yet about his own slaying of the giant, because he wished to test Prince Sigtryg's sincerity, and he was satisfied, for the prince burst out, "Would to God that I had gone to her before! but my father needed my help against foreign invaders and native rebels. I will go immediately and save my lady or die with her!" "No need of that, for I killed that giant," said Hereward coolly, and Sigtryg embraced him in joy and they swore blood-brotherhood together. Then he asked, "What message do you bring me, and what means her ring?" The other replied by repeating the Cornish maiden's words, and urging him to start at once if he would save his betrothed from some other hateful marriage.

Return to Cornwall

The prince went at once to his father, told him the whole story, and obtained a ship and men to journey to Cornwall and rescue the princess; then, with Hereward by his side, he set sail, and soon landed in Cornwall, hoping to obtain his bride peaceably. To his grief he learnt that the princess had just been betrothed to a wild Cornish leader, Haco, and the wedding feast was to be held that very day. Sigtryg was greatly enraged, and sent a troop of forty

Danes to King Alef demanding the fulfilment of the troth-plight between himself and his daughter, and threatening vengeance if it were broken. To this threat the king returned no answer, and no Dane came back to tell of their reception.

Hereward and Sigtryg

Sigtryg would have waited till morning, trusting in the honour of the king, but Hereward disguised himself as a minstrel and obtained admission to the bridal feast, where he soon won applause by his beautiful singing. The bridegroom, Haco, in a rapture offered him any boon he liked to ask, but he demanded only a cup of wine from the hands of the bride. When she brought it to him he flung into the empty cup the betrothal ring, the token she had sent to Sigtryg, and said, "I thank you, lady, and would reward you for your gentleness to a wandering minstrel; I give back the cup, richer than before by the kind thoughts of which it bears the token." The princess looked at him, gazed into the goblet, and saw her ring; then, looking again, she recognised her deliverer and knew that rescue was at hand.

Haco's Plan

While men feasted Hereward listened and talked, and found out that the forty Danes were prisoners, to be released on the morrow when Haco was sure of his bride, but released useless and miserable, since they would be turned adrift blinded. Haco was taking his lovely bride back to his own land, and Hereward saw that any rescue, to be successful, must be attempted on the march. Yet he knew not the way the bridal company would go, and he lay down to sleep in the hall, hoping that he might hear something more. When all men slept a dark shape came gliding through the hall and touched Hereward on the shoulder; he slept lightly, and awoke at once to recognise the old nurse of the princess. "Come to her now," the old woman whispered, and Hereward went, though he knew not that the princess was still true to her lover. In her bower, which she was soon to leave, Haco's sorrowful bride awaited the messenger.

Rescue for Haco's Bride

Sadly she smiled on the young Saxon as she said, "I knew your face again in spite of the disguise, but you come too late. Bear my farewell to Sigtryg, and say that my father's will, not mine, makes me false to my troth-plight." "Have you not been told, lady, that he is here?" asked Hereward. "Here?" the princess cried. "I have not heard. He loves me still and has not forsaken me?" "No, lady, he is too true a lover for falsehood. He sent forty Danes yesterday to demand you of your father and threaten his wrath if he refused." "And I knew not of it," said the princess softly, "yet I had heard that Haco had taken some prisoners, whom he means to blind." "Those are our messengers, and your future subjects," said Hereward. "Help me to save them and you. Do you know Haco's plans?" "Only this, that he will march tomorrow along the river, and where the ravine is darkest and forms the boundary between his kingdom and my father's the prisoners are to be blinded and released." "Is it far hence?" "Three miles to the eastward of this hall," she replied. "We will be there. Have no fear, lady, whatever you may see, but be bold and look for your lover in the fight." So saying, Hereward kissed the hand of the princess, and passed out of the hall unperceived by anyone.

The Ambush

Returning to Sigtryg, the young Saxon told all that he had learnt, and the Danes planned an ambush in the ravine where Haco had decided to blind and set free his captives. All was in readiness, and side by side Hereward and Sigtryg were watching the pathway from their covert, when the sound of horses' hoofs heard on the rocks reduced them to silence. The bridal procession came in strange array: first the Danish prisoners bound each between two Cornishmen, then Haco and his unhappy bride, and last a great throng of Cornishmen. Hereward had taken command, that Sigtryg might look to the safety of his lady, and his plan was simplicity itself. The Danes were to wait till their comrades, with their guards, had passed through the ravine; then while the leader engaged Haco, and Sigtryg looked to the safety of the princess, the Danes would release the prisoners and slay every Cornishman, and the two parties of Danes, uniting their forces, would restore order to the land and destroy the followers of Haco.

Success

The whole was carried out exactly as Hereward had planned. The Cornishmen, with Danish captives, passed first without attack; next came Haco, riding grim and ferocious beside his silent bride, he exulting in his success, she looking eagerly for any signs of rescue. As they passed Hereward sprang from his shelter, crying, "Upon them, Danes, and set your brethren free!" and himself struck down Haco and smote off his head. There was a short struggle, but soon the rescued Danes were able to aid their deliverers, and the Cornish guards were all slain; the men of King Alef, never very zealous for the cause of Haco, fled, and the Danes were left masters of the field. Sigtryg had in the meantime seen to the safety of the princess, and now placing her between himself and Hereward, he escorted her to the ship, which soon brought them to Waterford and a happy bridal. The Prince and Princess of Waterford always recognised in Hereward their deliverer and best friend, and in their gratitude wished him to dwell with them always; but he knew "how hard a thing it is to look into happiness through another man's eyes," and would not stay. His roving and daring temper drove him to deeds of arms in other lands, where he won a renown second to none, but he always felt glad in his own heart, even in later days, when unfaithfulness to a woman was the one great sin of his life, that his first feats of arms had been wrought to rescue two maidens from their hapless fate, and that he was rightly known as Hereward the Saxon, the Champion of Women.

King Horn

Hero-Myths & Legends of the British Race by Maud Isabel Ebbutt is an early twentieth-century anthology of retold medieval and later heroic narratives associated with Britain and its cultural orbit, first published by George G. Harrap around 1910. It gathers stories such as Beowulf, Havelok the Dane, Hereward the Wake, Robin Hood, Sir Gawain material and others, arranging them as a kind of prose "reader" in chivalric and legendary history.

King Horn is her prose adaptation of the Middle English chivalric romance King Horn, probably the oldest surviving romance in English, originally composed in the thirteenth century and itself derived from the earlier Anglo-Norman Romance of Horn.

The Royal Family of Suddene

There once lived and ruled in the pleasant land of Suddene a noble king named Murry, whose fair consort, Queen Godhild, was the most sweet and gentle lady alive, as the king was a pattern of all knightly virtues. This royal pair had but one child, a son, named Horn, now twelve years old, who had been surrounded from his birth with loyal service and true devotion. He had a band of twelve chosen companions with whom he shared sports and tasks, pleasures and griefs, and the little company grew up well trained in chivalrous exercises and qualities. Childe Horn had his favourites among the twelve. Athulf was his dearest friend, a loving and devoted companion; and next to him in Horn's affection stood Fikenhild, whose outward show of love covered his inward envy and hatred. In everything these two were Childe Horn's inseparable comrades, and it seemed that an equal bond of love united the three.

The Saracen Invasion

One day as King Murry was riding over the cliffs by the sea with only two knights in attendance he noticed some unwonted commotion in a little creek not far from where he was riding, and he at once turned his horse's head in that direction and galloped down to the shore. On his arrival in the small harbour he saw fifteen great ships of strange build, and their crews, Saracens all armed for war, had already landed, and were drawn up in warlike array. The odds against the king were terrible, but he rode boldly to the invaders and asked, "What brings you strangers here? Why have you sought our land?" A Saracen leader, gigantic of stature, spoke for them all and replied, "We are here to win this land to the law of Mahomet and to drive out the Christian law. We will slay all the inhabitants that believe on Christ. You yourself shalt be our first conquest, for you shalt not leave this place alive." Thereupon the Saracens attacked the little band, and though the three Christians fought valiantly they were soon slain. The Saracens then spread over the land, slaying, burning, and pillaging, and forcing all who loved their lives to renounce the Christian faith and become followers of Mahomet. When Queen Godhild heard of her husband's death and saw the ruin of her people she fled from her palace and all her friends and betook herself to a solitary cave, where she lived unknown and undiscovered, and continued her

Christian worship while the land was overrun with pagans. Ever she prayed that God would protect her dear son, and bring him at last to his father's throne.

Horn's Escape

Soon after the king's death the Saracens had captured Childe Horn and his twelve comrades, and the boys were brought before the pagan emir. They would all have been slain at once or flayed alive, but for the beauty of Childe Horn, for whose sake their lives were spared. The old emir looked keenly at the lads, and said, "Horn, you are a bold and valiant youth, of great stature for your age, and of full strength, yet I know you have not yet reached your full growth. If we release you with your companions, in years to come we shall dearly rue it, for you will become great champions of the Christian law and will slay many of us. Therefore you must die. But we will not slay you with our own hands, for you are noble lads, and shall have one feeble chance for your lives. You shall be placed in a boat and driven out to sea, and if you all are drowned we shall not grieve overmuch. Either you must die or we, for I know we shall dearly abide your king's death if you youths survive." Thereupon the lads were all taken to the shore, and, weeping and lamenting, were thrust into a rudderless boat, which was towed out to sea and left helpless.

Arrival in Westernesse

The other boys sat lamenting and bewailing their fate, but Childe Horn, looking round the boat, found a pair of oars, and as he saw that the boat was in the grasp of some strong current he rowed in the same direction, so that the boat soon drifted out of sight of land. The other lads were a dismal crew, for they thought their death was certain, but Horn toiled hard at his rowing all night, and with the dawn grew so weary that he rested for a little on his oars. When the rising sun made things clear, and he could see over the crests of the waves, he stood up in the boat and uttered a cry of joy. "Comrades," cried he, "dear friends, I see land not far away. I hear the sweet songs of birds and see the soft green grass. We have come to some unknown land and have saved our lives." Then Athulf took up the glad tidings and began to cheer the forlorn little crew, and under Horn's skilful guidance the little boat grounded gently and safely on the sands of Westernesse. The boys sprang on shore, all but Childe Horn having no thought of the past night and the journey; but he stood by the boat, looking sadly at it.

Farewell to the Boat

"Boat,' he said, 'which have borne me on my way,

Have you good days beside a summer sea!

May never wave prevail to sink you deep!

Go, little boat, and when you come home

Greet well my mother, mournful Queen Godhild;

Tell her, frail skiff, her dear son Horn is safe.

Greet, too, the pagan lord, Mahomet's thrall,

The bitter enemy of Jesus Christ,

And bid him know that I am safe and well.

Say I have reached a land beyond the sea,

Whence, in God's own good time, I will return

Then he shall feel my vengeance for my sire."

Then sorrowfully he pushed the boat out into the ocean, and the ebbing tide bore it away, while Horn and his companions set their faces resolutely towards the town they could see in the distance.

King Ailmar and Childe Horn

As the little band were trudging wearily towards the town they saw a knight riding towards them, and when he came nearer they became aware that he must be some noble of high rank. When he halted and began to question them, Childe Horn recognised by his tone and bearing that this must be the king. So indeed it was, for King Ailmar of Westernesse was one of those noble rulers who see for themselves the state of their subjects and make their people happy by free, unrestrained intercourse with them. When the king saw the forlorn little company he said, "Whence are ye, fair youths, so strong and comely of body? Never have I seen so goodly a company of thirteen youths in the realm of Westernesse. Tell me whence you come, and what you seek." Childe Horn assumed the office of spokesman, for he was leader by birth, by courage, and by intellect. "We are lads of noble families in Suddene, sons of Christians and of men of lofty station. Pagans have taken the land and slain our parents, and we boys fell into their hands. These heathen have slain and tortured many Christian men, but they had pity upon us, and put us into an old boat with no sail or rudder. So we drifted all night, until I saw your land at dawn, and our boat came to the shore. Now we are in your power, and you may do with us what you will, but I pray you to have pity on us and to feed us, that we may not perish utterly."

Ailmar's Decision

King Ailmar was touched as greatly by the simple boldness of the spokesman as by the hapless plight of the little troop, and he answered, smiling, "You shalt have nought but help and comfort, fair youth. But I pray you, tell me your name." Horn answered readily, "King, may all good betide thee! I am named Horn, and I have come journeying in a boat on the sea - now I am here in your land." King Ailmar replied, "Horn! That is a good name: mayst you well enjoy it. Loud may this Horn sound over hill and dale till the blast of so mighty a Horn shall be heard in many lands from king to king, and its beauty and strength be known in many countries. Horn, come you with me and be mine, for I love you and will not forsake you."

Childe Horn at Court

The king rode home, and all the band of stranger youths followed him on foot, but for Horn he ordered a horse to be procured, so that the lad rode by his side; and thus they came back to the court. When they entered the hall he summoned his steward, a noble old knight named Athelbrus, and gave the lads in charge to him, saying, "Steward, take these foundlings of mine, and train them well in the duties of pages, and later of squires. Take especial care with the training of Childe Horn, their chief; let him learn all your knowledge of woodcraft and fishing, of hunting and hawking, of harping and singing; teach him how to carve before me, and to serve the cup solemnly at banquets; make him your favourite pupil and train him to be a knight as good as yourself. His companions you mayst put into other service, but Horn shall be my own page, and afterwards my squire." Athelbrus obeyed the king's command, and the thirteen youths soon found themselves set to learn the duties of court life, and showed themselves apt scholars, especially Childe Horn, who did his best to satisfy the king and his steward on every point.

The Princess Rymenhild

When Childe Horn had been at court for six years, and was now a squire, he became known to all courtiers, and all men loved him for his gentle courtesy and his willingness to do any service. King Ailmar made no secret of the fact that Horn was his favourite squire, and the Princess Rymenhild, the king's fair daughter, loved him with all her heart. She was the heir to the throne, and no man had ever gainsaid her will, and now it seemed to her unreasonable that she should not be allowed to wed a good and gallant youth whom she loved. It was difficult for her to speak alone with him, for she had six maiden attendants who waited on her continually, and Horn was engaged with his duties either in the hall, among the knights, or waiting on the king. The difficulties only seemed to increase her love, and she grew pale and wan, and looked miserable. It seemed to her that if she waited longer her love would never be happy, and in her impatience she took a bold step.

Athelbrus Deceives the Princess

She kept her chamber, called a messenger, and said to him, "Go quickly to Athelbrus the steward, and bid him come to me at once. Tell him to bring with him the squire Childe Horn, for I am lying ill in my room, and would be amused. Say I expect them quickly, for I am sad in mind, and have need of cheerful converse." The messenger bowed, and, withdrawing, delivered the message exactly as he had received it to Athelbrus, who was much perplexed thereby. He wondered whence came this sudden illness, and what help Childe Horn could give. It was an unusual thing for the squire to be asked into a lady's bower, and still more so into that of a princess, and Athelbrus had already felt some suspicion as to the sentiments of the royal lady towards the gallant young squire. Considering all these things, the cautious steward deemed it safer not to expose young Horn to the risks that might arise from such an interview, and therefore induced Athulf to wait upon the princess and to endeavour to personate his more distinguished companion. The plan succeeded beyond expectation in the dimly lighted room, and the infatuated princess soon startled the unsuspecting squire by a warm and unreserved declaration of her affection. Recovering from his natural amazement, he modestly disclaimed a title to the royal favour and acknowledged his identity.

On discovering her mistake the princess was torn by conflicting emotions, but finally relieved the pressure of self-reproach and the confusion of maiden modesty by overwhelming the faithful steward with denunciation and upbraiding, until at last, in desperation, the poor man promised, against his better judgment, to bring about a meeting between his lovelorn mistress and the favoured squire.

Athelbrus Summons Horn

When Rymenhild understood that Athelbrus would fulfil her desire she was very glad and joyous; her sorrow was turned into happy expectation, and she looked kindly upon the old steward as she said, "Go now quickly, and send him to me in the afternoon. The king will go to the wood for sport and pastime, and Horn can easily remain behind; then he can stay with me till my father returns at eve. No one will betray us; and when I have met my beloved I care not what men may say."

Then the steward went down to the banqueting-hall, where he found Childe Horn fulfilling his duties as cup-bearer, pouring out and tasting the red wine in the king's golden goblet. King Ailmar asked many questions about his daughter's health, and when he learnt that her malady was much abated he rose in gladness from the table and summoned his courtiers to go with him into the greenwood. Athelbrus bade Horn tarry, and when the gay throng had passed from the hall the steward said gravely, "Childe Horn, fair and courteous, my beloved pupil, go now to the bower of the Princess Rymenhild, and stay there to fulfil all her commands. It may be you shalt hear strange things, but keep rash and bold words in your heart, and let them not be upon your tongue. Horn, dear lad, be true and loyal now, and you shalt never repent it."

Horn and Rymenhild

Horn listened to this unusual speech with great astonishment, but, since Sir Athelbrus spoke so solemnly, he laid all his words to heart, and thus, marvelling greatly, departed to the royal bower. When he had knocked at the door, and had been bidden to come in, entering, he found Rymenhild sitting in a great chair, intently regarding him as he came into the room. He knelt down to make obeisance to her, and kissed her hand, saying, "Sweet be your life and soft your slumbers, fair Princess Rymenhild! Well may it be with your gentle ladies of honour! I am here at your command, lady, for Sir Athelbrus the steward, bade me come to speak with you. Tell me your will, and I will fulfil all your desires." She arose from her seat, and, bending towards him as he knelt, took him by the hand and lifted him up, saying, "Arise and sit beside me, Childe Horn, and we will drink this cup of wine together." In great astonishment the youth did as the princess bade, and sat beside her, and soon, to his utter amazement, Rymenhild avowed her love for him, and offered him her hand. "Have pity on me, Horn, and plight me your troth, for in very truth I love you, and have loved you long, and if you will I will be your wife."

Horn Refuses the Princess

Now Horn was in evil case, for he saw full well in what danger he would place the princess, Sir Athelbrus, and himself if he accepted the proffer of her love. He knew the reason of the steward's warning, and tried to think what he might say to satisfy the princess and yet not be disloyal to the king. At last he replied, "Christ save and keep you, my lady Rymenhild, and give you joy of your husband, whosoever he may be! I am too lowly born to be worthy of such a wife; I am a mere foundling, living on your father's bounty. It is not in the course of nature that such as I should wed a king's daughter, for there can be no equal match between a princess and a landless squire."

Rymenhild was so disheartened and ashamed at this reply to her loving appeal that her colour changed, she turned deadly pale, began to sigh, flung her arms out wildly, and fell down in a swoon. Childe Horn lifted her up, full of pity for her deep distress, and began to comfort her and try to revive her. As he held her in his arms he kissed her often, and said:

"Lady, dear love, take comfort and be strong!

For I will yield me wholly to your guidance

If you will compass one great thing for me.

Plead with King Ailmar that he dub me knight,

That I may prove me worthy of your love.

Soon shall my knighthood be no idle dream,

And I will strive to do your will, dear heart."

Now at these words Rymenhild awoke from her swoon, and made him repeat his promise. She said, "Ah! Horn, that shall speedily be done. Ere the week is past you shalt be Sir Horn, for my father loves you, and will grant the dignity most willingly to one so dear to him. Go now quickly to Sir Athelbrus, give him as a token of my gratitude this golden goblet and this ring; pray him that he persuade the king to dub you knight. I will repay him with rich rewards for his gentle courtesy to me. May Christ help him to speed you in your desires!" Horn then took leave of Rymenhild with great affection, and found Athelbrus, to whom he delivered the gifts and the princess's message, which the steward received with due reverence.

Horn Becomes a Knight

This plan seemed to Athelbrus very good, for it raised Horn to be a member of the noble Order of Knights, and would give him other chances of distinguishing himself. Accordingly he went to the king as he sat over the evening meal, and spoke thus, "Sir King, hear my words, for I have counsel for you. Tomorrow is the festival of your birth, and the whole realm of Westernesse must rejoice in its master's joy. Wear you your crown in solemn state, and I think it were nought amiss if you should knight young Horn, who will become a worthy defender of your throne." "That were well done," said King Ailmar. "The youth pleases me, and I will knight him with my own sword. Afterwards he shall knight his twelve comrades the same day."

The next day the ceremony of knighting was performed with all solemnity, and at its close a great banquet was prepared and all men made merry. But Princess Rymenhild was somewhat sad. She could not descend to the hall and take her customary place, for this was a feast for knights alone, and she would not be without her betrothed one moment longer, so she sent a messenger to fetch Sir Horn to her bower.

Horn and Athulf Go to Rymenhild

Now that Horn was a newly dubbed knight he would not allow the slightest shadow of dishonour to cloud his conduct; accordingly, when he obeyed Rymenhild's summons he was accompanied by Athulf. "Welcome, Sir Horn and Sir Athulf," she cried, holding out her hands in greeting. "Love, now that you have your will, keep your plighted word and make me your wife; release me from my anxiety and do as you have said."

"Dear Rymenhild, hold you yourself at peace,' said young Sir Horn, 'I will perform my vow. But first I must ride forth to prove my might; I must conquer hardships, and my own worse self, Ere I can hope to woo and wed my bride. We are but new-fledged knights of one day's growth, and yet we know the custom of our state is first to fight and win a hero's name, then afterwards to win a lady's heart. This day will I do bravely for your love and show my valour and my deep devotion in prowess against the foes of this your land. If I come back in peace, I claim my wife."

Rymenhild protested no longer, for she saw that where honour was concerned Horn was inflexible. "My true knight," she said, "I must in sooth believe you, and I feel that I may. Take this ring engraved with my name, wrought by the most skilled worker of our court, and wear it always, for it has magic virtues. The gems are of such saving power that you shalt fear no strokes in battle, nor ever be cast down if you gaze on this ring and think of your love. Athulf, too, shall have a similar ring. And now, Horn, I commend you to God, and may Christ give you good success and bring you back in safety!"

Horn's First Exploit

After taking an affectionate farewell of Rymenhild, Horn went down to the hall, and, seeing all the other new-made knights going into the banquet, he slipped quietly away and betook himself to the stables. There he armed himself secretly and mounted his white charger, which pranced and reared joyfully as he rode away; and Horn began to sing for joy of heart, for he had won his chief desire, and was happy in the love of the king's daughter. As he rode by the shore he saw a stranger ship drawn up on the beach, and recognised the banner and accoutrements of her Saracen crew, for he had never forgotten the heathens who had slain his father. "What brings you here?" he asked angrily, and as fearlessly as King Murry had done, and received the same answer, "We will conquer this land and slay the inhabitants." Then Horn's anger rose, he gripped his sword, and rushed boldly at the heathens, and slew many of them, striking off a head at each blow. The onslaught was so sudden that the Saracens were taken by surprise at first, but then they rallied and surrounded Horn, so that matters began to look dangerous for him. Then he remembered the betrothal ring, and looked on it, thinking earnestly of Rymenhild, his dear love, and such courage came to him that he was able to defeat the pagans and slay their leader. The others, sorely wounded - for none escaped unhurt - hurried on board ship and put to sea, and Horn, bearing the Saracen leader's head on his sword's point, rode back to the royal palace. Here he related to King Ailmar this first exploit of his knighthood, and presented the head of the foe to the king, who rejoiced greatly at Horn's valour and success.

Rymenhild's Dream

The next day the king and all the court rode out hunting, but Horn made an excuse to stay behind with the princess, and the false and wily Fikenhild was also left at home, and he crept secretly to Rymenhild's bower to spy on her. She was sitting weeping bitterly when Sir Horn entered. He was amazed. "Love, for mercy's sake, why do you weep so sorely?" he asked; and she replied, "I have had a mournful dream. I dreamt that I was casting a net and had caught a great fish, which began to burst the net. I greatly fear that I shall lose my chosen fish." Then she looked sadly at Horn. But the young knight was in a cheery mood, and replied, "May Christ and St. Stephen turn your dream to good! If I am your fish, I will never deceive you nor do anything to displease you, and hereto I plight you my troth. But I would rather interpret your dream otherwise. This great fish which burst your net is someone who wishes us ill, and will do us harm soon." Yet in spite of Horn's brave words it was a sad betrothal, for Rymenhild wept bitterly, and her lover could not stop her tears.

Fikenhild's False Accusation

Fikenhild had listened to all their conversation with growing envy and anger, and now he stole away silently, and met King Ailmar returning from the chase.

"King Ailmar,' said the false one, 'see, I bring a needed warning, that you guard yourself, for Horn will take your life; I heard him vow to slay you, or by sword or fire, this night. If you demand what cause of hate he has, know that the villain woos your only child, fair Rymenhild, and hopes to wear your crown. E'en now he tarries in the maiden's bower, as he has often done, and talks with her with guileful tongue, and cunning show of love. Unless you banish him you are not safe in life or honour, for he knows no law."

The king at first refused to believe the envious knight's report, but, going to Rymenhild's bower, he found apparent confirmation, for Horn was comforting the princess, and promising to wed her when he should have done worthy feats of arms. The king's wrath knew no bounds, and with words of harsh reproach he banished Horn at once, on pain of death. The young knight armed himself quickly and returned to bid farewell to his betrothed.

Horn's Banishment

"Dear heart," he said, "now your dream has come true, and your fish must needs break the net and be gone. The enemy whom I foreboded has wrought us woe. Farewell, my own dear Rymenhild; I may no longer stay, but must wander in alien lands. If I do not return at the end of seven years take yourself a husband and tarry no longer for me. And now take me in your arms and kiss me, dear love, ere I go!" So they kissed each other and bade farewell, and Horn called to him his comrade Athulf, saying, "True and faithful friend, guard well my dear love. You have never forsaken me; now do you keep Rymenhild for me." Then he rode away, and, reaching the haven, hired a good ship and sailed for Ireland, where he took service with King Thurston, under the name of Cuthbert. In Ireland he became sworn brother to the king's two sons, Harold and Berild, for they loved him from the first moment they saw him, and were in no way jealous of his beauty and valour.

Horn Slays the Giant Emir

When Christmas came, and King Thurston sat at the banquet with all his lords, at noontide a giant strode into the hall, bearing a message of defiance. He came from the Saracens, and challenged any three Irish knights to fight one Saracen champion. If the Irish won the pagans would withdraw from Ireland; if the Irish chiefs were slain the Saracens would hold the land. The combat was to be decided the next day at dawn. King Thurston accepted the challenge, and named Harold, Berild, and Cuthbert (as Horn was called) as the Christian champions, because they were the best warriors in Ireland; but Horn begged permission to speak, and said, "Sir King, it is not right that one man should fight against three, and one heathen hound think to resist three Christian warriors. I will fight and conquer him alone, for I could as easily slay three of them." At last the king allowed Horn to attempt the combat alone, and spent the night in sorrowful musing on the result of the contest, while Horn slept well and arose and armed himself cheerily. He then aroused the king, and the Irish troop rode out to a fair and level green lawn, where they found the emir with many companions awaiting them. The combat began at once, and Horn gave blows so mighty that the pagan onlookers fell swooning through very fear, till Horn said, "Now, knights, rest for a time, if it pleases you." Then the Saracens spoke together, saying aloud that no man had ever so daunted them before except King Murry of Suddene.

This mention of his dead father aroused Horn, who now realized that he saw before him his father's murderers. His anger was kindled, he looked at his ring and thought of Rymenhild, and then, drawing his sword again, he rushed at the heathen champion. The giant fell pierced through the heart, and his companions fled to their ships, hotly pursued by Horn and his company. Much fighting there was, and in the hot strife near the ships the king's two sons, Harold and Berild, were both slain.

Horn Refuses the Throne

Sadly they were laid on a bier and brought back to the palace, their sorrowful father lamenting their early death; and when he had wept his fill the mournful king came into the hall where all his knights silently awaited him. Slowly he came up to Horn as he sat a little apart from the rest, and said, "Cuthbert, will you fulfil my desire? My heirs are slain, and you are the best knight in Ireland for strength and beauty and valour; I implore you to wed Reynild, my only daughter (now, alas! my only child), and to rule my realm. Will you do so, and lift the burden of my cares from my weary shoulders?" But Horn replied, "O Sir King, it were wrong for me to receive your fair daughter and heir and rule your realm, as you do offer. I shall do you yet better service, my liege, before I die; and I know that your grief will change ere seven years have passed away. When that time is over, Sir King, give me my reward: you shalt not refuse me your daughter when I desire her." To this King Thurston agreed, and Horn dwelt in Ireland for seven years, and sent no word or token to Rymenhild all the time.

Rymenhild's Distress

In the meantime Princess Rymenhild was in great perplexity and trouble, for a powerful ruler, King Modi of Reynes, wooed her for his wife, and her own betrothed sent her no token of his life or love. Her father accepted the new suitor for her hand, and the day of the wedding was fixed, so that Rymenhild could no longer delay her marriage. In her extremity she besought Athulf to write letters to Horn, begging him to return and claim his bride and protect her; and these letters she delivered to several messengers, bidding them search in all lands until they found Sir Horn and gave the letters into his own hand. Horn knew nought of this, till one day in the forest he met a weary youth, all but exhausted, who told how he had sought Horn in vain. When Horn declared himself, the youth broke out into loud lamentations over Rymenhild's unhappy fate, and delivered the letter which explained all her distress. Now it was Horn's turn to weep bitterly for his love's troubles, and he bade the messenger return to his mistress and tell her to cease her tears, for Horn would be there in time to rescue her from her hated bridegroom. The youth returned joyfully, but as his boat neared the shore of Westernesse a storm arose and the messenger was drowned; so that Rymenhild, opening her tower door to look for expected succour, found her messenger lying dead at the foot of the tower, and felt that all hope was gone. She wept and wrung her hands, but nothing that she could do would avert the evil day.

Horn and King Thurston

As soon as Horn had read Rymenhild's letter he went to King Thurston and revealed the whole matter to him. He told of his own royal parentage, his exile, his knighthood, his betrothal to the princess, and his banishment; then of the death of the Saracen leader who had slain King Murry, and the vengeance he had taken.

Then he ended, "King Thurston, be you wise, and grant my boon; repay the service I have yielded you; help me to save my princess from this woe. I will take counsel for fair Reynild's fate, for she shall wed Sir Athulf, my best friend, my truest comrade and my doughtiest knight. If ever I have risked my life for you and proved myself in battle, grant my prayer."

To this the king replied, "Childe Horn, do what you wilt."

Horn Returns on the Wedding-day

Horn at once invited Irish knights to accompany him to Westernesse to rescue his love from a hateful marriage, and many came eagerly to fight in the cause of the valiant Cuthbert who had defended Ireland for seven years. Thus it was with a goodly company that Horn took ship, and landed in King Ailmar's realm; and he came in a happy hour, for it was the wedding-day of Princess Rymenhild and King Modi of Reynes. The Irish knights landed and encamped in a wood, while Horn went on alone to learn tidings. Meeting a palmer, he asked the news, and the palmer replied, "I have been at the wedding of Princess Rymenhild, and a sad sight it was, for the bride was wedded against her will, vowing she had a husband though he is a banished man. She would take no ring nor utter any vows; but the service was read, and afterwards King Modi took her to a strong castle, where not even a palmer was given entrance. I came away, for I could not endure the pity of it. The bride sits weeping sorely, and if report be true her heart is like to break with grief."

Horn Is Disguised as a Palmer

"Come, palmer," said Horn, "lend me your cloak and scrip. I must see this strange bridal, and it may be I shall make some there repent of the wrong they have done to a helpless maiden. I will essay to enter." The change was soon made, and Horn darkened his face and hands as if bronzed with Eastern suns, bowed his back, and gave his voice an old man's feebleness, so that no man would have known him; which done, he made his way to King Modi's new castle. Here he begged admittance for charity's sake, that he might share the broken bits of the wedding feast; but he was churlishly refused by the porter, who would not be moved by any entreaties. At last Horn lost all patience, and broke open the door, and threw the porter out over the drawbridge into the moat; then, once more assuming his disguise, he made his way into the hall and sat down in the beggars' row.

The Recognition

Rymenhild was weeping still, and her stern husband seemed only angered by her tears. Horn looked about cautiously, but saw no sign of Athulf, his trusted comrade; for he was at this time eagerly looking for his friend's coming from the lofty watch-tower, and lamenting that he could guard the princess no longer. At last, when the banquet was nearly over, Rymenhild rose to pour out wine for the guests, as the custom was then; and she bore a horn of ale or wine along the benches to each person there. Horn, sitting humbly on the ground, called out, "Come, courteous Queen, turn to me, for we beggars are thirsty folk." Rymenhild smiled sadly, and, setting down the horn, filled a bowl with brown ale, for she thought him a drunkard. "Here, drink this, and more besides, if you wilt; I never saw so bold a beggar," she said. But Horn refused. He handed the bowl to the other beggars, and said, "Lady, I will drink nought but from a silver cup, for I am not what you think me. I am no beggar, but a fisher, come from afar to fish at your wedding feast. My net lies nearby, and has lain there for seven years, and I have come to see if it has caught any fish. Drink to me, and drink to Horn from your horn, for far have I journeyed."

When the palmer spoke of fishing, and his seven-year-old net, Rymenhild felt cold at heart; she did not recognise him, but wondered greatly when he bade her drink "to Horn." She filled her cup and gave it to the palmer, saying, "Drink your fill, and then tell me if you have ever seen Horn in your wanderings." As the palmer drank, he dropped his ring into the cup; then he returned it to Rymenhild, saying, "Queen, seek out what is in your draught." She said nothing then, but left the hall with her maidens and went to her bower, where she found the well-remembered ring she had given to Horn in token of betrothal. Greatly she feared that Horn was dead, and sent for the palmer, whom she questioned as to whence he had got the ring.

Horn's Stratagem

Horn thought he would test her love for him, since she had not recognised him, so he replied, "By St. Giles, lady, I have wandered many a mile, far into realms of the West, and there I found Sir Horn ready prepared to sail home to your land. He told me that he planned to reach the realm of Westernesse in time to see you before seven years had passed, and I embarked with him. The winds were favourable and we had a quick voyage, but alas! he fell ill and died. When he lay dying he begged me piteously, 'Take this ring, from which I have never been parted, to my dear lady Rymenhild,' and he kissed it many times and pressed it to his breast. May God give his soul rest in Paradise!"

When Rymenhild heard those terrible tidings she sighed deeply and said, "O heart, burst now, for you shalt never more have Horn, for love of whom you have been tormented so sorely!" Then she fell upon her bed, and grasped the dagger which she had concealed there; for if Horn did not come in time she had planned to slay both her hateful lord and her that very night. Now, in her misery, she set the dagger to her heart, and would have slain herself at once, had not the palmer interrupted her. Rushing forward, he exclaimed, "Dear Queen and lady, I am Horn, your own true love. Do you not recognise me? I am Childe Horn of Westernesse. Take me in your arms, dear love, and kiss me welcome home." As Rymenhild stared incredulously at him, letting the dagger fall from her trembling hand, he hurriedly cast away his disguise, brushed off the disfiguring stain he had put on his cheeks, and stood up straight and strong, her own noble knight and lover. What joy they had together! How they told each other of all their adventures and troubles, and how they embraced and kissed each other!

Horn Slays King Modi

When their joy had become calmer, Horn said to his lady, "Dear Rymenhild, I must leave you now, and return to my knights, who are encamped in the forest. Within an hour I will return to the feast and give the king and his guests a stern lesson." Then he flung away the palmer's cloak, and went forth in knightly array; while the princess went up to the watch-tower, where Athulf still scanned the sea for some sign of Horn's coming. Rymenhild said, "Sir Athulf, true friend, go quickly to Horn, for he has arrived, and with him he brings a great army." The knight gladly hastened to the courtyard, mounted his steed, and soon overtook Horn. They were greatly rejoiced to meet again, and had much to tell each other and to plan for that day's work.

In the evening Horn and his army reached the castle, where they found the gates undone for them by their friends within, and in a short but desperate conflict King Modi and all the guests at the banquet were slain, except Rymenhild, her father, and Horn's twelve comrades. Then a new wedding was celebrated, for King Ailmar durst not refuse his daughter to the victor, and the bridal was now one of real rejoicing, though the king was somewhat bitter of mood.

Horn's Departure

When the hours wore on to midnight, Horn, sitting beside his bride, called for silence in the hall, and addressed the king thus, "Sir King, I pray you listen to my tale, for I have much to say and much to explain. My name is in sooth Horn, and I am the son of King Murry of Suddene, who was slain by the Saracens. You did cherish me and give me knighthood, and I proved myself a true knight on the very day when I was dubbed. You did love me then, but evil men accused me to you and I was banished. For seven years I have lived in a strange land; but now that I have returned, I have won your fair daughter as my bride. But I cannot dwell here in idleness while the heathen hold my father's land. I vow by the Holy Rood that I will not rest, and will not claim my wife, until I have purified Suddene from the infidel invaders, and can lay its crown at Rymenhild's feet. Do you, Oh King, guard well my wife till my return."

The king consented to this proposal, and, in spite of Rymenhild's grief, Horn immediately bade her farewell, and with his whole army embarked for Suddene, this time accompanied by Athulf, but leaving the rest of his comrades for the protection of his wife.

The Apostate Knight

The wind blew fair for Suddene, and the fleet reached port. The warriors disembarked, and marched inland, to encamp for the night in a wood, where they could be hidden. Horn and Athulf set out at midnight to endeavour to obtain news of the foe, and soon found a solitary knight sleeping. They awoke him roughly, saying, "Knight, awake! Why sleep you here? What do you guard?" The knight sprang lightly from the ground, saw their faces and the shining crosses on their shields, and cast down his eyes in shame, saying, "Alas! I have served these pagans against my will. In time gone by I was a Christian, but now I am a coward renegade, who forsook his God for fear of death at the hands of the Saracens! I hate my infidel masters, but I fear them too, and they have forced me to guard this district and keep watch against Horn's return. If he should come to his own again how glad I should be! These infidels slew his father, and drove him into exile, with his twelve comrades, among whom was my own son, Athulf, who loved the prince as his own life. If the prince is yet alive, and my son also, God grant I may see them both again! Then would I joyfully die."

The Recognition

Horn answered quickly, "Sir Knight, be glad and rejoice, for here are we, Horn and Athulf, come to avenge my father and retake my realm from the heathen." Athulf's father was overcome with joy and shame; he hardly dared to embrace his son, yet the bliss of meeting was so great that he clasped Athulf in his arms and prayed his forgiveness for the disgrace he had brought upon him. The two young knights said nothing of his past weakness, but told him all their own adventures, and at last he said, "What is your true errand here? Can you two alone slay the heathen? Dear Childe Horn, what joy this will be to your mother Godhild, who still lives in a solitary retreat, praying for you and for the land!" Horn broke in on his speech with "Blessed be the hour when I returned! Thank God that my mother yet lives! We are not alone, but I have an army of valiant Irish warriors, who will help me to regain my realm."

The Reconquest of Suddene

Now the king blew his horn, and his host marched out from the wood and prepared to attack the Saracens. The news soon spread that Childe Horn had returned, and many men who had accepted the faith of Mahomet for fear of death now threw off the hated religion, joined the true king's army, and were rebaptized. The war was not long, for the Saracens had made themselves universally hated, and the inhabitants rose against them; so that in a short time the country was purged of the infidels, who were slain or fled to other lands. Then Horn brought his mother from her retreat, and together they purified the churches which had been desecrated, and restored the true faith. When the land of Suddene was again a Christian realm King Horn was crowned with solemn rites, and a great coronation feast was held, which lasted too long for Horn's true happiness.

Fikenhild Imprisons Rymenhild

During Horn's absence from Westernesse, his comrades watched carefully over Rymenhild; but her father, who was growing old, had fallen much under the influence of the plausible Fikenhild. From the day when Fikenhild had falsely accused Horn to the king, Ailmar had held him in honour as a loyal servant, and now he had such power over the old ruler that when he demanded Rymenhild's hand in marriage, saying that Horn was dead in Suddene, the king dared not refuse, and the princess was bidden to make ready for a new bridal. For this day Fikenhild had long been prepared; he had built a massive fortress on a promontory, which at high tide was surrounded by the sea, but was easy of access at the ebb; there he now led the weeping princess, and began a wedding feast which was to last all day, and to end only with the marriage ceremony at night.

Horn's Dream

That same night, before the feast, King Horn had a terrible dream. He thought he saw his wife taken on board ship; soon the ship began to sink, and Rymenhild held out her hands for rescue, but Fikenhild, standing in safety on shore, beat her back into the waves with his sword. With the agony of the sight Horn awoke, and, calling his comrade Athulf, said, "Friend, we must depart today. My wife is in danger from false Fikenhild, whom I have trusted too much. Let us delay no longer, but go at once. If God will, I hope to release her, and to punish Fikenhild. God grant we come in time!" With some few chosen knights, King Horn and Athulf set out, and the ship drove darkling through the sea, they knew not where. All the night they drifted on, and in the morning found themselves beneath a newly built castle, which none of them had seen before.

Horn's Disguise

While they were seeking to moor their boat to the shore, one of the castle windows looking out to sea opened, and they saw a knight standing and gazing seaward, whom they speedily recognised; it was Athulf's cousin, Sir Arnoldin, one of the twelve comrades, who had accompanied the princess there in the hope that he might yet save her from Fikenhild; he was now looking, as a forlorn hope, over the sea, though he believed Horn was dead. His joy was great when he saw the knights, and he came out to them and speedily told them of Rymenhild's distress and the position of affairs in the castle. King Horn was not at a loss for an expedient even in this distress. He quickly disguised himself and a few of his comrades as minstrels, harpers, fiddlers, and jugglers. Then, rowing to the mainland, he waited till low tide, and made his way over the beach to the castle, accompanied by his disguised comrades. Outside the castle walls they began to play and sing, and Rymenhild heard them, and, asking what the sounds were, gave orders that the minstrels should be admitted. They sat on benches low down the hall, tuning their harps and fiddles and watching the bride, who seemed unhappy and pale. When Horn sang a lay of true love and happiness, Rymenhild swooned for grief, and the king was touched to the heart with bitter remorse that he had tried her constancy so long, and had allowed her to endure such hardships and misery for his sake.

Death of Fikenhild

King Horn now glanced down and saw the ring of betrothal on his finger, where he had worn it ever, except that fateful day when he had given it as a token of recognition to Rymenhild. He thought of his wife's sufferings, and his mind was made up. Springing from the minstrels' bench, he strode boldly up the hall, throwing off his disguise, and, shouting, "I am King Horn! False Fikenhild, you shalt die!" he slew the villain in the midst of his men. Horn's comrades likewise flung off their disguise, and soon overpowered the few of the household who cared to fight in their dead master's cause. The castle was taken for King Ailmar, who was persuaded to nominate Sir Arnoldin his heir, and the baronage of Westernesse did homage to him as the next king. Horn and his fair wife begged the good old steward Sir Athelbrus to go with them to Suddene, and on the way they touched at Ireland, where Reynild, the king's fair daughter, was induced to look favourably on Sir Athulf and accept him for her husband. The land of King Modi, which had now no ruler, was committed to the care of Sir Athelbrus, and Horn and Rymenhild at last reached Suddene, where the people received their fair queen with great joy, and where they dwelt in happiness till their lives' end.

Legends of King Arthur

Folk-Lore and Legends: English is a late nineteenth-century anthology edited by Charles John Tibbitts and first published in London by W. W. Gibbings in 1890. It gathers a varied selection of English material, chapbook texts, local legends, fairy lore and giant tales, framed by an introductory note on the perceived "dying out" of traditional narratives in modern England.

Legends of King Arthur" appears as one of the closing pieces in the book and is Tibbitts's prose presentation of a Northumbrian sleeper-under-the-hill tradition associated with Sewingshields Castle. The story relates how a farmer and, in a variant, a shepherd accidentally find a subterranean hall where Arthur, Guinevere, their court and hounds lie in enchanted sleep.

Immemorial tradition has asserted that king Arthur, his queen Guinevere, court of lords and ladies, and his hounds, were enchanted in some cave of the crags, or in a hall below the castle of Sewingshields, and would continue entranced there till someone should first blow a bugle-horn that lay on a table near the entrance into the hall, and then "with the sword of stone" cut a garter, also placed there beside it. But none had ever heard where the entrance to this enchanted hall was, till a farmer at Sewingshields, about fifty years since, was sitting knitting on the ruins of the castle, and his clew fell and ran downwards through a bush of briars and nettles, as he supposed, into a deep subterranean passage. Full in the faith that the entrance into King Arthur's hall was now discovered, he cleared the briary portal of its weeds and rubbish, and entering a vaulted passage, followed, in his darkling way, the web of his clew. The floor was infested with toads and lizards, and the dark wings of bats, disturbed by his unhallowed intrusion, flitted fearfully around him. At length his sinking faith was strengthened by a dim, distant light, which, as he advanced, grew gradually lighter, till, all at once, he entered a vast and vaulted hall, in the centre of which a fire without fuel, from a broad crevice in the floor, blazed with a high and lambent flame, that showed all the carved walls and fretted roof, and the monarch and his queen and court reposing around in a theatre of thrones and costly couches. On the floor, beyond the fire, lay the faithful and deep-toned pack of thirty couple of hounds, and on the table, before it, the spell-dissolving horn, sword, and garter. The farmer reverently but firmly grasped the sword, and as he drew it leisurely from its rusty scabbard, the eyes of the monarch and his courtiers began to open, and they rose till they sat upright. He cut the garter, and, as the sword was being slowly sheathed, the spell assumed its ancient power, and they all gradually sank to rest, but not before the monarch lifted up his eyes and hands, and exclaimed:

"O woe betide that evil day

On which this witless wight was born

Who drew the sword - the garter cut,

But never blew the bugle-horn."

Of this favourite tradition, the most remarkable variation is respecting the place where the farmer descended. Some say that after the king's denunciation, terror brought on loss of memory, and the farmer was unable to give any correct account of his adventure, or the place where it occurred. All agree that Mrs. Spearman, the wife of another and more recent occupier of the estate, had a dream in which she saw a rich hoard of treasure among the ruins of the castle, and that for many days together she stood over workmen employed in searching for it, but without success.

Another version of the story has less of "the pomp of sceptred state" than the preceding, and has evidently sprung from a baser original, but its verity is not the less to be depended upon.

A shepherd one day, in quest of a strayed sheep on the crags, had his attention aroused by the scene around him assuming an appearance he had never before witnessed. There seemed to be about it a more than wonted vividness, and such a deep solemnity hung over its aspect, that its features became, as it were, palpably impressed upon his mind. While he was musing upon this unexpected occurrence, his steps were arrested by a ball of thread. This he laid hold of, and, pursuing the path it pointed out, found it led into a cavern, in the recesses of which, as the guiding line used by miners in their explorations of devious passages, it appeared to lose itself. As he approached, he felt perforce constrained to follow the strange conductor, that had so marvellously come into his hands. After passing through a long and dreary vestibule, he entered into an apartment in the interior. An immense fire blazed on the hearth, and cast its broad flashes with a wild, unearthly glare, to the remotest corner of the chamber. Over it was placed a huge caldron, as if preparations were being made for a feast on an extensive scale. Two hounds lay couchant on either side of the fire-place, in the stillness of unbroken slumber. The only remarkable piece of furniture in the apartment was a table covered with green cloth. At the head of the table, a being, considerably advanced in years, of a dignified mien, and clad in the habiliments of war, sat, as it were, fast asleep, in an arm-chair. At the other end of the table lay a horn and a sword. Notwithstanding these signs of life, there prevailed a dead silence throughout the chamber, the very feeling of which made the shepherd reflect that he had advanced far beyond the limits of human experience, and that he was now in the presence of objects that belonged more to death than to life. The very idea made his flesh creep. He, however, had sufficient fortitude to advance to the table and lift the horn. The hounds pricked up their ears most fearfully, and the grisly veteran started up on his elbow, and raising his half-unwilling eyes, told the staggered hind that if he would blow the horn and draw the sword, he would confer upon him the honours of knighthood to last through time. Such unheard-of dignities, from a source so ghastly, either met with no appreciation from the awe-stricken swain, or the terror of finding himself alone in the company, it might be of malignant phantoms, who were only tempting him to his ruin, became too urgent to be resisted, and, therefore, proposing to divide the peril with a comrade, he groped his darkling way, as best his quaking limbs could support him, back to the blessed daylight. On his return, with a reinforcement of strength and courage, all traces of the former scene had disappeared. The crags presented their usual cheerful and quiet aspect, and every vestige of the opening of a cavern was obliterated. Thus failed another of the repeated opportunities for releasing the spell-bound king of Britain from the "charmed sleep of ages." Within his rocky chamber he still sleeps on, as tradition tells, till the appointed hour; or if invited by his enchantress to participate in the illusions of the fairy festival, it has charms for him no longer. "Wasted with care," he sits beside her, the banquet untasted, and the pageantry unmasked.

St Herbert, the Hermit of Derwentwater

St Herbert, the Hermit of Derwentwater is one of the early chapters in Wilson Armistead's Tales and Legends of the English Lakes, first published in London by Simpkin, Marshall & Co. in 1891. The book is a prose collection of historical sketches, legends and romanticised narratives set around the Lake District.

Within this framework, the St Herbert story focuses on the figure of the Anglo-Saxon recluse associated with St Herbert's Island on Derwentwater. The tale blends hagiography and local legend.

Amongst the beautiful isles of Derwentwater, that named St. Herbert's Island deserves a more than ordinary notice, as well for its beauty as its historical associations. This insulated paradise includes an extent of four or five acres, well covered with wood, and is situated near the centre of the lake. It obtained its name from St. Herbert, a priest and confessor, who, "to avoid the intercourse of man, and that nothing might withdraw his attention from unceasing mortification and prayer," about the middle of the 7th century, chose this island for his lonely abode.

"St. Herbert here came,

And here for many seasons, from the world

Removed, and the affections of the world,

He dwelt in solitude."

The locality was well adapted to the severity of his religious life; he was surrounded by the lake, from whence he received his simple diet. On every hand the voice of waterfalls excited the most solemn strains of meditation - rocks and mountains were his daily prospect, inspiring his mind with ideas of the might and majesty of the Creator.

That St. Herbert had his hermitage on this island is certain from the authority of the venerable Bede, as well as from tradition, and nowhere could ancient eremite find more profound peace, or a place of so great beauty, whence to bear on the wings of imagination his orisons to heaven.

St. Herbert was particularly distinguished for his friendship to St. Cuthbert, bishop of Lindisfarne, with whom he was contemporary; and, according to a legendary tale, at the intercession of St. Herbert both these holy men expired on the same day, and in the same hour and minute, which, according to Bede, was in 678 or 687.

At Lindisfarne, expecting death,

The good St. Cuthbert lay,

With wasted frame and feeble breath;

And monks were there to pray.

The brotherhood had gathered round,

His parting words to hear,

To see his saintly labours crown'd,

And stretch him on the bier.

His eyes grew dim; his voice sunk low;

The choral song arose;

And ere its sounds had ceas'd to flow,

His spirit found repose.

At that same hour, a holy man,

St. Herbert, well renown'd,

Gave token that his earthly span

Had reach'd its utmost bound.

St. Cuthbert, in his early years,

Had led him on his way

When the tree falls, the fruit it bears

Will surely, too, decay.

The monks of Lindisfarne meanwhile,

Were gazing on their dead;

At that same hour, in Derwent isle,

A kindred soul had fled.

There is but little information on record respecting St. Herbert, and had it not been for his intimacy with St. Cuthbert, his name probably would not have been handed down to posterity at all. In truth, he did little more than pray and meditate on this spot. It was his wish to live and die unknown. Though one in spirit, St. Cuthbert and the Hermit of Derwentwater were entirely dissimilar in character. St. Cuthbert was bishop of Lindisfarne, an eminent preacher in his day, whose eloquence influenced the will of many, and whose active zeal contributed to the advancement of the then dominant church, of which he was one of the main pillars and rulers. St. Herbert was altogether a man of prayer. He retired from the world to this solitude, and passed his days in devotion. The two saints used to meet once a year for spiritual communion. Which had most influence with the Ruler of heaven we cannot say.

The venerable Bede writes thus of the Hermit of Derwentwater, "There was a certain priest, revered for his uprightness and perfect life and manners, named Herberte, who had a long time been in union with the man of God (St. Cuthbert of Farn Isle), in the bond of spiritual love and friendship. For living a solitary life in the isle of that great and extended lake, from whence proceeds the river of Derwent, he used to visit St. Cuthbert every year, to receive from his lips the doctrine of eternal life. When this holy priest heard of St. Cuthbert's coming to Lugubalia, he came after his usual manner, desiring to be comforted more and more, with the hope of everlasting bliss, by his divine exhortations. As they sat together, and enjoyed the hopes of heaven, among other things the bishop said, "Remember, brother, Herberte, that whatsoever you have to say and ask of me, you do it now, for after we depart hence, we shall not meet again, and see one another corporally in this world; for I know well the time of my dissolution is at hand, and the laying aside of this earthly tabernacle draws on apace.'

"When Herberte heard this, he fell down at his feet, and with many sighs and tears beseeched him, for the love of the Lord, that he would not forsake him, but to remember his faithful brother and associate, and make intercession with the gracious God, that they might depart hence into heaven together, to behold His grace and glory whom they had in unity of spirit served on earth; for you know I have ever studied and laboured to live according to your pious and virtuous instructions; and in whatsoever I offended or omitted, through ignorance and frailty, I straight-way used my earnest efforts to amend after your ghostly counsel, will, and judgment. At this earnest and affectionate request of Herbertes, the bishop went to prayer, and presently being certified in spirit that his petition to heaven would be granted, said, "Arise, my dear brother, weep not, but let your rejoicing be with exceeding gladness, for the great mercy of God has granted unto us our prayer.'

"The truth of which promise and prophecy was well proved in that which ensued; for their separation was the last that befell them on earth; on the same day, which was the 19th day of March, their souls departed from their bodies, and were straight in union in the beatific sight and vision; and were transported hence to the kingdom of heaven, by the service and hands of angels."

It is probable the hermit's little oratory or chapel might be kept in repair after his death, as a particular veneration appears to have been paid to this retreat, and the memory of the saint; for, at the distance of almost seven centuries, we find this place resorted to in holy services and processions, and the hermit's memory celebrated in religious offices. The remains of the hermitage are still visible;

and near to these hallowed ruins stands a small grotto of unhewn stone, called the New Hermitage, erected some years ago by Sir Wilfrid Lawson, to whose representative the island at present belongs. The dwelling of the anchorite consisted of two apartments, one of which, about twenty feet in length by sixteen in width, appears to have been his chapel; the other, whose dimensions are considerably less, was his cell.

The passion for solitude and a recluse life which reigned in the days of this saint, and was cherished by the monastic school, at first sight may appear to us uncouth and enthusiastic; yet when we examine into those times, our astonishment will cease, if we consider the estate of those men, who, under all the prejudices of education, were living in an age of ignorance, vassalage, and rapine; and we shall rather applaud than condemn a devotee, who, disgusted with the world and the sins of men, consigns his life to the service of the Deity in retirement. We may suppose we hear the saint exclaiming in *Young's Excursion* with the poet:

"Blest be that hand Divine, which gently laid

My heart at rest beneath this humble shade;

The world's a stately bark, on dangerous seas,

With pleasure seen, but boarded at our peril;

Here on a single plank, thrown safe on shore,

I hear the tumult of the distant throng,

As that of seas remote or dying storms;

And meditate on scenes more silent still,

Pursue my theme, and fight the fear of death.

Here, like a shepherd gazing from his hut,

Touching his reed or leaning on his staff,

Eager ambition's fiery chase I see;

I see the circling hunt of noisy men

Burst law's enclosures, leap the mounds of right,

Pursuing and pursued, each other's prey;

As wolves for rapine, as the fox for wiles,

Till Death, that mighty hunter, earths them all."

Wordsworth has the following beautiful lines on the Hermit of Derwentwater:

"If you, in the dear love of some one friend,

Hast been so happy that you know what thoughts

Will sometimes, in the happiness of love,

Make the heart sink, then will you reverence

This quiet spot; and, stranger, not unmoved

Will you behold this shapeless heap of stones,

The desolate ruins of St. Herbert's cell.

There stood his threshold; there was spread the roof

That sheltered him, a self-secluded man,

After long exercise in social cares,

And offices humane, intent to adore

The Deity with undistracted mind,

And meditate on everlasting things

In utter solitude. But he had left

A fellow-labourer, whom the good man loved

As his own soul. And when, with eye upraised

To heaven, he knelt before the crucifix,

While o'er the lake the cataract of Ladore

Pealed to his orison, and when he paced

Along the beach of this small isle, and thought

Of his companion, he would pray that both

(Now that their earthly duties were fulfilled)

Might die in the same moment. Nor in vain

So prayed he! As our chroniclers report,

Though here the hermit numbered his last hours,

Far from St. Cuthbert, his beloved friend,

Those holy men died in the self-same day."

The Compassion of Constantine

The Compassion of Constantine appears in Maud Isabel Ebbutt's Hero-Myths & Legends of the British Race, first published by George G. Harrap & Company in London in 1910 as part of Harrap's "Myths and Legends" series, with later reprints through the 1910s and 1920s.

Ebbutt's episode draws on the medieval legend-cycle surrounding the Emperor Constantine's conversion, particularly the strand preserved in John Gower's Confessio Amantis, which presents Constantine as an exemplar of "true charity" and pity towards the poor and sick.

Youth of Constantine

Constantine the great was the eldest son of the Roman Emperor Constantius and the British Princess Helena, or Elena, and was brought up as a devout worshipper of the many gods of Rome. The lad grew up strong and handsome, of a tall and majestic figure, skilled in all warlike exercises, and, as he fought in the civil wars between the various Roman emperors, he showed himself a bold and prudent general in battle, a friendly and popular leader in time of peace. The popularity of the youthful Constantine was dangerous to him, and he needed, and showed, great skill in evading the deadly jealousy of the old Emperor Diocletian, and the hatred of his father's rival, Galerius. At last, however, his position became so dangerous that Constantius felt his son's life was no longer safe, and earnestly begged him to visit his native land of Britain, where Constantius had just been proclaimed emperor and had defeated the wild Caledonians. The excuse given was that Constantius was in bad health and needed his son; but not until the young man was actually in Britain would his anxious father avow that he feared for his son's life.

Acclaimed Emperor

When the half-British Constantius died, Constantine, who was the favourite of the Roman soldiery of the west, was at once acclaimed as emperor by his devoted troops. He professed unwillingness to accept the honour, and it is said that he even tried in vain to escape on horseback from the affectionate solicitations of his soldiers. Seeing the uselessness of further protest, Constantine accepted the imperial title, and wrote to Galerius claiming the throne and justifying his acceptance of the unsought dignity thrust upon him. Galerius acquiesced in the inevitable, and granted Constantine the inferior title of "Cæsar," with rule over Western Europe, and the wise prince was content to wait until favouring circumstances should destroy his rivals and give him that sole sway over the Roman Empire for which he was so well fitted. He had now reached the age of thirty, had fought valiantly in the wars in Egypt and Persia, and had risen by merit to the rank of tribune. His marriage with Fausta, the daughter of the Emperor Maximian, and his elevation to the rank of Augustus brought him nearer to the attainment of his ambition; and at length the defeat and death of his rivals placed him at the head of the world-wide empire of Rome. It is to some period previous to Constantine's elevation to the supreme authority that we must refer the following story, told by Gower in his "Confessio Amantis" as an example of that true charity, which is the mother of pity, and makes a man's heart so tender that:

"Though he might himself relieve,

Yet he would not another grieve,"

but in order to give pleasure to others would bear his own trouble alone.

Becomes a Leper

The noble Constantine, Emperor of Rome, was in the full flower of his age, goodly to look upon, strong and happy, when a great and sudden affliction came upon him: leprosy attacked him. The horrible disease showed itself first in his face, so that no concealment was possible, and if he had not been the emperor he would have been driven out to live in the forests and wilds. The leprosy spread from his face till it entirely covered his body, and became so bad that he could no longer ride out or show himself to his people. When all cures had been tried and had failed, Constantine withdrew himself from his lords, gave up all use of arms, abandoned his imperial duties, and shut himself in his palace, where he lived such a secluded life in his own apartments that Rome had, as it were, no lord, and all men throughout the empire talked of his illness and prayed their gods to heal him. When everything seemed to be in vain, Constantine yielded to the prayer of his council, that he would summon all the doctors, learned men, and physicians from every realm to Rome, that they might consider his illness and try if any cure could be found for his malady.

Rewards Offered for his Cure

A proclamation went forth throughout the world and great rewards were offered to any man who should heal the emperor. Tempted by the rewards and the great fame to be won, there came leeches and physicians from Persia and Arabia, and from every land that owned the sway of Rome, philosophers from Greece and Egypt, and magicians and sorcerers from the unexplored desert of the east. But, though Constantine tried all the remedies suggested or recommended by the wise men, his leprosy grew no better, but rather worse, and even magic could give him no help.

Again the learned men assembled and consulted what they should advise, for all were loath to abandon the emperor in his great distress, but they were all at a loss. They sat in silence, till at last one very old and very wise man, a great physician from Arabia, arose and said, "Now that all else has failed, and naught is of any avail, I will tell of a remedy of which I have heard. It will, I believe, certainly cure our beloved emperor, but it is very terrible, and therefore I was loath to name it till every other means had been tried and failed, for it is a cruel thing for any man to do. Let the Emperor dip himself in a full bath of the blood of infants and children, seven years old or under, and he shall be healed, and his leprosy shall fall from him; for this malady is not natural to his body, and it demands an unnatural cure."

Constantine Assents Regretfully

The proposal was a terrible one to the assembly, and many would not agree to it at first, but when they considered that nothing else would heal the emperor they at length gave way, and sent two from among themselves to bring the news to Constantine, who was waiting for them in his darkened room. He was horrified when he heard the counsel they brought, and at first utterly refused to carry out so evil a plan; but because his life was very dear to his people, and because he felt that he had a great work to do in the world, he ultimately agreed, with many tears, to try the terrible remedy.

A Cruel Proclamation

Thereupon the council drew up letters, under the emperor's hand and seal, and sent them out to all the world, bidding all mothers with children of seven years of age or under to bring them with speed to Rome, that there the blood of the innocents might prove healing to the emperor's malady. Alas! what weeping and wailing there was among the mothers when they heard this cruel decree! How they cried, and clasped their babes to their breasts, and how they called Constantine crueller than Herod, who killed the Holy Innocents! The eastern ruler, they said, slew only the infants of one poor village, but their emperor, more ruthless, claimed the lives of all the young children of his whole empire.

Constantine is Conscience-stricken

But though the mothers lamented bitterly, they must needs bow to the emperor's decree, whether they were lief or loath, and thus a great multitude gathered in the great courtyard of the imperial palace at Rome: women nursing sucking-babes at the breast, or holding toddling infants by the hand, or with little children running by their sides, and all so heart-broken and woebegone that many swooned for very grief. The mothers wailed aloud, the children cried, and the tumult grew until Constantine heard it, where he sat lonely and wretched in his darkened room. He looked out of his window on the mournful sight in the courtyard, and was roused as from a trance, saying to himself, "O Divine Providence, who have formed all men alike, lo! the poor man is born, lives, suffers, and dies, just as does the rich; to wise man and fool alike come sickness and health; and no man may avoid that fortune which Nature's law has ordained for him. Likewise to all men are Nature's gifts of strength and beauty, of soul and reason, freely and fully given, so that the poor child is born as capable of virtue as the king's son; and to each man is given free will to choose virtue or vice. Yet you give to men diversity of rank, wealth or poverty, lordship or servitude, not always according to their deserts; so much the more virtuous should that man be to whom you have put other men in subjection, men who are nevertheless his fellows and wear his likeness. Thou, Oh God, who have put Nature and the whole universe under law, would have all men rule themselves by law, and you have said that a man must do to others such things as he would have done to himself."

His Noble Resolve

Thus Constantine spoke within himself as he stood by the window and looked upon the weeping mothers and children, the very sentinels of his palace pitying them, and trying in vain to comfort them; and a strife grew strong within him between his natural longing for healing and deliverance from this loathsome disease which had darkened his life, and the pity he felt for these poor creatures, and his horror at the thought of so much human blood to be shed for himself alone. The great moaning of the woeful mothers came to him and the pitiful crying of the children, and he thought, "What am I that my health is to outweigh the lives and happiness of so many of my people? Is my life of more value to the world than those of all the children who must shed their blood for my healing? Surely each babe is as precious as Constantine the

Emperor!" Thus his heart grew so tender and so full of compassion that he chose rather to die by this terrible sickness than to commit so great a slaughter of innocent children, and he renounced all other physicians, and trusted himself wholly to God's care.

He Announces his Determination

He at once summoned his council, and announced to them his resolution, giving as his reason, "He that will be truly master must be ever servant to pity!" and without delay the anxious mothers were told that their children were free and safe, for the emperor had renounced the cure, and needed their blood no longer. What raptures of rejoicing there were, what outpouring of blessing on the emperor, what songs of praise and thanks from the women wild with joy, cannot be fully told; and yet greater grew their joy and thankfulness when Constantine, calling his high officials, bade them take all his gathered treasures and distribute them among the poor women, that they might feed and clothe their children, and so return home untouched by any loss, and recompensed in some degree for their sufferings. Thus did Constantine obey the behests of pity, and try to atone for the wrong to which he had consented in his heart, and which he had so nearly done to his people.

The Victims Sent Home Happy

Home to all parts of the Roman Empire went the women, bearing with them their happy children, and the rich gifts they had received. Each one thanked and blessed the emperor, and sang his praises, where before she had passed with tears and bitter curses on his head; each woman shared her joy with her neighbours; and the very children learnt from their mothers and fathers to pray for the healing of their great lord, who had given up his own will and sacrificed his own cure for gentle pity's sake. Thus the whole world prayed for Constantine's healing.

A Vision

Lo! it never yet was known that charity went unrequited and this Constantine now learnt in his own glad experience; for that same night, as he lay asleep, God sent to him a vision of two strangers, men of noble face and form, whom he reverenced greatly, and who said to him, "O Constantine, because you have obeyed the voice of pity, you have deserved pity; therefore shalt you find such mercy, that God, in His great pity, will save you. Double healing shalt you receive, first for your body, and next for your woeful soul; both alike shall be made whole. And that you mayst not despair, God will grant you a sign - your leprosy shall not increase till you have sent to Mount Celion, to Sylvester and all his clergy. There they dwell in secret for dread of you, who have been a foe to the law of Christ, and have destroyed those who preach in His Holy Name. Now you have appeased God somewhat by your good deed, since you have had pity on the innocent blood, and have spared it; for this you shalt find teaching, from Sylvester to the salvation of both body and soul. You will need no other leech." The emperor, who had listened with eagerness and awe, now spoke, "Great thanks I owe to you, my lords, and I will indeed do as you have said, but one thing I would pray you - what shall I tell Sylvester of the name or estate of those who send me to him?" The two strangers said, "We are the Apostles Peter and Paul, who endured death here in your city of Rome for the Holy Name of Christ, and we bid Sylvester teach and baptize you into the true faith. So shall the Roman Empire become the kingdom of the Lord and of His Christ." So saying, they blessed him, and passed into the heavens out of his sight, and Constantine awoke from his slumber and knew that he had seen a vision. He called aloud eagerly, and his servants waiting in an outer room ran in to him quickly, for there was urgency in his voice. To them Constantine told his vision and the command which was laid upon him.

Sylvester Summoned

Messengers rode in hot haste to Mount Celion, and inquired long and anxiously for Sylvester. At last they found him, a holy and venerable man, and summoned him, saying, "The Emperor calls for you: come, therefore, at once." Sylvester's clergy were greatly affrighted, not knowing what this summons might mean, and dreading the death of their dear bishop and master; but he went forth gladly, not knowing to what fate he was going. When he was brought to the palace the emperor greeted him kindly, and told him all his dream, and the command of the Apostles Peter and Paul, and ended with these words, "Now I have done as the vision bade, and have fetched you here: tell me, I pray, the glad tidings which shall bring healing to my body and soul." When Sylvester heard this speech he was filled with joy and wonder, and thanked God for the vision He had sent to the emperor, and then he began to preach to him the Christian faith: he told of the Fall of Man, and the redemption of the world by the death and resurrection of Jesus Christ, of the Ascension of Jesus and His return at the Day of Judgment, of the justice of God, who will judge all men impartially according to their works, good or bad, and of the life of joy or misery to come. As Sylvester taught, the monarch listened and believed, and, when the tale was ended, announced his conversion to the true faith, and said he was ready, with his whole heart and soul, to be baptized.

Constantine Baptized

At the emperor's command, they took the great vessel of silver which had been made for the children's blood, and Sylvester bade them fill it with pure water from the well. When that was done with all haste, he bade Constantine stand therein, so that the water reached his chin. As the holy rite began a great light like the sun's rays shone from heaven into the place, and upon Constantine; and as the sacred words were being read there fell now and again from his body scales like those of a fish, till there was nothing left of his horrible disease; and thus in baptism Constantine was purified in body and soul.

William of Cloudeslee

*William of Cloudeslee, in Maud Isabel Ebbutt's Hero-Myths &
Legends of the British Race, works as a bridge between medieval
outlaw balladry and an early twentieth-century idea of "national
character." Ebbutt treats William as a companion figure to Robin
Hood, another marksman-outlaw whose loyalty to friends and
family sits uneasily alongside his rebellion against authority.*

*William's story helps to sketch a mythic lineage for the British Isles
in which bravery, skill and stubborn integrity recur from age to
age. She streamlines and dignifies the older ballad material so that
it reads less as tavern entertainment and more as a semi-heroic
episode, suitable for young readers who are being offered a usable
past. The violence and rough justice of the original tradition are
softened, but not wholly removed; instead they are reframed as the
necessary risks taken by a man who refuses to abandon his own.*

Introduction

The outlaw of medieval England has always possessed a potent
charm for the minds of less rebellious persons. No doubt now the
attraction has somewhat waned, for in the exploration of distant
lands and the study of barbaric tribes, men can find that breadth of
outlook, that escape from narrow conventionalities, which they

could formerly gain only by the cult of the "noble outlaw." The romance of life for many a worthy citizen must have been found in secret sympathy with Robin Hood and his merry band of banished men, robbing the purse-proud to help the needy and gaily defying law and authority.

To the poor, however, the outlaw was something more than an easy entrance to the realms of romance; he was a real embodiment of the spirit of liberty. Of all the unjust laws which the Norman conquerors laid upon England, perhaps the most bitterly resented were the forest laws, and resistance to them was the most popular form of national independence. Hence it follows that we find outlaw heroes popular very early in our history—heroes who stand in the mind of the populace for justice and true liberty against the oppressive tyranny of subordinate officials, and who are always taken into favour by the king, the fount of true justice.

Famous Outlaws

There is some slight tinge of the "outlaw hero" in Hereward, but the outlaw period of that patriot's life is but an episode in his defence of England against William the Norman. There is a fully developed outlaw hero, the ideal of the type, in Robin Hood, but he has been somewhat idealized and ennobled by being transformed into a banished Earl of Huntingdon. Less known, but equally heroic, is William of Cloudeslee, the William Tell of England, whose fame is that of a good yeoman, a good archer, and a good patriot.

The Outlaws

In the green forest of Englewood, in the "North Country," not far from the fortified town of Carlisle, dwelt a merry band of outlaws. They were not evildoers, but sturdy archers and yeomen, whose outlawry had been incurred only for shooting the king's deer. Indeed, to most men of that time—that is, to most men who were not in the royal service—the shooting of deer, and the pursuit of game in general, were not only venial offences, but the most natural thing in life. The royal claim to exclusive hunting in the vast forests of Epping, Sherwood, Needwood, Barnesdale, Englewood, and many others seemed preposterous to the yeomen who lived on the borders of the forests, and they took their risks and shot the deer and made venison pasty, convinced that they were wronging no one and risking only their own lives. They had the help and sympathy of many a man who was himself a law-abiding citizen, as well as the less understanding help of the town mob and the labourers in the country.

The Leaders

While the outlaws of merry Sherwood recognised no chief but Robin Hood and no foe but the Sheriff of Nottingham, the outlaws of Englewood were under the headship of three famous archers, brothers-in-arms sworn to stand by each other, but not brothers in blood. Their names were Adam Bell, William of Cloudeslee, and Clym of the Cleugh; and of the three William of Cloudeslee alone was married. His wife, fair Alice of Cloudeslee, dwelt in a strong house within the walls of Carlisle, with her three children, for they were not included in William's outlawry. It was possible thus for her to send her husband warning of any attack planned by the Sheriff of Carlisle on the outlaws, and she had saved him and his comrades from surprise already.

William Goes to Carlisle

When the blithe spring had come, and the forest was beautiful with its fresh green leaves, William began to long for his home and family; he had not ventured into Carlisle for some time, and it was more than six months since he had seen his wife's face. Little wonder was it, then, that he announced his intention of visiting his home, at the risk of capture by his old enemy the Sheriff. In vain his comrades dissuaded him from the venture. Adam Bell was especially urgent in his advice that William should remain in the greenwood.

"You shall not go to Carlisle, brother, by my advice, nor with my consent. If the sheriff or the justice should know that you are in the town short would be your shrift and soon your span of life would end. Stay with us, and we will fetch you tidings of your wife."

William replied, "Nay, I must go myself; I cannot rest content with tidings only. If all is well I will return by prime tomorrow, and if I fail you at that hour you may be sure I am taken or slain; and I pray you guard well my family, if that be so."

Taking leave of his brother outlaws, William made his way unobserved into the town and came to his wife's dwelling. It was closely shut, with doors strongly bolted, and he was forced to knock long on the window before his wife opened the shutter to see who the importunate visitor was.

"Let me in quickly, my own Alice," he said. "I have come to see you and my three children. How have you fared this long time?"

"Alas!" she replied, hurriedly admitting him, and bolting the door again, "why have you come now, risking your dear life to gain news of us? Know you not that this house has been watched for more than six months, so eager are the sheriff and the justice to capture and hang you? I would have come to you in the forest, or sent you word of our welfare. I fear—oh, how I fear!—lest your coming be known!"

The Old Woman's Treachery

"Now that I am here, let us make merry," said William. "No man has seen me enter, and I would fain enjoy my short stay with you and my children, for I must be back in the forest by prime tomorrow. Can you not give a hungry outlaw food and drink?"

Then Dame Alice bustled about and prepared the best she had for her husband; and when all was ready a very happy little family sat down to the meal, husband and wife talking cheerily together, while the children watched in wondering silence the father who had been away so long and came to them so seldom.

There was one inmate of the house who saw in William's return a means of making shameful profit. She was an old bedridden woman, apparently paralysed, whom he had rescued from utter poverty seven years before. During all that time she had lain on a bed near the fire, had shared all the life of the family, and had never once moved from her couch. Now, while husband and wife talked together and the darkness deepened in the room, this old impostor slipped from her bed and glided stealthily out of the house.

News Brought to the Sheriff

It happened that the king's assize was being held just then in Carlisle, and the sheriff and his staunch ally the justice were sitting together in the Justice Hall. There this treacherous old woman hurried with all speed and pushed into the hall, forcing her way through the crowd till she came near the sheriff. "Ha! what would you, good woman?" asked he, surprised. "Sir, I bring tidings of great value." "Tell your tidings, and I shall see if they be of value or no. If they are I will reward you handsomely." "Sir, this night William of Cloudeslee has come into Carlisle, and is even now in his wife's house. He is all alone, and you can take him easily. Now what will you pay me, for I am sure this news is much to you?" "You say truth, good woman. That bold outlaw is the worst of all who kill the king's deer in his forest of Englewood, and if I could but catch him I should be well content. Dame, you shall not go without a recompense for your journey here and for your loyalty." The sheriff then bade his men give the old woman a piece of scarlet cloth, dyed in grain, enough for a gown, and the treacherous hag hid the gift under her cloak, hastened away to Alice's house, and slipped unperceived into her place again, hiding the scarlet cloth under the bed-coverings.

The Hue and Cry

Immediately he had heard of Cloudeslee's presence in Carlisle the sheriff sent out the hue and cry, and with all speed raised the whole town, for though none hated the outlaws, men dared not refuse to obey the king's officer. The justice, too, joined the sheriff in the congenial task of capturing an outlaw whose condemnation was already pronounced. With all the forces at their disposal, sheriff and justice took their way towards the house where William and Alice unconscious of the danger besetting them, still talked lovingly together.

Suddenly the outlaw's ears, sharpened by woodcraft and by constant danger, heard a growing noise coming nearer and nearer. He knew the sound of the footsteps of many people, and among the casual shuffling of feet recognised the ominous tramp of soldiers.

"Wife, we are betrayed," cried William. "Here comes the sheriff to take me."

The Siege of the House

Alice ran quickly up to her bedchamber and opened a window

looking to the back, and saw, to her despair, that soldiers beset the house on every side and filled all the neighbouring streets. Behind them pressed a great throng of citizens, who seemed inclined to leave the capture of the outlaw to the guard. At the same moment William from the front called to his wife that the sheriff and justice were besieging the house on that side.

"Alas! dear husband, what shall we do?" cried Alice. "Accursed be all treason! But who can have betrayed you to your foes? Go into my bedchamber, dear William, and defend yourself there, for it is the strongest room in the house. The children and I will go with you, and I will guard the door while you defend the windows."

The plan was speedily carried out, and while William took his stand by the window Alice seized a pole-axe and stationed herself by the door. "No man shall enter this door alive while I live," she said.

The Attack

From the window Cloudeslee could perceive his mortal enemies the justice and the sheriff; and drawing his good longbow, he shot with deadly aim fair at the breast of the justice. It was well for the latter then that he wore a suit of good chain-mail under his robes; the arrow hit his breast and split in three on the mail.

"Beshrew the man that clad you with that mail coat! You would have been a dead man now if your coat had been no thicker than mine," said William.

"Yield yourself, Cloudeslee, and lay down your bow and arrows," said the justice. "You cannot escape, for we have you safe."

"Never shall my husband yield; it is evil counsel you give," exclaimed the brave wife from her post at the door.

The House is Burnt

The sheriff, who grew more angered as the hours passed on and Cloudeslee was not taken, now cried aloud, "Why do we waste time trifling here? The man is an outlaw and his life is forfeit. Let us burn him and his house, and if his wife and children will not leave him they shall all burn together, for it is their own choice."

This cruel plan was soon carried out. Fire was set to the door and wooden shutters, and the flames spread swiftly; the smoke rolled up in thick clouds into the lofty bedchamber, where the little children, crouching on the ground, began to weep for fear.

"Alas! must we all die?" cried fair Alice, grieving for her children.

William opened the window and looked out, but there was no chance of escape; his foes filled every street and lane around the house. "Surely they will spare my wife and babes," he thought; and, tearing the sheets from the bed, he made a rope, with which he let down to the ground his children, and last of all his weeping wife.

He called aloud to the sheriff, "Sir Sheriff, here have I trusted to you my chief treasures. For God's sake do them no harm, but wreak all your wrath on me!"

Gentle hands received Alice and her babes, and friendly citizens led them from the press; but Alice went reluctantly, in utter grief, knowing that her husband must be burnt with his house or taken by his foes; but for her children she would have stayed with him. William continued his wonderful archery, never missing his aim, till all his arrows were spent, and the flames came so close that his bowstring was burnt in two. Great blazing brands came falling upon him from the burning roof, and the floor was hot beneath his feet. "An evil death is this!" thought he. "Better it were that I should take sword and buckler and leap down amid my foes and so die, striking good blows in the throng of enemies, than stay here and let them see me burn."

Thereupon he leaped lightly down, and fought so fiercely that he nearly escaped through the throng, for the worthy citizens of Carlisle were not anxious to capture him; but the soldiers, urged by the sheriff and justice, threw doors and windows upon him, hampered his blows, and seized and bound him, and cast him into a deep dungeon.

The Sheriff Gives Sentence

"Now, William of Cloudeslee," said the sheriff, "you shall be hanged with speed as soon as I can have a new gallows made. So noted an outlaw merits no common gibbet; a new one is most fitting. Tomorrow at prime you shall die. There is no hope of rescue, for the gates of the town shall be shut. Your dear friends, Adam Bell and Clym of the Cleugh, would be helpless to save you, though they brought a thousand more like themselves, or even all the devils in Hell."

Early next morning the justice arose, went to the soldiers who guarded the gates, and forbade them to open till the execution was over; then he went to the market-place and superintended the erection of a specially lofty gallows, beside the pillory.

News is Brought to the Greenwood

Among the crowd who watched the gallows being raised was a little lad, the town swineherd, who asked a bystander the meaning of the new gibbet.

"It is put up to hang a good yeoman, William of Cloudeslee, more's the pity! He has done no wrong but kill the King's deer, and that merits not hanging. It is a foul shame that such injustice can be wrought in the king's name."

The little lad had often met William of Cloudeslee in the forest, and had carried him messages from his wife; William had given the boy many a dinner of venison, and now he determined to help his friend if he could. The gates were shut and no man could pass out, but the boy stole along the wall till he found a crevice, by which he clambered down outside. Then he hastened to the forest of Englewood, and met Adam Bell and Clym of the Cleugh.

"Come quickly, good yeomen; you tarry here too long. While you are at ease in the greenwood your friend, William of Cloudeslee, is taken, condemned to death, and ready to be hanged. He needs your help this very hour."

Adam Bell groaned. "Ah! if he had but taken our advice he would have been here in safety with us now. In the greenwood there is no sorrow or care, but when William went to the town he was running into trouble." Then, bending his bow, he shot with unerring aim a hart, which he gave to the lad as recompense for his labour and goodwill.

The Outlaws Go to Carlisle

"Come," said Clym to Adam Bell, "let us tarry no longer, but take our bows and arrows and see what we can do. By God's grace we will rescue our brother, though we may abide it full dearly ourselves. We will go to Carlisle without delay."

The morning was fair as the two yeomen strode from the deep green shades of Englewood Forest along the hard white road leading to Carlisle Town. They were in time as yet, but when they drew near the wall they were amazed to see that no entrance or exit was possible; the gates were shut fast.

Stepping back into the green thickets beside the road, the two outlaws consulted together. Adam Bell was for a valiant attempt to storm the gate, but Clym suddenly bethought him of a wiser plan.

Clym's Stratagem

He said, "Let us pretend to be messengers from the king, with urgent letters to the justice. Surely that should win us admission. But alas! I forgot. How can we bear out our pretence, for I am no learned clerk. I cannot write."

Said Adam Bell, "I can write a good clerkly hand. Wait one instant and I will speedily have a letter written; then we can say we have the king's seal. The plan will do well enough, for I hold the gate-keeper no learned clerk, and this will deceive him."

Indeed, the letter which he quickly wrote and folded and sealed was very well and clearly written, and addressed to the Justice of Carlisle. Then the two bold outlaws hastened up the road and thundered on the town gates.

They Enter the Town

So long and loud they knocked that the warder came in great wrath, demanding who dared to make such clamour.

Adam Bell replied, "We are two messengers come straight from our lord the king." Clym of the Cleugh added, "We have a letter for the justice which we must deliver into his own hands. Let us in speedily to perform our errand, for we must return to the king in haste."

"No," the warder replied, "that I cannot do. No man may enter these gates till a false thief and outlaw be safely hanged. He is William of Cloudeslee, who has long deserved death."

Now Clym saw that matters were becoming desperate, and time

was passing too quickly, so he adopted a more violent tone. "Ah, rascal, scoundrel, madman!" he said. "If we be delayed here any longer you shalt be hanged for a false thief! To keep the king's messengers waiting thus! Canst you not see the king's seal? Canst you not read the address of the royal letter? Ah, blockhead, you shalt dearly abide this delay when my lord knows thereof."

Thus speaking, he flourished the forged letter, with its false seal, in the porter's face; and the man, seeing the seal and the writing, believed what was told to him. Reverently he took off his hood and bent the knee to the king's messengers, for whom he opened wide the gates, and they entered, walking warily.

They Keep the Gates

"At last we are within Carlisle walls, and glad thereof are we," said Adam Bell, "but when and how we shall go out again Christ only knows, who harrowed Hell and brought out its prisoners."

"Now if we had the keys ourselves we should have a good chance of life," said Clym, "for then we could go in and out at our own will." "Let us call the warder," said Adam. When he came running at their call both the yeomen sprang upon him, flung him to the ground, bound him hand and foot, and cast him into a dark cell, taking his bunch of keys from his girdle. Adam laughed and shook the heavy keys. "Now I am gate-ward of merry Carlisle. See, here are my keys. I think I shall be the worst warder they have had for three hundred years. Let us bend our bows and hold our arrows ready, and walk into the town to deliver our brother."

The Fight in the Market-place

When they came to the market-place they found a dense crowd of sympathizers watching pityingly the hangman's cart, in which lay William of Cloudeslee, bound hand and foot, with a rope round his neck. The sheriff and the justice stood near the gallows, and Cloudeslee would have been hanged already, but that the sheriff was hiring a man to measure the outlaw for his grave. "You shall have the dead man's clothes, good fellow, if you make his grave," he said.

Cloudeslee's courage was still undaunted. "I have seen as great a marvel ere now," he said, "as that a man who digs a grave for another may lie in it himself, in as short a time as from now to prime."

"You speak proudly, my fine fellow, but hanged you shall be, if I do it with my own hand," retorted the sheriff furiously.

Now the cart moved a little nearer to the scaffold, and William was raised up to be ready for execution. As he looked round the dense mass of faces his keen sight soon made him aware of his friends. Adam Bell and Clym of the Cleugh stood at one corner of the market-place with arrow on string, and their deadly aim bent at the sheriff and justice, whose horses raised them high above the murmuring throng. Cloudeslee showed no surprise, but said aloud, "Lo! I see comfort, and hope to fare well in my journey. Yet if I might have my hands free I would care little what else befell me."

The Rescue

Now Adam said quietly to Clym, "Brother, do you take the justice, and I will shoot the sheriff. Let us both loose at once and leave them dying. It is an easy shot, though a long one."

Thus, while the sheriff yet waited for William to be measured for his grave, suddenly men heard the twang of bowstrings and the whistling flight of arrows through the air, and at the same moment both sheriff and justice fell writhing from their steeds, with the grey goose feathers standing in their breasts. All the bystanders fled from the dangerous neighbourhood, and left the gallows, the fatal cart, and the mortally wounded officials alone. The two bold outlaws rushed to release their comrade, cut his bonds, and lifted him to his feet. William seized an axe from a soldier and pursued the fleeing guard, while his two friends with their deadly arrows slew a man at each shot.

The Mayor of Carlisle

When the arrows were all used Adam Bell and Clym of the Cleugh threw away their bows and took to sword and buckler. The fight continued till midday for in the narrow streets the three comrades protected each other, and drew gradually towards the gate. Adam Bell still carried the keys at his girdle, and they could pass out easily if they could but once reach the gateway. By this time the whole town was in a commotion; again the hue and cry had been raised against the outlaws, and the Mayor of Carlisle came in person with a mighty troop of armed citizens, angered now at the fighting in the streets of the town.

The three yeomen retreated as steadily as they could towards the gate, but the mayor followed valiantly armed with a pole-axe, with which he clove Cloudeslee's shield in two. He soon perceived the object of the outlaws, and bade his men guard the gates well, so that the three should not escape.

The Escape from Carlisle

Terrible was the din in the town now, for trumpets blew, church-bells were rung backward, women bewailed their dead in the streets, and over all resounded the clash of arms, as the fighting drew nigh the gate. When the gatehouse came in sight the outlaws were fighting desperately, with diminishing strength, but the thought of safety outside the walls gave them force to make one last stand. With backs to the gate and faces to the foe, Adam and Clym and William made a valiant onslaught on the townsfolk, who fled in terror, leaving a breathing-space in which Adam Bell turned the key, flung open the great ponderous gate, and flung it to again, when the three had passed through.

Adam and the Keys

As Adam locked the door they could hear inside the town the hurrying footsteps of the rallying citizens, whose furious attack on the great iron-studded door came too late. The door was locked, and the three friends stood in safety outside, with their pleasant forest home within easy reach. The change of feeling was so intense that Adam Bell, always the man to seize the humorous point of a situation, laughed lightly. He called through the barred wicket:

"Here are your keys. I resign my office as warder—one half-day's work is enough for me; and as I have resigned, and the former gate-ward is somewhat damaged and has disappeared, I advise you to find a new one. Take your keys, and much good may you get from them. Next time I advise you not to stop an honest yeoman from coming to see his own wife and have a chat with her."

Thereupon he flung the keys over the gate on the heads of the crowd, and the three brethren slipped away into the forest to their own haunts, where they found fresh bows and arrows in such abundance that they longed to be back in fair Carlisle with their foes before them.

William of Cloudeslee and his Wife Meet

While they were yet discussing all the details of the rescue they heard a woman's pitiful lament and the crying of little children. "Hark!" said Cloudeslee, and they all heard in the silence the words she said. It was William's wife, and she cried, "Alas! why did I not die before this day? Woe is me that my dear husband is slain! He is dead, and I have no friend to lament with me. If only I could see his comrades and tell what has befallen him my heart would be eased of some of its pain."

William, as he listened, was deeply touched, and walked gently to fair Alice, as she hid her face in her hands and wept. "Welcome, wife, to the greenwood!" he said. "By heaven, I never thought to see you again when I lay in bonds last night." Dame Alice sprang up most joyously. "Oh, all is well with me now you are here; I have no care or woe." "For that you must thank my dear brethren, Adam and Clym," said he; and Alice began to load them with her thanks, but Adam cut short the expression of her gratitude. "No need to talk about a little matter like that," he said gruffly. "If we want any supper we had better kill something, for the meat we must eat is yet running wild."

With three such good archers game was easily shot and a merry meal was quickly prepared in the greenwood, and all joyfully partook of venison and other dainties. Throughout the repast William devotedly waited on his wife with deepest love and reverence, for he could not forget how she had defended him and risked her life to stand by him.

William's Proposed Visit to London

When the meal was over, and they reclined on the green turf round the fire, William began thoughtfully, "It is in my mind that we ought speedily to go to London and try to win our pardon from the king. Unless we approach him before news can be brought from Carlisle he will assuredly slay us. Let us go at once, leaving my dear wife and my two youngest sons in a convent here; but I would fain take my eldest boy with me. If all goes well he can bring good news to Alice in her nunnery, and if all goes ill he shall bring her my last wishes. But I am sure I am not meant to die by the law." His brethren approved the plan, and they took fair Alice and her two youngest children to the nunnery, and then the three famous archers with the little boy of seven set out at their best speed for London, watching the passers-by carefully, that no news of the doings in Carlisle should precede them to the king.

Outlaws in the Royal Palace

The three yeomen, on arriving in London, made their way at once to the king's palace, and walked boldly into the hall, regardless of the astonished and indignant shouts of the royal porter. He followed them angrily into the hall, and began reproaching them and trying to induce them to withdraw, but to no purpose. Finally an usher came and said, "Yeomen, what is your wish? Pray tell me, and I will help you if I can; but if you enter the king's presence thus unmannerly you will cause us to be blamed. Tell me now whence you come."

William fearlessly answered, "Sir, we will tell the truth without deceit. We are outlaws from the king's forests, outlawed for killing the king's deer, and we come to beg for pardon and a charter of peace, to show to the sheriff of our county."

The King and the Outlaws

The usher went to an inner room and begged to know the king's will, whether he would see these outlaws or not. The king was interested in these bold yeomen, who dared to avow themselves law-breakers, and bade men bring them to audience with him. The three comrades, with the little boy, on being introduced into the royal presence, knelt down and held up their hands, beseeching pardon for their offences.

"Sire, we beseech your pardon for our breach of your laws. We are forest outlaws, who have slain your fallow deer in many parts of your royal forests." "Your names? Tell me at once," said the king. "Adam Bell, Clym of the Cleugh, and William of Cloudeslee," they replied.

The king was very wrathful. "Are you those bold robbers of whom men have told me? Do you now dare to come to me for pardon? On mine honour I vow that you shall all three be hanged without mercy, as I am crowned king of this realm of England. Arrest them and lay them in bonds." There was no resistance possible, and the yeomen submitted ruefully to their arrest. Adam Bell was the first to speak. "As I hope to thrive, this game pleases me not at all," he said. "Sire, of your mercy, we beg you to remember that we came to you of our own free will, and to let us pass away again as freely. Give us back our weapons and let us have free passage till we have left your palace; we ask no more; we shall never ask another favour, however long we live."

The king was obdurate, however; he only replied, "You speak proudly still, but you shall all three be hanged."

The Queen Intercedes

The queen, who was sitting beside her husband, now spoke for the first time. "Sire, it were a pity that such good yeomen should die, if they might in any wise be pardoned." "There is no pardon," said the king. She then replied, "My lord, when I first left my native land and came into this country as your bride you promised to grant me at once the first boon I asked. I have never needed to ask one until today, but now, sire, I claim one, and I beg you to grant it." "With all my heart; ask your boon, and it shall be yours willingly."

"Then, I pray you, grant me the lives of these good yeomen." "Madam, you might have had half my kingdom, and you ask a worthless trifle." "Sire, it seems not worthless to me; I beg you to keep your promise." "Madam, it vexes me that you have asked so little; yet since you will have these three outlaws, take them." The queen rejoiced greatly. "Many thanks, my lord and husband. I will be surety for them that they shall be true men henceforth. But, good my lord, give them a word of comfort, that they may not be wholly dismayed by your anger."

News Comes to the King

The king smiled at his wife. "Ah, madam! you will have your own way, as all women will. Go, fellows, wash yourselves, and find places at the tables, where you shall dine well enough, even if it be not on venison pasty from the king's own forests."

The outlaws did reverence to the king and queen, and found seats with the king's guard at the lower tables in the hall. They were still satisfying their appetites when a messenger came in haste to the king; and the three North Countrymen looked at one another uneasily, for they knew the man was from Carlisle. The messenger knelt before the king and presented his letters. "Sire, your officers greet you well."

"How fare they? How does my valiant sheriff? And the prudent justice? Are they well?"

"Alas! my lord, they have been slain, and many another good officer with them."

"Who has done this?" questioned the king angrily.

"My lord, three bold outlaws, Adam Bell, Clym of the Cleugh, and William of Cloudeslee."

"What! these three whom I have just pardoned? Ah, sorely I repent that I forgave them! I would give a thousand pounds if I could have them hanged all three; but I cannot."

The King's Test

As the king read the letters his anger and surprise increased. It seemed impossible that three men should overawe a whole town, should slay sheriff, justice, mayor, and nearly every official in the town, forge a royal letter with the king's seal, and then lock the gates and escape safely. There was no doubt of the fact, and the king raged impotently against his own foolish mercy in giving them a free pardon. It had been granted, however, and he could do nought but grieve over the ruin they had wrought in Carlisle. At last he sprang up, for he could endure the banquet no longer.

"Call my archers to go to the butts," he commanded. "I will see these bold outlaws shoot, and try if their archery is so fine as men say."

Accordingly the king's archers and the queen's archers arrayed themselves, and the three yeomen took their bows and looked well to their silken bowstrings; and then all made their way to the butts where the targets were set up. The archers shot in turn, aiming at an ordinary target, but Cloudeslee soon grew weary of this childish sport, and said aloud, "I shall never call a man a good archer who shoots at a target as large as a buckler. We have another sort of butt in my country, and that is worth shooting at."

William of Cloudeslee's Archery

"Make ready your own butts," the king commanded, and the three outlaws went to a bush in a field close by and returned bearing hazel-rods, peeled and shining white. These rods they set up at four hundred yards apart, and, standing by one, they said to the king,

"We should account a man a fair archer if he could split one wand while standing beside the other." "It cannot be done; the feat is too great," exclaimed the king. "Sire, I can easily do it," said Cloudeslee, and, taking aim very carefully, he shot, and the arrow split the wand in two. "In truth," said the king, "you are the best archer I have ever seen. Can you do greater wonders?" "Yes," said Cloudeslee, "one thing more I can do, but it is a more difficult feat. Nevertheless I will try it, to show you our North Country shooting." "Try, then," the king replied, "but if you fail you shall be hanged without mercy, because of your boasting."

Cloudeslee Shoots the Apple from his Son's Head

Now Cloudeslee stood for a few moments as if doubtful of himself, and the South Country archers watched him, hoping for a chance to retrieve their defeat, when William suddenly said, "I have a son, a dear son, seven years of age. I will tie him to a stake and place an apple on his head. Then from a distance of a hundred and twenty yards I will split the apple in two with a broad arrow." "By heaven!" the king cried, "that is a dreadful feat. Do as you have said, or by Him who died on the Cross I will hang you high. Do as you have said, but if you touch one hair of his head, or the edge of his gown, I will hang you and your two companions." "I have never broken my pledged word," said the North Country bowman, and he at once made ready for the terrible trial. The stake was set in the ground, the boy tied to it, with his face turned from his father, lest he should give a start and destroy his aim. Cloudeslee then paced the hundred and twenty yards, anxiously felt his string, bent his bow, chose his broadest arrow, and fitted it with care.

The Last Shot

It was an anxious moment. The throng of spectators felt sick with expectation, and many women wept and prayed for the father and his innocent son. But Cloudeslee showed no fear. He addressed the crowd gravely, "Good folk, stand all as still as may be. For such a shot a man needs a steady hand, and your movements may destroy my aim and make me slay my son. Pray for me."

Then, in an unbroken silence of breathless suspense, the bold marksman shot, and the apple fell to the ground, cleft into two absolutely equal halves. A cheer from every spectator burst forth deafeningly, and did not die down till the king beckoned for silence.

The King and Queen Show Favour

"God forbid that I should ever be your target," he said. "You shall be my chief forester in the North Country, with daily wage, and daily right of killing venison; your two brethren shall become yeomen of my guard, and I will advance the fortunes of your family in every way."

The queen smiled graciously upon William, and she bestowed a pension upon him, and bade him bring his wife, fair Alice, to court, to take up the post of chief woman of the bedchamber to the royal children.

Overwhelmed with these favours, the three yeomen became conscious of their own offences, more than they had told to the royal pair; their awakened consciences sent them to a holy bishop, who heard their confessions, gave them penance and bade them live well for the future, and then absolved them. When they had returned to Englewood Forest and had broken up the outlaw band they came back to the royal court, and spent the rest of their lives in great favour with the king and queen.

Historical Notes

This section contains some brief biographical notes about the original collectors and their books featured in this collection. These notes have been adapted from those primarily on Wikipedia along with other supporting sources and notes.

Joseph Jacobs (1854-1916)

Joseph Jacobs was an Australian-born folklorist, literary critic, historian, and social scientist whose work helped shape the modern understanding of English and European folk traditions. Born in Sydney in 1854 to a Jewish family of Prussian descent, Jacobs was educated first in Australia and later in England, where he attended St. John's College, Cambridge. From early on, he showed a keen interest in history, languages, and the stories that bind cultures together.

Though he trained as a scholar of literature and history, Jacobs is best remembered as one of the foremost collectors and editors of English folklore. His work revived and popularised many of the world's best-loved fairy tales, including *Jack and the Beanstalk, Goldilocks and the Three Bears, The Three Little Pigs, Jack the Giant Killer*, and *The History of Tom Thumb*. These tales first appeared in *English Fairy Tales* (1890) and *More English Fairy*

Tales (1893), collections that combined careful research with vivid retelling. His editions became definitive for generations of English-speaking readers, shaping how these stories are still told today.

Jacobs's passion for comparative folklore led him beyond England's borders. He compiled and edited collections of Jewish, Celtic, Indian, and European fairy tales, introducing readers to the breadth of the world's oral traditions. His work was distinguished by a desire to preserve the tone, humour, and moral imagination of the original storytellers, rather than smoothing them into Victorian gentility. In this, Jacobs differed from contemporaries like the Brothers Grimm or Andrew Lang, striving instead for authenticity and cultural respect.

Beyond his collections of tales, Jacobs was an active editor and scholar. He produced critical editions of *The Fables of Bidpai* and *The Fables of Aesop*, wrote extensively on the migration and transformation of folklore motifs, and edited several versions of *The Thousand and One Nights*. He was deeply involved with The Folklore Society in England and served as editor of its journal, *Folklore*. His expertise and editorial rigor helped to formalize folklore studies as a serious academic discipline.

Jacobs also made important contributions to Jewish scholarship and cultural history. In 1896, he travelled to the United States to lecture on The Philosophy of Jewish History at Gratz College in Philadelphia and before audiences of the Council of Jewish Women in New York, Philadelphia, and Chicago. Four years later, he moved permanently to America to take up the role of revising editor for the monumental *Jewish Encyclopaedia* (1901–1906), overseeing contributions from more than six hundred writers and scholars. He also worked closely with the Jewish Publication

Society and the American Jewish Historical Society, helping to advance Jewish intellectual life in the English-speaking world.

Joseph Jacobs married Georgina Horne, with whom he had two sons and a daughter. He continued writing and editing until his death at his home in Yonkers, New York, on 30 January 1916, aged sixty-two.

During his lifetime, Jacobs was recognized as one of the leading folklorists of his generation, a scholar who bridged cultures and preserved voices from the deep past. His collections remain some of the most beloved in the English language, cherished both for their storytelling charm and their deep respect for the traditions they represent.

Selected Bibliography:

- English Fairy Tales (1890)
- Celtic Fairy Tales (1892)
- More English Fairy Tales (1893)
- Indian Fairy Tales (1892)
- The Fables of Aesop (1894)
- Europa's Fairy Book (1916)
- Jewish Fairy Tales and Legends (1919, posthumous)
- The Fables of Bidpai (1895)
- The Thousand and One Nights (editor, various editions)
- The Story of Geographical Discovery: How the World Became Known (1899)
- The Jews of Angevin England: Documents and Records from Latin and Hebrew Sources (1893)
- Studies in Biblical Archaeology (1894)

Maud Isabel Ebbutt (born 1867)

Maud Isabel Ebbutt was a British writer and folklorist best known for her 1910 collection *Hero-Myths and Legends of the British Race*, a sweeping retelling of the legendary and heroic tales that shaped the cultural imagination of Britain. Although relatively little is known about her personal life, Ebbutt's writing places her firmly among the early twentieth-century authors who sought to make the mythic past vivid and accessible to general readers, particularly at a time when Britain was rediscovering its Celtic, Anglo-Saxon, and Norse heritage through scholarship, art, and literature.

Born in 1867, likely in England, Ebbutt came of age during a period of intense interest in folklore and national identity. The late Victorian and Edwardian eras saw a flourishing of mythological studies, with writers such as Andrew Lang, Charles Squire, and Joseph Jacobs adapting traditional tales for new audiences. Ebbutt's contribution to this tradition is distinctive for its intellectual depth and for the moral and philosophical reflections that accompany her storytelling.

Her best-known work, *Hero-Myths and Legends of the British Race* (1910), blends literary retelling with historical and cultural commentary. The book draws upon sources ranging from the Beowulf epic and the Arthurian romances to medieval chronicles and Norse sagas, presenting them as expressions of the ideals and values of the peoples who told them. Ebbutt viewed myth not merely as entertainment but as a moral and cultural mirror, reflecting the evolving character of a nation and its people.

In her introduction, she quotes Thomas Carlyle's dictum, "Hero-worship endures forever while man endures," using it as the guiding principle for her study of heroism through the ages. For

Ebbutt, each generation's heroes revealed the spirit of their age: the Saxons' admiration for strength, the Normans' reverence for loyalty, and the English yeoman's love for justice embodied in the figure of Robin Hood. Her prose combines scholarly precision with romantic idealism, suggesting that myth endures because it speaks to the timeless human need for moral exemplars and stories that elevate the spirit.

Hero-Myths and Legends of the British Race was published as part of the popular *Myth and Legend in Literature and Art* series by George G. Harrap & Co., which aimed to present the world's mythologies in an accessible form for general readers and students. Ebbutt's volume remains one of the finest examples in the series for its elegant narrative and thoughtful introduction. Her work stood at the crossroads of literature and cultural history, bridging Victorian moral earnestness with Edwardian curiosity and early twentieth-century scholarship.

As she herself wrote, "To every age, and to every nation, there is a peculiar ideal of heroism, and in the popular legends of each age this ideal may be found."

Selected Bibliography

- Hero-Myths and Legends of the British Race (London: George G. Harrap & Co., 1910) – Part of the Myth and Legend in Literature and Art series.
- "Introduction to Hero-Myths and Legends of the British Race," in which Ebbutt discusses heroism, national identity, and moral philosophy (1910).
- Myths and Legends of the Middle Ages (attributed, London: Harrap, c. 1911), possibly a companion or derivative volume within the same series, though attribution remains uncertain.

- Articles and essays on British folklore and mythology (uncollected, early twentieth century; several reprinted in educational anthologies of myth and legend during the 1910s–1920s).

Andrew Lang

Andrew Lang (1844–1912) was a Scottish poet, novelist, literary critic, and anthropologist, best known for his prolific literary output and his contributions to the field of folklore studies.

Andrew Lang was born on March 31, 1844, in Selkirk, Scotland, to John Lang, a town clerk, and Jane Plenderleath Sellar Lang. He was the eldest of eight siblings. Lang received his early education at the Selkirk Grammar School before attending the Edinburgh Academy and later the University of St. Andrews, where he studied classics and modern literature.

Lang began his literary career as a journalist and editor, contributing articles, essays, and reviews to various newspapers and magazines. He gained recognition for his literary criticism, demonstrating a keen intellect and a deep understanding of literature, folklore, and mythology.

Lang's interests were diverse, and he wrote extensively on a wide range of subjects, including poetry, fiction, history, anthropology, and psychology. He was a prolific author, producing numerous works across multiple genres throughout his lifetime.

One of Lang's most significant contributions to scholarship was his work in the field of folklore studies. He was deeply fascinated by the oral traditions and folk beliefs of different cultures, and he devoted much of his career to collecting, researching, and analysing folktales, myths, and legends from around the world.

Lang's "Fairy Books" series, which included collections such as "The Blue Fairy Book" (1889), "The Red Fairy Book" (1890), and "The Green Fairy Book" (1892), among others, became immensely popular and influential. These collections featured fairy tales from various cultural traditions, translated and adapted for English-speaking audiences, and helped to preserve and popularize many classic folk stories.

In addition to his contributions to folklore studies, Lang wrote numerous other books on diverse subjects. He authored poetry collections, such as "Ballads and Lyrics of Old France, " (1872) and "Rhymes à la Mode, " (1884), which showcased his talent for verse.

Lang also wrote historical works, biographies, literary histories, and novels, including "The Monk of Fife, " (1895), a historical novel set in the time of Joan of Arc. He was a versatile writer, capable of tackling both fiction and non-fiction with equal skill and enthusiasm.

In 1875, Andrew Lang married Leonora Blanche Alleyne, with whom he had four children. Blanche, as she was commonly known, was a talented author and translator in her own right, and she often collaborated with Lang on his literary projects.

Andrew Lang's legacy as a writer, folklorist, and scholar endures through his extensive body of work, which continues to be studied, admired, and enjoyed by readers around the world. His contributions to folklore studies helped to popularize the study of folk traditions and fairy tales, shaping the way these stories are understood and appreciated to this day. Lang's influence on literature, anthropology, and cultural studies remains significant, and his works remain important sources for scholars and enthusiasts interested in the rich tapestry of human culture and imagination.

Selected Bibliography:

Fairy Books - Lang's "Coloured Fairy Books" are among his most celebrated works, each named after a different colour:

- The Blue Fairy Book (1889)
- The Red Fairy Book (1890)
- The Green Fairy Book (1892
- The Yellow Fairy Book (1894)
- The Pink Fairy Book (1897)
- The Grey Fairy Book (1900)
- The Violet Fairy Book (1901)
- The Crimson Fairy Book (1903
- The Brown Fairy Book (1904)
- The Orange Fairy Book (1906)
- The Olive Fairy Book (1907)
- The Lilac Fairy Book (1910)

Other Notable Works:

- The Blue Poetry Book (1891): A collection of poems suitable for children.
- The True Story Book (1893): A compilation of historical narratives presented in a storytelling format.
- The Red True Story Book (1895): Continuation of historical tales aimed at younger readers.
- The Animal Story Book (1896): Stories centred around animals, blending fact and fiction.
- The Arabian Nights Entertainments (1898): Lang's rendition of the classic Middle Eastern tales.
- The Book of Romance (1902): A collection of romantic tales from various traditions.

- The Red Book of Animal Stories (1899): Further animal-centric tales for children.

Scholarly and Literary Criticism:

- Custom and Myth (1884): Essays exploring the origins of various customs and myths.
- Myth, Ritual and Religion (1887): A two-volume work examining the connections between mythology, rituals, and religious practices.
- Books and Bookmen (1886): Essays on literary topics and book collecting.
- Letters to Dead Authors (1886): Imaginary letters addressed to famous authors of the past.
- Homer and the Epic (1893): A study of Homer's works and their place in epic literature.

Translations:

- The Odyssey of Homer (1879): Prose translation in collaboration with S.H. Butcher.
- The Iliad of Homer (1883): Prose translation with Walter Leaf and Ernest Myers.

Charles John Tibbitts

Charles John Tibbits (31 January 1861 – 7 July 1935) was a British journalist, newspaper editor and legal writer whose best-known legacy for folklorists is the compact Folk-Lore and Legends series issued by W. W. Gibbings in the late nineteenth century. He was born in Chester, the youngest son of George Tibbits, a solicitor, and his wife Mary Myddleton, and was baptised at St John the Baptist's, Chester, in 1863. Educated first at Albion House School in the city, he matriculated at Oxford in October 1880 with the initial intention of entering the Church, and took his BA in 1886. Instead of a clerical career, however, he "wandered into journalism", beginning on local papers as reporter, sub-editor and finally editor, before moving to London after about three years "to find fortune".

In London Tibbits joined Harmsworth Publications and became assistant editor to Alfred Harmsworth, contributing stories and articles across a wide range of London newspapers. In 1895 he was appointed editor of the *Weekly Dispatch*, a mass-circulation Sunday paper, which he remodelled and enlarged, notably introducing more pictorial material. He also edited the short-lived *Women's Weekly* between 1896 and 1900, part of the expanding market in periodicals aimed at women readers. His editorship of the *Weekly Dispatch* was marked by a robust style of investigative and campaigning journalism; in 1901 he and a reporter, Charles Windust, were convicted of contempt for publishing prejudicial material about an ongoing criminal case, and both served six weeks' imprisonment. Tibbits nonetheless retained his post until 1903, and continued thereafter to publish articles on social questions and occasional short fiction in leading magazines.

Alongside his newspaper work, Tibbits developed a strong interest in popular narrative and cheap print, which fed directly into his folklore editing. For W. W. Gibbings he compiled a sequence of small, uniform volumes under the collective banner *Folk-Lore and Legends*, beginning with regional anthologies on Germany, Oriental traditions, Scotland and Ireland (all 1889), and followed by further volumes on England, Scandinavia, and Russian and Polish material (1890). His own introductory notes make clear that he was not a field collector; instead he drew on chapbooks and earlier scholarly or semi-scholarly collections, selecting stories he regarded as representative and re-presenting them for a late-Victorian Anglophone readership. In the Russian and Polish volume, for example, he states that the tales are "selections made from the Russian chap-book literature, and from the works of various Russian and Polish collectors of Folklore" such as Afanasiev and Glinski, and that he includes chapbook tales of foreign origin where they have been naturalised into local custom and belief.

His editorial stance balances a preservationist instinct with a willingness to adapt. In his English volume he remarks that "the old English Folklore Tales are fast dying out" under the pressure of "remorseless 'progress'" and the struggle for existence, and that he has tried to offer "some of the best specimens" of the national tradition. At the same time, he acknowledges that he has taken pains to use the earliest printed forms he could find for nursery tales, while making such "excision and slight alteration" as he deemed necessary. This mixture of fidelity and light redaction is characteristic of his approach: he treats folklore as a national literary inheritance that can and should be tidied for general readers without, in his view, losing its essential character.

The *Folk-Lore and Legends* series proved durable, and has been repeatedly reprinted and mined for later anthologies, often with Tibbits identified as editor rather than author. Modern platforms and booksellers still group him with other classic folklore compilers, and digital projects such as Project Gutenberg and LibriVox continue to circulate his volumes widely. Although he never had the status of a professional folklorist in the academic sense, his work sits at an important intersection between nineteenth-century journalism, the late-Victorian taste for "myths and legends" in small gift-books, and the broader popularisation of international folk narrative for English readers.

In the early years of the twentieth century Tibbits shifted focus again, qualifying as a solicitor and writing on legal matters for British and American journals. His book *Marriage Making and Marriage Breaking* (1911) entered contemporary debates over the reform of divorce law, combining legal exposition with social commentary. He thus occupies an unusual position: a figure who moved between professions, from would-be clergyman to journalist, editor, folklore anthologist and legal writer, always working at points where specialist knowledge was translated into forms accessible to a general public.

Tibbits's personal life also connected him with the world of popular fiction. In 1896 he married the novelist Annie Olive Brazier at St Marylebone, London; she later published a sequence of sixpenny novels under the name Annie O. Tibbits, and reference works on Edwardian fiction treat her as a significant minor figure in that field. The couple lived first in Kensington, later in Woodside Park, Barnet, and had three children: Arthur Christopher, Eleanor Mary and Isabella Margaret Myddleton. Tibbits was a member of several London clubs, including the Press,

National Liberal and Savage Club, and listed fishing and chess among his recreations. He died at Barnet, Hertfordshire, on 7 July 1935.

Selected bibliography:

Folk-Lore and Legends series (W. W. Gibbings and associated publishers)

- Folk-Lore and Legends: Germany (1889)
- Folk-Lore and Legends: Ireland (1889)
- Folk-Lore and Legends: Oriental (1889; sometimes cited as 1892 in later issues)
- Folk-Lore and Legends: Scotland (1889)
- Folk-Lore and Legends: English (1890)
- Folk-Lore and Legends: Russian and Polish (1890)
- Folk-Lore and Legends: Scandinavian (1890)

Related story collections and series

- Terrible Tales: German (1890)
- Terrible Tales: French (1890)
- Terrible Tales: Italian (1890)
- Terrible Tales: Spanish (1890)

Later and non-folklore works

- Archipropheta (1906), Nicholas Grimald; translated by Charles John Tibbits
- Marriage Making and Marriage Breaking (1911)

Flora Annie Webster Steel

Flora Annie Webster Steel (1847–1929) was an Anglo-Indian writer, folklorist and educationalist whose work sits at the knotty intersection of empire, women's labour and the preservation of oral tradition. She was born at Sudbury Priory, Middlesex, the third child of George Webster and Isabella MacCallum, into a comfortable but not grand English household. In 1867 she married Henry William Steel of the Indian Civil Service and followed him to northern India, living for some twenty-two years, mostly in the Punjab. Unlike the stock figure of the idle "memsahib" she later mocked, Steel immersed herself in local languages and customs, moving between British administrative circles and Punjabi villages. The birth of her daughter brought her into women's domestic spaces, and from that position she began to learn vernaculars, collect stories and observe the textures of everyday life.

Her official role as Inspectress of Government and Aided Schools in the Punjab gave her a formal framework for this curiosity. Steel travelled extensively, assessing village schools and agitating for improvements in basic education, especially for girls. At the same time she built relationships with figures such as John Lockwood Kipling, head of the Lahore School of Art and father of Rudyard Kipling, and the civil servant-ethnographer Richard Carnac Temple. With Temple she produced *Wide-Awake Stories: A Collection of Tales Told by Little Children, Between Sunset and Sunrise, in the Panjab and Kashmir* (1884), a substantial volume of orally narrated tales recorded from local informants, which already shows her instinct to present Indian narrative traditions as vigorous and self-sufficient rather than as mere "background" to British rule.

Steel's best-known folkloric work, *Tales of the Punjab: Told by the People* (1894), grew directly from these years of listening and note-taking. The book offers a large selection of Punjabi folk narratives, framed for Anglophone readers but strongly marked by dialect, proverbial speech and local humour, with illustrations by J. Lockwood Kipling and learned notes by Temple. Although she does not operate as a "scientific" folklorist in the later academic sense, Steel takes care to present the tales as living performances rather than curiosities, insisting in her prefaces and practice that they have been "told by the people" and not invented by her. Her later collection *English Fairy Tales* (1918), retelling stories from her own culture with equal energy, sits interestingly alongside the Punjabi material; together they make her one of the few nineteenth-century writers to mediate both Indian and English folk traditions for a broad juvenile and family readership.

Folklore was only one strand of Steel's output. She also wrote Anglo-Indian fiction that probed the tensions of colonial life, beginning with the short-story collection *From the Five Rivers* (1893) and continuing through novels such as *On the Face of the Waters* (1896), an ambitious narrative of the 1857 uprising, and *The Hosts of the Lord* (1900), centred on Christian missionary work. These works earned her a reputation, sometimes grudging, as a major interpreter of India for British readers; critics and later scholars have repeatedly described her as the "female Kipling," a label she reportedly disliked, not least because it framed her as derivative of a male contemporary rather than as an independent voice. Modern criticism has tended to treat her instead as a writer who negotiates uneasily between complicity in imperial structures and an often sharp critique of colonial arrogance, especially where women and lower-caste Indians are concerned.

Steel also produced one of the most influential domestic manuals of the Raj, *The Complete Indian Housekeeper and Cook* (1888), co-authored with Grace Gardiner. Intended as an instructional guide for British women running households in India, it covers everything from supervising servants to dealing with climate, illness and food. The book went through many editions and was widely read, earning her the description "the Mrs Beeton of British India." For all its briskly imperial assumptions, the manual also functions as an inadvertent ethnography of domestic colonial life, recording the practical interdependence between British employers and Indian staff. In this sense it stands alongside the folktale collections as a record of cross-cultural contact, though of course written firmly from the coloniser's side of the relationship.

After returning from India in 1889, Steel settled first in Scotland and later in Gloucestershire, where she continued to publish prolifically: further novels, story collections, a popular history *India Through the Ages: A Popular and Picturesque History of Hindustan* (1908), children's books such as *The Adventures of Akbar* (1913), and finally her autobiography *The Garden of Fidelity* (1930), completed shortly before her death. She died on 12 April 1929 at her daughter's home in Minchinhampton. Her reputation has since moved in and out of focus: celebrated in her own time, then overshadowed, and now the subject of renewed scholarly interest, including studies by Daya Patwardhan and Violet Powell and a growing body of postcolonial criticism that reads her fiction and folktale collections as complex documents of British women's writing under the Raj.

Selected bibliography:

Folklore and fairy-tale collections

- Wide-Awake Stories: A Collection of Tales Told by Little Children, Between Sunset and Sunrise, in the Panjab and Kashmir (with Sir Richard Carnac Temple), Education Society's Press, Bombay, 1884.
- From the Five Rivers (short stories rooted in Punjabi life), 1893.
- Tales of the Punjab: Told by the People (also issued as Tales of the Punjab: Folklore of India), with illustrations by J. Lockwood Kipling and notes by R. C. Temple, Macmillan, London, 1894.
- English Fairy Tales, illustrated by Arthur Rackham, 1918.
- A Tale of Indian Heroes, 1923.

Anglo-Indian fiction and short-story collections

- Miss Stuart's Legacy (novel), 1893.
- The Flower of Forgiveness (stories), 1894.
- The Potter's Thumb (novel), 1894.
- Red Rowans (novel), 1895.
- On the Face of the Waters (novel of the 1857 uprising), 1896.
- In the Permanent Way, and Other Stories, 1897.
- In the Tideway, 1897.
- Voices in the Night (stories), 1900.
- The Hosts of the Lord (novel on missionary work), 1900.
- In the Guardianship of God (novel), 1903.
- A Book of Mortals (stories), 1905.
- A Sovereign Remedy (novel), 1906.
- A Prince of Dreamers (novel), 1908.

- King-Errant (novel), 1912.
- The Adventures of Akbar (children's historical novel), 1913.
- The Mercy of the Lord (novel), 1914.
- Marmaduke (novel), 1917.
- Mistress of Men (novel), 1918.

Non-fiction, domestic and historical

- The Complete Indian Housekeeper and Cook: Giving the Duties of Mistress and Servants, the General Management of the House, and Practical Recipes for Cooking in India (with Grace Gardiner), first edn 1888; frequently reprinted.
- India (dramatic or historical sketches), 1905.
- India Through the Ages: A Popular and Picturesque History of Hindustan, 1908.

Autobiography

- The Garden of Fidelity: Being the Autobiography of Flora Annie Steel, 1847–1929, Macmillan, London, 1930.

Juliana Horatia Ewing

Juliana Horatia Ewing (née Gatty, 3 August 1841 – 13 May 1885) was an English writer of children's literature whose work sits at a crossroads between domestic realism, moral tale and literary fairy story. Born at Ecclesfield, near Sheffield, she was the second of the ten children of the Reverend Alfred Gatty, vicar of Ecclesfield, and Margaret Gatty, herself a successful writer for the young. Educated at home, she grew up in a household steeped in books and informal performance. Andersen, the Grimms and other nineteenth-century storytellers were part of the family reading, and Juliana, nicknamed "Aunt Judy" by her siblings for her mimicry and narrative flair, very quickly became the natural storyteller of the nursery. This mixture of Anglican piety, literary culture and playful theatre shaped both the tone and the moral texture of her later work.

Ewing's first stories appeared in Charlotte Mary Yonge's Anglican girls' magazine *The Monthly Packet* while she was still young, but her main professional home became *Aunt Judy's Magazine*, founded and initially edited by her mother in 1866, then later by Ewing and her sister. The magazine published many of her best-known tales, including "The Brownies," "Lob Lie-by-the-Fire" and the stories later gathered in *Old-Fashioned Fairy Tales*. In 1867 she married Major Alexander Ewing of the Army Pay Corps and went with him to Fredericton, New Brunswick, for two years, an experience preserved in her letters home and echoed in some of her fiction; on their return she spent much of the 1870s in the garrison town of Aldershot. Failing health meant she could not accompany him to later postings in Malta and Ceylon, and in her final years the couple lived in Somerset and then Bath, where she died after surgery in 1885 and was buried at Trull.

Her fiction covers a broad range, from relatively realistic narratives of English middle-class childhood such as *Mrs Overtheway's Remembrances*, *A Flat Iron for a Farthing* and *Six to Sixteen* to more concentrated novellas like *Jackanapes* and *The Story of a Short Life*, which explore courage, loss and the ethics of self-sacrifice against military or quasi-military backgrounds. Contemporary readers valued her for her unusually acute understanding of children's inner lives, a sympathy that is often combined with a clear admiration for discipline and duty, and with a steady Anglican didacticism. This blend of tenderness and firmness, domestic detail and moral seriousness, gives her work a distinctive tone within late Victorian children's writing.

Within that body of work, the fairy-tale and folklore material occupies a special place. Stories such as "The Brownies," "Lob Lie-by-the-Fire" and the tales collected in *Old-Fashioned Fairy Tales* draw explicitly on British and northern European folk motifs: brownies, house-elves, nixies, hill-folk and other supernatural beings. Ewing did not usually transcribe oral tales in the manner of later folklorists; instead she re-imagined folkloric figures within crafted literary narratives for magazine and book publication. Critics have noted how accurately she handles details of brownie and "lob" lore, and how she uses these beings to dramatize questions of labour, gratitude and the ethics of domestic life. In this sense she stands as an important mediating figure, transmitting folk materials into a new, highly self-conscious genre of Victorian children's fantasy.

Her most overtly fairy-tale collection, *Old-Fashioned Fairy Tales* (first published in book form in the 1880s after serialisation in *Aunt Judy's Magazine*), consists of original stories that imitate the forms and moral logic of traditional "wonder tales" while addressing quite specific nineteenth-century concerns: temperance, industry, charity and the right exercise of authority. The title is a playful misdirection; these are not retellings of familiar plots, but new inventions shaped by an intimate knowledge of fairy-tale conventions. Similarly, the volume *Lob Lie-by-the-Fire, The Brownies and Other Tales* brings folkloric sprites into the sphere of the Victorian parlour and farmhouse, tying household prosperity and social harmony to the treatment of invisible helpers and marginal figures. Through such work Ewing helped to naturalise fairy beings within English domestic fiction for children.

Her influence reaches surprisingly far beyond the printed page. The term "Brownies" for the younger section of the Girl Guides originates directly from her story "The Brownies," adapted by Robert Baden-Powell as a model of helpful, unseen service for junior Guides in the 1910s. This single tale thus helped to translate an item of folklore, refracted through her moral storytelling, into a lasting institutional identity for generations of girls. More broadly, her fiction remained in print well into the twentieth century, often in school and gift editions illustrated by artists such as Randolph Caldecott, and it has continued to attract critical attention as part of the formation of modern British children's literature. Her sister's memoir *Juliana Horatia Ewing and Her Books* fixed a powerful image of her as both devout and imaginative, and recent scholarship has revisited her as a key late-Victorian figure in the literary reshaping of folk and fairy materials for child readers.

Selected bibliography:

Primary works (fairy-tale and folklore-related)

- "The Brownies" (first published 1870; often reprinted in The Brownies and Other Tales).
- "Lob Lie-by-the-Fire; or, The Luck of Lingborough" (1873; later in Lob Lie-by-the-Fire, The Brownies and Other Tales).
- The Brownies and Other Tales (London: 1870).
- Lob Lie-by-the-Fire, The Brownies and Other Tales (various editions; e.g. Roberts Brothers, Boston, 1890).
- Old-Fashioned Fairy Tales (stories written mainly in the early 1870s for Aunt Judy's Magazine; collected volume first issued in the 1880s, often dated 1882; later reprinted by the Society for Promoting Christian Knowledge and others).

Individual fairy-tale and legend pieces, many first appearing in magazines and later gathered into collections, for example:

- "Kind William and the Water Sprite" (1869)
- "Amelia and the Dwarfs" (1870)
- "The Nix in Mischief" (1870)
- "The Hillman and the Housewife" (1870)
- "The Neck: A Legend of a Lake" (1870)
- "The Fiddler in the Fairy Ring" (1873).

Other major children's works

- Aunt Judy's Tales (1859) and Aunt Judy's Letters (1862; both associated with the family pseudonym and Aunt Judy persona).
- Mrs Overtheway's Remembrances (1869).

- A Flat Iron for a Farthing; or, Some Passages in the Life of an Only Son (1872).
- Six to Sixteen: A Story for Girls (1875).
- Jan of the Windmill: A Story of the Plains (serial 1872–73; book 1876).
- Jackanapes (1879; often issued with Caldecott illustrations).
- Daddy Darwin's Dovecot (1884).
- The Story of a Short Life (1885).
- Miscellanea and Last Words: A Final Collection of Stories (posthumous collections).

Wilson Armistead

Wilson Armistead (1819–1868) was a Leeds Quaker, businessman and prolific writer whose work ranged from fierce abolitionist polemic to devotional compilations and, importantly for folklore studies, a substantial volume of Lake District legends. He was born on 30 August 1819 in Leeds to Joseph and Hannah Armistead, a Quaker family rooted in the industrial district of Holbeck, where the family's brush, flax and mustard businesses stood near the Friends' meeting house on Water Lane. The combination of mercantile routine and Quaker piety shaped his life: he remained a manufacturer and oil merchant in Leeds while devoting much of his energy, and ultimately his health, to religious and humanitarian causes. In 1844 he married Mary Bragg of Allonby, Cumberland; the couple had five children, and their household became a centre of Quaker and reform activity in the town.

Armistead is best known to historians as a leading British abolitionist. In Leeds he helped organise and sustain the Leeds Anti-Slavery Association, wrote an astonishing quantity of anti-slavery material, and turned his skill as a compiler into a weapon against the slave system. His major work, *A Tribute for the Negro* (1848), runs to over 500 pages and sets out both an argument against ideas of racial inferiority and a long series of biographies of Black writers, leaders and thinkers; it was widely subscribed and praised by contemporaries in the transatlantic abolitionist movement. He followed this with tracts and books such as *Memoirs of Paul Cuffe, a Man of Colour, Calumny Refuted by Facts from Liberia, Slavery Illustrated in the Histories of Zangara and Maquama, The Crowning Crime of Christendom* and the series of Leeds Anti-Slavery Tracts, later collected under the striking description *Five Hundred Thousand Strokes for Freedom.*

Armistead even travelled to the United States in 1850, reporting his experiences in a long sequence of articles for *The British Friend*, which mix scenic description with sharp accounts of slavery and race prejudice.

Alongside his abolitionist work, Armistead was an industrious historian of Quakerism. Joseph Smith's *Descriptive Catalogue of Friends' Books* (1867) lists more than forty titles under his name, about half of them dealing with slavery and the rest with Quaker biography and doctrine. He edited an annotated edition of *George Fox's Journal*, wrote *Memoirs of James Logan* (a major study of the Pennsylvania statesman and Friend), and produced a biography of the Philadelphia Quaker reformer Anthony Benezet. His six-volume *Select Miscellanies* gathered anecdotes, doctrinal reflections, extracts from journals and poems into pocket-sized collections designed for "desultory readers", an early attempt to meet a mass audience with short, varied religious reading. Across these projects one can see the same habits at work: he draws together scattered texts, supplies connecting commentary, and frames the whole as a moral and educational resource.

It is within this wider pattern of compilation that Armistead's contribution to folklore belongs. In the early 1850s he brought out *Tales and Legends of the English Lakes and Mountains*, published by Longmans under the pseudonym "Lorenzo Tuvar" and described on the title page as "collected from the best and most authentic sources". Contemporary bibliographical notes state that he compiled the book largely to raise funds for American anti-slavery bazaars, which ties the folklore project directly to his reform work. Later catalogues give Manchester publisher A. Heywood & Son and a notional date of 1852; by the later nineteenth century the collection was circulating in various issues, often shortened to *Tales and Legends of the English Lakes*, and is now classified straightforwardly under "Folklore – England – Lake District".

Tales and Legends of the English Lakes offers a mixture of prose narratives, verse and topographical sketches rooted in the landscape of the Lake District. Armistead gathered stories of local ghosts, battles, saints and lovers from guidebooks, antiquarian histories and oral traditions, then rewrote them in a Victorian romantic register that dwells on the scenery while preserving a good deal of local colour. The result is not "fieldwork" in the later ethnographic sense, but it does what much nineteenth-century regional folklore aimed to do: fix in print a set of stories associated with particular fells, tarns and valleys, and embed them in a narrative of place that middle-class readers could visit, read about and imaginatively claim. Through this volume, Armistead stands as a significant early mediator of Lake District legend, sitting somewhere between the collector of folk tradition and the romantic populariser.

In his last years Armistead's energies were increasingly taken up by relief work for formerly enslaved people in the United States after the Civil War. As treasurer of the Leeds Freedmen's Aid Association he organised subscriptions and in 1866 oversaw a remittance of £1,000 to the American Freedmen's Aid Commission in New York, a substantial sum raised from Leeds and district. He continued to speak, write and organise on anti-slavery matters until shortly before his death, and was chosen to present an address of welcome to the American abolitionist William Lloyd Garrison during his visit to Leeds in October 1867. By this time, however, years of overwork and financial strain had taken a toll on his health.

Armistead spent his later life in the Little Woodhouse area of Leeds, then at Beech Grove Terrace, and finally at "Virginia Cottage" (later "Virginia House"), an ironically named property whose earlier owner had prospered from Virginian slave-grown tobacco. The house now forms part of Lyddon Hall on the University of Leeds campus. He died at home on 18 February 1868, aged forty-nine, with peritonitis recorded as the cause of death, and was buried in Woodhouse Cemetery, close to the places where he had worshipped and campaigned. A memorial from the Leeds Freedmen's Aid Association described him as "the heart of the anti-slavery party in Leeds"; to that we might add that he was also a quiet but important figure in the nineteenth-century effort to gather and preserve local legend, leaving behind a Lake District folklore collection that still circulates today.

Selected bibliography:

Folklore and regional legend

- Tales and Legends of the English Lakes and Mountains, collected from the best and most authentic sources, under the pseudonym "Lorenzo Tuvar". London: Longmans & Co, c.1852–55. Often cited as Manchester: A. Heywood & Son, 1852.
- Later issues as Tales and Legends of the English Lakes. Various reprints, including London, 1891 and modern facsimile and digital editions.

Abolitionist works and writings on race

- Memoirs of Paul Cuffe, a Man of Colour. London, 1840.
- A Tribute for the Negro: Being a Vindication of the Moral, Intellectual, and Religious Capabilities of the Coloured

Portion of Mankind; with Particular Reference to the African Race. London: William Irwin, 1848.

- Calumny Refuted by Facts from Liberia; with Extracts from the Inaugural Address of President Roberts, an Eloquent Speech of Hilary Teage, and Extracts from a Discourse by H. H. Garnet. Leeds / London, 1848.
- Slavery Illustrated in the Histories of Zangara and Maquama, Two Negroes Stolen from Africa. Leeds, 1849.
- The Crowning Crime of Christendom; or, A Review of the African Slave Trade. Leeds, 1850.
- Leeds Anti-Slavery Tracts (often cited under the collective description Five Hundred Thousand Strokes for Freedom). Leeds, 1853.
- Further Testimonies for Freedom, 1859.
- Facts versus Fiction – Will the "Nigger" Work? Leeds, 1863.
- Public Libraries for Liberia and Sierra Leone. 4to pamphlet, 1865.

Quaker biography and religious compilations

- Editor, Journal of George Fox, with historical and biographical notes. London, 1852.
- Memoirs of James Logan: A Distinguished Scholar and Christian Legislator, Secretary, Chief Justice, and for Two Years Governor of Pennsylvania. London: Charles Gilpin, 1851.
- Select Miscellanies, Chiefly Illustrative of the History, Principles and Practices of the Society of Friends. 6 vols, London, 1851–52.
- Life of Anthony Benezet, Philadelphia Quaker and anti-slavery advocate. London, 1859.

Other notable works

- The Garland of Freedom: A Collection of Poems, Chiefly Anti-Slavery. 3 vols, edited by Armistead, Leeds, c.1853; issued with the Leeds anti-slavery tracts.
- Reminiscences of a Visit to the United States, in the Summer of 1850. Originally serialised in The British Friend (1850–53), later printed in book form for private circulation.

About the Editor

Clive Gilson was born in 1962 into a household steeped in sport and rhythm. His father was a senior amateur and lower-league professional footballer, while his mother, equally formidable, was an award-winning ballroom dancer. Their spirited household didn't just hum with ambition, it danced to it.

After earning a degree in History from Leeds University, Clive took an unexpected turn into the then-nascent world of information technology in the late 1980s. Yet, the call of story and stage never left him. Alongside a thriving tech career, he freelanced as a journalist and book reviewer, earning one small by-line in the national press, and also spent over a decade performing in village halls and professional theatres across the south of England.

A true inheritor of his family's sporting zeal, Clive later pivoted into live sports broadcasting. In the 1990s, he became a trusted rugby 'stato' for the BBC, ITV, EuroSport, and TVNZ, bringing insight and analysis to major tournaments including the Heineken Cup, Six Nations, World Sevens, and Rugby World Cups.

As a writer, Clive has made his mark across genres. His debut novel, *Songs of Bliss*, was published in 2017, followed by *A Solitude of Stars* in 2019. Since then, he has released three acclaimed short story collections, *The Mechanic's Curse*, *The Insomniac Booth*, and, in 2025, *Melodies in Black Ink*.

He is also an award-winning poet and the author of a biography detailing the life of a former professional footballer, namely his father. Since 2018, Clive has served as Managing Editor of the Firesides Tales Project, a global storytelling initiative that has published over 30 collections of folktales, fairy tales, myths, and legends from around the world.

Today, Clive continues to write fiction rich in folklore, memory, and quiet transformation, combining his deep love of narrative with a lifelong fascination with the human spirit.

For more about his work, visit clivegilson.com, where stories are always waiting to be found.

ORIGINAL FICTION BY CLIVE GILSON

- *Songs of Bliss*
- *Out of the Walled Garden*
- *The Mechanic's Curse*
- *The Insomniac Booth*
- *A Solitude of Stars (Cry Havoc, part 1)*
- *A Symphony Of Sorrows (Cry Havoc, part 2)*
- *Melodies In Black Ink*
- *Acts Of Faith*

AS EDITOR – *FIRESIDE TALES* – *Western Europe*

- *Tales From the Land of Dragons* – Welsh Folk & Fairy Tales
- *Tales From the Land of The Brave* – Scottish Folk & Fairy Tales
- *Tales From the Land of Saints And Scholars* – Irish Folk & Fairy Tales
- *Tales From the Land of Hope And Glory* – English Folk & Fairy Tales
- *Tales from Gallia* – French Folk & Fairy Tales

AS EDITOR – *FIRESIDE TALES* – *Northern Europe*

- *Tales From Lands of Snow and Ice* – Scandinavian Folk & Fairy Tales
- *Tales From the Viking Isles* – Icelandic Folk & Fairy Tales
- *Tales From the Forest Lands* – Finnish Folk & Fairy Tales
- *Tales From the Old Norse* – Scandinavian Folk & Fairy Tales
- *Tales from Germania* – German Folk & Fairy Tales

AS EDITOR – *FIRESIDE TALES* – *Southern Europe*

- *Tales From the Land of Rabbits* – Spanish & Portuguese Folk & Fairy Tales
- *Tales Told by Bulls and Wolves* – Italian Folk & Fairy Tales
- *Tales of Fire and Bronze* – Greek Folk & Fairy Tales

AS EDITOR – *FIRESIDE TALES* – *Eastern Europe*

- *Tales From The Samodivi* – Balkan Folk & Fairy Tales
- *Tales From the Land of the Strigoi* – Romanian Folk & Fairy Tales

- *Tales Told by the Wind Mother*– Hungarian Folk & Fairy Tales

AS EDITOR – *FIRESIDE TALES* – *North America*

- *Okaraxta* - Tales from The Great Plains
- *Tibik-Kìzis* – Tales from The Great Lakes & Canada
- *Jóhonaa'éí* –Tales from America's Southwest
- *Qugaaĝix̂* - First Nation Tales from Alaska & The Arctic
- *Karahkwa* - First Nation Tales from America's Eastern States
- *Pot-Likker* - Folklore, Fairy Tales, and Settler Stories from America

AS EDITOR – *FIRESIDE TALES* – *Africa*

- *Arokin Tales* – Folklore & Fairy Tales from West Africa
- *Hadithi Tales* – Folklore & Fairy Tales from East Africa
- *Inkathaso Tales* – Folklore & Fairy Tales from Southern Africa
- *Tarubadur Tales* – Folklore & Fairy Tales from North Africa
- *Elephant And Frog* – Folklore from Central Africa

AS EDITOR – *FIRESIDE TALES* – *Middle East*

- *Tales From The Meddahs* – Turkish Folk & Fairy Tales
- *Tales From The Hakawati* – Arabic Folk & Fairy Tales
- *Tales Told By Balebos & Gusan* – Jewish & Armenian Folk & Fairy Tales

AS EDITOR – *FIRESIDE TALES* – *Asia & The Far East*

- *Tales Told By The Kathaakaar* – Folk & Fairy Tales from India
- *Tales Of The Gùshì Yuan* – Chinese Folk & Fairy Tales

AS EDITOR – *FIRESIDE TALES* – *Animal Tales*

- *Dog Tails* – Folk & Fairy Tales featuring our canine chums
- *Cat Tails* – Folk & Fairy Tales featuring our feline friends
- *Horse Tails* – Folk & Fairy Tales featuring our equine friends
- *Pig Tails* – Folk & Fairy Tales featuring our porcine friends

AS EDITOR – *FIRESIDE TALES – South & Central America*

- *Tales From The Caribbean* – Folk & Fairy Tales from Caribbean islands
- *Tales From Central America* – Central American Folk & Fairy Tales
- *Tales Told From South America* – South American Folk & Fairy Tales

509

Reviews

I have edited Clive Gilson's books for over a decade now – he's prolific and can turn his hand to many genres. poetry, short fiction, contemporary novels, folklore, and science fiction – and the common theme is that none of them ever fails to take my breath away. There's something in each story that is either memorably poignant, hauntingly unnerving, or sidesplittingly funny - *Lorna Howarth, The Write Factor*

*Ragged A**** Ruffian* reviewed on Amazon in the United Kingdom on 27 January 2021 - A truly heartwarming, interesting, story with a wonderful narrative. Unquestionably a splendid read

A Solitude of Stars: With deft turns of phrase and an imagination that would make Philip K. Dick jealous, Gilson foresees a dystopian future, the seeds of which are definitely being sown right now. The story is a chilling glimpse of what may come to pass, warmed by a thread of love that raises the narrative beyond despair. I found the stories disturbing and breath-taking in equal measure. The Apparat and Dirigiste tribes are ranging across our solar system seeking peace by waging war, raising the question; is humanity actually capable of peace? A riveting read. - *Rob Swan, The Write Factor*

Songs of Bliss gripped me from the start - I had to read right to the end. Loved the humour. Impressed by the surprising empathy that I felt for rather - on the face of it - unlikeable characters. Look forward to seeing it in print. - *Maighdean-Mhara, commenting on Authonomy*

I just wanted to thank you once more for your help acquiring this beautiful collection. It's found a new home at the top of my library. I've already stumbled onto some wonderful stories in a couple of the collections, and I can't wait to get more. Have a wonderful holiday and a great new year... - *Richer Daniel Laporte, California, December 2021*

Melodies In Black Ink: A collection of darkly captivating short tales, each inspired by the melodies that move us, the lyrics that linger, and the stories hidden between the notes.

Gilson (editor of the international Fireside Stories series) offers a dark, poignant collection of genre-crossing stories, all inspired by songs, that explore the fragile intersections of love, loss, resilience, and the shadows we carry. Ranging from children with superpowers to accounts of blossoming love, abusive relationships, unexpected pregnancies, and the isolating rhythm of a machine-driven society, Gilson's stories capture raw textures of the human experience in a key suggested by their musical inspirations, which include lushly brooding tracks from Kate Bush, This Mortal Coil, Angel Olsen, The Cure, and Youssou N'Dour (the sublime "7 Seconds," a duet with Neneh Cherry.) Gilson has a gift for moment-to-moment storytelling that grips and then lingers, like Gorilla Glue stuck to one's fingertips, resisting even the harshest solvents of reason.

Life goes wrong in unpredictable yet resonant ways throughout these 26 compact tales, and Gilson's vivid portrayals of scenery and emotion make it easy to lose oneself in these narratives, drowning in a wave of feeling that refuses to let go. From the Scottish Highlands to space travel to the blood-soaked earth of Danish-Viking battlefields—told from the perspective of Ulfhednar and his sacred wolf, Ulric—these stories span wide imaginative terrain. Despite some big ideas and SF elements, characterization is compelling. "The Jakey and the Nae Chancer" introduces Elliot and Fiona, who have perfected the art of detachment, the latter of whom "was almost certain that her heart was too delicate to risk breaking again." One of the most heart-wrenching stories, "Be Well," is inspired by a devastating loss. It's a piece that does more than tug at the heart, it reaches in and seizes hold with unrelenting intensity.

Adding a unique dimension, each story concludes with a toast to the song and artist that inspired it, an invitation to experience these briskly potent stories on another sensory level, with a soundtrack tying words to melody, emotion to rhythm. Melodies in Black Ink is not light reading—but it is deeply moving, with haunting emotional rewards.

Searing, surprising stories of urgent feeling, inspired by beloved songs.

Tales From The Land Of Hope & Glory

The US Review of Books
Professional Reviews for the People

Melodies in Black Ink: This work is not just another set of tales linked together by a myriad of characters who sometimes appear in more than one narrative. In fact, this is much more than just another short story collection. It is also a reflective, musical journey. Accompanying each story is an explanation of the song that inspired the writing. Most impressive is the wide expanse of musical genres, artists, and songs included in this book. From Wardruna to Metric to Blue Oyster Cult to Dot Allison, the book's audience will experience a musical journey unlike any other. The incorporation of the notes discussing each inspirational song provides an informative background. It also provides historical context, along with the author's personal anecdotes, about each song.

What makes this book even more realistic is its honest, vulnerable, and sometimes gritty portrayal of the characters and their existences. One story in which all of these themes and characteristics culminate is "Going Underground." It is a story in which even the main character's name, Daniel Grimes, reflects the character's harsh, gritty environment and existence, as well as the difficult decisions Daniel must make. Daniel embodies rebellion against the status quo after having lived a life in which he originally "played by the rules. All it got him were ration credits and a little coin, enough to rent a bedsit and eat slop." "Going Underground" is a daring story with a dystopian tone. Deepening that dystopian tone is the fact that the author cleverly disguises the story's time period, and the tale can be read as either occurring in the past, the present, or the very near future.

Music lovers will appreciate this book because of the role music plays in each and every story. The stories, too, are a testament to not only the power of music but also of the necessity of interdisciplinary studies and the humanities. The stories are a novel type of ekphrastic writing in that, rather than responding to visual art, the stories are responses to music. The fluid, poetic writing in each story mirrors the magic and lyricism inherent in the songs the author utilizes. These stories are powerful, emotional, and moving. Most of all, they are beautifully and unquestionably human.

RECOMMENDED by the US Review

Book review by Nicole Yurcaba

9 781915 081711